Kepler One
The Choosing
Book one in the Kepler One series.

Copyright ©2017 by TP Keane

www.tpkeane.com
Massachusetts, USA

First Edition
Printed in the United States of America
Cover Design by
http://lorainelotter.wixsite.com/rynkatryn

Library of Congress Cataloguing-in-Publication Data Available
Library of Congress Control Number:
2017903420

ISBN: 978-0-9971793-4-7
10-ISBN: 0997179341

To my amazing parents, Noel and Pauline
Burke, whose continued support and
encouragement has spurred me ever onwards.

Chapter 1

My mother coughed all night in the room next to mine as death came to wrap its sticky black claws around her. Death was slow to finish the job, however, too weary and overworked in the pit of depravity that was my home. Such was the nature of Tier Five, so dark, decaying, and cold, that even the Grim Reaper was condemned to an eternity of relentless servitude here.

The sound of her struggling to breathe brought tears to my eyes and a tightness in my chest. I wanted it to stop, so desperately I wanted it to stop, but who was I to do anything about it? I was Zoe Ruthland, a Tier Five and lowlife according to what was left of humanity; not worth the precious oxygen I breathed. Like most things in my life, I was powerless to do anything but wait as the cancer slowly took her.

I listened to her convulsing in wet, unyielding hacks, and I knew each one caused her pain. I worried that the next one would be worse, or wouldn't come at all. It played on my mind, maddening me to near the point of insanity, so I did the only thing I could do. I turned over in my cot and plugged my ears with my fingers, trying to squeeze out the sound. Still I heard her coughing, and I couldn't take it anymore. Anger, fear, frustration, whatever it was that built up inside me, made me want to slam my fists against the thin wall between us and shout at her to "be quiet for five minutes, so I could sleep."

No sound escaped my lips. These might be the last days I had with my mother, and I couldn't have my memories tainted with regret. I lay there my eyes shut tight, listening to her slowly die, and wondered when *my* time would come. Thirty? Forty? I was only sixteen, but the radiation from above ground had reached us all, seeping into the food, the air, the water, and even our threadbare clothes. People were dying younger and younger every year; my mother was only forty-five.

Despite her deterioration, the radiation counter on my wall reassured me that not much had changed since I looked at it last. There was still not enough to kill me outright, but enough to shorten my life considerably, as it had shortened hers. Not many lived past the age of sixty in Bunker Twelve, if it could be called living. Whenever my time might be, I was resolved that it would *not* involve any children of my own. Feeling tears run along the side of the oxygen-generating mask which rarely left my face, how could I do *this* to them?

What remained of the human race lived in an old bunker constructed by an older government. We survived in a tomb of concrete walls stained brown by contaminated groundwater, or at least those were the colours of the walls *I* saw. Hydroponic gardens sustained us, but rumours spread about how the radiation had wilted and turned our *Garden of Eden* sour. I wasn't sure the rumours were true, but I suspected they might be from the horrendously rotted taste of our meal bars.

Our scientists made inoculations for the necessary things that couldn't be found beneath the ground, like sunshine. Their main task, however, was to find a cure for the radiation, something that would help our bodies overcome the poison we were all bathed in. They had failed, and no one believed they would succeed. It was for that very reason the lottery was to take place tomorrow, and, unbelievably, *I* had been selected to be in the running.

The World Confederate Council, WCC, had succumbed to the popular demand that a spaceship must be prepared for the inevitable evacuation of Earth. The WCC had many delusions, the first being that there was a "world" outside of our bunker to council over. The second, that they could undo the damage man and his weapons had done to our Earth.

Reluctant to give up on curing the cancer infecting us all, and with nowhere to send the refugees, the WCC had pushed back on the idea of a spaceship for as long as it could. It wanted to reserve the last resources so the scientists could continue to fail. But like my mother, the Earth was on its deathbed, and we, like rats on a sinking ship, must now clamber to get off, or drown.

I wasn't sure I wanted to go.

I stared up at the yellowed ceiling of my quarters for what seemed like the entire night. Like I had done countless nights before, my eyes followed the lines of the number twelve branded in black on its surface. Running from murderers who would kill me to sell my organs was all I knew in life, but it was familiar. Even though it felt like a prison at times, this was the only home I had ever known and I would miss parts of it.

I would miss my mother most of all, and couldn't bring myself to think of her lying in bed with no one to help her, no one to feed her or bring her water, and no one to shed a tear by her side when death finally came for her. She told me how she never wanted to be alone in her last moments, and that weighed heavily on my chest. She was my last living relative. My father died from a brain tumour some three years earlier and I was the only one of their allotted "two children limit," fulfilled; a dying legacy to mill among the other condemned. But how could I leave her?

My anxiety made my legs restless, so I got up. I must have paced my bare room a hundred times before I found myself looking into a small tarnished mirror on the wall. My reflection stared back at me. Dark rims under green eyes, dulled too early with life experience, were the tell-tale signs that I hadn't slept for many nights. My shoulder-length blonde hair was lank, dirty, and unwashed; as was every other citizen's in Bunker Twelve. We drank only enough contaminated water to stave off dehydration, nothing else.

As I stared at my gaunt face, it occurred to me that I was nothing like my father. His brown, dying eyes still haunted me to this day, and I was glad to see no resemblance. While my memories painted him as a strong and kind man, I was thin and weak. With little to eat, there was only enough to sustain our bodies, not make them grow strong. I was also mature enough that I could no longer pass as his son, unfortunately for me. As a boy, there was less chance of being raped, but the risk wasn't eliminated altogether. At least that was the case for Tier Five citizens, the lowest of the low.

I was one of those citizens, put here by birthright. With only five tiers, those closest to Tier One resided deeper into the Earth's crust and were shielded better from the radiation. They received more food and medicine, too. Council members of the WCC spent their final days on silk sheets many miles below me, while my mother struggled to breathe in the smoggy clouds of their society, pleading with me for medicine to ease the pain.

I didn't have any medicine, and every day I had to watch her turn her head away as tears streamed down her grey-tinted cheeks. Each morning she woke, I watched my mother endure another day of agony. If it were me, I would want someone to put me out of my misery, but I couldn't bring myself to do that for her.

My parents had taught me to see the value of life, even in one as pitiful as my own. Contrary to the thieving, murdering culture of those around me, they taught me compassion and kindness. I even spoke differently to everyone on Tier Five. While we weren't so removed from our former lives above world, about four generations, that we had lost the accents and cultures of our home countries, most citizens of Tier Five only had a basic grasp of proper English. *That* skill was lost to criminal factions who invented their own secret language, and parentless children who were never taught any better.

My parents had insisted that I speak as though I were a Tier One, but they taught me too well. While others might have the resolve to end their parent's misery with a pillow, I could not, and I resented them for it. I resented them for not making me stronger, more callous; for not helping me survive in the world that *they* had condemned me to.

I balled my fist and slammed it into the speckled mirror. It cracked, and shards of glass crashed onto the cement floor, echoing loudly against the walls. I heard my mother's coughing stop for a moment, as if she was going to do the motherly thing and get out of bed to check on me, but the coughing returned. I was left alone in the insipid surroundings of my room, knuckles bleeding.

The lottery, a chance to leave death and live somewhere other than Tier Five. I wanted to go now, I was so sick of death, but if I was selected, how could I leave my mother like this? I plopped myself back onto my bed again and sagged against the wall, wrapping a dirty rag around my knuckles. *They won't choose me, I'm a Tier Five*, I thought. I was positive then that my worry, anxiety, and even my hopefulness, was for nothing. Like the food and the medicine, places on the only means to escape this hell would be already taken by the children of the elite. The lottery was only a façade to appease those who might argue.

Only teenagers were eligible for this opportunity, because they were old enough to be trained how to operate a spaceship, but still young enough that the radiation wouldn't yet have done too much damage. They would also be most likely to survive the journey and repopulate another world. I closed my eyes and lay back in my bed, visualising what that new world might look like. Air, not tainted with the smell of plastic, warm sunshine bathing my skin, and food, sweet food, as far as the eye could see.

An unsettling thought made its way into my mind then. *Maybe there was no new world? Maybe the WCC was sending a group of teens into space so the citizens wouldn't lose hope. A sacrifice, a cull to ease the demand on our limited resources.* If that was the case, most, if not all, of the disposable candidates would be chosen from Tier Five. I would have no choice but to leave my mother and die in whatever vacuum of space I was sent to.

"A fitting end to a miserable life," I whispered.

Somehow I slept after that, comforted that my life would continue to be predicable in its task to always disappoint. Morning came before I was ready for it. The wail of the seven a.m. alarm rang through the corridors of Tier Five. I could almost hear the collective groans as people dragged themselves out of bed, groggy from poor air and malnutrition. For what? There was no work on Tier Five, only crime. The powers-that-be, however, saw fit that all tiers should retain some normality and routine. Waking everyone in the mornings was the impractical habit they clung to. Not everyone obeyed.

A heaviness settled into my body. It made it difficult for me to dress in my Tier Five uniform of black trousers and a grey tunic. It wasn't so much a uniform as it was a way to sort out the different privileges of Bunker Twelve. The tiers were also a way to keep order on a desperate world. Anyone judged to have broken a law was moved up a level, closer to the surface of the Earth and the radiation. There were no laws on Tier Five. How could there be with no punishment worse than what we were already living? We were left to survive, beg, borrow, or steal our way through life. Many did those things, and worse.

It was rare that anyone got promoted to a better level. In my lifetime, and my parents' too, there had only been three people. Deemed essential to the running of Bunker Twelve, they had secured their comfort by whatever made them special. I wasn't special, nor was anyone I knew. With the same noose around their necks as I had around mine, many had tried to sneak past the security separating our tiers; all were shot dead for their efforts.

My home was a dangerous place, and I learned from a young age to trust no one. If anyone found out about my entry into the lottery, they would kill me to take my place, so I kept it a closely guarded secret, even from my mother.

A computer screen flashed to life on one of my water-stained walls, the cracking, fizzing noise drawing me out of my thoughts. It flickered for a moment, and long lines distorted the pixelated face that came into focus.

"Good morning, Zoe Ruthland. May you find health this day," it cooed.

I hated the disconnected cheeriness the bunker computers used. Even more so, I hated the greeting that everyone seemed brainwashed into repeating. May you find health this day . . . ridiculous!

"Actually, I won't find health this day, computer. I think you'll find that I'll be more contaminated today than I was yesterday," I said, pulling frayed shoes onto my feet.

"I don't understand the question. Please rephrase and try again," it sung.

"Oh, shut up."

The androgynous face on the computer blinked at me and smiled, its dark hair, slicked back so I couldn't tell if it was long or short. Its avatar appeared delicate and its movements were feminine. A slight tilt of its head as it talked, the sweet smile framed with glossy lipstick, and the dark brown eyes edged with mascara, all indications that it was female. Its longer nose and strong jaw, however, were features more suited to a man. I couldn't fathom why an artificial intelligence would have eccentricities like this, but it did. Perhaps it was an effort on the programmer's part to humanise it, give it a personality. Despite the programmer's best efforts, its sickly sweet smile never faltered and its eyes blinked too deliberately to be natural.

"Why haven't you switched off, computer? What do you want?" I snapped.

"Today is the lottery," it answered. "Congratulations, Zoe. The president has asked that you please make your way to the Central Pavilion after your breakfast."

President James Tucker, the ruler of what was left, had more important things to do than ask me to "please" make my way to the Central Pavilion. I wasn't even sure he knew I existed. I'd often seen his ruddy jowls wobble on the computer screen as he lectured us on how to ration more effectively.

Right on cue, a small compartment opened beneath the screen. Resting inside was the same deep-purple nutrition bar I had eaten three times a day for the past sixteen years. I picked it up and the compartment closed. It fit neatly into the palm of my hand, not big enough to reach the edges. *How much of this should I ration?*

I slid my rebreather off long enough to take a bite, then grimaced and replaced it again. The meal bar smelled as disgusting as ever, like putrefied flesh and rotting fruit. It was the sandy texture held together with gelatine that was the worst part, however. A true appetite suppressant.

With a splutter, the computer screen went blank, and I was alone again.

"The lottery," I huffed, taking another bite.

There had been talk of the spacecraft from workers on other tiers. If there was one thing Tier Five's were good at, it was circulating rumours. The ship, named Kepler One, was said to be so technologically advanced that it surpassed anything here in Bunker Twelve. Of course, citizens from Tier Five never got anywhere near it, not even to help with the construction. Perhaps we were too stupid, or maybe too untrustworthy.

The rumours, however, gave me a small amount of hope that maybe our journey into space wasn't the cull I was expecting. *Why would they exhaust such huge amounts of resources only to let it drift off into space?* As I took another bite of my breakfast, I allowed some part of me to believe it, if even just to linger a moment longer in the feeling. It was rare that I got to feel hope.

I finished my meal bar before going next door to where my mother lay in her bed. All citizens had their own room from the age of ten. Some children ended up on the opposite side to their family, and that afforded them little comfort or protection. The rooms were small, no larger than a prison cell, and I was fortunate that mine was next door to my mother's. At least, I *had* thought myself fortunate before the cancer. Now I wasn't too sure.

As her door slid open, some part of me hoped to find that she was no longer breathing, while another part shuddered to think it . . . but she was alive. Her thin frame was swallowed by the small cot, and her hair had all but fallen out. Her lips were permanently blue despite her rebreather. The cancer in her lungs still sucked at what little life she had left, like a greedy child on a mother's teat. Her green eyes, my green eyes, had sunken into her skull, and there was no part of her now that I wanted to remember as my mother. She was remains, bones and skin unable to move onto the next life.

"Zoe," she whispered, stretching an emaciated hand toward me.

"Mom, rest," I said, rushing over to grab her hand.

It wasn't often that my mother recognised me through the delirium of pain, or rather it wasn't often that she had the energy to call my name. It felt bittersweet that now, on the day I might leave her forever, she retrieved some modicum of what she was like before. I helped her eat whatever food she could tolerate. Each movement she took, that I made her take, was met with a gasp of pain.

"Medicine," she said, her eyes pleading with me as she refused her food.

I already knew what she wanted before she asked, and I couldn't help her. I had tried to barter for some medicine, but I had nothing to offer. I tried to steal it, but I wasn't a very good thief and nearly lost my life in the process. I had humiliated myself and begged in the corridors for someone to help, but my pleading went unanswered. I had tried *everything*, and now she was still asking. I couldn't bear it any longer.

"Okay, Mom, okay," I whispered. "I'll get you some medicine."

She smiled, and a tear escaped the corner of her eye running slowly over her sunken cheek and across the crescent-moon birthmark on the right side of her jaw. I hated to see her cry, but seeing her cry from the false hope I had given her was intolerable.

I left. Either I was going to whatever hell the WCC planned for the lottery winners, or I would come back and end her suffering myself. It was unthinkable, but I was desperate, and she was in so much pain.

Joining the throngs of other people in the corridor, I blended into the sea of grey as we made our way down to the Central Pavilion. Even if this *was* a suicide mission, I didn't care anymore. I just didn't want to be *here*.

Chapter 2

"Zoe!"

I knew that high-pitched voice instantly. Jason, a tow-headed, thirteen-year-old boy with more enthusiasm than sense, pushed his way through the crowd toward me. Beneath his translucent blinking mask a broad smile stretched across his thin face as bony arms waved frantically in the air. A few seedy characters threw him sideway glances, but said nothing. Today he was safe from attack as the lottery had occupied everyone's minds.

"You hear?" he said, his voice breaking. "I got chosen to go spacing. Won't that be cool? I tinking what it like. I tinking if I fly the ship. You tinking they'd let me fire blasters?" Blasters were what most Tier Five citizens called guns. "Maybe us two will go. It be so cool, you and me. Was you chosen, too?"

"Whoa, calm down," I said, shushing him.

We hadn't reached the safety of the Central Pavilion yet, but I nodded in reply. Although he was only slightly better at English than the rest of Tier Five, he still hadn't mastered it properly. At least he understood me well enough that I didn't have to don the dialect of my ilk. Both his parents had died of radiation poisoning by the time he was six. He lived only three cubicles away from me and had only spoken in grunts when I first met him, his parents unable to speak much better. I adopted him as a brother, taught him English as best I could, cared for him and made sure he wasn't left to starve by the greedy bastards that would steal the food from his mouth.

Jason was excitable at the best of times, but today he was nearly bursting at the seams. He had turned thirteen only two days ago and had become eligible for the lottery.

"You have to keep quiet," I whispered.

"I can't," he said, his voice breaking into a squeak as he squeezed my arm, his left hand missing half a pinky finger from a fight he lost as a child. "Spacing, just tink it. And the ship will have its own breathers. We won't be wearing these tings no more." He flicked his mask with his finger.

"Jason, you know there are only fifteen spots, and those will probably be taken up by Tier One and Two kids."

Jason glared at me before shoving me roughly into the shoulder of a sourly-looking man. The man growled and flashed a knife at me from his under his tunic. I apologised to him and moved Jason and myself farther from his reach.

"Don't be saying that," Jason said, furrowing his brow, oblivious to the danger we narrowly avoided. "I'll no listen. I got a chance to fly, same as any of them others. President Tucker said it."

"Okay, okay," I said. "I just don't want you to get your hopes up, that's all."

Jason focused on the crowd ahead with a steely look in his eyes, his lips firmly pursed together. He knew, just as much as I did, that the lottery was most likely rigged, as was everything else in this hellhole. But the chance to escape Earth was only ever going to happen once, and his name *was* on the list of hopefuls, as was mine.

Our river of grey tunics flowed through two rusted metal gates which were flanked either side by Tierless soldiers. The Tierless were a group of citizens dedicated to protecting the people and their resources. They wore black uniforms and large guns crossed their broad chests. They also wore disgusted and disapproving glares as they stared at us.

The soldiers were called Tierless because they milled through all five levels, having no true home to speak of, only a compound they slept in between shifts. They were formidable, bore no allegiances with any particular tier, and were always at the ready to take down a usurper. The only corridors the Tierless were absent from were those in my home, where we were left to protect ourselves.

Watchful drones buzzed above our heads as Jason and I passed through the gate. Each drone hummed at a different pitch to the next, creating an off-key symphony in the unusual doldrum of Tier Five. I called them eyeballs because they were circular in appearance with hundreds of swivelling, twisting camera lenses inside a glass dome. They were also about as useful as a floating eyeball.

Those reliable rumours told how these drones would alert the Tierless to crimes on other tiers with a long, piercing wail. The few drones on Tier Five, however, seemed content to just watch. Not many survived. They were beaten, broken, and disassembled by the filth that lived there on a regular basis. Those that I saw stayed high in the air, out of reach, and took only sweeping passes over our world. Here, however, as we descended the cracked and broken concrete stairs, they were numerous and hovered closer to our heads.

All of the concrete on the upper level was cracked and crumbling; the walls, the ceiling, everything. I often wondered if it would collapse altogether. As we descended, the fissures became smaller and the walls less stained with the faecal-coloured poison seeping in from the deadly world none of us had ever seen.

Normally the five levels never met, but today was different. Our grey coalesced with the green tunics from Tier Four as we ambled down another wider, less broken, set of steps. Orange tunics of Tier Three and blue tunics of Tier Two joined us as we descended deeper into the Earth. This was my first time leaving Tier Five and it was strange to see colours other than grey. I couldn't keep my eyes off them. One or two citizens in orange caught me looking and returned my stare with wary, terrified glances. Of course they would. I was a Tier Five, a murderer in their eyes.

The four lines of colours automatically separated themselves from one another, not wanting to be contaminated by the filth that walked beside them. I noted that the Tier Two masks blinked faster than the rest of ours, their cheeks seemed fuller and pinker, too.

Tier One wouldn't be joining us on the journey down the cement steps. They lived next to the Central Pavilion, only a stone's throw from the impenetrable doors of the labs containing medicines, and next to the hydroponic pods that farmed our food. Already waiting, they wore neatly pressed white tunics and contemptuous smiles upon their smug faces as we entered.

The only robots in Bunker Twelve tottered amidst the sea of white and catered to their every whim. Left over by the government which constructed the bunker, their blank and rusted faces were bare and corroded, the last hints of paint long since peeled away. Unnecessary, and decrepit as the bunker itself, they had become a status symbol among the Tier Ones, nonetheless.

The room was dominated by twelve large pillars holding up a lofty domed ceiling, and I marvelled at its beauty and cleanness. Everything was white, save for the riffraff making their way in. There were many doors leading out of the Central Pavilion. The most dominant of which were the large metal doors reaching half way to the ceiling. They whispered at the secrets of the magic-men we called scientists. Beyond the doors, tablets, medicines, maybe even cures to certain ailments. I practically salivated at the thought, but those doors would never open for me, I knew this.

We gathered around a raised, circular platform in the centre of the room and waited. Separated into segments by the colour of our tunics, the ceiling reverberated the excited whispers of each tier. Five large screens hung from the ceiling, facing each gathering of colour. Smiling sweetly on the screens was the bunker's avatar.

"Please, come in and find a place," he said in a light, airy voice repeatedly. "May you all find health this day."

The screen was immaculate. There were no cracks, no distorted pixels, and no filth coating it in a layer of grime. The colours were vibrant and the avatar was clear. What was also clear was that the fact that the avatar was male, but far more feminine and beautiful than most women. I turned to Jason to ask what he thought of it. Despite my question and the exhilaration around him, however, Jason still wouldn't look at me. A pang of regret made guilt my only companion. *Who was I to take away his hope?*

"Jason, I'm sorry," I said quietly. "You're right. You have every chance to be selected and I shouldn't be so negative. How about I cross my fingers and toes for you, so you win?"

Jason looked me up and down suspiciously with his pale blue eyes. I crossed my fingers, toes, legs, and arms to prove it to him. I even crossed my eyes, and he laughed.

"Let's two of us cross," he said mimicking me. "We be two times luckier, or both as stupid-looking."

It was my turn to laugh, but all I could muster was a smile. My mind was still on my mother. I wondered if, in the excitement of the day, I could sneak into one of the scientist's labs to steal some medicine. I would never have another opportunity to be in Tier One again. The doors, like the entrance to the different levels, were closely guarded by the Tierless, however. I knew I couldn't slip past them, I'd most likely get shot. *Then* who would look after my mother?

The computer avatar above us went silent, staring at us with its perfect smile and beautiful brown eyes. I waited expectantly, but I was the only one. The noise of the crowd escalated with excitement.

"Ladies, gentlemen, and children," a voice boomed over the cacophony. "May you all find health this day."

Clad in a niveous tunic and trousers, which were dangerously stretched at the seams, President Tucker strode in from a side door and made his way to the raised stage. He opened his arms wide as if waiting for a fanfare, which never came, and tilted his ginger head at people as he passed by. His ruddy jowls bulged when he smiled, and his small eyes all but disappeared beneath a hooded brow. Austerity seemed to agree with the president.

"What a joyous day. What a momentous occasion," he said, spinning once on the platform to greet us all. "I know you're all very excited to begin the lottery, so I won't delay any longer. But I do have one or two words to say." A few people groaned.

"For so long we've just survived, struggled beneath the ground that poisons us." I rolled my eyes. Not one of the many inches around his waist suggested he had struggled much. "And now, at last, there's hope. I'm pleased to announce that the spaceship, Kepler One, has finally been completed. Within its cargo bay rests our best chance of survival.

"We've developed a technology and designed a mechanism that will terraform a new world to make it habitable for us. It means that we'll be able to breathe an otherwise poisonous atmosphere, eat the local food, and drink the waters that would have killed us before."

Excited whispers began to animate the faces around me.

"It has taken some time and considerable resources, but I can confirm that under *my* government, life away from our dying Earth is now possible. I have worked tirelessly to bring this to you, my people."

Jason and I squeezed each other's hands, our legs uncrossed and we focused on the portly man. This was new. The spacecraft had been rumoured to be an escape pod only, but now it was clearly so much more than that. A plan, a tangible plan to save humanity was sitting somewhere in its cargo bay. Even though I knew the president to be neither an engineer nor a scientist, I didn't care that he took credit for the work. My shock and excitement was echoed by all but the Tier One citizens, who undoubtedly already knew about it.

"Until now, we were faced with one dilemma," he continued. "We didn't have a suitable world nearby. We needed one with the necessary resources to survive and those worlds have always been unreachable to us. With a recent technological breakthrough in wormhole travel, however, crossing vast amounts of space is now possible."

The whispers and excitement dulled the president's otherwise booming voice.

"What the heck are wormholes?" I whispered to Jason.

He shrugged. "Who cares?"

"Please, please, I ask for calmness," President Tucker said, wafting the air up and down with his fat hands and the buzz of the eyeballs eventually became audible again. "There is an issue, however. Only one attempt can be made to reach the planet, Kepler 452b, as we don't have the resources to construct another spacecraft on Earth. But don't lose hope," he said, seeing our collective jaws drop. "If you turn your eyes to the screen above us—"

The computer's avatar disappeared and in its place was a live feed of the Kepler One. A cylindrical room appeared, its walls densely decorated with pipes that clung to it. They joined and separated from each other, disappearing behind the concrete in a confusing network of metal. Some hissed and spat hot liquids, forming violent puffs of smoke that drifted up beyond the screen as if they were clouds.

People, as small as ants, scurried at the bottom, lifting heavy equipment into the air using drones donned with large claws instead of cameras. Right in the centre of the room, however, was the most magnificent sight I had ever seen. By the sounds of the gasps around me, it was a wonderment the others weren't expecting, either.

Resting on eight black thrusters, each ten times my size, was the Kepler One spacecraft. I had visualised it as a bucket of bolts held together with tape and luck, but this citadel was a far cry from the shanty I dreamed up.

Sleek lines cumulated into a lethal point many miles above the workers. Everything and nothing reflected off its mirrored exoskeleton, which moved and swirled as though it was liquid. There were no windows on its eddying metal hull, just silver. It reminded me of an arrowhead made of mercury, although how it kept its shape, I had no idea.

A series of moving rings surrounded the ship, running up and down its length, slipping over one another slowly, their movements precise. The tinny, fluid sound of metal sliding on metal reminded me of knives being sharpened and it made my throat go dry. For all its beauty, this ship had an air of deadliness about it.

Frozen to the spot in abject awe and disbelief that anything so beautifully dangerous could have come from the cesspit of Bunker Twelve, the Central Pavilion reverberated the hum of the Kepler One. It lulled us all into silence, and I basked in its power.

"There it is folks," the president continued, his voice snapping me out of my stupor. "The Kepler One. And inside its cargo bay are machines, goliaths to be exact, capable of mining and extracting the natural resources of a planet at tremendous speeds. When our intrepid explorers land on Kepler 452b, they will initiate a pre-programmed command which will set these behemoths to their task of constructing more ships. These ships will then be sent back to Earth and we will *all* travel to our new home."

Another wave of delighted cries was silenced by the president's large hand.

"Those lucky few who take on this mission hold all of our lives in their hands. Therefore, they must be fit enough to endure the hardships of space travel in general, and the toll such a voyage will take on their bodies. If they are *not*, if they're sick, our hope dies with them, so, we must pick only the healthiest.

"The chosen will enter cadet training, but there's only room for the top fifteen on this spacecraft. They will endure rigorous testing to determine who the better candidates are. The rest, I'm afraid, will be returned to their tier."

I swallowed the dryness in my throat. I was so close, so close to escaping.

"And now, we come to the time of choosing," the president said, sweeping his hand over the crowd slowly. Jason squeezed my arm again, his excitement digging his nails into my bicep. "The process is simple. I ask all those selected for the lottery to step forward to the edge of the stage. A technician will take a sample of your blood and those deemed healthy enough will move onto cadet training."

Jason and I stared at each other for a moment. We watched as a few white tunics followed the president's beckoning before uncrossing ourselves completely and making our way toward the stage. My heart thumped hard against my chest, and I wasn't sure if it was because of excitement or fear. Not all the children of age had been selected, and envious eyes followed us as we made our way up, burning into our backs. There was only Jason and me from Tier Five, a handful from tier four, three, and two, while the vast majority came from Tier One. Also joining us were five Tierless soldiers, who remained stoic and emotionless while the rest of us fidgeted nervously.

"Welcome to you all," President Tucker said, casting a sparing glance at us. "Now, if you would please roll up your sleeves, we can begin. You'll be glad to know that the results of the blood test are instantaneous. If the haemovac light turns green, you move onto the next stage. If it turns red, you must return to your family and friends."

My fingers fumbled with the frayed edge of my sleeve as I rolled it above my elbow. Jason had no such trouble; his skinny arm was bare and thrust forward in seconds.

A bespectacled man, with uncombed, sparse hair and a long white coat, began the blood testing with a Tier Three boy on the opposite side of the stage to me. Pressing a finger-sized cylindrical haemovac into the crook of the first hopeful's arm, a small hiss sounded out in the silenced room. A high-pitched beep followed that, and then the light turned red.

"Oh, I'm sorry," President Tucker dramatized, shaking his head in commiseration as if it were a game show. "Thank you for participating. Please return to your tier."

The boy looked confused, rubbed his arm, and returned to the sea of orange. Next came a tall Tier One boy whose stubbly chin bore the tell-tale signs of adulthood. The haemovac hissed, beeped, and turned green.

"Oh my, congratulations. I had no idea," President Tucker avowed, fanning his face dramatically. "Come, come up onto the stage. Please welcome the first winner of the lottery. My handsome son, Liam Tucker."

Liam bore the president's trademark red hair and hooded brow, so there was no mistaking him as a Tucker. Unlike his father, however, he was probably the thinnest Tier One citizen I had ever seen. Liam rubbed his arm, bowed his head, and stood next to his father, who clapped histrionically.

The president's enthusiasm was met with silence, and the technician moved on. Three more were rejected and told to return to their families. They did so with disgruntled stares at Liam. Then came one of the Tierless. He held his arm out and muscles bulged under tattooed skin.

I disliked tattoos. They were an aimless display of bravado and stupidity as far as I was concerned. Men on Tier Five with sloping foreheads and gormless smiles tattooed themselves with marks, brandishing the number of people they'd murdered for all to see. This soldier's tattoos, however, weren't crudely drawn like those on Tier Five. Nevertheless, he was the embodiment of the violent, Neanderthalesque persona which often accompanied his kind. The only thing harder than his physique was his stare at the technician, who was only doing his job.

The soldier didn't flinch as the haemovac took his sample. He didn't rejoice along with the rest of us as the light turned green, either. He sneered and eyed the other hopefuls with a look that suggested *he* was going to be in charge and no one had better question it.

"Commander Nathan McCall, everyone."

Even the president took a step away from the commander as he stood in front of Liam, purposefully blocking the boy from view. The two were comparable in height, but that was as far as the similarities went. Nathan's hair was blond, cut close to his head, and his powerful physique was wide enough to obscure Liam's slight frame completely. I didn't like the look of him, tattoos or no tattoos.

Three more were rejected, then a tier four girl was accepted. Another two Tierless were sent back to their duties, and five more Tier Ones along with them. The technician was only four people away from me now, three away from Jason. I felt Jason's fingers wrap around my hand as another Tierless held out his muscular arm. The light turned green.

"Congratulations, Lieutenant Tristan Grayson," the president declared.

"You mean, Lieutenant Reject," Nathan said with a snigger.

I saw the lieutenant clench his jaw muscles and flare his nostrils at the comment, but he said nothing. He shifted the large gun across his chest and joined the other lottery winners on stage, standing behind his commander. Tristan was taller than Nathan, not as bulky but still formidable in stature. His tussled brown hair matched his eyes, which were framed with a dark scowl. Despite the scowl, I was instantly drawn to him, like something about him, something beyond the corporeal, was familiar to me. It was a ludicrous notion, but there nonetheless.

My attention was brought back to the technician, only one person away from Jason now. An Asian girl in blue smiled sweetly at him as he pressed the haemovac into her arm.

"Ouch!" she squeaked.

The light turned green.

"Please welcome Larissa Chang from Tier Two," the president announced.

A rancorous applause sounded out from those in blue. Larissa waved to them before skipping to join her fellow lottery winners on stage. Larissa must have been popular, and I began to wonder if other tiers had the luxury of a social life. There was no such thing in Tier Five. Anyone allowed into my home would sooner slit my throat for my belongings than shake my hand.

Jason was next. There were only two of us from Tier Five, and I could feel all eyes on our grubby, grey backs. I squeezed his free hand to reassure him. The haemovac hissed, beeped, and I held my breath.

It turned red.

"No!"

The word slipped out of my mouth without me realising.

"Oh, I'm sorry, son. Please return to your tier."

Jason looked at me, his eyes wide, disbelieving, and tears brimmed at the edges. Jason was one of the healthiest kids I knew in Tier Five, I had made sure of it. *How could this be?* I knew how, because the lottery was rigged. There was no way a Tier Five would ever be given an opportunity like this.

"Don't worry. I'll be with you soon enough."

Jason eventually nodded, defeat clearly etched on his face. He rubbed his arm and melted back into the grey. I held out my arm and watched as the haemovac touched my pale skin. It hissed and something sharp prick me, then came the beep.

"Congratulations," the president boomed. "Please welcome Zoe Ruthland from Tier Five."

I stood momentarily stymied, not knowing if I was living a dream or a nightmare. Did the light really turn green? *I can't go. What about my mother? What about Jason? Who will look after him if he's sick?* I scanned the crowd for my only friend and found his masked face staring back at me. He smiled from ear to ear and nodded reassuringly as if to say, what you waiting for?

Amidst the silence, I turned to the president and made my way numbly on stage. I hid behind the tallest of the Tierless, Tristan, and tried to melt into the background. I was sure someone made a mistake, that they would find their error and send me back to

Tier Five at any moment. The technician unwaveringly carried on testing the hopefuls, dismissing a lot of them.

Joining me on stage next was a heavy-set Tier One boy, Otto, probably the youngest of us all and the most nervous. His bowl-cut, sandy hair did nothing to appease the roundness of his face. He looked at me with wide blue eyes and I knew what he was thinking. It was the same thing everyone thought about a Tier Five citizen. She's going to stab me and take my valuables.

I smiled at him and gave him a reassuring nod. He whimpered and moved away.

"Oh, I'm sorry. Please return to your tier."

"No, wait! That's not fair. Why should I have to stay when the likes of *her* gets to go?" a boy in white screamed, pointing at me. "She's too thin and weak anyhow. Send her back to the filth she deserves to be in and I'll go in her place. She's useless, all her kind are. That's why they dress them in grey, so they can blend in with the useless dirt. Shadow!"

The boy spat in my direction, but his spittle didn't reach me. Shadow was the nickname they gave Tier Five citizens. I hated it. It meant that we weren't real, we were only shadows that appeared, made no difference to the world, then died in the light of others more deserving.

All eyes were on me, even Tristan's. His dark stare raked over me as if to size me up, and he didn't look impressed. A heat rose in my cheeks and a nervous flutter started in my stomach, but it wasn't because of Tristan's gaze. I could feel a fight coming on; I had seen enough of them in my tier to recognise the beginnings, but I was no good at fighting. I had received enough beatings to know that, too.

"I'm sorry, John. But you're not healthy enough to be selected," the president sympathised.

"Why? Why am I not healthy enough? There's nothing wrong with me," he yelled. "Go ahead, scan me and you'll see."

The technician glanced back at the president, his eyes magnified comically by his thick glasses. The president sighed and nodded. Pockets were searched and the technician's balding head was scratched, but eventually he produced a small rectangular box, brimming with lit buttons. I'd never seen a working portable scanner before; they were privileges kept for other tiers. It did no good to have them on our tier regardless. Even if we knew what was wrong with us, Tier Five citizens didn't have the means to do anything about it. Better to live in happy ignorance than fear a death that was inevitable.

The technician inserted the haemovac into the box and examined the results.

"The genetic decoder finds a seventy-six percent likelihood that he will develop diabetes by the age of forty-three," he announced, his voice nasally and indistinct.

"*Might* develop," the boy protested. "*Might.* There's no guarantee that I will, and I'll probably be dead at forty-three anyhow. So what does it matter? I'm healthy *now*."

"My dear boy," the president said, sighing. "If the rescue part of the mission should fail, then the future of the human race will be carried on by the lottery winners. Your diabetes is a genetic burden that the future of humanity doesn't need to bear. Thank you for taking part, please return to your tier."

The boy named John balled his fists so hard that they shook. His face turned red and his clenched teeth grinded together audibly. His eyes bore down on me like a crazed animal ready to pounce on his prey. He wanted me dead, I could see it in his eyes. Nathan was the only thing standing between us. The Tierless commander cocked his head over his shoulder to look at me. He smirked before stepping aside.

"If they can do without my genes, they don't need *hers* either."

He took off running and I froze in my spot. I could see the hate in his eyes as he raised a fist above his shoulder. Inside I screamed, but the frost gluing me to the ground had frozen my vocal cords shut, too, and nothing came out. He careened past Nathan, who made no effort to stop him, and I waited for the pain to come.

Without warning, the butt of a rifle slammed into the side of John's face with a palpable thump. He cried out and crumpled to the ground where the force of the assault had thrown him. Standing over him was the Tierless lieutenant, Tristan, scowling more darkly than I had ever seen anyone scowl before.

"Take the boy away," President Tucker said with a waft of his hand, "and let us continue."

Three Tierless soldiers picked up the semi-conscious boy under his arms and dragged him back toward the gathering of white tunics. I could feel a tremble start in my fingers and legs as the angry stares of every tier rested on me. It was clear that no one wanted to see me up here.

"Thank you," I whispered to Tristan as the hissing, beeping, and cheering of the day's events continued.

Tristan looked back at me and raised one eyebrow.

"You're gonna have to fight your own battles or you'll never survive training," he said, his accent listing, smooth, and with light drawl on the O's and A's.

He turned his broad back to me again and focused his attention on the technician. I hid behind him for as long as I could, dodging the stares of those who wanted me to drop out of the running, or die. I could do neither. I had to escape from death; from my mother's death. Was I the cold-hearted murderer they thought me to be by leaving my beloved mother to her fate? Or was I the coward they all knew me to be, truly no better than the dirt under their shoes?

A cold sense of aloneness washed over me when I realised all the hopefuls had been selected. There were twenty-three in all, and I was the *only* Tier Five. I felt the wet bristles of an imagined brush painting its large, red target on my back, and the sensation started a rise of panic in my stomach.

Chapter 3

After a quick parade around the Central Pavilion, President Tucker led the mishmash of hopefuls through the triple-locked metal doors of the labs. I passed between the stoic soldiers either side of the door with my eyes firmly on the ground, expecting them to shoot me for trespassing as I crossed the threshold. They didn't, and I couldn't believe my luck.

The cheers and applause from outside died as the large doors groaned closed behind us. The lack of an audience did nothing to dampen the president's enthusiasm as he proceeded to congratulate us again and again. I stayed near the back of the group and marvelled at my clean surroundings, acutely aware of every layer of grime incrusted on me.

Everything gleamed. Workers milled in pristine white lab coats, red coloured rebreathers covered their clean faces, and polished shoes squeaked on the glossy painted floor. Glass containers, which swished multi-coloured liquids continuously, sat on the white tables. Networks of glass tubes twisted and turned around each other, each dripping or evaporating various concoctions in an orchestra of bubbling and hissing.

From the corner of my eye I spotted rows of shelves weighed down with translucent boxes containing small white tablets, and my heart did a flip. No one was paying attention to me. The president had captivated them all, or entrapped them, with his long-winded explanation of how the labs worked. *If I don't make it onto the spacecraft, this might be my only chance to help my mother*, I thought.

I glanced around at my fellow hopefuls and, reassured that their eyes weren't on me, I slipped behind a large table supporting one of the glass tube sculptures. So far, so good. No one had spotted my surreptitious movement. Heart beating wildly and keeping as low as I could, I slunk between one table and another in the direction of the tablets. It was painfully slow going, or perhaps it wasn't and time had just ground to a halt as I measured my next move. Every fibre of my being told me to turn back, but I kept going. I reached the wall without anyone noticing and smiled at my good fortune again.

My smile faded quickly. For a long time I stared at the rows of plastic containers from my crouched position, indecision freezing me to the spot. I wondered if I should abandon my plan. I had the opportunity to do so much more than be a Tier Five, a thief. I could help save them all, not just my mother. As if to remind me of my real duty, my mother's hypoxic face flashed in my mind and the sound of her pleading for medicine knocked me back into reality. *Stop being so naïve*, I scolded. *You're not going to pass the training because* they *won't let you.*

33

I was resolved then, I had to help my mother, but it left me with another problem. I didn't know which tablets to take, not that it mattered much. Something was better than nothing, wasn't it? The sound of glass shattering as a scientists dropped one of his experiments made me jump, and before I realised what I was doing, I grabbed a fistful of whatever tablets were in front of me.

"Old habits die hard, do they?"

I spun around to face the voice, fear turning the blood in my veins to ice.

Nathan's strong hand grabbed my upper arm and picked me up off the ground roughly. Glaring hazel eyes and a malicious smirk sent a stone of dread plummeting into my stomach. He dug his fingers into the arm holding the tablets and squeezed as hard as he could, making me gasp. My hand opened automatically and the tablets fell to the ground, bouncing out my guilt on the hard floor with a *tick, tick, tick*.

"Please," I begged quietly.

"Harder for Shadows to hide in the bright lights, isn't it?" he said, before wheeling me around to face my fellow hopefuls. "Is this really the kind of scum we want to start a new civilisation with?" he roared, shaking me roughly. "She's nothing more than a thief, a liar, and will probably kill us all in our sleep. Are you all so naïve that you think she's harmless by the fact that she's so pathetically wretched looking? That's how these Tier Fives lull you into a false sense of security. I've seen it hundreds of times. Don't be fooled. Her grimy hands will slit your throat sooner than any of the others standing next to you. I say we send her back to the filth and take that John guy instead. At least we can trust him."

Nathan shook me harder still, as if to dislodge any other contraband from my person. I cried out in pain as his cruel grip twisted my arm further. There were no objections to his maliciousness from the others.

"Why did you steal?" President Tucker asked, ambling his way through the crowd toward me.

"To sell, no doubt. She knows she's not going to make it through the cadet training, so she thought she'd make a quick buck or two selling anything she could swipe."

"Thank you, commander. But I asked the girl."

Tears brimmed at the edges of my eyes. *How could I have been so stupid?* Even if I did make it through now, they would hate me even more, and I'd never be able to gain their trust. A sea of judging, disapproving, faces confirmed my fear and waited for my answer.

"My mother is dying," I said more quietly than I intended. "She's in a lot of pain and I can't afford the medicine to help her die in peace." Never having said it out loud before, the words struck my heart deeply and a tear escaped. The condemning stares didn't relinquish their disapproval, however, and Nathan snorted.

"So, that makes it okay to steal from the rest of us, does it?" he snapped.

I shook my head and he twisted my arm more, making me cry out.

"Let her go, commander," President Tucker said. "That's an order."

Nathan glared at the rotund man for a moment. With a huff of indignation, he shoved me roughly and

I fell to the ground holding my arm where the skin burned. I buried my face in my other hand and cried as quietly as I could. *They'll send me back now. How can I face* her *with nothing?*

"Dear child," the president said, bending down and lifting my chin in his large hand. "There's no need to steal. All families of the lottery winners will be given food and the best medical treatment, as compensation for the loss of their children, you understand? As long as you remain a cadet, your mother will have her medicine."

As long as I remain a cadet! If that was true, I would do anything they asked of me. I would dance through fire, thrust my arm into acid, anything other than go back to her with empty hands. I couldn't listen to her coughing for another night, and I couldn't bring myself to kill her either.

"And my brother, too?" I pleaded more than asked. "He was selected, but wasn't healthy enough. Will they find out what's wrong with him and help?" Even though he wasn't my real brother, I was hoping they wouldn't find out and just take my word for it.

"Of course, my dear," he replied.

I flung my arms around the president's thick neck and hugged him tightly. I couldn't help it. The relief, the burden which had just been lifted from my shoulders, changed everything. I never knew the heaviness of it before, not until it was gone.

Tears streamed down my face, and through them I could see the rest of the hopefuls looking at me with curious expressions. I must have been something of an oddity to them—a Tier Five who was a terrible thief and cried for her family. The only person who wasn't whispering behind his hand, or staring open-mouthed at me, was Tristan. His expression was stony, unreadable, and I worried about what that meant.

"Well, yes, okay. That's enough of that then," the president said, coughing once as he pried me off. He dusted my grey stains from his white tunic, then reached out and helped me up. He kept hold of my hand and marched me to the front of the crowd, wherein he continued his speech.

"Here is our first stop," he announced, gesturing at a single, opaque glass door. "You'll each be examined more thoroughly by the technician and decontaminated before we move any further."

"I thought the h-h-haemovac tested our health?" the boy called Otto interrupted.

It was only then anyone realised Otto had a stammer. His voice trailed off toward the end of his sentence, and he turned his attention to the floor as our eyes found him.

"Indeed, it does," replied the president. "But there are a great many things that can't be determined by a simple blood test. For one, we must see that you're all capable of carrying children. The radiation has made many of us infertile, and it would do no good to reserve a precious space for someone who can't, well . . . you know."

Otto looked embarrassed at the president's answer. No doubt, as a Tier One, he was too young to know much of these things. I wasn't. I learned about sex as a young child in Tier Five, but I was one of the fortunate ones. I learned about it from my parents instead of from a man I didn't know in the middle of the night. Unlike some of the wretched peers I grew up with, my parents didn't use me as a commodity.

The president ushered us through the door before anyone had the chance to ask more questions. Inside, two rows of red chairs lined the white walls of a tiny waiting room. There wasn't enough seats for us all, so I decided to lean into a corner, fearful I would be asked to give up a seat to a higher tier and suffer further humiliation.

The president spun his thick finger around the room and selected five candidates to be scanned first. After disappearing beyond a metal door, a deep whirring noise hummed through the walls of the waiting area. Whispers between the Tier Ones grew louder, and I overheard them congratulating each other. From the snippets of conversations they didn't know I was listening to, I heard them speak softly about the results of their last scan which assured them of a clean bill of health. I'd never seen the inside of a Medbay, never mind had a scan.

After about thirty minutes, the president returned along with the five cadets. Each smiled broadly and were dressed in a new uniform; a red tunic and black trousers. They gleamed as if they were made new again. Their hair was shiny and loose as though it had been washed, and their skin glowed in apparent cleanness.

"Please put your hands together to welcome the first five cadets."

The president's announcement was met with only a few claps.

"Right, next we'll have, Commander McCall, Jax Thornton, Zoe Ruthland, Sarah Davies, and Sam Wilkens."

My heart leapt into my mouth when I heard my name. I didn't know who the other three were and glanced around to find them as I made my way toward the president. Following me was a young, mousy-haired girl from Tier One who ignored me, and a sly looking older boy from tier four. The boy was sickly pale, and his complexion wasn't helped by the greasy, black hair dangling limply over his indigo-blue eyes. His tight, thin lips parted into a smile, revealing broken yellow teeth on his rodentine face. I nodded politely and turned away.

Although I didn't like Nathan, there was something more sinister about Sam's lingering gaze, and I quickened my step to move closer to the Tierless commander. Walking alongside him was a tall Asian boy, his hair spiked and dyed green at the tips. He was gangly, but walked with a certain swagger and broad smile under his mask. It was odd to see people smiling. No one smiled for good reason on Tier Five, but rather than raising suspicion, it made me like this Tier Three guy the president called Jax.

"This way," our rotund leader touted.

We were shown into a large, white room with five hovering beds attached to the centre of hollowed machines. The machines hummed quietly, like monsters waiting to roar, and supported an array of blinking lights. The hole where the scanner would slide over the bed, yawned as though it would swallow its victim whole. It scared me because it looked so advanced and incomprehensible, and I had no idea if being scanned would hurt. By the looks of it, my imagination told me it would. That fear was assuaged by the larger concern of what it might reveal, however.

"Please go behind the curtain and take off all clothing and jewellery. Then lie on the bed and the technician will call out instructions over the intercom," he said on his way out of another door, leaving us all stunned.

Take off what *now?*

The curtains he referred to were opaque and only came to the edge of each bed. A quick glance either side and all would be revealed. A shake started in my fingers and I balled my fists to hide it. When the Tier One girl and I met eyes, I could see my trepidation mirrored in her expression. We said nothing as we selected two beds beside one another.

My anxiety was made worse when Jax entered the cubical next to mine. Disrobing in front of a boy was asking for trouble in my tier, and it went against every instinct of self-preservation I had. *Get a grip and do it for mom*, I thought. I was just grateful it wasn't Nathan who lay the other side of me, or worse, Sam. That pleasure belonged to Sarah.

I undressed as quickly as I could, hoping to get it over and done with. Wearing only my rebreather, I lay on the soft mattress and tried not to think about the cold air flowing over my naked body. My thoughts were interrupted when over the edge of the curtain, Jax's head appeared as he lay down on his bed. The opaque material separating the two of us didn't quite hide everything. I covered myself with my hands even though I knew it wouldn't help much. Thankfully, he kept his eyes focused on the ceiling above.

"Okay, take off the rebreathers and we can begin," the nasal voice of the technician announced over a loudspeaker. "This will only take a few moments. You might feel some symptoms of oxygen deprivation, but you'll all be fine."

Oh sure, just take off the one thing that's stopping us from suffocating, I thought sarcastically. Bunker Twelve's carbon dioxide scrubbers had functioned at only twenty percent for the past ten years and only slightly more before that. They were on the brink of a complete system failure and nothing the engineers tried could fix them.

I took a few last breaths and did as the technician asked. The air in Medbay was stale, thick, and choking, like trying to breathe through a wet sock. It smelled of rust, death, and decay. Within minutes, the drowning sensation tried to persuade me to jump off the scanner and claw my way to the surface of the ocean I imagined was drowning me. I wasn't the only one.

We all breathed heavily, trying to fill our lungs with something, anything. I'd been without my rebreather before and seemed to fair out the best. It wasn't uncommon to have your rebreather stolen in the middle of the night in Tier Five. Chasing down a thief without a rebreather was a lot harder than just lying on a bed, so panic didn't overwhelm me.

The machines whirred into action, and a clear hood ran up the length of my body, covering my head. Much to my surprise, it didn't hurt as the scanner hovered over me, touching me with only its bright blue lights. It didn't feel like anything at all, really.

Although my lungs began to ache, my attention was grabbed by the sound of someone breathing more rapidly than the rest of us. Jax's jaws were clenched, his shoulder muscles taunt, and sweat beaded his forehead.

"Are you okay?" I said through the cover.

I wasn't sure if it was the distortion from the plastic hoods or the dizziness spinning my head, but for one fleeting moment Jax looked afraid.

"I'm fine," he said through his teeth.

I saw him swallow deeply, as if his throat had gone dry.

"You sure? Is there—"

"I said, I'm fine," he said, turning to look at me.

His brown eyes burned into mine in a deadly warning. I couldn't help but try to cover myself more and slink down the table. For someone who had been so happy entering the room, he had changed his tune in a hurry. Thankfully his scathing looks didn't last long. The scanners beeped and a fine mist filled the hood, obscuring my view of Jax.

An orange light slowly ran the length of me, tingling my skin all the way up and down. As it ran over my face, I closed my eyes and allowed myself a moment to enjoy the pleasant sensation. It was a damn sight better than succumbing to the desperate, hypoxic insects that crawled under my skin.

As I lay there, I felt something change. My hair didn't stick to my head anymore, like it normally did. It flowed like some kind of wonderful silk gown. I ran my fingers through it and marvelled at how it shined in the harsh light of the scanner. Even through the mist, I'd never seen it so clean.

The scanner beeped again, and the clear hood whooshed back into its yawning mouth. We were left confused and naked on the beds longer than I would have liked.

"What the hell was that?" Nathan said.

"Decontamination, complete," an androgynous voice replied.

"I think mine's broken." Sarah laughed nervously. "It didn't do anything."

I glanced over at her. She was right. It seemed that her scanner hadn't removed the years of grim from her skin like mine had. Although I had thought Tier One's to be the cleanest citizens in Bunker Twelve, next to me her face appeared sooty. Even Sam, whose head lifted off his bed to examine her better, was more waxen but cleaner now that his skin wasn't blemished with dirt.

"You must be too filthy for it," Sam said, wheezing in the thin air with a wide grin revealing his white, but still broken, teeth. "Maybe I should lick you clean?"

"Shut up," Jax snapped.

Jax's forehead was creased and dotted with more sweat than before. He was clearly uncomfortable. Perhaps he didn't like scanners, or maybe he just didn't like being naked. Whatever was making him so angry, I knew it probably had little to do with Sam's disgusting remark.

"You may replace your rebreathers and put on the uniforms provided," the technician said.

A small drawer on the side of my scanner popped open. I secured my rebreather and dressed as fast as I could. Two things bothered me as I did. The first, that Jax was still breathing too rapidly into his mask. If he wasn't careful he'd hyperventilate. Through the curtain, I could see his silhouette lean heavily on the scanner bed. The second, was that Sarah, by the sound of the racket she was making, had started to bang her scanner with her fist, or kick it, or both.

"There's no uniform," she yelled.

"Sarah, please put on your original uniform."

The technician's voice bore no tell-tale signs of why Sarah didn't get decontaminated, why she didn't get a red uniform like the rest of us, but we already knew why. I heard her fumble in her cubical, small sobs beginning to echo around the quiet room. My own grey uniform lay in a crumpled heap on the floor, and I was glad to leave it there.

When we were dressed, the curtains retracted of their own accord. Against the stark whiteness of Sarah's tunic, her bloodshot eyes and blotchy skin stood out. For a while there was silence as we waited for the voice to speak over the intercom again. Jax's breathing had returned to normal, giving Sarah the floor to sniffle and hiccup in her breaths.

A door opened and the president came in, his thick eyebrows knitted together.

"Thank you for participating, Sarah. Please make your way back to your family," he said, a wide sweep of his hand directing her toward a different door than the one we had entered.

"Why? What's wrong with me?" Sarah choked out.

James Tucker folded his hands in front of him, all grandeur of his office gone.

"You can't have children," he said flatly. "I'm sorry, my dear."

"What? But I don't understand," she wailed. "I've had scans before, and they were all fine."

"Things change, my dear, things change," he replied, resting his large hand on her back to guide her out of the door. Sarah protested, cried, but she left.

"One down, only seven left to go," Nathan said while the president escorted the sobbing girl out. "How long you going to last, Shadow? Not many going to root for a thief like you."

I felt my cheeks burn.

"*I'll* root for you," Sam said, smiling at me. Bile made itself known in my stomach as he edged closer. He leaned into my neck and sniffed my hair, then eyed me up and down slowly. "You clean up well, for a Shadow."

"No amount of decontamination can get rid of what she is," Nathan said with a sneer.

I said nothing. This was the way things were going to be, and I knew it. I was going to be the outlet for their fear, their insecurity, and everything else, but I wasn't going to let it stop me from being here. I was going to endure whatever they threw at me. I had to, for my mother and for Jason.

Chapter 4

After our medical, the president ushered us into a WCC conference room, although it wasn't being used for a conference today. Tottering automatons placed porcelain plates onto the table in front of us. Each supported a heap of food the likes of which I had never seen before.

Warm green vegetables piled high on a plate too small for the meal, and a mound of paste covered in steaming, brown sauce spilled over the edges. A slab of something else oozing blood sat beneath it all. It dripped, steamed, and set my stomach growling so loudly I was sure the others heard it, too.

Sets of silver knives and three-pronged utensils rested at either side of my plate, like an army of shining soldiers waiting to be commanded. My hands glided over them, not daring to pick up any for fear I would choose the wrong one and embarrass myself.

Two glasses, one filled with water and the other with a deep red liquid, headed our dining experience. I left those, too, expecting the water to be contaminated like it was on Tier Five. But when the others drank without hesitation, it made me wonder if the WCC had the pleasure of unsullied water, too. It would explain why they always looked cleaner and healthier than the rest of us. The idea made my curiosity turn prickly.

The barbed notions in my head were disturbed by the divine smell of the food beneath my nose, however, and I couldn't resist its succulence anymore. Resorting to using my fingers—as was customary on Tier Five—I picked up the meat and began to devour every last morsel. I couldn't get it into my stomach fast enough, and my rebreather spent more time on the table than on my face. Even the suffocating, rusty smelling air of Bunker Twelve couldn't dissuade my enthusiasm. Whatever these things were, I would die happy with the memory of their taste on my lips.

Someone coughed and the sound was a little too deliberate and harsh to be natural. My mouth bulging and my fingers dripping, I looked up. It was only then I noticed everyone was staring at me.

"Pig!" Nathan said, his lip curling with disgust.

I felt my cheeks burn as the others stared at me with the same repulsion as Nathan. The others had attacked their meal with more delicacy, refinement, and used the utensils I knew nothing about. I had given myself away as the animal they all suspected I was.

I put down the slab of meat and looked around for something to wipe the gristle from my face and hands.

"You don't need to be such an ass about it, Nathan. It's not her fault she doesn't know what a knife and fork are. Here, sweetie, use this. It's called a napkin," Larissa said, handing me a square of white fabric.

Larissa had soft brown eyes and a warm smile. I could see why she was so popular. Not only was she incredibly pretty, but she was also the kindest person I had ever met. Kinder than I could ever be, and the epitome of what my parents wanted in a daughter.

Tier Five had hardened me too much to be that kind, and part of me felt jealous of Larissa. I took the napkin, regardless, and wiped my hands and mouth. I forced a smile through my embarrassment before replacing my rebreather.

Nathan snorted and focused his attention on his meal again, for which I was grateful. I kept quiet as the others resumed eating, directing my attention to the room around me for fear eye contact would goad another insult from someone.

I couldn't help noticing my other table neighbour, Otto. He spent his time edging as far away from me as possible without falling off his chair. For a boy of his admirable size, he ate very little; deciding to push the food around his plate instead. Perhaps it was my close proximity to him or my table manners that made him lose his appetite.

The conference room, according to the president, was where the bloated council members spent their lives eating and making laws that were irrelevant to the lowliest of us all. Admittedly, he didn't use those words exactly, but that fact could hardly be left out because in a world where starving to death was a daily occurrence, the thinnest council members would be considered obese by most.

My hunger had blinded me to the lavishness of my surroundings. The conference room was a cocoon of sky-blue, right down to the carpet beneath our feet and the filigree pattern of the cushions under our rumps. Six flowing, white drapes spilled from a grand chandelier on the lofted ceiling. They fell down the walls in such a coordinated manner that it looked as though a master painter had intentionally slopped his paint to create a masterpiece. It was beautiful, large, but hollow.

From what I saw, much of the WCC headquarters was equally decadent in its appearance. Even the white table we dined at reflected the harsh lights off its varnished surface as though the stars themselves resided within. I imagined the council members arguing their cases in raving, fist-shaking debates, food flying from their mouths and sullying its cleanness.

The table was simple, solid, and ornately decorated with carvings around the edges. The only blemish, a circular indentation not made of wood, perhaps plastic, rested under my plate. Although it was only a table, and something I shouldn't be so enamoured with, I had never seen anything so beautiful before, nor did I expect I would see it ever again once I failed their tests.

I couldn't help staring at it, however, and wondered where it had come from. I guessed it was a relic from the old world, from before the meteorites and the bombs. Part of me longed to see that world, while another part of me purposefully latched onto the president's bellowing voice to anchor me to this reality. Wishing for the impossible never lead to anything but disappointment.

The president regaled all who would listen with stories of his rise to power from Tier Two. His flabby cheeks wobbled as he shook his head while remembering his struggles. Those closest to him had no choice but appear to be listening, nodding politely with apathetic smiles painted on their faces. The rest ignored him and continued with their meals in varying ferocity.

I listened and attempted to eat my own meal with more refinement this time. After a while I pushed my plate away and leaned back in my chair. My belly ached uncomfortably and I began to feel the stirrings of nausea. My discomfort, however, wasn't because I had shovelled in more food than I had seen in my entire lifetime. It was because *this* amount of food existed in the first place.

It wasn't until the plates, still loaded with uneaten meats and vegetables, sunk beneath the table through the plastic indents below them, that my anger made itself known. Even without asking, I knew where the waste was going; the grinding, munching, machine I heard beneath the table was a dead giveaway, too.

I felt sickened. Tier Fives were the leftovers of society, fed on the leftovers of the WCC's gluttony, plates and all. The prickly anger began to boil over as I watched the president sucking the gristle off his fat fingers before leaving half his meal to the disposal unit. His wastefulness stoked the fires of my rage. I tried to contain myself, but memories of going to bed with an aching belly, crying because of the hunger, only served to enrage me further.

I hadn't realised I was clenching the table so fiercely until I felt Larissa's hand gently touch mine.

"Are you okay?" she whispered, her delicate brow creased with concern.

I snapped out of my thoughts, flinching away from her touch. I nodded and tried to force a smile again. I could tell by the worry in her expression that

I wasn't very convincing. It was no wonder. I had never felt such overwhelming fury before, and that was saying a lot coming from a Tier Five.

"Well, after the previous Minister for Prevention of Disease and Disabilities passed away from malaria, I was appointed his replacement. And so began my career in the WCC, and my rise to president of Bunker Twelve," the president said with a chortle.

I couldn't take his windbaggery anymore.

"Why have I never seen food?" I asked, my tone intentionally low and warning.

"I beg your pardon?" he said, appearing taken aback.

"In all my years living in Tier Five, I've never seen real food before. Why? Why is it that we're stuck up there, next to the radiation, next to death, while the rest of Bunker Twelve hides behind the shield of our cancer-ridden bodies?" I felt my blood begin to churn wildly as my mother's face flashed in my mind. "Why is it that you've left us to die by our own hands, or by disease, while you get *fat* off of the food that's meant for all of us?"

The other cadets stared at me with open mouths, Otto leaned away and kept a firm grip of his dinner knife. Only Tristan and Nathan seemed unperturbed by my outburst; Nathan stretching his arms behind his head, content to observe, while Tristan cocked his head sideways as if my outburst was more curious than alarming. The president, however, rested his hands on his large belly and gave me a look soaked in pity.

"The balance of our resources is delicate, Zoe," he began. "You're right, it's not fair. It's not equal, and there are those who miss out in the basics of life because of it.

"The tier system is in place for a reason, however. The most useful citizens, those who govern, who might cure us or develop technology to increase our chances of survival, reside in Tier One. They continue our fight to live. Their children are educated with the knowledge of past failings and successes so the same mistakes aren't repeated in an infinite spiral of failure.

"I ask you, what would be the point in having a scientist capable of saving the world if he dies of starvation or cancer before he can achieve this? The tier rankings denote a citizen's ability to help us survive and, as such, resources are filtered through them in the same manner.

"But it wasn't always that way," he added quickly, seeing my rage flare. "In the beginning, Tier Five was solely meant for criminals. The homeostasis of our world couldn't survive if we allowed thievery or murders to go unchecked. There was no place but the uppermost level to put them. Tier Five was never meant to be inhabited. It was meant for storage, but what could we do?

"Over time, the inmates started having children of their own. And those children are, *you* are, the innocent victims in a system on the brink of collapse.

"Many Tier Five citizens had more than the allotted two children allowed to them, too. Their population grew, but their resources did not. Meal bars were the only way we could keep them alive. As the radiation levels on the surface continued to rise because of degrading nuclear powers stations above ground, so too do the levels in Bunker Twelve. Our world is in the last throes of its life and there's little room for generosity."

"But you have *so much* of it here," I said, my voice quieter than I had intended. "My father died, living his last days in an agony I wouldn't wish on my worst enemy. There was nothing my mother nor I could do but watch him suffer until his heart stopped beating, and he had a strong heart. How is that fair?"

"Should have stuffed a pillow over his face," Nathan scoffed.

I stood abruptly, my chair smacking the floor behind me. I could feel my fingernails digging painfully into my palms as I clenched them tighter and tighter. He was right, I should have had enough courage to put my father out of his misery; my mother, too. I was a coward, I was weak, and I hated that he knew it about me. I hated his short blond hair, his stupid hazel eyes, and the arrogant demeanour he always carried himself with.

"SHUT UP!" I yelled. "What do *you* know about it anyway? You've probably never loved anything in your whole life. I don't think you even know what love is."

I hadn't seen him get up and make his way toward me, but Tristan suddenly appeared beside me and grabbed my shoulders firmly. He spun me around to face him, interrupting the slew of insults I aimed at Nathan. His dark eyes probed mine, searching perhaps for my attention. That still rested firmly on Nathan, who picked at his teeth with his nails and appeared unruffled by my words.

"Stop," Tristan said to me. His voice was cool and deep. "You're here to help your mom, right?" My eyes snapped back to his instantly. I nodded. "Do you wanna get thrown outta here before you even start? 'Cos that's what's gonna happen if you carry on. They're looking for team players. So play nice, or you might as well stop wasting everyone's time and go back to Tier Five now."

Tristan let his hands slide off my shoulders and scrutinized me one more time before he returned to his chair. His words made the reality of my situation clearer than my reason ever could.

The WCC held all the cards. If they asked me to jump into a canyon, I would plummet to my doom. If they asked me to crawl, I would get onto my belly as fast as I could. If they asked me to strip naked in a room with four strangers, I would do it every time. My mother and Jason were depending on me, and my anger had put their lives in danger.

"Sorry," I said to Nathan, bile raising in the back of my throat. He shrugged and carried on picking his teeth. "I'm sorry to you, too, President Tucker. It's not my place to question how Bunker Twelve works. I should just be glad that it *does* work."

"Yes, well, I do understand your frustration, and it *has* been an eventful day," the president said, mopping his ruddy face with a napkin. "I'm sure you could all do with some rest. Lord knows you'll need it tomorrow when you begin your training. To that end, I think it's about time I showed you to the Tierless compound. This is where you'll spend the next six weeks learning all there is to know about space travel, terraforming, and leadership. Won't that be exciting?"

No one answered.

I took my place at the back of the crowd where I belonged and followed the president out of the conference room. I kept my head down, abashed at my rude and stupid behaviour. I'd have to do better at being nice, being compliant, no matter how right I was. Being nice was a foreign concept to me, however, and I wasn't sure I could pull it off.

We cut through the WCC corridors painted in swirling patterns of gold and red, and rounded on a set of imposing metal doors. Through them, a large dark hall with tall ceilings and poor lighting yawned to welcome us. Hoops dangled from the ceiling in rows of three and four, reminding me of nooses. Tierless soldiers, young and old, punched thick bags and wrestled each other to the ground in a bizarre dance of fists and kicks. Automatons, painted all black, ducked, dived, and ran through a concrete maze as soldiers tracked them down and shot them with their pulse rifles.

The air was rent with the sound of combat until we entered. The Tierless stopped their training and in silence watched us pass, a scowl on each of their faces.

"So, this is the Tierless training facility." Sam's voice whispered far too closely to my ear. I jumped and moved away from him. "Guess they're not happy about having to leave it."

Sam's indigo eyes slid between me and the soldiers. Despite the fact that there was something about this guy which ran the wrong way over my spine, I could ill-afford to shun a new friend.

"Why do they have to leave?"

Encouraged by my speaking to him, Sam slunk closer to me.

"You don't expect they can just make another wing for us out of thin air, do you?" he said. "This is all we got, Bunker Twelve. Nothing more. They're the only ones with the facilities to train us, so we're taking over. Doesn't matter to them anyway, they're used to not having a home, but I thought you'd have figured it out by now. Not too clever, are you?" I had to control myself with that comment. "But don't worry about it. Stick by me and just keep looking pretty. I'll do the thinking for both of us."

The part inside of me that wanted to slap him across his face churned wildly. *I'm not stupid, I've just never been outside of Tier Five before.* That thought was more unsettling than it ought to be, because it was the truth. I was at a severe disadvantage to the rest of the group. While they all had some form of education, I couldn't read or write. Although my parents spoke more eloquently than most Tier Fives, they had never taught me that skill. There wasn't a lot of call for it in my world, but I suspected it was vital skill needed to fly a spacecraft.

The rest of the cadets were also more "worldly," if it could be called that seeing as how our world consisted of only five tiers. However small it was, they *all* seemed to know more about the other tiers than me. Did that make me stupid? Less repulsed by the metaphorical arm Sam put over my shoulders—however much the thought made me shudder—I smiled.

We entered the only other corridor at the far end of the hall. The president waved us past a large room clad in metal, even down to the walls, tables, and chairs. He called it The Tin and told us that this was where we would eat. A portly, middle-aged man with a balding head and missing one arm, stood behind a hole in the metal wall. Disgruntled and disabled, with the name Al sewn onto his shirt, he was clearly in no fit state to work as a soldier. I wondered if this was the kind of jobs Tierless veterans got when they retired. I couldn't see Tristan or Nathan being content to serve food like this man, and assumed him to be the exception to the rule of dying young from combat or disease.

Solid, windowless doors lined the rest of the hallway. It was dark, and were it not for the glow of keypads lighting our path, I wouldn't have been able to see much. From behind some of those locked doors, I heard the gentle whirr of machinery and the hushed murmur of voices. The whirr was too quiet to be alarming and the murmurs incoherent enough to disinterest me.

At the end of the corridor, the president swung open a heavy metal door revealing a dark, dreary room with little furniture. Fifteen cots hovered against the walls left and right, with fifteen metal lockers at their foot. Aside from that, there was nothing but the concrete walls and floors. The beds weren't all that different from those on Tier Five, save for the fact that ours didn't hover. They were all broken, worn, torn asunder for parts and left dead on the ground.

"Now, you'll notice that there aren't enough cots," the president began. "With limited resources, we could only spare enough for those actually travelling on Kepler One. Unfortunately, some of you will have to sleep on the floor until such time as one becomes available."

"What do you mean, becomes available?" Larissa asked with a tone of suspicion.

"Well, there will be eliminations. Some of you will return home and some will, eh—"

"Will get recycled into hydroponic nutrients," Nathan said, smiling and looking directly at me.

"Is that l-likely to happen?" Otto asked, his eyes wide with terror.

"No! No, no, of course not," the president said, pulling on the sleeve of his white tunic and avoiding Otto's eyes. "But I suppose accidents *do* happen. In any event, you'll be meeting your trainer tomorrow, General Cormac Stonewall. He'll be able to tell you more about it than I. So, I suggest you all tuck yourselves in for the night and be ready for him first thing in the morning."

President Tucker did an awkward regal wave and turned to leave. Before disappearing through the door again he stopped to hug his son, whispering something into his ear. Liam moved away from his father, narrowing his eyes and clenching his sinewy hands together. The president looked disappointed with his reaction and ambled hesitantly out of the room.

"You hear that, Shadow?" Nathan said, plopping himself onto the nearest bed and leaning back to get comfortable. He aimed a sharp, cold smile at me through his mask. "Accidents *do* happen."

Despite my fists clenching so tightly that my knuckles turned white, I said nothing to him. I avoided looking in his direction and instead found the nearest bed to me and sat gingerly on the edge.

"Oie! Who said you get a bed?"

The voice came from a girl about my age whom I knew to be a Tier One. Her curly brown hair jostled

58

as she shook her head at me. From the lottery, I vaguely remembered her name was Ariel.

"I'm not sleeping on the dirty floor," she shrieked. "That's a Shadow's place."

"Hey! Leave her be," Sam said.

I glanced beside me. Sam had procured the bed next to mine and sprawled himself across the length of it, smiling suggestively. He flicked his tongue across his lips and winked.

"It's okay, you can have it," I said to Ariel.

Ariel threw a disgusted look in Sam's direction, but took the bed regardless. It was the only one left, so it was either that or the floor and she had already objected to the latter.

Those who had foot lockers took out the nightclothes provided, a white t-shirt and black loose trousers, and changed. The rest of us gathered at the top of the room, forming a neat line of bodies like those in a mass grave. I joined them, finding a spot on the end of the line, and curled my arm under my head to fall asleep.

The others eventually settled and an awkward quiet filled the room. The quiet was disturbed some time later when Otto began sniffling and whimpering about how he "wanted to go home now." I didn't bother to turn around and try to comfort him. I was too tired, and he'd probably freak out on me anyhow.

I blocked out his sobbing, closed my eyes, and for the first time in I didn't know how long, fell asleep without the sound of my mother dying.

Chapter 5

"MORNING, MAGGOTS!"

The voice was loud, male, and made my spine snap to attention instantly. I leapt up from the floor, my fists clenched and ready for the fight I was expecting; a matter of reflex more than anything. But there was no fight to avoid.

Instead, a man wearing the same black uniform as the Tierless, save for a gold stripe over one shoulder, glared at the cadets still cowering below their blankets; all save me, Tristan, and Nathan.

The man's accent was similar to Tristan's, but far stronger. He was elderly, perhaps mid-fifties, and his frame was solid and imposing. His gunmetal-grey hair was neatly shorn on both sides, and stood to attention on the top of his head. He struck me as a man not accustomed to emotions or compassion.

It wasn't often I saw someone with as many wrinkles as he had, and I could only presume that *this* was General Stonewall. The most peculiar thing about his appearance, however, was the fact that his eyes were milky white. He was blind, or almost blind.

Disabled people never faired out too well on my tier. Any disfigurement, or mutation from the radiation, usually ended in a mercy killing . . . if anyone cared enough. So I was surprised to see someone like him in charge.

Standing behind the imperious general was a younger man with a nose and forehead that seemed too large for the rest of his face. His curly, brown hair swayed as he darted his narrowed eyes between us all. The smaller man whispered into the ear of the general. His stare lingered on me, and the general nodded.

"My name is General Cormac Stonewall and this is Captain Michael Stansfield. It appears that we got off on the wrong foot, so allow me to be clear. When I say, morning maggots, it ain't a code to fix your hair or do your nails, you shower of snivelling, pathetic ingrates. It means get your asses outta bed, NOW!"

The room, or perhaps just my ears, rang with the cadence of the general's bellow. Bed clothes were flung into the air and boots scrabbled and squeaked on the cement floor as the others clambered to stand to attention.

"Do you know why I called y'all maggots?" the general asked amidst the commotion.

"Yes, Sir," Nathan and Tristan answered in unison.

The general walked down the centre of the room with a confidence that belied his disability. He stopped in front of Tristan, then turned and faced him as though he could see.

"Well, Lieutenant Grayson, why don't you enlighten me and tell me why y'all are maggots?" he asked.

Tristan's eyes remained fixed on the general's forehead. He tensed his fists and clenched his jaw muscles. Swallowing slowly, he had the look of a man who was incredibly incensed.

"Because that's what we are, Sir," he shouted. "We're the lowest of the low, the bottom of the food chain. Nothing more than the maggots that feed off the discarded leftovers of society."

"That's right, Tristan," the general said, continuing his walk down the centre aisle toward me. "Only something so pathetic would cower the way y'all did. Of course, I expected more from the two Tierless, but I was hoping there'd be a few of you long enough off their momma's teat that y'all would have some kinda backbone. It seems, however, there ain't none but one."

General Stonewall, hands clasped behind his back, took long strides in my direction and stopped an inch short of head-butting me.

"What's your name and what tier did you come from?"

"Zoe Ruthland," I replied, my fists still clenched. "Tier Five."

I could feel everyone's eyes on me. Over the general's shoulder Nathan glared, his eyes burgeoning some kind of renewed hatred for me. Tristan, on the other hand, kept his focus on the wall opposite him and ignored the inquest.

"Good," General Stonewall said after a moment's hesitation, slapping me on the shoulder and nearly sending me toppling to the ground. "You're gonna need that backbone of yours. Although, you could do with working on those muscles. You ain't nothing but skin and bones. In fact," he said, turning to the rest of the cadets, "y'all are gonna to need some of Zoe's gumption, because y'all are in for a world of hurt."

The general made his way to the top of the room again, where the penumbra was starker. He only stopped when his captain touched his arm. Had it not been for him, the general might have walked straight into the far wall. Instead, he turned to face us. I was convinced, then, that the general had *some* sight and his captain was nothing more than a guide dog.

"From now on, there ain't no more tiers or Tierless," the general ordered. "There ain't no more mommy or daddy neither. All you maggots got are the walls around you and each other. You're the crew of Kepler One until such time as you are not. Your training will start after breakfast and won't end until you're on that ship, or back in your tiers.

"Understand, this ain't gonna be easy, but giving up *ain't* an option either. You *will*, each and every one of you, follow my orders and complete your training. You'll undergo rigorous testing until the weak have been weeded out from the strong. You'll be scored on your ability, and those with the lowest scores will be sent home.

"I should also tell y'all, that this ain't just physical testing. There's more to starting a new civilisation than being able to lift twice your body weight. Even the strongest of you might be sent back because of your lack 'a smarts, so don't get too cocky."

The general swept the room with a raised eyebrow and a knowing smile. He paused on Triston momentarily, his smile fading.

"Right! Get yourselves up and outta the barracks," he barked. "Then make your way to The Tin because breakfast is waiting, and it ain't getting any tastier."

The general and his guide dog left the barracks. As soon as the doors closed behind them, there was a desperate scrabble to get dressed. Along with the other floor-dwellers, I had no such issues as I had slept in my clothes. I waited and trailed behind the cadets as we made our way into The Tin.

I ate alone, the weary glances of the others telling me they didn't fancy my company. I didn't feel much like company anyhow. I had nothing to talk about with these people, and they had nothing in common with me. After all, I wasn't here to make friends.

It was difficult to swallow the food Al had slopped oatmeal wordlessly onto my plate, not just because I was tightly wound with anxiety, but also because I was still disgusted with how much went to waste afterward. Despite what the president had said, I still thought the amount of food provided was excessive and could have been distributed more fairly, but my thoughts were soon interrupted.

The *thud, thud* sound of slow, deliberate footsteps approaching behind me made the hairs on back of my neck stand on end. I froze, clenching my spoon so hard that my knuckles turned white, and waited for whatever trick or punishment the cadets wanted to spring on me. Without warning, a meal bar dropped from above my head and landed on my half empty plate, splashing its watery contents onto my jacket.

"Thought you'd prefer this," Nathan said, "seeing as how you don't like real food."

"Knock it off," Tristan said, glaring at him from another table.

"What?" Nathan replied, shrugging innocently and rounding my table until he faced me. "She's obviously not used to real food. I was just trying to be helpful."

For a while, I almost thought Nathan *was* trying to be helpful in the only way a rude and gruff Tierless soldier could, but then I saw the corners of his mouth twitched as if he was trying desperately not to smile. The Tin went quiet as everyone waited for my response. Most, by the looks on their faces, were expecting me to take the knife beside by my plate and sink it into Nathan's chest.

"Thank you," I said, locking eyes with him. "But I'm perfectly capable of looking after myself."

Nathan hesitated, raking his eyes over me before shrugging.

"Whatever. I tried," he said, making his way toward a table where Sam and a dark-skinned girl sat. "Can't have the Shadow disappear, now can we?"

Bizarrely, the meal bar *did* look enticing, but that was his point, wasn't it? Nathan wanted me to stay the pathetic, ignorant little Shadow so I would fail their training and "disappear," as he put it.

I pushed it to the side and went to wipe the food from my tunic only to realise it was clean. I was sure the slop had sullied my tunic, but I couldn't find a single drop of oatmeal. I shook my head and instead, forced more Tierless food down my throat. It wasn't as lavish as the food in the WCC, but it still tasted better than meal bars.

After breakfast we were ushered into one of the side rooms along the corridor. In it, rows of individual desks and chairs striated across a dull room with little more than a singular lightbulb in the ceiling to illuminate it. Harsh lines of shadows painted the dusty room an eerie atmosphere, and the lab coat-clad, fidgeting technician waiting inside reminded me of a ghost rattling his chains.

Looking sheepishly at each other, we took our seats. Somehow I ended up in the front, right under the nose of the technician. He paid me no attention, however, too busy diving into his pockets and scratching his head.

A hum of whispers began to fill the room as we waited.

"Yes! Yes, okay! Settle down now and give me a minute," he said.

The whispers continued between the cadets; between everyone save me. I was seated between Otto and a Tier Two, sable-haired girl named Thelma. Neither had any inclination of engaging me in small talk, and I was perfectly happy to ignore them, too.

The growing noise irritated the technician. He huffed in exacerbation, his thick glasses sliding down his nose with the effort. Even through his rebreather I heard his dry nose whistles becoming louder. His face reddened and this made his demeanour more comical than threatening.

"Sit down and shut up!" he yelled.

His assertiveness took me by surprise. Judging by sudden silence and the rows of open mouths, it took everyone else by surprise, too. With one finger he pushed his glasses back into their original position and smiled awkwardly.

"Right!" he said, clearing his throat. "Right. Well, em, it might interest you all to know that I'm not actually a technician at all. My name is Professor Salinski. My father was Professor Salinski, too, as was his before him. It seems, however, that my name is too much for the president to remember."

It didn't surprise me that the president was so dismissive. After all, it would be far easier to claim the accolades of the professor if no one knew who he really was.

"The general has asked me to let you all know that you'll be training with him in the gym this afternoon. Please don't be late . . . he hates it when people are late." The professor carried a genuine look of concern. "So, today, we'll be starting your academia training."

A screen, the width and height of the wall behind the professor, flashed to life. The white glow dispelled the creepy shadows and dowsed us all in an eye-burning brightness. Displayed on the screen was a succession of lines and shapes that I didn't understand.

"As you can see here," the professor began, "Kepler 452b is over fourteen hundred light-years away from us. This is the planet we'll, hopefully, be settling on. It's also about, em, sixty percent larger than Earth, and its sun is bigger, too. Can anyone tell me what that might mean for you?"

"It means that g-gravity will be stronger, and it w-will be w-warmer, too," Otto replied.

"Correct," the professor said, patting Otto awkwardly on his head. "That's why you must undergo environmental training . . . so you can become accustomed to the new conditions.

"To that end, I have, em, modified your uniforms. They're embedded with micro-nanites that can increase the weight of the tunic, while at the same time increase temperature to eventually match the new world."

"What are nanites?" Larissa asked.

"Eh, good question," the professor responded. "It's a relatively new technology we've developed consisting of, in the case of your tunics, microscopic robots that can alter their density and form, among other things."

I looked at my sleeve and ran the material between my fingers to examine it for any tell-tale signs that he was telling the truth. It appeared no different from my grey tunic, other than the fact that it was clean and not frayed at the edges.

"This technology has helped us conquer wormhole travel, too," he added, picking up a small hand-held monitor and tracing his fingers over it.

Slowly, I felt a weight begin to increase on my shoulders, arms, chest, and legs. My uniform hummed as a warmth spread over my body. A few people cried out in alarm.

"Don't be scared," the professor said, waving a hand in the air. "It's only me. The settings will be increased daily until you reach the, em, same parameters as the planet. For now, you may remove your tunics at night only. All other activities must be done wearing them. That includes, em, physical training. It will harder, but the sooner you get used to it, well, the better.

"Oh, as an added bonus, the nanites will also clean everything they touch, including you."

I wasn't the only one wearing a look of horror on their face. As it was, the uniform was evoking a suffocating feeling in me, but the notion of little robot creepy crawlies scuttling all over my body made me shiver. I wasn't sure it was an idea I could ever get used to, but I had to try.

I sat up straight ignoring the heat and focusing on the professor. Taking a styli, the professor scribbled various shapes onto the screen. I didn't understand them, but I pretended that I did. It was the only way I was going to survive training long enough for my mother to die in peace.

"So, as some of you may know," the professor began, "Kepler 452b was discovered over a hundred years before the, em, asteroids hit Earth, before the destruction caused society to fail and nuclear war to break out. Being more than fourteen hundred light-years away from us, the planet was unreachable, until now."

The professor paused for dramatic effect, which did nothing to pique the interest of anyone other than Otto.

"You see, using the nanite technology, I've managed to create a quantum beam, if you will. This is a stream of energy created and carried by the nanites which can traverse a wormhole. If you look here at this diagram," he said pointing to a thin, long line on the board. "If we are here, at point A, and the planet we want to get to is all the way down the other end, at point B, it would take thousands of years to reach it using conventional engines. However, by using a wormhole, we can bend the fabric of space and time to shorten the distance." Like capturing the head of a snake, the professor's styli touched the board and shifted point A, bending the thick black line over on itself until it lay on top of point B, effectively folding the line in half. "Using the quantum beam to punch a hole into space, we can jump from point A to point B in an instant."

"Oh my . . . You've created a Jump Drive!" Otto said in awe. "W-will we get to visit the ship and see it before we go?" Otto asked.

"At some stage, yes," the professor replied.

"And what about the gravity and the r-radiation?" Otto asked, his expression more sombre now.

"Radiation?" Larissa said.

"Yeah, I'd like to know about that, too," Sam said.

"Right, yes, of course," the professor said, raising one finger in the air and returning to the board. He decorated his diagram with swirls and more strange markings, and continued with gusto. "As you can imagine, such forces are liable to, em, tear the ship in half, but you needn't worry. We've created the world's first inertial dampener—a force field. This will protect the ship from most of the damage. However." He looked around the room over his thick glasses, adding in a graver tone, "However, the force field is not sufficient to protect organic materials from both the radiation bombardment naturally found at the event horizon and, among other things, the gravitation forces that would, well . . . pull you apart, for want of a better expression. Therefore, you will all be in stasis while you travel."

"Wait. Are you kidding me?" Nathan interrupted. "You're going to hurtle us through a wormhole . . . in a freezer? Who's going to fly the ship?"

As much as I disliked Nathan, I almost felt like cheering him on then. By the looks on all of the other pale faces, I wasn't alone.

"The ship's android will follow predetermined flight parameters and will adjust for any unforeseen circumstances," he answered confidently. His confidence wasn't catching and whispers crescendoed from the back of the room.

"Ship's android?" I asked over the din. The only androids I'd ever seen were the rusted bolt-bags in Tier One. I had absolutely no confidence that they would work long enough to see us safely to the other side of this wormhole.

"Yes," he replied. "A new, state-of-the-art android is being created solely for the purposes of this flight. Essentially it's the ships computer, and the computer is it. Both are one in the same being. There are a few tasks during your journey that need to be done by hand, so an android is essential."

The professor accessed some files on the screen and brought up a bizarrely grotesque image. Splayed on a metal table were the innards and workings of a mechanical man. Its silver bones gleamed in the harsh lights of whatever lab it was in, and were surrounded by pumping, turning, and undulating tubules and mechanisms that looked distinctly human. Its head lay adjacent to its arms with no eyes, no skin, just a metal skull. As if it was the android's blood, the parts were coated in a transparent green goo.

"Gross," Thelma muttered under her breath.

"You won't be in a freezer, by the way," the professor added. "You'll be encased in a bio-static gel that will provide all of your nutrition and oxygen needs. There will be no freezing involved. The stasis pods are also designed to be independent from the ship and can eject at the command of the android . . . should there be a problem."

"Oh, great," Thelma shouted, throwing her arms into the air. "So, we're going to be living in goo and if it all goes horribly wrong we'll be chucked out into space at the whim of a computer? Left to drift until we die?"

The room erupted into cries of alarm and shouts of anger. Fists were balled and waved in the air, someone yelled something about being a "sacrificial lamb." I closed my eyes and tried to block out the noise. The professor's laconic attempts to calm them all coalesced into the timbre. It sounded like a thousand buzzing bees, each stinging my own fearful nerves inside. The image of my mother's emaciated face, her tears, and the blue tinge around her lips was all I could think about.

"SHUT UP! ALL OF YOU!" I shouted, standing and spinning round. "What made you think this was going to be easy?" A sea of blank, astonished faces stared back at me. "Did you honestly think the worst thing that was going to happen was the training? We're going into space. Space, people! We're travelling through a wormhole, something that has never been tested. It's *going* to be dangerous and, yes, we may not survive . . . but what's the alternative?

"The Earth is dying, and every last soul in this wretched place is counting on us to save them. *Us!* This is it, *we* are it. Our world and our species die with us if we don't succeed. So, if you haven't got the stomach for it, move over and let someone braver take your place. If, on the other hand, you're here to save the people you love, then shut up and listen to the man."

I took one last scathing look around and found that Tristan was the only one whose mouth wasn't agape. He was smiling at me and nodded approvingly in my direction when our eyes met. I felt a small heat flush my cheeks, and I sat down quickly again to hide it. His handsome smile annihilated my resolve to stay mad at everyone.

"Yes, well, thank you, em, Zoe, isn't it?" the professor asked. I nodded. "It's always good to keep the larger picture in mind. I think it's best to spare you *every* detail for the moment. It's already been an overwhelming day for you all.

"So, with that rousing speech, let us begin with your academia." The professor waved his hand over the board and it cleared. He scribbled furiously, then turned back to me. "Just so I can get an idea of where to, em, begin, I'm going to ask you to solve some simple math problems. Zoe, if you will?"

My heart leapt into my mouth and my cheeks burned more intently. I looked left and right, hoping someone else's hand was raised, only to be met with rows of expectant faces staring back at me. After my "big speech" it seemed that the role of sacrificial lamb was edging my way.

"I, I, can't," I whispered.

"What's that?" the professor asked, cupping his ear.

"I can't," I repeated, somewhat louder.

"Nonsense, it's a simple question, one that I'm positive you can answer. Just read the problem and visualise it in your head," he said, taking me by the arm and making me stand up.

"I can't," I said more forcefully, pulling my arm away.

"Zoe, you're a smart girl. I'm sure that if you—"

"I SAID I CAN'T," I yelled. "I can't do the stupid math problem because . . . because I can't read."

There was no avoiding it. I plopped myself back into my chair and rested my elbows on the table, burying my head in my hands. They would send me back now, I was positive. My mother would die in pain and Jason wouldn't get the help he needed. They would both die, because I wasn't good enough.

"Right. I see," the professor said solemnly. "I was aware different tiers would have varying degrees of education, but I'm afraid I wasn't expecting this. I'm not quite sure where to go from here."

The room was silent. It surprised me because I was expecting someone to shout "send her home," but no one did, not even Nathan.

"Okay. So, I think it's probably best to, em." I squeezed my head waiting for his response and began to hate the dithery way he talked. "Give you two weeks to get a grasp of reading. If you can prove yourself by then, I won't send you home. Two weeks. Okay? Maybe some of your fellow cadets can help you."

I looked up at the professor and had never wanted to hug someone more in my life. I restrained myself and nodded instead. Breathing a sigh of relief, I smiled at Otto beside me. He looked away and raised his hand to answer the question.

My heart sank, and I chastised myself for getting my hopes up. No one was going to help me. They were going to sit back and watch me fail, then step over me to take my place. I was on my own. My only hope was to teach myself and pray my other scores would be good enough to keep me in the top fifteen. But hope was a foolhardy notion in a place like Bunker Twelve.

Chapter 6

Lunch came and went. I ate hardly anything and, for a change, I wasn't the only one. Thelma, Larissa, Otto, and Liam all seemed to have lost their appetite to the extra weight and heat of their uniforms, not to mention the recent topic of conversation.

The only ones predictably unperturbed by it all were Tristan and Nathan. Tristan sat on his own away from the group, while Nathan sat beside his newly formed clique. It consisted of Sam, a dark-skinned girl called Emily, a few others I didn't know, and a doe-eyed wisp of a boy called Chuck. It was a motley bunch, none fitting the other in appearance, demeanour, or tier. But then again, I was hardly the authority on fitting in.

After lunch the other cadets made their way toward the gym. Reluctantly I followed, not wanting to physically exert myself in any way, shape, or form today as the weight of my tunic was heavy enough. Tristan followed me.

"Hey," he said, grabbing my elbow.

I stopped and raised my fists. The only time I was stopped in a corridor was on Tier Five, and that was never for a good reason.

"Whoa, take it easy," he said, holding his hands in the air in surrender. "I just wanna warn you that the general will be expecting you to spar today, but I can see you're set for that." Tristan smiled handsomely, but his words made my innards run cold despite my warm uniform.

"I don't know how to fight," I said, panic steeling itself in my heart. A thousand different scenarios ran through my mind at once, but in each of them I ended up lying on the ground bleeding, or dead. My fear shackled my ability to walk, and soon the others had passed by Tristan and me, leaving us alone in the corridor.

"But you're a Tier Five," he said with a small laugh of disbelief. "I thought you all knew how to fight."

"No, no," I replied, shaking my head repeatedly. "If you're smart, you never fight; fighting gets you killed in Tier Five. Only a moron would take their chances in a battle of fists and shanks."

"Well, how *did* you how bad it is. There's no way you can avoid it."

"I fight dirty and run away," I replied, holding onto my elbows to stop myself shaking.

Tristan rested a hand on my shoulder, squeezing it slightly. It was a gesture I assumed he meant to be reassuring, but it wasn't. No one, besides my family, had ever given a damn about me before, and his concern was troubling. I felt the familiar swell of suspicion rise inside.

"Well, do that then," he said, letting go of my shoulder. "Kick 'em in the nads, then keep out of their reach."

"Why are you helping me?" I asked, narrowing my eyes.

"Believe it or not, Zoe, we gotta lot more in common than you think," he replied.

"Like what?"

"Like the fact that we're both late," he said, turning away from me and making his way toward the gym. "The rest is for another day. Right now we better get our asses to the general before he chops 'em off."

I followed him into the gym which echoed the grunts and groans of Tierless soldiers still training in its periphery. The general *was* waiting for us and I heard Tristan swear under his breath as we entered.

"Well, well, well," he said. "Would you look what the cat drug in. Pardon me for interrupting your lunch, ladies, but if it ain't too much trouble . . . GET YOUR ASSES OVER HERE, NOW!"

Tristan and I sprinted over to the general. We fell in line with the other cadets, and I heard Sam snigger under his breath after someone else tutted. Tristan stared at the wall opposite him like he had done in the morning. I wasn't sure if it was his training or some kind of self-defence against the general's disapproval. Whatever it was, I did the same.

"Captain," the general said, half-turning to his dog. "Correct me if I'm wrong, but I was sure I said not to keep me waiting. Ain't that what I said?"

"Yes, Sir," the captain replied.

"Well, it seems that these two were busier than a cat covering crap on a marble floor," he said, taking a step toward Tristan. "What in the world was so important that you kept me waiting, boy?"

"Sorry, Sir. It won't happen again," Tristan answered.

"You're damn right it won't happen again. 'Cos the next time you're late, you're outta here. Ya hear me? Thirty laps around the gym, boy, and not a word of complaint."

"Yes, Sir," Tristan replied, saluting the general and jogging toward the far wall.

"It wasn't his fault," I said. "I kept him talking."

I kicked myself inside. It was bad enough lugging the weight of our uniforms around, but running in it was an unbearable thought. I wasn't sure I'd be able to do it, and I prayed the general hadn't heard me. Tristan threw me a sideways glance as he left, his brow furrowed and his lips mouthed, *shush*.

"Well, girl, I thought you'd be smarter than that," the general said. My heart sank. "Haven't got the good sense God gave a rock, have you?"

My mouth opened to fire an insult back, but then closed again.

"Ain't no one looking out for no one in this place," he said. "I thought you of all people would know that, coming from Tier Five and all. Listen to me and listen good 'cos I'm only gonna say this once. This is a competition. People are gonna start getting ruthless and pretend to be your friend, only to cut you off at the legs. Keep your wits about you and trust no one, ya hear?"

The general nodded toward Tristan, and the gesture confused me. Tristan's advice on fighting was more than I was expecting from anyone. *How could Tristan's help be bad? Maybe he* wanted *to make me late.* The thought didn't seem to sit right, but it was the only one I could think of.

I glanced at Tristan running around the gym. He was fit and, even though his breathing was laboured, seemed strong enough to handle the run with the extra weight. He was so much stronger and faster than me, why would he try get me into trouble? *Because he only has to get rid of seven people,* I thought. The easiest way to ensure he got on the Kepler One was to pick off the weakest first . . . me.

"Seeing as how you say you're responsible for this," the general continued, "you're up first."

"What?" My mouth went suddenly dry.

"Nathan and Zoe will be first to spar," he announced. "Marked on the floor is a red circle. Sparring takes place within that circle. If you manage to get your opponent outside it or knock your opponent out, you win. Your scoring starts today, and diving will only get you another match. Each cadet must win at least one fight this week or be sent back to his or her tier."

"But I . . ." My mind raced with fear and wouldn't stop running. "I, I, don't know how to fight. You haven't taught us yet."

"Exactly," he replied. "I need to see what I'm working with. If you can't survive here, you ain't gonna survive on another planet. Only the Almighty knows what's waiting for y'all on Kepler 452b. Could be barren, could be all kinds of unfriendly critters. It's an older solar system, so chances are there's some kinda life, and that life might be hostile. Now, get into the circle girl and show me what you're made of."

My legs moved toward the centre of the circle, but my mind screamed at them to run away. They didn't listen and sooner than I would have liked, I found myself face to face with Nathan McCall. His eyes narrowed and raked me up and down as he swaggered around me, circling like a predator. His fists clenched and a smirk spread slowly across his face.

The other cadets stood just outside the red line. Most held an expression of concern, but I knew it wasn't for my wellbeing. They were, most likely, worrying about who was up next.

"Ready, Shadow?" Nathan said, his fists now hovering in front of his face. I copied him, taking a long uneven breath, and readied myself as best I could.

"Spar!" the general shouted.

Without warning, Nathan thrust his fist toward my face. I tried to dodge it, but was too slow. A blinding, white light filled my vision, and I crumpled to the ground. Pain etched its way from my temple to my jaw. That was when his foot pounded into my stomach, forcing my breath to leave my body. I couldn't inhale, I couldn't see; I was stunned by the pain as he slammed his elbow down on my spine. I cried out.

"Oh, come on," Nathan jeered. "Get up and fight, will you? It's no fun when it's so easy."

I tried to beg him to stop, but I couldn't gather enough breath. Soon came to know that it would have done me no good anyhow. Nathan was merciless.

Pushing myself up off the ground, his knee viciously collided with my jaw. My rebreather was knocked from my face and pain consumed me as I flew backwards, head first. The ground was hard, cold, and painful as I skidded along it, and the metallic taste of blood filled my mouth.

"Nathan wins," the captain announced.

I rolled onto my side, clutching my stomach and jaw as I gasped for air. The red tape on the floor met my eyes. He had knocked me out of the ring. Agony scored its claws along my body and the fluttering feeling of desperation, devoured me. *I'm never going to win a fight and I'll be sent home . . . my mother will be sent home,* I thought. I reached for my blood-splattered mask and pushed it back over my mouth.

"Next match, Angelo and Zoe."

"But I . . ." I couldn't speak. It was too painful and there wasn't enough air in my lungs yet. All I could do was roll onto my hands and knees and look at the general as I wheezed. His dog saw me and whispered into his ear.

"That's right, Zoe. Your punishment is to stay in the ring until you win," the general said. "You ain't gonna be late again, are ya?"

There was nothing else for it. This was my place on the Kepler One crew; on the ground, beaten and defeated.

Tears made their way to the edges of my eyes as I crawled back into the ring on hands and knees, desperately trying to breathe and regain some strength. Teetering on unsteady feet again, and sobbing quietly, I squared off against the boy called Angelo. His skin was tanned and healthy. His brown hair matched his brown eyes, and his muscles were more developed than mine. I lifted my mask to wipe blood from my mouth before raising my fists in front of my face.

"Spar!"

Angelo was trained in some kind of fighting technique. He came at me with whirling kicks and punches. I couldn't avoid them, I couldn't stop them, and I found myself on the ground once more, but this time I was still inside the circle. Blissful respite came when Angelo stopped hitting me and I gasped through the pain as it receded a little.

"What are you waiting for?" the general demanded.

"She's down," Angelo said, his accent heavy with the sound of another language.

"She ain't outside the circle and she ain't unconscious either, is she?"

"No, but—"

"But nothing. Finish her off. You can't leave an enemy alive to come at you another day. Finish it!"

My eyes went wide as Angelo came toward me.

"*Lo siento*," he whispered before kicking me in the stomach over and over again.

I cried and tears streamed down my face as pain filled my body. Between his assaults I crawled toward the blurry, red line. I didn't want to fight, I couldn't fight. My only chance was to get outside the circle. After a few more agonising kicks to my legs and back, I stretched my hand out and touched the line.

"She's outside," Angelo said, relief clear in his voice. "She's outside, and I'm done."

"She cheated," Nathan shouted. "She reached over the line herself."

Along with the pain, a well of anger surged through my body. Nathan didn't have to tell him; I was sure his dog would have anyhow. I hated Nathan then, with every ounce of my being. He was scum, and I wanted to revert to my Tier Five heritage and kill him. I wanted to throttle him until his smug face turned blue.

Before I could, my tunic was suddenly grabbed by two strong hands, and I was lifted clean off the floor. My legs and arms dangled limply as the general shook me.

"What were you thinking?" he demanded. "Better to be knocked unconscious than be labelled a cheat. If there's one thing I hate more than chickens, it's cheats. Y'all gotta trust each other on this mission, and how's anyone gonna trust a cheat?"

I tried to answer him, but all my energy was taken up with trying to stay conscious. From behind the general, I saw a Tristan shaped silhouette continue to do his laps. He didn't look to see what was going on, he just kept running.

"Stand on your feet, cadet," the general demanded, setting me down again.

My legs wobbled, I stumbled, but I stood.

"Next up, Zoe and Amile," he said, making my stomach sink into my boots.

I turned to face my opponent. She was smaller than I, frail, a bag of twitches and nerves. If I was ever going to be able to beat anyone in combat, it would be her, but I was so dizzy and weak I could barely stand. I ambled toward her, stumbling sideways and landing in Larissa's arms instead. She helped me to my feet again.

"You can do this," she whispered into my ear. "Don't think of her as a person. Just keep punching."

Larissa gave me an encouraging smile, and I was immediately suspicious again. *Why was she trying to help me?* Regardless of her motives, she was right. I had to think of Amile as my enemy, nothing else. Breathing heavily, I turned to her, fists raised.

"Spar!"

I lunged at her, my fist trying to make contact with her face. I missed and only barely stopped myself from bulldozing out of the ring. Her foot found the back of my knee and I crumpled to the ground again. Spinning around, I caught her leg just as it was about to hit my face. I slammed my elbow onto the top of her knee, and she cried out in pain, hobbling backwards. Dragging myself to my feet, I lunged at her again. This time my fist found her temple, and it felt good to inflict pain.

A new surge of something powerful coursed through my beaten body, giving me more energy than I had ever known. I hit her again and again, screaming with every punch as my frustrations and anger took over. I felt stronger every time my knuckles crunched into her skull. I was possessed. I was someone else, someone more powerful than Zoe Ruthland.

I didn't stop when she fell to the floor either, the unfairness of my life, my family's life, fuelling my rage in a torrent of fury. I couldn't see her through my tears, couldn't hear the other cadets because of my screams. It wasn't until a pair of arms, stronger than mine, pulled me off Amile that I stopped.

I wiggled out of his grip and whirred around to find Nathan staring at me with wide eyes. Without thinking, I kicked him as hard as I could between the legs. He cried out in pain and crumpled to the floor. On his way down, my knee met his nose. He howled in pain as blood gushed from it.

"Zoe, stop this right now." The general's voice was loud and authoritative. I stopped fighting. I breathed heavily through my mask, my eyes burning with tears, my raw fists ready for the next fight.

"What do you think you're doing?" he asked, squaring up to me. I didn't back down, I audaciously took a few steps toward him.

"Fighting, like you said," I replied through my teeth. "Leaving no enemy alive."

"Someone get a medic, QUICK," he shouted to the room.

I heard a pair of boots scurry off through the gym.

"I don't need a medic," I snapped. "I'm fine."

The general's milky eyes glared at me as though he could see right through me.

"The medic *ain't* for you," he said in a low voice.

I looked down at my feet, at Nathan who was still clutching his balls and holding his nose beneath his rebreather. I didn't think he deserved a medic.

My attention was drawn away from Nathan as the rest of the cadets circled Amile. I couldn't see through them, but it was clear she was still on the ground. Someone was crying while another person was ordering everyone to *give her some air*. My heart leapt into my throat.

A medic rushed into the gym, dressed in a white lab coat and a red facemask. The sea of bodies covering Amile parted way for him, and I collapsed to the ground with what I saw. Amile was shaking all over, like she was fitting. Her face was a bloody mess and bore no resemblance to her former self. One of her legs was bent the wrong way, and cadets pinned her down so she didn't do any more damage to herself as she convulsed. All the while, bloody bubbles frothed at her mouth, drowning her.

The medic ran a hand-held scanner over her body and turned to the general.

"She has massive cranial haemorrhaging, General," he said. "I'm not sure there's anything we can do for her."

"No! No, you have to," I said, looking frantically between the medic and the general. Neither acknowledged me. "Please, help her," I begged.

After a few more full body jolts, Amile stopped convulsing and became eerily still. The scanner in the medic's hand sounded alarms, and its lights flashed wildly. Even from where I stood, I could see that Amile wasn't breathing.

I had never killed anyone in my life, and a sickening coldness froze me to the spot. My breathing quickened and my hands shook uncontrollably. A Tier Five killer to the core, but I hadn't meant to be.

I waited for the medic to do something.

"Let her go in peace then," the general said quietly.

"No, no, no, no," I screamed, running to Amile and kneeling beside her. "I didn't mean to . . . you can't die, Amile. Please wake up, wake up."

I shook Amile roughly to wake her, but there was nothing left; no life inside her beaten corpse. My blood-stained tears dripped onto her tunic as I put the heels of my hands on her chest and tried to revive her. Her body bounced limply with every compression.

"HELP ME!" I roared at the medic.

There was only silence; a bone-chilling reverence to the Grim Reaper as he came and finalised my terrible deed. Had he been as quick with my mother, none of this might have happened.

"Help me," I whispered, refusing to let death have the last word. My pleading went unanswered. Sobbing uncontrollably, I collapsed onto the ground next to her. "I didn't mean to. I'm sorry. I'm sorry. I'm so sorry."

Eventually, the crowd around us dispersed. They left the gym under the mournful umbrella of quiet sobs and grief-stricken whispers as I continued to atone for the worst thing I had ever done. A stretcher came, and medics lifted Amile's body onto it. Her arms fell limply over the sides until the medics enclosed her in a green bag destined for the hydroponics bay. They hoisted her from my view on the ground.

My deed was done, and could never be undone.

"Please, tell her I'm sorry," I called after them, defeated, nonsensical, and sobbing on the floor.

Amile was carried beyond the gym doors and, as was with everyone who died in Bunker Twelve, would be recycled into nutrients for our food. My stomach churned and lurched. I doubled over and vomited. I heard the general order someone to take Nathan to the Medbay.

Hunkered on my knees and holding my stomach, the general's well-worn boots stopped in front of my nose. I didn't look up, but I felt him contemplating me for a moment. Then he turned and left without a word.

After what seemed like the longest time, the only sound left in the large hall was the rhythmic pounding of Tristan's boots and my weeping. I saw him looking at me, but he didn't say anything. He just kept running. My heart ached more than my body hurt as I was left alone to process what I had just done. I couldn't reconcile it, I couldn't believe it. After everything my parents had taught me, when it boiled down to it, I was no better than the monsters I was trying to escape.

Chapter 7

Knowing that Amile was soon to be part of my meals, the food I ate that evening sat in my stomach like lumps of lead. My jaw and lip throbbed too much to eat anyhow, and my whole midsection had turned purple with bruises. But I didn't mind the pain. In some small way it was retribution for what I had done to Amile.

I sat in The Tin, slipping a cup of water under my mask, pressing the rim into my cut lip whenever I felt like the pain just wasn't enough. My stomach growled from hunger, and the gnawing ache added to the hefty toll I had to pay.

"May you find health this day," Nathan said, sneering at me as he passed.

His nose was still swollen, his gait somewhat wider, and his words weren't meant in kindness. The maliciousness in his voice told me it was a dig at the fact that I was a murderer, and my victim would never find health again.

"May you find health this day," Sam copied as he, too, passed by with an empty try.

"May you find health this day," Emily said.

One by one, the cadets lined up to wish me health. All, that was, except Tristan, who seemed to only pay attention to his meal. Even Otto, whose tray shook wildly as he passed by, wished me health this day, lacing it with as much venom as a scared, young boy could. I kept my eyes focused on the table in front of me and took their invectives to some dark place inside where I could mull over them time and again when needed. It was the least I could do to honour Amile.

When they were done, I waited in The Tin for everyone to leave. I didn't want to face their stares as well as their words as I tried to sleep that night, not that I would sleep much. Tristan was last to get up. He stopped at my table and sat opposite me.

"You gotta let it go," he said, his voice calm.

"I don't know what you're talking about," I replied, wanting to be left alone.

"Yes you do," he said, resting his hand on mine. I flinched as he touched my bruised knuckles, but I didn't pull away. "I know what it's like to kill someone. Remember, doing terrible things doesn't make you a terrible person. You just gotta do what you gotta do, and if she had been stronger she would have done the same to you. You can't care about 'em . . . the cadets, that is. You gotta just look out for yourself."

I pulled my hand away.

"I'm not like you," I said, more quietly than I had intended. "You have orders to blame. I don't. I was only supposed to knock her out, but I killed her . . . I *killed* her."

"Death is death in this place," he replied, standing to leave. "Whether you kill someone by accident or shoot an eight-year-old girl because she was in the wrong place at the wrong time . . . it doesn't matter. You gotta let it go so you can save the rest of them left behind. Wallowing in your own self-pity when the world is relying on you is just plain selfish."

My bottom lip quivered, and my eyes filled with tears as I watched him leave. I couldn't understand why he was he was saying these things to me. I had just killed someone, and as far as I was concerned I was allowed to feel upset. I wasn't some kind of robot like him, all stern and emotionless. I had a heart, it was hurting, and self-pity was my only friend right now.

I swore at him under my breath, but he didn't hear. He was long gone by that point, and I knew it. I crossed my arms on the table and rested my forehead on them. Blocking out the world, I pretended I was back in my small room, next to my mother who was slowly dying of cancer. I felt strangely at ease with the memory, but I still couldn't stop the tears from falling.

They came in the form of a tsunami taking over everything inside me, including my breathing. Long deep sobs echoed in the empty room as I cried for Amile, for Jason, and for my mother. Having kept my emotions in-check for so long—for fear another Tier Five would see them as weakness—I'd never cried so hard before. It felt good, freeing.

My dehydrated body eventually ran out of tears, but the sadness and shame still crushed my heart. I knew I couldn't avoid my fellow cadets forever, so I got up, wiped my cheeks tersely with my sleeve, and headed to the barracks.

The room was silent as wary, angry stares followed me into the room. Ignoring them, I made my way to the top to find a spot next to the others on the floor. Before I reached them, however, Nathan stood and blocked my path, carrying a wicked smile.

"That's your bed over there," he said, pointing to the bed next to Tristan, the one Amile used to sleep in. "You eliminated her fair and square, so it's yours."

"I don't want it," I whispered.

"Nonsense," he said, taking me by the elbow and directing me forcefully toward the bed. "You deserve it because now there's only six to get rid of. You did us all a favour really."

I snatched back my arm and shoved him in the chest with both hands as hard as I could. Nathan stumbled backwards and looked at me with a bewildered expression.

"I said, I don't want it," I shouted, my face burning with anger. "Leave me alone or I'll kick your other ball into your stomach."

Tristan sniggered and covered his rebreather with his hand as Nathan shot him a pointed look. Despite Nathan's death-glare, Tristan let out a small laugh, but quickly concealed with a cough.

"Please, it's not as if you actually care about Amile," Nathan said, looking at me with as much hatred and repugnance as I'd seen on anyone. "You're a Tier Five, isn't killing people what you do for a hobby?"

I stared at his boots, unable to look him in his face. As much as I tried to prevent it, a tear escaped and rolled down my cheek. I wrapped my arms around my stomach trying not to vomit again, and willed my bottom lip to stop quivering. It didn't.

"I *do* care," I said in a pathetic whisper. "I've never killed anyone before. Please, just let me pass."

Nathan stood his ground for what seemed like a long time, seemingly stunned by my reaction.

"Fine," Nathan said in a tone more gentle than I was expecting. "I was only trying to help."

Nathan sidestepped out of the way and allowed me to continue toward the top of the room. The other floor dwellers were about as welcoming as Nathan, however. In unified hatred or fear of me, they got to their feet and locked arms, barricading me from their spot. Otto stood in the centre of the human wall, his eyes wide and his legs visibly shaking.

"It's f-f-f-f-f-f-full," he said with a wobble in his voice.

It didn't take a genius to realise what was going on. Either someone had put them up to this or they truly didn't want me lying next to them. I wasn't surprised. If I were sleeping next to a killer I might have some misgivings, too. Even so, I couldn't help but feel the gap between me and the other cadets widen.

"Hey, Zoe," Tristan called out, gesturing toward the bed next to his. "I promise I don't bite."

For a long time I stared at the empty bed. Amile's indentation was still vaguely visible on the pillow. Taking a deep breath, I turned my back to the human wall and sat on the cot next to Tristan. The other cadets resumed their business and got ready for bed.

As harsh as Tristan had been about getting over it, I was glad I was sleeping next to him. He didn't hate me, he wasn't scared of me, and it helped that I thought he wasn't all that bad looking. Not that it mattered much because it was clear he didn't have any feelings for me, if he had any feelings at all.

I settled uneasily into my new bed. Snores from Otto, and a few others, filled the empty space between me and the walls as I lay awake for what seemed like hours. They kept me company as the night was eventually choked by the coldness of early morning. For the longest time I thought I was the only one still up, but I was wrong.

"Hey, Zoe," Tristan whispered.

I looked over to see him propped up on one elbow and looking at me.

"Yeah," I replied.

Without warning, he threw his blanket off and sat on the bed next to me. I was confused, not knowing what to do. Should I sit up, should I stay lying down? It wasn't often that a shirtless man sat on the edge of my bed, or ever actually. *What does he want?*

"You remember when I told you that we were more alike than you knew?" he said.

"Yeah," I said, deciding I should prop myself onto my elbows.

"Well I, em, I guess that . . ." Tristan fiddled with the edges of my blanket like he was nervous. It was endearing and completely out of character from what I knew of him. "See, you and me, we're the same."

"Tristan, what the heck are you talking about? We're nothing alike," I said with a sigh, exasperated and tired.

"But we are," he insisted. "I've never told anyone this before because I didn't want people to treat me any different. I wanted to be a Tierless, just like everyone around me . . . but I ain't."

"Well, if you're not a Tierless, what are you?"

"I'm a Tier Five," he replied quietly. "When I was young, maybe six or seven, my mother struck a deal with the general. He needed more soldiers, and my mother needed food or medicine, I can't remember which. So she traded me."

Tristan smiled weakly and focused on the thread he was pulling.

"That's awful," I said, sitting up properly and resting my hand on his knee.

"It ain't really," he said. "I think my mother was pregnant, or maybe just had a baby. I ain't too sure. I don't remember much about my parents, but I *do* know they couldn't take care of two kids. So they kinda did me a favour really.

"I remember bits of my life in Tier Five. Growing up with the general was tough, but a damn sight better than staying there. I remember the days where there was nothing to eat and . . . well, let's just say that most of my memories ain't good, you know?"

I did know. Those kinds of memories were all I knew, until the lottery.

"Why are you telling me this? You don't have to," I questioned, my suspicion rising again.

"This is gonna be an unfair battle for you," he said. "I just wanted you to know that, well, you ain't alone here. You can trust me."

Tristan grinned sheepishly before squeezing my hand and returning to his own bed without another word. I watched him turn over, pull the covers above his shoulders, and appear to fall asleep as though he hadn't said anything to me at all. It was the strangest conversation I'd ever had, and ended even more strangely . . . abrupt, almost.

Regardless, it seemed the general was wrong; not everyone was out for themselves. I smiled and the feeling of loneliness faded. Tristan knew me, he understood where I'd come from and what I was so desperately fighting for. If there was anyone here I should be able to trust, it should be him.

Over the next two weeks I got better at not getting beaten to a pulp while sparring, but not by much. I even managed to win a few matches. Although, I wasn't sure if that was because I was getting better, or if everyone else was still too scared of me to fight properly.

Oddly, the only cadet I had never seen fight was Liam, the president's son. He trained on his own, hitting the Tierless punch bags with little more effort than a seven-year-old girl. It seemed that his linage absolved him of the need to train like the rest of us. The others grumbled and questioned it among themselves, but the general ended all griping with a hard slap at the back of each head.

Apparently, I was quite a good shot with a pulse rifle, too. Holding such a lethal weapon made me nervous beyond belief, but my nerves seemed to sharping my aim. Droid after scurrying droid fell as I chased them through the maze. Their dented, worn bodies were nothing more than empty carcasses made mobile by the most minimal of technologies. It meant that they could take hit after hit without needing repairs. It wasn't something I enjoyed, not after Amile, but something I knew I was good at, and I needed all the high scores I could get.

My bruises turned yellow, and with my lip crusted over I was an attractive sight to behold. On more than one occasion Nathan commented on how I looked like a disfigured blowfish. I ignored him. I didn't care what he called me anymore because now I had a friend, Tristan. Albeit a distant and not very talkative friend. His interaction with me was little more than a couple of sentences a day and the odd nod of encouragement. As much as I would have liked more, I appreciated what I got nonetheless.

I felt myself getting stronger, too. Perhaps it was because my hunger overcame my disgust at eating the Amile-tainted food. After all, I wasn't going to be of any use to my mother or Jason if I just wasted away, now was I?

Making use of the Tierless's limited library, which consisted of nothing but martial arts books, I tried to teach myself how to read by associating the pictures with words. Not being able to decipher which word was the item I was looking at, meant I was failing miserably at the task. I wanted to ask Tristan if he would help, but I got the distinct impression that he was only there for moral support. Anything more than that and his eyes glazed over and all conversation would stop. He was odd that way, but at least he didn't want me to fail like the rest of the group.

Our uniforms increased in weight daily, and although it made little difference to Nathan and Tristan, the rest of us struggled. Otto, in particular, seemed to carry a permanent look of a torture across his face. I felt bad for him. He still cried every night, wanting to go back to his parents. Everyone ignored him, calling him a *baby* behind his back and sometimes to his face. But in the silence of the night, his weeping coalesced with our own thoughts and fears and no one said a word to him. No one offered him a supportive hug either. It seemed that his candour was more than they wanted to handle.

From the sidelines, it was easy to see people starting to turn on each other. They would dig at each other with snide remarks, or study in secret and lead their supposed friends to believe that they weren't. I was glad they cared too little to bother with me. Even Sam appeared to prefer the company of his cot neighbour, Ariel, to me . . . much to her obvious disgust.

Sam didn't ingratiate himself with others so much as he tried to melt himself onto their backs, fronts, wherever he could gain purchase. Even Nathan seemed to have tired of his company. Sam and his cronies, Emily, Simon, and Chuck, stuck together and whispered in darkened corners. They often eyed a specific person and laughed like hyenas as if they were planning to do something to them. I suspected it was only to psyche-out their competition more than anything.

Simon was taller than Sam, stockier, too, with broad shoulders and brown hair. He was a Tier Three, and always had a distrusting look in his eyes. Chuck, on the other hand, couldn't have been more than fourteen, and from the look of his thin build, must have been a tier four. His dark skin seemed a permanent shade of grey, and his fingers always fiddled with the hem of his tunic. His awkward smiles were apparent when Sam's group laughed at someone. It was clear he didn't belong, but at least he had someone to help him.

Professor Salinski's lessons introduced the mathematics and theory behind his wormhole travel.

From my understanding of it, and my understanding was limited at best, the quantum beam would punch open the fabric of space and stabilise the tear. Using two nanite probes, one that would navigate the wormhole to the other side while the other remained at the entrance, the beam between them would hold the wormhole open until we crossed. Like a tightrope traversing the great unknown, our ship will travel along the beams path using conventional nuclear engines.

Today's lesson on finding wormholes, however, was infinitely more complicated than just crossing the swirling, crushing throat of a wormhole. According to research done before the war—and the information stored was sparse at best—wormholes exist naturally in the universe. That's not to say they were open and sucking in all matter around them, rather their potential existed.

Dotted throughout the vacuum of space are many surges, or gatherings, of negative energy—an indicator of an opening to a wormhole. Through the manipulation of quantum fields, this opening can be widened large enough to allow a spacecraft to pass through it.

Using the probe on the far end, the destination of the wormhole can be determined by examining the star pattern on the other side. If it wasn't in the correct direction, the probe would retract, the wormhole close, and we would search for a different opening.

Having no control over the exit or the length of the wormhole, the Kepler One would have to make a series of jumps, hopping from one point in the galaxy to the next until we reach Kepler 452b: A journey the professor expected would take us just under a year to complete.

"A year?" Sam asked, his voice raising.

"Well, searching for wormholes using the nuclear engines is a slow job," the professor replied. "And there's no guarantee that we'll be able to find the, em, next wormhole easily. It might involve some hunting."

No one seemed overly pleased about how long it was going to take. I didn't expect to be on the ship, so it didn't matter much to me.

The professor proceeded to cover every inch of the board, trying to explain to us the randomness of these wormholes. I could read a few words, but I was too slow to keep up and a sense of hopelessness flooded me. It had been two weeks and I was still no closer to figuring out how to read than I was walking on the moon.

I couldn't help but imagine my mother, cast into the abysmal surroundings of Tier Five again, her face contorted in pain. I couldn't imagine going back to eating nothing but meal bars for the rest of my life either. I didn't know what to do, and for the rest of the lesson I was consumed by my failure.

Mid-training exams were creeping up. Even if I got the highest scores in everything else, there was no way I would pass without learning how to read, and leaving at the half-way point was *not* an option for me.

My despair was interrupted by the sudden wave of excitement in the room. From the snippets of conversations I heard, the figured it would be easier to understand the concept if we actually went to see the ship. My mouth dropped open and I couldn't help but grin from ear to ear as we were herded into two lines. Even if I never made it to the end, at least I would get to see history in the making . . . literally.

"Okay, settle down," the professor said, waving his hands in the air as we gathered behind him. "You must remember that it's not finished yet, okay? So don't be alarmed if there are, em, bits missing."

I wasn't sure anyone cared, or heard the professor. At his signal they followed him out of the room like a line of red-coated ducklings following their mother. Even though I kept to the back of the group, I, too, was swept up by the palpable excitement in the air. My exhilaration was only slightly dampened by the fact that I was stuck following Nathan's broad frame.

We were led out of the Tierless compound and through Tier One, where we received a plethora of imperious stares down powdered noses. Nathan, in his usual charming fashion, stared back at them, even baring his teeth at one. Alarmed, the onlookers melted into other gatherings of Tier Ones and whispered feverously among themselves.

"So, it's not just me your always that nice to!" I said, hoping he wouldn't hear me. He did. Nathan glared at me over his shoulder but said nothing as we continued to follow the others.

Soon we came to the Central Pavilion and it confused me somewhat. Although the room was large, it certainly wouldn't be large enough to fit a spacecraft. Building something so big, for so long, would have created a lot of noise in that area, too. I was pretty sure it would have been heard even in Tier Five. Residing at the bottommost level of Bunker

Twelve, there was nowhere else to go but the Central Pavilion.

"Right," the professor said, ushering us toward the far wall. A lone and pathetic, tarnished metal door, complete with a rusted five spoke handle, was the only feature on it. "As you can imagine security is pretty tight, so I ask you all to stay together and please don't wander off or you'll be shot . . . I'm serious." The professor skimmed us with an over-the-glasses stare that meant business. "The president and I are the only ones with, em, access to the Kepler One. So if you get left behind, that's where you stay. Do I make myself clear?"

"What about the workers?" Larissa asked. "Surely they have to come and go?"

"Like I said," he said, leaning over to conceal a keypad on the side of the door before punching in a code. "Anyone left behind, stays behind."

I wondered then if that was the fate of the workers; to be plucked from their tiers like the Tierless and condemned to spend their lives away from their families. I also wondered what their fate would be once the ship was built. Would they be returned to their tiers? Would they stay where they are? Would they disappear?

A small panel above the keypad opened and the professor stuck his thumb into a hole in the centre. After a moment, a resounding clunk echoed in the Central Pavilion and the five point handle turned of its own accord. Another clunk and the door swung open.

"Quickly now. Come on, in you get," he said, almost pushing us inside.

The room was tiny and we all barely fit before the door started to close behind us again. I had the misfortune of being pressed up against Nathan. What was worse, we were face to face and I found it hard to avoid looking at him. As if to make me more uncomfortable, he blatantly and unapologetically stared at me the whole time.

"Sorry," I whispered, hoping my apology would make him stop.

Nathan didn't respond, he didn't move, he just kept looking at me. I knew he hated me, but there was very little I could do about our closeness in that moment. Surely he understood?

"Pardon me, excuse me," the professor said, squeezing through the crowd to the far wall.

We all shifted to let him pass and that meant I was crushed against Nathan more. At one point someone bumped into the back of my knees and my legs buckled. Before I collapsed to the ground and could be trampled by everyone, Nathan caught me around my waist with both arms and held me upright. He didn't let me go, either, he just held me there while the professor initiated a retinal scan at another panel. At least, that was what I thought the professor did. I wasn't paying attention. All my concentration was focused on Nathan's face.

He slowly, deliberately, scanned my cheeks, my chin, my eyes, as he held me against him. His lips twitched, but he said nothing. He made me incredibly nervous, and I wasn't sure if it was in a completely bad way this time. As I found my feet again, I apologised and pulled away. Nathan let me go and turning his attention toward the professor. I followed his gaze.

The professor's glasses rested on the top of his head as he peered into a box fastened to the side of the wall. Without warning, the wall jerked and cracked into five equal segments. Under the chest-rumbling sound of unseen gears, each segment truncated slowly behind the other walls, twisting and opening in a spiral. The grinding of gears finally stopped with a reverberating *clunk*, and a dark chasm yawned in front of us.

The cavernous tunnel wasn't a haphazardly hewn burrow of mud and rocks, like I expected. It's rounded, metal walls were tarnish and reminiscent of old world technology—clunky and large with thick wires dangling everywhere. Water dripped from the ceiling onto electrified rails, illuminating the tunnel in a shower of sporadic blue sparks. When it did, I saw the inaccuracy of the tunnels construction; twisting and dipping where it should be straight, before it disappeared into darkness.

I was expecting some slithering, spikey monster to emerge from inside. Instead, a whooshing sound, which began almost inaudibly at first, became gradually louder and louder as something mechanical came toward us. A freezing breeze gathered strength and tussled the hair of those standing closest to the tunnel entrance. Larissa and Otto let out an alarmed cry as the beast I imagined emerged, only it wasn't a beast.

A windowless ball which fit the tunnel perfectly screeched to a halt at the wall. Its bulbous corroded exterior protruded slowly into our small room as it gently bumped to a halt. It hummed, hissed once and made everyone jump, including me which unfortunately drew Nathan's stare again. I ignored him.

After a moment, a small tube protracted from inside the machine and the professor placed his finger into it.

"Ouch," he said, taking back his finger and sucking on it. "DNA identification," he explained to those around him as the doors slid open. "Right, into the tram then please. One at a time. There's plenty of room up the front."

If whoever built this place wanted to keep the riffraff out, they did a damn good job of making it as difficult as possible to get in. I'd known some very talented thieves in Tier Five, but even they would struggle with this security.

Inside, the tram had one large viewer on the wall in front of us, displaying the gawping maw ahead. As I entered and wrapped my hand around a small leather belt dangling from the ceiling, I thought it very clever of them to hide the entrance in plain sight. No one would have guessed at what lay behind that unassuming door. The fact that there were no Tierless guarding it either, was pure genius as far as I was concerned.

We were jolted violently and I stumbled backward as it began gathering speed. A hand, placed momentarily on the small of my back, pushed me forward again and stopped me from falling. I looked back and was surprised to find that it was Nathan helping me. As sparks from under the carriage lit the tram in intermittent flickers, his eyes, still hard and staring, rested on me.

"Thanks," I said. He didn't answer.

Wary, I turned my attention back to the viewer which revealed the impossible speeds that melted the tunnel walls into a blur of metal. My stomach churned as we tipped on our side, the force of our speed keeping our tram pinned against the wall as we rounded a corner. Larissa, standing beside me, grabbed my free hand and squeezed it tightly, her eyes wide and her face pale.

"In the era the bunker was created, about the twenty-first century, the world was an unstable place," the professor began, unaffected by the speed, his thick glasses sheening a flash of blue occasionally and obscuring his eyes behind it. "Because of that, the government saw the need for a bunker to protect politicians, rulers, great artists, and the foremost minds of their time. But, em, only a catchment of those people were actually saved when the asteroids hit.

"You see, em, the bunker was left unused for a long time. So, to cover the costs of keeping it, the government rented it out, if you will, as a base for research and development."

Although I was sure none of us, bar Otto, had any interest in his story, listening to the professor was comforting. It distracted me from the tilting, tipping, falling sensation of the tram.

"The main project here was the advancement of space travel and the discovery of new worlds," he continued. "I tell you the innovations created in these bunkers were astounding."

"These?" I asked quickly. "You mean there's more than one?"

The professor paused, perhaps for a bit too long.

"There used to be," he said. "Before the war. But Bunker Twelve is the only one left now. This was where the scientists and engineers lived and developed their technology. The launch bay, where we're going now, is where they built and tested the first spacecrafts."

"So the quantum b-beam has been tested before?" Otto interrupted.

"Earlier, more unstable versions have," he said as the tram began to slow. "But we've come a long way since then. Leaps and bounds."

The tram came to a stop with a small bump, making us stumble forward a step. I let go of Larissa's hand as its doors slid open and we exited. We emerged into an enormous cylindrical room and I couldn't help but stare at my surroundings as I followed the others out.

The room stretched from where we stood, up into the depths of a darkness my eyes couldn't penetrate. It was decidedly colder here. Even with my temperature-adjusted tunic, my skin prickled with the chill and curls of breath frosted my mask.

The air hummed with the harmony of people, drones, and the deep, soothing tones of the Kepler One. To say that I felt insignificant next to such a beautiful and enormous behemoth was an understatement. It looked just like it had on the screen, only its shell shone more brightly and the spinning, sliding rings around it sounded more like the dropping of a sharpened guillotine.

The Kepler One loomed over us like the giant's beanstalk in tales of old, and I was sure one of the rings would come loose and decapitate us at any moment. It's dangerous beauty terrified me, but it made it real. This was the Kepler One and we were *really* going into space . . . at least the others were.

People in green overalls and white hardhats, watched us with suspicion as we encroached into their sanctum. Some of them carried clipboards, while others hauled equipment on hovering flatbeds. All of them looked ill and undernourished, but that didn't' surprise me. Judging by the cold and the void of darkness above us, I doubted there was much between us and the irradiated surface of Earth.

"Welcome to the launch bay," the professor touted, making his way to the ship. "This is where you'll launch and begin your journey to Kepler 452b. This chamber is like, em, the barrel of a gun, and when your thrusters ignite you'll be shot through the atmosphere and into space."

The thrusters he referred to weren't exactly high technology. They were eight cylinders of highly explosive fuel which, when lit, would propel us out of Earth's gravity. An umbilical and last hurrah to the old world. They contained only enough fuel for one launch, after which they would disengage and the nuclear engines would take over. This solidified our inability to explore alternative planets along the way, and delay Bunker Twelve's rescue.

"The rings you see spinning around the spacecraft are what generates the inertial dampener. It acts like a shield and makes it streamline in any environment as well as impervious to the gravitational forces of the wormhole . . . to a certain degree, of course. Isn't that exciting?"

"Fan-bloody-tastic," Emily said with a snort. "Can't wait."

I swallowed the dryness in my throat. Although he tried his best to dumb it down for those of us who would never be able to comprehend the complexity of this ship, I was still lost. To me, the whole idea was incomprehensible.

The professor ignored Emily and continued toward the ship. Higher up, drones passed equipment seemingly right through the solid walls of the Kepler One. Like pebbles dropping into a puddles, they disappeared with little more than a ripple. In the same way, the silver walls above the thrusters parted in two as though they were curtains made of water. A grated gang plank protracted from inside, and ground to a halt a few feet in front of us.

"This way," the professor said, guiding us inside.

"W-where did this, I mean, how . . ." Otto stammered, the wonderment in his young face giving a sparkle to his eyes. "W-we have barely enough t-to survive. Where d-did this all come from?"

"Most of the resources were obtained before the nuclear war," the professor replied, only glancing over his shoulder at us as we followed him onto the gangway. "So you can thank the previous rulers of this country for it all."

It had never occurred to me, before he said it, to wonder what part of Earth we were buried under. It never seemed important. Not until now, when we would eventually emerge from our hiding place and see what was left. An odd sense of grief struck me as I realised we would be the first humans to witness the devastation left in the wake of the bombs. We might very well be the last to see its scarred surface, too.

"What country are we under?" I questioned, absently reaching a hand to stroke the undulating hull of the Kepler One as we passed through its doors. It was cool and more solid than I was expecting.

"Bunker Twelve is buried beneath the island of Manhattan, in America. I think that was its name. The Kepler One will launch from an area once called Central Park," he answered. "But where we are doesn't matter anymore. There's nothing left of the old world above except ghosts."

The inside of the Kepler One surprised me. It was more boring than I imagined. I thought it would be more like Tier One, full of unnecessary decoration and embellishments. Aside from the dark grated flooring underfoot, the ship was an homage to the mundane. Beige, curving, walls, punctuated with severe white lights, ran on forever either side of me. And that was it, nothing more. Regardless of its austerity, however, the solidity of the ship exuded a power that kept me in awe of it.

"About a third of the space on this ship is taken up by the two engines; the jump drive, and a nuclear powered engine," he said.

"Sorry, why can't we just use the jump drive again?" I questioned, feeling a heat rise in my cheeks for not remembering something important.

"If we approach or leave a planet using only a wormhole, we might end up inside the core or splattered on its surface," he said patiently. "Manoeuvring around a gravitational pull that strong must be done using slower engines."

"Of course it does," I answered, feeling stupid. This was something we had covered in class and I already knew it. "Can we see it? The jump drive, I mean."

The professor nodded, grinning broadly as our attention finally focused only on him. He guided us through more corridors—which looked identical to the last—and I worried that I might end up lost, forever wandering the crazy wonderland of mirrored passageways.

A gentle hum, the same hum I heard from outside the ship, grew in volume as we came closer to the source. It throbbed in slow rhythmic beats now, and I felt the reverberations through my feet. A wide room opened up to reveal the metallic heart of the ship in all its spherical, glory.

The jump drive was enormous, at least five times my height with wires that glowed in a patchwork of sigils.   They traversed its curved surface in wild complex of patterns. Piping and tubules skewered the behemoth at regular intervals and branched into a network of smaller wires, which then disappeared into the walls of the ship.

"Engineering," the professor declared. "Those of you lucky enough to become an engineer will work from this station. All, that is, except the chief engineer who will remain on the bridge. This is where you will programme and initiate your flight, among other things."

It was a job involving complicated mathematics I wasn't intelligent enough to understand. I didn't fancy being an engineer much anyhow. Right below the suspended ball, and far too close to it for my liking, was the engineer station, complete with four chairs. Presumably this is where they would be strapped in for launch.

"And this," the professor said, standing on one of the chairs to pat the behemoth in a slow circular motion like it was a cherished pet. "This is the jump drive. Using it, we can tunnel through the universe to create our wormholes."

"Is that safe?" Thelma asked, crossing her arms over her chest as he hopped off the chair again. "No offense or anything, but are you sure we won't, like, destroy the universe in the process?"

"Quite sure," he answered, leading us out of engineering again. "Believe it or not, we've been working on this for longer than you've been alive. Come, please keep up. We only have a short time to see everything. I must have you back to the general after lunch."

The mere thought of the general put a damper on my excitement. I wanted to stay on the ship and explore more of it instead of being shouted at by that cantankerous windbag.

We rounded another indiscernible corridor, and I was struck by one particular door on the left. With no markings, its most striking feature was its vibrant yellow colour. It was out of place in the sea of beige and piqued my interest.

"What's in here?" I asked, stopping and pointing to the door.

"That's where the nuclear engines are kept," the professor answered over his shoulder, still walking.

"Aren't you going to show it to us then?" I said, surprised by my own belligerent tone.

"That room is shielded with lead to protect you all from the radiation," he said, not waiting for us. "Only droids can enter it safely. If I open that door, you would die within seconds of exposure. That's not exactly a smart move on my part, now is it?"

The others pushed past me and I felt like an idiot.

"No, of course not," I said, swallowing deeply.

The professor brought us into an elevator which climbed the heights of the Kepler One at alarming speeds. There was little more room than in the entrance to the tram, but at least I wasn't squashed up against Nathan this time. I clung to a rail fastened to one of the beige walls and did my best to keep my footing as the elevator suddenly stopped and then sped in a horizontal direction. Thankfully the ride was short and soon we milled into another beige corridor.

"Here we are," the professor sang, waving his hand over a door embossed with the number fifteen in large black figures. "This is one of the entrances to the cargo hold, which takes up the majority of the Kepler One."

The doors swhoosed open seamlessly, and we all caught our breaths. I stepped onto the grated platform beyond the door and held the railing in front of me firmly. We were on the fifteenth floor, and below us, more grated platforms snaked around the walls of a giant chasm within the ship.

Cumulating in lines inside the chasm, and swaying on hangers, were hundreds of mechanical monsters of every size. Some even reached our towering heights while others occupied only the first few floors below. Each was adorned with a variety of shovels, tank tracks, or thick tree-trunk legs, and enormous drill bits that I imagined could easily find the centre of the Earth. Some of these monsters had smaller beasts dangling from their dark metal armour, like puppets hanging from a hook. They, too, had a variety of tools instead of limbs. I had never seen anything like it before.

"W-what are these?" Otto asked beside me, his voice full of wonderment.

"These are the excavators and ship builders," the professor replied matter-of-factly. "These are the machines that will find the resources on the new world and build the rescue ships. Their tasks have already been programmed, and they will perform their duties automatically once activated."

From the size of them, I could imagine them leaving whole worlds flattened, pillaged, and left for dead. I wondered, for just a moment, if it was such a good idea to let them loose on the new world. Smarter people than I had created them, however, and I assumed they knew the planet's tolerance for destruction.

"All auxiliary personnel will be seated here for take-off," the professor said.

He gestured toward three dark-grey chairs securely fastened to the wall beside us and I thought it almost symbolic really. The auxiliary crew, those with no specific purpose other than to be extra DNA or an extra pair of hands, left strapped next to the rest of the cargo. I wouldn't have minded being an auxiliary crew member, but I knew it was unlikely to happen.

Stealing one last glance at the metal leviathans, I followed the professor out of the cargo hold. The passageways were becoming easier to figure out now that I knew the centre of the ship was hollow.

Rounding a bend, the professor ran his hand over a small panel on a blaringly white door. It opened and revealed a predominantly white room with several beds wrapped tightly in white linen. One of the beds was attached to the same kind of body scanner I remembered from my first day as a cadet. I remembered how vulnerable I felt that day, too, and was only slightly amused to find that I felt no different today.

Liam stepped into the room, leaving the rest of us congregating around the door. He ran his hand over a multitude of cupboards hiding bottles of pills and vials of medicines behind opaque glass. His red hair and tunic contrasted brightly against all the white, but he seemed peaceful, happy to be there, even.

"This is Medbay," the professor said, following Liam inside. "This is where your medic will stay. It's stocked with the most advanced equipment and supplies which should last at least a few years, well beyond your time on the planet."

The professor's choice of words struck me as odd.

"What do you mean, well beyond our time on the planet? Surely we'll be there for more than a few years?" I asked, narrowing my eyes as the professor began to lead us toward the back of Medbay.

"Sorry, em, I meant well beyond your time there *alone* . . . until we arrive there, too," he answered, hurrying toward a series of rooms with nothing but transparent plastic for walls. They looked sturdy enough, and each had a keypad on the outside of their doors, but privacy was obviously not a factor in their design. "These are the isolation chambers. I don't expect you'll need them, but these are here in case one of you contract a contagious disease, or something. After all, we have no immunity to the potential microbes on the new planet.

"And if you see here," he said, gesturing to a gathering of people huddled around a metal table inside one of the chambers. "We're temporarily using one of the chambers as a clean room to construct the ship's android."

Spread across the table were the same mechanical workings as we saw earlier. Only now its arms, legs, and torso were being slowly covered by a skin, of sorts. White humming machines, complete with a nozzle underneath, hovered over the droid and sprayed coating after coating of an alabaster substance onto its body. Metallic ribs slowly disappeared before our eyes, as did the gooey wires traversing its abdomen, hidden beneath this pale membrane. The only part of this android which appeared complete was its head. It smiled at us while perched on a block at the end of the table.

This droid wasn't like the automatons' on Tier One. It could have easily passed for human, if it wasn't so perfect. A floppy wave of dark hair fell over one of its brown eyes. Although its nose was slightly longer than it ought to be, it was still sleek, thin, and elegant, and brought an aspect of imperfect perfection to its features. Rose red lips parted slightly to greet us, revealing flawless white teeth. It was the spitting image of the bunker avatar and those same mascara-lined brown eyes that had followed me around my room in Tier Five, followed me again.

"So, he will have access to the whole ship, including personal files?" Tristan asked.

"Yes, and no," the professor answered as we gathered closer to the plastic wall for a better look. "There's only so much information we can download into its brain. It can access all that through the ship, though, but we've limited the mobile bot's memory to only what's necessary."

Necessary, I thought. *Who decides what's necessary? Is it necessary to know if one of us has more to lose than the others? Is it necessary to try to save us all and risk the ship should it come to it?* The android's disassociated smile made me wonder if he might let us die out of spite, or logic, or whatever motivated a robot to turn on its masters.

"Hello!" the android said in a tinny voice, blinking only once.

"How exciting, his first word," the professor almost squeaked. "Hello there."

The professor waved at the robot, but it didn't respond. It stared blankly at us before closing its eyes and dropping its smile. The people working around the table cursed, one of them flinging his arms in the air in exasperation. I was guessing they weren't expecting it to shut down. Perhaps there was an overload somewhere? It didn't reassure me that the android would be ready for our flight, but then again, I didn't have to worry about that. It wasn't as if I was going to be on the Kepler One as it took off.

The professor ushered us out of Medbay as the workers threw scathing looks in our direction, like it was our fault the android had malfunctioned. As we made our way back toward the tram, he explained that the levels above us weren't ready for viewing yet: Too many wires and hazards lying around. Judging by the equipment still sailing through the uppermost walls of the ship as we left the Kepler One, I figured he wasn't exaggerating.

He did describe the three levels we hadn't seen, however. Above the Medbay lay the security level, where we could find the armoury, equipment, and the brig. Jail cells, as unnecessary as the isolation chambers apparently, but there nonetheless. That was also where the terraforming machine was located, but it was under lock and key, inaccessible even to the professor. It made sense really. Without it, there was no mission, so every precaution had to be taken.

Above the security deck were our quarters, a gym, and the stasis chamber, where we would sleep as we jumped from one wormhole to the next. Above that again, and at the topmost layer of the Kepler One, was the command deck, which included the bridge.

I was only slightly disappointed that I wouldn't get to see the whole ship, but as we barrelled down the tunnel toward the Central Pavilion again, I couldn't help but be overwhelmed with what we did see. How the human race had evolved since our time as cavemen was astonishing, but yet, we hadn't evolved enough to have stopped the war, nor could we save the Earth. I wondered then, would we ever?

Chapter 8

The first thing which alerted me that something was terribly wrong was the fact that the gym was empty of all Tierless soldiers as we entered. Void of the normal din of grunts and shouts, only the sounds of our boots and the hum of a couple of nearby drones reverberated as we formed our usual two rows and stood to attention.

The second thing that alarmed me was the fact that General Stonewall waited quietly as we filled in, his lapdog ever-hovering by his side. General Stonewall's nature was anything but patient from what I knew of him.

"Good afternoon, Maggots," he bellowed. "I hope y'all are well rested. Never one to be accused of being a procrastinator, I'll get to the point. We'll be starting your *most important* testing today . . . endurance."

The sensation of my heart growing wings and fluttering about my chest like a frantic bird trying to escape its cage, consumed me instantly. I thought I might pass out as fear washed the heat from my body.

"Why do w-we need endurance, exactly?" Otto asked, raising his shaking hand only as far as his ear.

The general narrowed his eyes in the direction of the voice. He took two long strides toward Otto, only Otto was more to his right and the general didn't seem to notice. His dog took hold of the crook of his arm and tugged him slightly into place. The general shrugged off the captain roughly and literally growled at him.

"I know where the kid is," he snapped.

General Stonewall stepped to the right and lined his eyes up with Otto, who by now was sweating profusely beneath his bowl-cut hair.

"If you should fall off a mountain, it's my job to make sure that you can hold on long enough for the rest of them to save your fat ass," he said, gritting his teeth together. Otto flinched at the insult. "It's also my job to make sure you ain't gonna die of a heart attack after climbing said mountain. Endurance is what's gonna keep y'all going. It's gonna stop y'all from giving up and lying down to die like a mangy dog. Don't get me wrong, I don't give a bare-ass flick about your lives save for one aspect of it. If *you* die, we *all* die. And that I do care about."

The general leaned in closer to Otto, actually touching noses with him and squaring off in an overtly aggressive manner.

"There ain't no room for fragile flowers in this group. Understand, son?"

"Y-yes," Otto whispered, closing his eyes as tears escaped.

"WHAT?"

"YES, SIR!" he bellowed, without a hint of a stammer.

Satisfied, the general resumed his original position next to his guide dog. He scanned the rest of us and curiosity had me wondering how much he could actually see. But even if he was completely blind, he was still a formidable man and I wasn't about to test him.

"Today's trial will be final," he began. "Y'all are gonna hang from the hoops on the ceiling for five minutes. If you can't manage five minutes, the only place for you to go is to plummet to the ground where you'll most probably break something. And if you fall, you'll also be sent back to your tier. This is a do or die situation kids!"

Frantic whispers crescendoed, and the general acknowledged them with a nod. I couldn't help but look up at the small hoops no bigger than my head, dangling fifteen feet off the cement floor. My fluttering heart became manic and my palms began to sweat.

"I expect that most of you will have trouble with this, but this is something you gotta overcome. You gotta keep holding on as if your life depended on it, 'cos someday it might. You gotta fight past that little voice in your head telling you to let go. Doing everything you can to survive, and doing only what your head says you can do, are two *very* different things. One will keep you alive, while the other will kill us all. I need to see that y'all have that gumption before I send *anyone* into space."

The captain strode over to the far wall and pressed a green button on a large panel of blinking lights. Slowly the ropes began to lower.

"Find a spot and prepare yourselves," the general ordered.

We fanned out and found our places beneath the hoops. No more than five feet away, and surrounding me, were Tristan, Nathan, and Otto. The two Tierless kept their focus on the ropes as they stopped an inch above our heads. Otto whimpered beside me; his hands looking sweatier than mine as he rubbed them repeatedly on his tunic.

"You'll be okay," I said to him. "Just hold on."

"I c-c-can't do it," he replied, his lip quivering. "I'm too heavy. I'll never be able to h-h-hold myself up."

I glanced at Tristan. He had slipped his arm through the hoop, hitching his elbow on the plastic rim, and wrapped his hand around the rope.

"Look, do it this way," I said, mimicking Tristan. "The hoop is too thick to hold onto for long and your hand will lose its grip."

Otto followed my instructions and for the first time since we met, he smiled at me.

Without warning, the hoops suddenly jerked and the ropes began to retract. I held on for dear life as my weight put pressure on my shoulder and wrist. It didn't take long to reach the dizzying heights of the gym ceiling, and it took more than a few breaths to steady my nerves. Already my hand had turned a light shade of blue as the rope choked off the blood supply . . . but I was still holding on.

I heard Otto whimper again. He was moving and twisting, trying to relieve the pain in his arm.

"Don't," I told him. "Just accept the pain and stay still. Moving will only make it worse." Otto nodded and stayed perfectly still, sniffles the only noise he made as tears streamed down his cheeks.

I willed my own body to go limp. The pain in my arm made it almost impossible, so I tried to think of something other than the numbness spreading over my fingers. It was Larissa who distracted me. She was gently swinging herself back and forth on the hoop, humming like she might be brushing her hair. I didn't know if her laissez-faire attitude was a ploy to throw off the other competitors around her or if she was just freakishly strong. Either way, she was the only one who seemed to be enjoying it.

It irked me beyond belief to see the two Tierless dangling calmly on their ropes. Their eyes were closed as if they were asleep, while all around them people groaned and cried. They were so similar in physique, but completely different in nature. I wondered how that could be if they were both brought up the same way.

Then I remembered Tristan hadn't been brought up that way. He still had memories from his life in Tier Five, dark memories I knew only too well. I also began to wonder how different he might have been if his parents had kept him. Would we have ever met? He certainly wouldn't have been so brawny, and his skin would lack the healthy glow it had now, but I was sure he would still be as handsome. His nose was perfectly straight, and his chin was angular and strong. No amount of malnutrition could hide that.

"Zoe, I can't hold on," Otto whimpered beside me.

Otto's entire head had gone bright red and sweat poured from his brow now, making his hair stick to his face. His free hand was gripping his other arm that quivered with the effort of holding on.

"If I could j-just switch arms."

Otto started to grab for the rope with his other hand.

"No, don't move," I said, the pain in my arm returning and making me clench my teeth. "If you switch, you'll lose your grip. Just keep going. You can do it, Otto. I know you can."

Otto shook his head, his eyes wide with fear as he glanced at the ground beneath him.

"Look around you," I said, gesturing with my head to the others. Some had grabbed onto the hoop only and were now paying for their mistake. "You're still up here, Otto. You haven't fallen yet. We must be four minutes into it at this stage and your grip isn't slipping like the rest of them. So if they can do it, you can, too."

"I, I, no, I can't do it. Zoe, I can't."

"You *can,* Otto. Fight for one more second. If you don't fall, fight for another second, and then another. It's all that's left; seconds. Okay?"

Otto nodded, his lips pursed together and his eyes squeezed hard.

Suddenly, a scream filled my ears and turned my blood to ice. From the corner of my vision I saw Chuck, the boy with a shock of black hair, plummet to the ground. I closed my eyes as his body met with the hard cement with a sickening thud. The fall was instantly followed by the sounds of snapping and a blood-curdling scream. I opened my eyes just enough to see the boy's slight frame writhing in pain. Both of his legs were twisted in a way they were never meant to go.

"Concentrate," I told Otto. "Don't look at him. Just concentrate on holding on."

Otto was crying out loud now, so were a few others as the medics came to take Chuck away. His screams grew fainter as he was carried through the corridors, but no matter how faint they became, I could still hear them in my mind. The scene was all too close to my last memory of Amile and I found myself desperately trying to not cry.

"Time's up. Well done, the rest of you," the general eventually boomed from below us.

After a sudden clunk our ropes began to descend toward the ground again. My boots touched the ground, and I unfurled the rope from around my purple hand allowing the blood to rush back. The pain was unbearable. I cradled my arm close to my stomach and doubled over, waiting for it to pass. A severe case of pins and needles followed that, and Otto verbalised my discomfort in loud wailing cries.

"You did good," Tristan said from behind me, his voice calm.

"I, well, I mean . . ." I stuttered, awkwardly. "I just copied you, that's all," I said, standing again and pretending that my arm wasn't on fire.

"Good, I was hoping you would," he said with a coy smile, resting his hand on the small of my back.

A faint redness flushed his cheeks and Tristan slipped his hand away quickly, his fingers accidentally brushing my waist under my dishevelled tunic. I was expecting a tingle to shoot through my skin as he touched me; a jolt of electricity, anything. There was nothing, and that confused me.

"Why do you think I stood beside you?" he asked.

My mouth opened to say something, but nothing came out. I hadn't realised that he had stood there on purpose. Even if I did, I wasn't sure I'd have figured out he was trying to help me without being too obvious. I also wondered if my feelings for him were more indicative of a friendship than of someone I truly fancied. I was disappointed the dong of truth that came with that thought.

"Line up, Maggots!"

Tristan turned away and followed the general's orders without hesitation. I straightened my tunic and fell into line with the others, avoiding the bloodstain Chuck had left behind.

"Endurance is the most important thing y'all are gonna learn," the general said. "Your brain is gonna tell you that you can't do stuff. It's gonna try to convince you that there has to be another way, an easier way. I'm here to tell you that there ain't no other way. It's *all* gonna be hard, and the sooner you reconcile that with your mind, the sooner y'all can get over it. Your body will do as your mind tells it. And if it tells you to let go, y'all will end up like Chuck . . . with two broken legs and a one way ticket back to momma."

We all glanced at the door Chuck had departed through. He wasn't someone I would call a friend, or even an acquaintance, but I hated to see anyone's hopes of escaping this Prison of Hades dashed.

"Get yourselves ready for dinner," the general said. "Tomorrow ain't gonna be any easier, and y'all could do with some shuteye."

"Yes, Sir," we replied in unison.

After one last intense stare, the general strode out of the gym, reluctantly accepting his captain's gentle nudges toward the door. Not really knowing what to say to each other, we all followed Tristan and Nathan as they made their way to The Tin. I took my usual place at the back, behind Larissa.

"You did really well," I called after her.

Larissa turned to look at me. Her eyes raked over me as if she was determining if I was being sarcastic or genuine.

"Thanks," she replied, flashing a smile. "So did you."

Larissa waited for me to catch up. We walked together down the corridors while the others went ahead.

"I did okay, but you didn't seem to be bothered by it at all."

"Yeah, I guess it's 'cos I'm weirdly strong," she said with a snort of laughter. "You know, the boys were scared of me as a kid 'cos I could always beat the crap out of them."

I laughed, picturing her raising her fists over her head triumphantly as she peaked a mound of unconscious boys. Maybe that was the reason she was so popular in her tier. Her kindness and strength had seen her become a hero to them.

"Wish I was that strong," I muttered.

"But you are," she replied, resting a hand on my arm. "You came from nothing and have probably lived a more horrible life than any of us can imagine. Everyone either feared you or had something against you when you first came here, but you stuck it out. You never gave up, you never let them bring you down. Not only that, but I saw you helping Otto even though he stood against you with the others. It takes strength not to succumb to bitterness, and *that's* what I admire about you the most. Living the life you had, it would be easy to become bitter and selfish, but you didn't."

I didn't know what to say. My cheeks warmed and my vision blurred with unshed tears. No one had ever said such nice things about me before.

"Thanks," I said quietly, unable to make my voice any louder.

Larissa smiled and wrapped an arm around my shoulders, squeezing me tightly.

"Come on, you big soppy mess, or the boys will eat our dinner, too," she said, letting go of me.

We walked in silence after that and I couldn't help but smile. I wondered if this was what having a friend was like. Although Jason was my friend, he was also my brother, someone who had no choice but to like me. Larissa, on the other hand, didn't depend on me for anything. She could have ignored me in the corridor and kept walking.

Of course, she was completely wrong. I wasn't strong at all, and I *was* bitter about things. Being bitter only aided vengeance, however, and vengeance got people killed. My life had taught me to keep all that inside, put one foot in front of the other and just keep going. There was no conscious effort on my part to be the bigger person. Still, if Larissa wanted to think that of me, who was I to argue?

I followed the sumptuous smell of dinner into The Tin. My stomach rumbled and I hastily grabbed a tray of food from Al. I sat in the usual corner by myself and tucked into the meal that, today, actually resembled real food. Hanging from the rafters worked up a serious appetite.

"M-mind if I join you?" Otto asked.

I turned to find him standing beside me, his metal tray shaking slightly in his grip and an anxious look fretting his round face. My mouth full, I nodded and gestured to the chair beside me.

"She says it's okay," he shouted back to the table of people he normally sat with.

Without warning, they each picked up their trays and followed him toward my table. After a few moments of shuffling and pushing, they sat down. I didn't know what was happening. I thought they were going to ambush me, or something worse. I swallowed the food in my mouth with great difficulty.

"What do you want?" I asked, staring at them all.

"Some help," Otto replied. "I p-propose that we allow Zoe into our secret group. All those in favour, say a-aye."

Each of his friends raised their hand without hesitation. "Aye."

"What group? What the hell are you talking about?" I said, becoming more wary with each smile that flashed in my direction. "I don't want to be part of any group. I just want to be left alone."

"But you need help to r-read, right?" Otto said before I could stand and move to another table. "We can help you with that."

My guard was immediately raised.

"But you don't like me, Otto. None of you do," I said. "Why would you help me?"

"You know, at first we were t-t-terrified of you," he began. "I thought you'd slit my throat in the m-middle of the night just to eliminate me."

"I thought you'd sprout claws and gut us all," Jax said.

I remembered Jax from the body scanners on the first day; a gangly Asian boy with green tipped, spikey hair who smiled broadly.

"But we r-realise now that we w-were wrong," Otto interpreted.

"What changed your minds?" I said, pushing my food around the tray with my fork. "Why aren't you all scared of the big, bad Tier Five anymore?"

"Because you helped me," Otto said, his pale-blue eyes fixed resolutely on mine. "You didn't have to. You could have just let me fall, and then there would have been two of us eliminated. B-but you didn't. So we've had a meeting, and we've decided that you're part of our group now."

"What do you do in this group?" I asked, curiosity piquing my interest.

"Well, for you, w-we'd help you read and in exchange you could help us learn to f-fight and get stronger."

"Isn't that cheating?" I asked, looking at the sea of hopeful faces. "We're supposed to earn our places by ourselves. General Stonewall said so."

"The two Tierless have had a lifetime of training and good food," Jax interjected. "Even Sam and his little band of cretins have had a better head-start than you. And there's no way we can compete against the likes of Larissa."

"It's about the survival of the fittest. We're just levelling the playing field, that's all," said the girl who sat beside me in class. Thelma, I think her name was. "In the end, doesn't that make us more likely to survive, if we band together instead of fighting against each other? Doesn't that make us the fittest?"

She was right, of course, but if I learned anything on Tier Five it was that everyone had an angle and nothing was done out of the goodness of anyone's heart. Regardless of what this little group's real reason for including me was, I *did* need their help.

"All right. When do we start?"

"Tonight at three a.m.," Otto replied, a wide grin spreading over his face. "When e-everyone else is asleep and the drones leave to recharge. We'll meet in the usual place."

Chapter 9

I never fancied myself much as a teacher. Sherpa of folks as meek as myself, maybe, but I always thought myself too stupid or inexperienced to be anything other than the fodder for whatever life created or destroyed around me. So before bed, and with Otto's permission, I told Tristan about their secret group hoping he would help.

"Sorry. Ain't interested," he answered.

His response shocked me, and for a long time my mouth stayed open, unable to close itself. I stared dumbly at the floor as he finished dressing for bed. My mouth opened and closed silently as slipped under his sheets.

"Why won't you help us?" I finally asked.

"Why should I?" he replied. "Listen, I don't mean to sound harsh or anything, but what's the point? Really? Everyone keeps telling you that this is a competition. Why would I wanna help my competitors? I mean, it kinda sounds crazy to me."

"But you're helping me?"

"Yeah, but you're different," he said, fixing his pillow and closing his eyes.

"How? How am I different?"

Tristan opened his eyes again and stared at the ceiling, letting out a long, exhausted sigh.

"You're different 'cos I think you can actually make it. *Those* guys are a lost cause and can offer me nothing in return. Don't get me wrong. I really wish it wasn't the case.

"If you get involved with them, you'll only get your heart broken when they fail. And they'll do nothing but drag you down with them, too," he said, turning his back to me to end the conversation. "You gotta make smart choices here, Zoe. And figuring out who's most beneficial to befriend is more important than you realise."

My brain couldn't comprehend the words he was saying. I had pictured Tristan as this hero, the strong silent type who helped people without the need to brag about it, but the words coming out of his mouth smashed that image like a rock through a glass window. He wasn't the strong silent type at all; he was just the silent self-serving type. I wondered how he saw my friendship benefiting him. What was he after? My anger surged, and I nearly ripped my night clothes as I pulled them on.

"What's the matter?" Nathan called from across the room. "Lovers have a tiff?"

"Get lost," I replied hotly.

Nathan's was the last voice I wanted to hear right now. I lay in my bed, pulled the covers up to my nose, and mulled over the disappointment fuelling my anger. The lights went out like clockwork at eight p.m., like they did every night. This was Bunker Twelve's method to conserve energy. Anyone left milling around after curfew had to do it in the dark.

All my energy, however, was spent trying to figure out what Tristan meant.

He's right, I thought. *Otto might not make it through the selection process, and if I spend my nights helping him, I'll only lose out on sleep and time I could use to better myself.* I needed to learn how to read, however, and Otto was the only one offering. *Could I be selfish and use Otto to get what I needed, only to leave without returning the favour?* I already knew the answer. I knew what it was like to be left behind, forgotten, with no one to help, and I wasn't going to do that to anyone.

It took a long time to fall asleep, but no sooner had I closed my eyes, then I was being woken again by a sweaty hand shaking my shoulder. I sat bolt-upright and balled my fist, waiting for my eyes to adjust to the darkness and find the face I needed to clobber.

"Zoe, it's m-m-m-me," Otto whispered.

"Oh, sorry."

Otto gave a nervous smile and gestured for me to follow him. The cement floor was cold on my feet as he led me out to the corridor. It was eerily quiet, deserted even by the drones. Never having lived in a tier where drones hung around, I had no idea that three in the morning was recharging time, but we weren't left completely unsupervised. Whispers travelled from the end of our corridor through the still air and reached my ears.

"Tierless," Otto mouthed, pointing to the end of the corridor.

A patrol? He stopped and waited until it was quiet once again. Beckoning me with a wave of his hand, we continued to tiptoe past the heavy doors of the

Tierless compound. I expected Otto to turn toward the gym, but instead he sized up one of the doors and punched a few buttons on the illuminated keypad beside it. It beeped and swung open.

"How do you know the code?" I whispered.

"Same way any o-other self-respecting nerd would; I hacked it," he replied, grinning from ear to ear.

I gained a new admiration for Otto then. He may not have been the most formidable cadet physically, but anyone able to hack a secure door inside the Tierless compound was a damn sight more valuable in my book.

Inside, the room appeared to be used for storage. Along with countless dusty boxes, there was a tattered punch-bag, with more tape than covering, swinging from the ceiling, and a glitching electronic whiteboard leaning against the far wall. There wasn't a lot of room, but someone had attempted to clear some space by stacking the dusty boxes against the wall, leaving the floor clear.

"Welcome to Afterhours, where you can meet the bottom-dwellers and the most piteous of the pathetic."

It was Thelma who greeted me. She slumped her pear-shaped frame against the boxes and stared at me with as much welcome as a Tier One would have for a meal bar. Standing next to her were five others I didn't recognise, save for two, Angelo and Jax. Angelo's brown eyes flashed sheepishly at me.

"What are you doing here?" I asked him, remembering how he had beaten me near to death when we fought. "Need help with your left hook?"

"Sorry about that, *chica*," he mumbled, toeing some imaginary dirt on the ground. "I tried to stop the fight. And I'm here because you're not the only one who needs help with reading."

I nearly laughed, but caught myself before I did. Angelo was a Tier Two and far more educated than I ever could be, yet here he was, needing the same help. As much as I didn't want to be cocky, knowing it gave me hope that I had a chance to be part of the Kepler crew, however small.

"I don't know why you've brought me here, Otto," I said, turning to him. "Angelo is a far better fighter. Why not just let him teach you?"

"Em, well . . ."

Otto scratched his head and bit his lip as his brain overtly tried to find the right words.

"It's okay, you can say it. I'm a bad teacher," Angelo replied, throwing his hands into the air. "I've tried and tried to teach them what I know, but I always end up shouting at everyone and sending them back to the barracks in tears."

"I see. And you think I'll be any better?"

"Can't be much worse," Thelma replied with a sharpness in her voice.

"Oh, shut up," Angelo retorted. "Maybe if you spent more time paying attention instead of moaning, you might have learned something."

"Well, maybe if you knew your lefts from your bloody rights I might not be so confused," she shouted back, taking a few steps toward him and squaring off.

"Yeah, well, there's only so much you can teach a *cerdo*," he replied, bringing his face an inch from hers and gritting his teeth.

"You watch your filthy mouth," she shouted. "I know what that means."

The two stared at each other as though their next move determined whether or not they would kill each other.

"Get a room," someone pipped in from behind them.

"Shut up," they said in unison.

"Okay," I said, slipping myself between Thelma and Angelo. "How about we just leave it there, before someone says something they'll *really* regret."

Thelma huffed and stomped off to the other side of the room. Angelo cursed at her under his breath in Spanish and did the same. I turned my attention back to Otto.

"I'm not sure I'll be any good at teaching them," I said. "I'll try, but I can't promise anything."

"That's good enough for me," he answered.

"Keep your wrists straight," I shouted. "Punch your opponent with the first two knuckles only. They're the strongest and will do most damage. If you punch with the rest, you'll only end up breaking your wrist."

The Afterhours group replied with a "Yes, ma'am."

I hated it, but for some reason it motivated them, so I didn't argue.

"If your stance is too narrow you'll become unstable," I called, shoving Jax only a little and sending him to the ground. Remarkably his green-spikey hair never moved as he tumbled. "Wider stance, one foot in front of the other, not side by side."

It was only a little more than they knew already. Even still, over the past few days I began to see the improvements slowly but surely. They were becoming stronger. Otto didn't cry anymore, and Thelma swore less at Angelo.

"Yes, ma'am."

"Spell benefit," Otto shouted over the huffing and puffing of the group.

"B-E-N-I-F-I-T," I replied.

"No, give me ten," he answered.

I swore and dropped to the ground for ten press-ups.

"Spell benefit," he repeated when I'd finished.

It was a game we played. No one could stop practice until I spelled ten words correctly. Until then, they had to keep punching and kicking the air, no matter how long it took. So far, I had spelled every word incorrectly, at least once. It had been a trying few days and they had worked hard. So hard that during the rare instances when I removed my rebreather, the stench of sweat in the room choked out any other odour.

"Oh my *God*," Thelma shrieked. "Spell the word already, I'm tired."

"Leave her alone," Angelo snapped. "She's doing her best."

I smiled. It might have been the first time in my life, aside from my parents, that anyone had stuck up for me. As nice as it was that Angelo showed me kindness, it only added extra pressure to get the word right.

"B-E-N-E-F-I-T," I said.

Everyone collapsed to the ground in a heap of panting, sprawling bodies.

"Well do . . . done," Otto said between wheezes.

"I think we should take a break," I said, feeling sorry for the group.

No one answered, but agreement was audible in their gasps. Everyone, that was, save Angelo. He was already quite fit, so the extra time working out hardly knocked a feather out of him.

"Zoe, can I talk to you for a minute?" he asked, taking my arm and leading me to the side of the room where the others were less likely to hear.

"Sure. Are you okay?"

"I'm fine. This isn't about me," he whispered, glancing behind him at the others. "It's about your friend, Tristan."

I stayed quiet, but raised an eyebrow at Angelo. I wasn't sure how he knew Tristan, nor could I fathom what he might have to say about him. Whatever it was, Angelo seemed deeply concerned.

"I know you and Tristan are friends, and I'm happy you've found someone you can rely on," he began, not looking me directly in the eye. "But I've heard things about him, things damning enough that I wouldn't want to be so close."

I opened my mouth to defend Tristan, but Angelo signalled for me not to speak, so I didn't. I wanted to hear what he had to say so I could refute everything and prove him to be the harbinger of nothing more than malign gossip.

"The Tierless don't have homes or families in other tiers because they must remain impartial. It's the way things have always been for them. Their loyalty must always remain with the ruling *Jefe* . . . sorry, boss," he added after seeing my confusion.

"But I've heard that Tristan isn't Tierless-born. He was born to a mother and a father on Tier Five."

"I know," I said, crossing my arms in front of my chest. "But I don't see how being born on Tier Five would make you untrustworthy or any less entitled to have friends."

"Right, yes, I know you're Tier Five, too," Angelo said nervously. "But that's not what I meant."

"Well, you'd better get to what you mean and tell me who spread these rumours about him, too. Otherwise, you and I are going to have problems," I said, leaning forward and narrowing my eyes.

"Do you remember when he was first selected?" I nodded, remembering the lottery. "You remember what Nathan called him?"

"I remember that Nathan was being an ass and called him Lieutenant Reject, if that's what you mean?"

"*Si*, I mean, it kind of is, yes, but it's not just that," Angelo said.

It seemed that my glaring had made Angelo incredibly nervous and he lost some power of speech.

"Would you just say it already?"

The others, having regained their breath, glanced at me. Angelo leaned in closer.

"Tristan isn't as honourable as he might seem," Angelo whispered. "He was reprimanded for excessive use of force and even suspended for . . ." Angelo lowered his voice and leaned closer. "Murder. They say he was trained by the general himself and he treated Tristan like a son. But about a year ago, after the murder, the general didn't want anything to do with Tristan anymore. He dropped him like a hot coal and only tolerates him now. The rest of the

Tierless soldiers think Tristan is some kind of soulless robot. They don't trust him, and neither should you, *chica*."

I didn't know what to say. Angelo was painting Tristan as some egotistical, sociopathic automaton. Tristan had already told me that he had killed people, one of them a little girl if I remembered right. He was only doing his job, surely? It wasn't his fault that people were desperate and chanced their luck by stealing. I had tried it myself. It was the government's fault for hoarding all the best food and medicine.

My anger boiled my innards. Tristan was the first to befriend me, and not because he wanted anything from me in return unlike the Afterhours club did. He helped because I was a fellow Tier Five and he knew the darkness I had come from. I was sure of it. Maybe the general dropped Tristan because he still showed some loyalty toward Tier Five citizens. The general didn't seem the type to tolerate disobedience.

I picked Angelo up by his red tunic and slammed him against the wall. Angelo wasn't a small guy, but I had grown stronger since my arrival in the Tierless compound. Although my arms still quivered, I was able to keep him pinned through the force of sheer outrage alone.

"You don't know the first thing about him," I yelled through clenched teeth. "You don't know what it was like to live in that hellhole. You don't know anything."

"Okay, okay," Angelo said, gasping and grabbing onto my hands, trying to pry them off.

"Who told you all of this? Who's going around spouting this utter B.S.? Was it Nathan?"

I could see it in his eyes, a sliver of uncertainty mixed with fear. Whoever told Angelo these things was someone he didn't want to get on the bad side of. I didn't have to guess the answer; I already knew. Even still, I waited for him to admit it, stretching out his discomfort as retribution. Angelo eventually nodded and I let go of his tunic. He dropped the inch to the ground, leaning against the wall and gasping for breath.

"Of course Nathan would say that." I almost laughed. "Tristan is Nathan's biggest competition here. He's trying to get rid of him. Nathan's a snake, a weasel, and a liar. In the future you should consider your source before you spread lies because it makes you look just as bad, if not worse as the liar."

"I was only trying to help," Angelo said sheepishly, righting his tunic and taking a step away. By now the group was on their feet and staring at us.

"Help?" I screeched. "Tristan has never done anything to hurt anyone here. In fact, he was the only one to befriend me in the beginning. Nathan, on the other hand, has done nothing but wished us all to fail. Haven't you heard him constantly talking about how many are left to be eliminated? Don't you realise *you're* the ones he's talking about? And you've all heard him threaten to kill me *accidentally*. What does that say about him?" No one answered. "Don't let words sway your opinion of people. Let their actions speak for their character instead . . . just as yours have spoken about you, Angelo."

I spun on my heels and crossed the small dusty room, shoving the door open as hard as I could. It slammed against the wall outside, the noise echoing loudly in the stillness of the night. Before it had a chance to swing closed again I stormed out, fists balled and in a seething rage that threatened to consume me.

Clenching my teeth until my jaw ached, I thundered toward the barracks, bursting through the door with no regard for my fellow cadets sleeping there. Quickly finding Nathan's bed in the darkness, I watched him for a beat as he lay on his back, breathing steadily with his eyes closed, and imagined the contempt with which he dreamed. *How does he sleep so well?*

"Zoe, what are you doing?" Tristan whispered from the other side of the room.

I ignored him. I tore over to Nathan's bed, grabbed his blanket, and ripped it off. Just as Nathan began to stir I leapt on top of him and straddled him with my knees pinning down his arms. He struggled under me, still groggy from sleep and not knowing what was happening. Before he realised and could overpower me, I bunched his white t-shirt in one hand and balled my other fist above my shoulder before slamming it into his face as hard as I could.

A sharp heat burned through my knuckles, but I ignored it. Nathan cried out and struggled to free himself. I smiled and hit him again and again, revelling in my dominance over a pathetic bully like him. He deserved every bone-crunching blow. I hit him in the chest, walloped him across his face, and crushed his arms beneath my legs, twisting to make it as painful as possible.

Without warning, a pair of powerful arms wrapped themselves around my waist and lifted me into the air. I fought against Tristan, trying to wriggle free from his grip and pummel Nathan a few more times. Someone switched on the lights and revealed my handiwork in delicious detail. I grinned with satisfaction when I saw Nathan's eye already puffing and his lip bleeding beneath his facemask. A hysterical laugh bubbled in my throat, and I heard the madness of it. Release, sweet release from my oppression.

"What was that for?" he yelled, holding his face.

"You know what it was for," I shouted unreservedly at him. "Is that how you think you're going to earn your place on the spacecraft, slandering people's character so we turn against them? Or maybe it's because you don't want anyone looking at *your* character, you weasely pathetic excuse for a human being, you waste of resources."

I became aware that I was calling him the names I had heard all too often in Tier Five. My breath hitched in my chest, and I sobered from the madness. This wasn't just about Tristan, it was about me, too. I was defending Tier Fives. I was defending my friend like I had wished a thousand times for someone to defend me. But I would never let on, not now that I had gone too far.

"That's enough," Tristan said calmly. "Everyone, go back to bed."

I objected in as many swear words as I knew, but Tristan's grip was too strong for me to argue. He pulled me out of the room and into the gym, dropping me unceremoniously onto the concrete floor. He circled me, pursing his lips together while shaking his head.

"What were you thinking?" he whispered. "What on Earth would make you do that?"

"He was spreading rumours about you," I shouted, my anger not allowing me to speak normally. "He wants everyone to turn against you. He's a *liar*, and I won't let him do it."

Tristan ran his hands through his brown hair, his muscles visibly tensing.

"He ain't lying," he said with a tone of resignation.

"What? What do you mean? He said you were a murderer, that the general wanted nothing to do with you anymore, that you were untrustworthy."

Tristan flopped down and sat cross-legged beside me on the concrete floor. His shoulders slumped and his gaze found an invisible speck of dirt in front of him.

"I *am* all of those things," he said quietly. "Everyone in Tierless has had to shoot someone at some point; it's part of our job."

"But Nathan made it sound like it wasn't part of your job, that you did it maliciously. He said the general brought you up like a son, but now he doesn't want anything to do with you because of it."

"What's between the general and me is gonna stay between us, and it ain't no one's business. But it seems that Nathan got what he wanted from you," he said, locking eyes with me.

"What do you mean?"

"Well, you've attacked him, unprovoked. If he reports you, you're outta here," he said, standing to walk away again. "He's had it in for you since the start, Zoe, and now you've played right into his hands. I wouldn't be surprised if he told your friends these things, knowing full well they'd tell you about it and you'd get all riled up. There's no room for

145

volatile personalities on this mission. The president knows it, and Nathan knows it, too."

Tristan lowered his voice for the last part and the gravity of its meaning became clear. A coldness weighed heavily in the pit of my stomach. Tristan was right. I had been played, and now my poor mother, and Jason, would suffer for my naiveté.

"I told you to be careful about befriending people," he said quietly. "I told you something bad would happen if you trusted people who ain't like you and me."

Tristan squeezed my shoulder sympathetically before leaving me alone in the gym. I sat on the cold cement, agog and pale.

"What have I done?"

Chapter 10

I couldn't swallow breakfast again that morning. The lump permanently stuck in my throat wouldn't allow me. My aversion to food was only partly due to the fact that we were meant to be starting mid-training exams today. The results would dismiss the two cadets with the lowest scores, a fact that had everyone whispering in low voices in The Tin.

I glanced at Nathan. His eye was still puffy, but his lip seemed to have recovered well enough that no one could tell, aside from a small cut, that I had split it last night. Sitting on his own today, his former clique—Sam, Simon, and Emily—appeared not to his taste any longer. He had become isolated from the rest of the cadets recently, too; choosing to be on his own rather than interact. I supposed their already healthy fear of him wasn't helped by my reaction to the rumours he started either.

As much as I wanted to smirk and revel at his unpopularity while a small gathering of cadets were content to share *my* table, I knew I couldn't. If I wanted to stay a cadet, I would have to swallow my pride and beg him not to report me for my outburst.

I picked up my tray and walked over to him. Behind me, everything went silent.

"Mind if I sit here?" I asked quietly.

Nathan looked up at me. His hazel eyes—one now rimmed with a deep purple—narrowed. He didn't say anything for a moment, the food in his mouth still bulging at the side of his cheek. He swallowed as though his meal had suddenly gone dry.

"So long as you promise not to hit me again," he said, pointing a fork to the chair opposite him.

"I can't promise you anything," I said, sitting down, "but I'll do my best."

Nathan looked at me, studying me for a moment. I wasn't sure if he actually found my answer funny or if he thought it would just be better to smile, but he did. It hit me then that this was the first time I had ever seen him smile instead of sneer. If he wasn't such a horrible prick, he would have been quite handsome.

"Listen, I just wanted to say I'm sorry," I said, pushing my food around the tray. "I shouldn't have punched you."

Nathan dropped his fork and it clattered loudly. Everyone in The Tin looked in our direction, but he didn't seem to care.

"You're right," he said loud enough for all to hear. "You shouldn't have jumped me while I was sleeping. That's a coward's attack, and it's the kind of thing your boyfriend would do. If you want to beat on me, fine! Just do it when I'm awake."

Nathan stood, his chair screeching on the floor, and left The Tin without letting me say anything. I clenched my fists desperately trying not to slam them on the table. I was only trying to apologise, even though he deserved everything he got. If anything, he should be apologising to Tristan, but instead Nathan managed to insult him, yet again.

My anger wouldn't let that sit, so I followed him into the hall. I wasn't perturbed by the fact that Nathan's broad frame exuded a darkness that challenged the gloomy corridor. My anger made me impervious to it as I stomped after him.

"Why are you so mean to me?" I shouted after him. "Why are you saying these things about Tristan? He's never done anything to you."

"How do you know?" Nathan shouted, stopping dead and wheeling around on me. "I've known him since we were little, you've known him for all of two and a half weeks. But I guess that makes *you* the expert, right? I guess you know how the world works, too, and who's pulling your puppet strings, don't you? Because you're Zoe Ruthland, all-knowing and all full of . . ."

He stopped short of swearing, but I knew what he meant to say.

"I'm not all-knowing, but I'm not stupid either. I can think for myself," I roared back. "And there's no one pulling my strings. Everything I've done was because I wanted to do it. If I wanted to go home right now, I could."

"Really? Well, if that's what you believe then you're more stupid than I realised," he said, breathing heavily through his nostrils and stepping closer to me. His powerful chest heaved up and down with the effort of containing himself and I started to become nervous. "We all have puppet strings, because we all have something to lose. Why do you think you were chosen to be in the lottery? Because you're *special*?

Do you think it was an accident *you* got chosen instead of the other Tier Five boy? You think it was coincidence that the president knew *your* name and not his? Tell me, what does he have to lose? His parents?"

"That doesn't matter," I said, feeling uncertainty creeping into my gusto.

"Of course it matters. It *all* matters. And I'm guessing by your non-answer that he had nothing to lose," Nathan said, standing upright, crossing his arms triumphantly across his broad chest. "You think any of us were chosen randomly? Of course we weren't!"

"Jason is sick," I shouted, wanting to slap him across his face. "He wasn't chosen because there's something wrong with him, not because his parents are dead."

"Convenient that only one of you got chosen, isn't it? You heard the president. His treatment only continues while you're a cadet. And let's not even pretend that he's your real brother. Another lie from a Tier Five!"

Fear erupted inside my stomach. *How did he know? Did the others know, too? Did the president know?* But the president wouldn't waste valuable resources on a Tier Five if he didn't have to. No, Nathan was just guessing and I had to shut him down.

"You *shut up!*" I yelled. "You don't know the first thing about me or my life. And for your information, I chose to stay even while you were being a complete ass to me."

"You. Chose. Nothing," Nathan shouted. "We were selected because we could be controlled. Because we had something they could hold over our heads. That's why you were picked, that's why you had no choice but to become a cadet. That's also the reason why you *can't* leave. Who else would risk their lives for this pathetic human race? Every one of us has something to lose. Everyone save your boyfriend, that is, and that's what makes him so dangerous."

"He's *not* dangerous, and he's *not* my boyfriend," I said.

Nathan dropped his arms and clenched his fists. For a moment I thought he was going to hit me. I backed away. Even though I had punched him and gained the upper hand once or twice, it had never been a fair fight, not even in the gym when I had kicked him in his privates. The way he leaned toward me now, his glare only an inch from my face, I knew I was no match for him. He was stronger, without question, and an uppercut from him would surely knock me out. I began to wonder why he had never done it before. I also began to wonder what a mean-spirited twat like him could have to lose.

"Oh, but he *is* dangerous, and not just because he has no tether to this world. There's a devil about him, too. Why do you think I warned your friend, Angelo, about him?"

"Because you wanted to slander his name and turn us all against him. Maybe it's *you* who has nothing to lose, and you're reflecting your own issues on him."

My voice went quiet toward the end of my sentence as my bravery left me. If looks could kill, Nathan would have murdered me then. He stepped away, his head shaking and his mouth open.

"Stupid, little girl," he whispered, turning and walking down the corridor.

"Are you going to report me?" I called after him.

Nathan didn't answer.

If someone had asked me the questions, I probably would have passed the test with flying colours. As it was, I only managed to answer half of Professor Salinski's questions. Even at that, I wasn't sure I had understood them correctly. One thing was for certain, if it hadn't been for Otto's teaching, I wouldn't have answered any of them at all.

As much as I wanted to believe Tristan's theory, I couldn't leave my new friends to fend for themselves. I owed Otto, big time, so I decided to keep training them even after the exams. I still hadn't decided if I should continue to be their friend, however. Everyone warned me that this was a competition, and that people would turn on me . . . and they had. Angelo, the unsuspecting pawn in Nathan's plan, Tristan who befriended me but refused to help me, and Otto who helped for a price, were my prime examples.

After my argument with Nathan, however, I felt more disheartened about our mission than ever. If we were the saviours of humankind, what did this kind of behaviour say about us? I couldn't believe humanity would boil down to courageousness derived from fear and self-servitude. Without some kind of camaraderie and compassion, the human race would inevitably be lead to its own demise again, regardless of the planet it was on.

During the test I couldn't stop thinking about what Nathan had said about the president. How could anyone have orchestrated our selection? I wasn't special, as Nathan had pointed out so callously. No one knew who I was, who my family were, or even if I would take any bait they put in front of me. *How could they have known I, a Tier Five, would want to save my family instead of just myself?*

There were a damn sight more Tier Fives who would have used the opportunity to better themselves and then run when it got too tough. I wasn't like the rest of Tier Five, my parents schooling saw to that. It was by their teachings, too, that I came to care about Jason, instead of just leaving him to fend for himself. *Why did they have to be so different?*

Regardless of my confusion, the day's testing continued. The general conceived an assault course worthy of the description. We dived through tunnels filled with blinding smoke, swung from ropes as Tierless soldiers threw objects at us to knock us off, and sparred with each other until half of us were unconscious on the floor or in Medbay.

Thankfully, I dodged most of my attacks and my senses weren't knocked from me. Otto, on the other hand, spent a good twenty minutes drooling on the floor at one point. Our training had toughened him up, and while other cadets gave up and cowered in the corner, he spent a few moments regaining his footing before carrying on. I was proud of him, proud of all of them. Even if they didn't make it, they showed real courage by their actions.

It came to my attention, as I knocked a teary, red-headed girl to the floor, that I hadn't seen Liam during the second half of the testing. He'd been sitting in front of me during the professor's exams, but after that point he had disappeared.

"Have you seen Liam?" I whispered to Angelo.

Angelo was winning his fight against a lanky, sour-faced girl in the sparring ring next to mine. Packed together in the gym like sardines, but within the confines of our own red sparring circle, Angelo was close enough to hear me.

"Ha, don't make me laugh, *chica*," he replied. "You won't see him here."

"Why not?" I said, dodging the feeble attack my opponent threw at me.

Angelo raised an eyebrow and smirked.

"Come on, Zoe, you know he's the president's son," he said. "The High and Mighty Lord Tucker wouldn't be seen dead dirtying himself next to the likes of us. You know he's got a thing about germs, right? He doesn't touch anything or anyone if he can help it . . . not even his *papi*."

I tried to recall ever seeing Liam shake a hand or brush someone's shoulder, but failed. Liam was so good at hiding in a crowd that I had paid little to no attention to his idiosyncrasies, or him in general. He always curled up in his bed at night long before the rest of us and was up before the alarms went off. I thought it was because he didn't want to be around us, but now I was wondering if it was because he wanted to use the bathrooms first . . . before we all came in and sullied it.

"This ain't Sunday tea," the general shouted in my ear. "Quit your yappen' and start fighten'."

"General Stonewall, where's Liam?" I asked, dropping my guard and facing the milky-eyed goliath.

The girl I was sparring with seized the opportunity to strike. Pain shot through my jaw as her fist collided into it. I stumbled a few steps, holding my chin in my hand.

"Yes!" she shouted, pointing to my feet. "I won!"

I looked down. My left foot had stepped outside the red circle. She *had* won.

"You can't afford distractions, Zoe," the general said, turning away from me. "Concentrate on yourself and don't worry about what the others are doing."

"No! Liam should train like the rest of us . . . or does the president's son get special treatment?"

The words echoed in the hall and brought the huffing, crying, and grunting to a stop.

"What?" the general demanded, wheeling toward me again.

"She said—" his faithful dog began.

"I heard her, you idiot. I'm blind, not deaf," he interrupted.

This was the first time the general had admitted his disability in front of the cadets. My outburst had silenced the group, but his admission had removed all sound from the world, or so it seemed. The general ran his broad hand through his spikey hair, clenching his jaw tight. Without warning, he grabbed me by my upper arm and pulled me behind him toward the gym door.

"You stay where you are," he shouted at his dog, pointing back at him without looking.

His dog obeyed, and the general continued to drag me, bumping me into a few cadets who were too slow to hustle out of his determined path. Slapping his free hand against the door and swinging it open, he shoved me through it. I tripped over my own feet and landed in a heap on the ground.

"Girl, if you wanna survive this training and get on that ship, you gotta listen to the right people," the general said, closing the door behind him. "I donno who's filling your head with nonsense, but you need to quit going 'round your ass to get to your elbow. Just fall in line and trust that there ain't no fricken conspiracy to uncover."

"And who are the *right* people, exactly?" I asked, picking myself off the floor to face the general. "How am I supposed to know who they are? So far, the president seems to have slipped his son into our merry band of misfits, and Liam doesn't seem to be required to train like the rest of us. Should I trust the president?

"Then there's you." I stepped closer to the general, hoping he would feel the anger boiling in me. "You're our trainer, our guide, but you're as blind as a bat in a tar pit." The general flinched at my words. "Even with that, I'm sure you can't possibly miss the fact that Liam is exempt to every rule you've laid down. You do nothing to fix it, and you expect us to turn a blind eye, too?" I winced at the unintended pun. "Should I trust you?

"Then there's your son, Tristan, or your step-son. You shun him as though he were a leper, and the Tierless all hate him, but he has been nothing but kind to me. Who do I trust there, the opinion of many or my own gut? I'm actually pretty tired of people not saying what they really mean. So if you don't mind, General Stonewall, I would very much like for you to tell me *exactly* who you think I should trust?"

The general didn't speak for a long time. He always had an air of power and unquestioning authority about him, but after my little speech his shoulders slumped, his barrel-chest deflated, and his face seemed more lined than ever. It was as if pointing out his disability and the flaw behind his orders had removed the façade that he was, well, *more* than us.

"I donno," he said softly. "It was all straight in my head once. But then again, I was able to read people before . . . before I started going blind. I ain't gonna lie, Zoe. Corruption has been around for as long as I can remember, maybe even since the dawn of man. From when he was young, I tried to teach Tristan how to spot it, how not to fall into its trap, but . . ." The general leaned against the wall behind him, and let out a long, weighty sigh.

"But what?" I asked, willing the answer to come from him.

"But I failed," he replied. "I didn't teach him these things so he could use them against people. I taught him so he could be better than those who did. I wanted him to lead the cadets and start our new world without corruption. I guess he didn't see how that could benefit *him*."

The general sounded as if he was talking about someone else, not the Tristan I had come to care about, and I *had* come to care about him. Something else the general said struck a chord with me, however.

"We only found out about Kepler One a short while ago. How can you have trained him from a young age?"

It was a simple question, but one that made the general's eyes widen and his mouth drop open slightly. He caught his breath and froze. I waited and stayed as quiet as a mouse, not wanting him to have any excuse to be distracted.

"Zoe, you ain't gonna be fooled by nothing," the general started. "But I can't answer that."

"Why not?"

"'Cos I just can't, okay?" he said, running his hand through his hair again. "There's some things you just gotta accept here, Zoe . . . please."

I had never heard him say *please* in all the time I knew him, and he didn't strike me as the type who would say it easily. It was like he was begging me to let it drop. If I was smart and wanted on that ship, I knew by his worried tone that I'd have to let that one go . . . for now.

"Believe it or not, I actually kinda like you . . . even if you *can* start an argument in an empty house. You're strong, determined, and honest as a nun in a confession box. We need that in the new world. But you're naïve, too, and that worries me."

The general smiled and for the first time I saw a man, not a warrior nor a leader, but a human being with all the capabilities of love, fear, compassion, and the emotions one wouldn't expect to find in a robot. This man, however, seemed frailer to me now, drained of life's vigour.

"Why would you care?"

"Why wouldn't I?" he said, standing and reaching for my shoulder, squeezing it hard. "You, Zoe, are everything I wanted Tristan to be. I tried so hard to make him a good leader, but I guess I forgot the compassion side of things. Tristan is the best soldier this old general could ever want, but he follows orders regardless of their morality. You don't. And you ain't afraid to stand up for what you believe neither."

His words shocked me, and beneath my rebreather my mouth opened to say something in Tristan's defence, but nothing came out. Of all the things I was expecting to happen after he flung me out of the gym, *this* was not one of them. The general's expression was genuine and his words sounded sincere. I believed that he found what Tristan was missing in me. Although, I didn't truly agree with him, nor did I have any intention of leading anything.

"So," I said with a grin. "If that's what you think of me, I'd love to know what you think of Nathan."

"Ha." The general smiled broadly, letting go of my shoulder and turning to where he thought the door was. He was off by a foot. "That boy makes my ass itch, but he's a good boy. Contrary as a cat licking a porcupine, but good."

"Are you sure we're talking about the *same* guy?" I said, taking his elbow and guiding him to the door.

"Don't," he snapped, pulling his arm away. "I can do it."

The general slid his hand along the wall until he reached the divide between the doors. Feeling his way along the seam, he repositioned himself again. If I didn't know any better, I'd swear his eyesight had gotten worse over the past week. He straightened his uniform and pushed open the doors like a man on a mission, taking long strides inside. His vulnerability stayed outside in the corridor, with me.

Chapter 11

Combat, Environmental, and Academia trials were over. As far as I knew, no one had succumbed to the added gravity or increased temperature of our suits, so I was guessing we all passed Environmental. I wasn't too worried about the combat side of things either. Even though I had lost a match to the teary red-head while I argued with the general, I had won or drawn all the rest of my matches. No, my main concern was the academic side of things. With only fifty percent of the questions answered, the highest score I could get was half as good as everyone else. My only hope was I had done well enough in combat that it would bring up my scores and I wouldn't be kicked out.

A cold stone of dread landed squarely in my stomach, making the warmth drain from my face. *What if I failed?* I hadn't thought about returning to Tier Five in a long while. I was getting used to not living in the catchbasin of crime and deviancy. More than that, I was actually starting to believe that I *could* make it. What a fool I was. I should have been more realistic. I should have been planning my return to Tier Five all this time and working out how I would kill my mother.

My mother. I hadn't thought about her, or Jason, in a long time either. They were constantly on my mind when I was living in Tier Five. Here, in the self-contained world of the Tierless compound, I had allowed myself to pretend. My make-believe world didn't have a sick mother, didn't have a brother depending on me. All it had was me, my trials, and the other cadets. I looked at them and wondered which of them would get the boot alongside me.

A few days after the trials, we had been brought into a little used room of the Tierless compound. Inside, a row of niveous chairs lined pristine white walls like it was the waiting room of Heaven itself. A brown door at the far end, with the president's name engraved on a gold plate at its centre, was all that marred the snowiness; that, and the fidgeting cadets in red and black sitting in the chairs.

Tristan sat next to the brown door, Liam sitting beside him. Neither seemed in any way anxious about meeting with the president to get their results. It didn't surprise me at all. Liam, being the president's son, would have an automatic pass. Tristan was so adept at everything he did that I was as sure he would pass, too. Which meant there were two less spaces for the rest of us, average Joe's.

"You'll do fine," a deep voice said from beside me.

Nathan's hazel eyes rested sheepishly on mine as I glared at him. Only a light discolouration remained under his eye from the shiner I'd given him.

"Can you just *not* talk to me right now?" I snapped.

Nathan raised his arms in surrender and leaned back into his chair. For some unknown reason, he'd been nicer to me over the last few days and it made me suspicious of him. I double checked to make sure there wasn't a sneer beneath his rebreather before I turned away again. Surprisingly, there wasn't. If anything, he looked a little hurt that I had been so offhand, but I couldn't spare the effort it required to be nice to him at the moment. It was taking everything I had to not chew off my own lip.

As I gnawed on it again, the president's door swung open and Angelo came storming out. His brown eyes shone with tears, and his fists shook as he clenched them tightly. I stood as he came closer.

"Angelo, what happened?"

"I'm out, *chica*," he replied, his bottom lip quivering slightly.

"What? B-b-but why?" Otto asked from the side.

"Turns out I'm dyslexic."

"Dys-what?" I said, my mouth open.

If Angelo couldn't pass, as good a fighter as he was, then what chance did I have?

"Dyslexic," Otto answered. "It's where h-he sees letters backward and confuses his left and r-right."

"*No passa nada*," Angelo said, taking the last few steps to the exit of Heaven's waiting room. He rested his hand on the handle and paused for a moment to look at me. "It doesn't matter. I'll get there eventually, won't I, Zoe? When you get to the new planet, promise you'll send back those ships for us. Promise, and I can leave here with some *esperanza*, some hope."

"I . . ."

The truth was, I didn't know if I'd even pass the exams. How could I make a promise I couldn't keep? Angelo looked on the brink of desperation. He was my friend. How could I *not* promise?

"Of course I will," I said, willing my voice to sound confident. "I'll send the first one back for you."

From my periphery I saw a few mouths drop open. I was sure they thought it egotistical of me to assume I'd make it through. But this wasn't about ego; this was about comforting a friend as he was cast back into hell.

Angelo nodded. A meek smile crossed his lips, and a tear rolled down his cheek. He pulled open the door and left the room before anyone else could see, leaving me alone with the weight of my promise and the eyes of everyone on me.

"You did a g-good thing," Otto said.

"Did I?"

I sat back down in my chair and wondered if I should have made that promise at all. I had given Angelo the same false hope I had given my mother the last time I saw her. I was never going to make it onto the Kepler One, surely they knew that?

The nervous twitches of the other cadets returned, along with the silence as Sam was called into the president's office next. I hated the silence; it gave me too much time to think. Instead, I watched Sam skulk his way across the room. A broken-toothed smile flashed back at his cronies, Simon and Emily, sending a cold shiver up my spine.

For whatever reason, I still detested everything about him, even the way he walked. It was unfair to him, but I couldn't help it. My reaction was instinctual, or guttural, or something else I couldn't explain, but it was there nonetheless.

As Sam closed the door behind him, Tristan's expression caught my attention. His lips were pursed and one eyebrow was raised in an, *I told you so,* sort of way. I didn't have to guess what he *told me* about. He'd warned me that making friends with the other cadets would weigh me down, and it had. I could physically feel the burden of my mother, Jason, and now Angelo, as a heaviness on my chest. But why else were we here if not to carry the burden of hope as we tried to save the human race?

I ignored Tristan's disapproval and focused instead on what was to come. No one knew really. All we were told was to wait in the room and the president would speak to us one at a time. He would disclose our results and ask us a few questions about our training . . . whatever that meant.

It wasn't long before Sam came out again. A broad grin stretched under his rebreather, accentuating his rotentine face. My stomach sank; he'd obviously passed. I didn't wish ill upon him, but if there was one cadet I could live without on the new planet, it would have been Sam. It also meant there was one less space for me to try and squeeze myself into.

"Zoe Ruthland!" the president bellowed from inside his office.

My heart flipped inside my chest. I stood and tried my best to walk casually toward the door. I failed miserably as the toe of my boot caught on my other heel, and I stumbled a few steps. Thankfully, I didn't end up sprawled across the white carpet underfoot. Sam caught my arm as he passed by, but not just to steady me. He leaned in far too closely for my liking and whispered into my ear.

"You can thank me properly later."

Sam let go of my arm and sat with his cronies again. They pressed him for information in urgent whispers, but he kept his indigo eyes fixed on me. He wasn't allowed to tell anyone what had happened inside. It was one of the rules the general's dog had barked at us before leaving us to our fate and the buzzing of an ever watchful drone above our heads was all the reason Sam needed to obey. I began to wonder if I had been called next because of something Sam had said to the president. *I won't be thanking you for anything,* I thought.

The president's office was a cocoon of red, gold, and comfort. Like the inside of a womb belonging to a mammoth beast, it encased me in a warmth not usually found in Bunker Twelve. Plump, golden couches pressed against deep-red walls adorned with gilded veins mapping an indiscernible pattern across it. A crystal chandelier, not so big it would overtake the splendour of the room but big enough that it couldn't be missed, dangled from the fingers of four ceiling-dwelling, golden cherubs. Their plump faces gleamed with the smiles forced upon them, and their unblinking eyes followed me into the room.

"Ah, Zoe. May you find health this day. Please, come in and sit down," the president trumpeted.

With great effort, he lifted himself off his seat as a means of greeting me. His podgy hand reached across a wooden table and gestured to a simple, white chair on the other side. I tentatively sat on the edge and nerves clammed my mouth shut tight.

"Now, let me see," he said, sitting again and flicking a thick finger across an electronic tablet on his desk. "General Stonewall has had nothing but the highest of compliments for you. Coming from *him*, that says a lot." I smiled. I wasn't expecting the general to say anything about me at all. I was glad he did, though, because it couldn't hurt my chances of passing, and I needed all the help I could get. Maybe he knew it, too, and that was the reason he intervened. "He says you show great promise and would be one of three cadets he would recommend for moving on to the next phase. That being said, I'm afraid it's not up to just him."

The president looked meaningfully at me. I understood from the beginning that the decision would have little to do with who the best cadets might be and more to do with who the *president* wanted. I itched to argue the unfairness of being the sole decider of our fates. A dictator, however, rarely saw the validity in an argument geared at relieving him of his power. If I wanted to get onto that ship, I couldn't argue, so instead, I smiled at him and said nothing.

"The technician has also complimented you." I bit my tongue at the president's wilful ignorance of the professor's title. "He said you show great promise and you're a hard worker. Your understanding of wormhole mechanics is second to none, and your mechanical reasoning abilities are in the top ten percent of the class. Your test scores, however, say otherwise. So, I'm not exactly sure where he's getting his information."

I swallowed hard. Here it was. Here was the point when the president would tell me that I had to return to Tier Five. My hands gripped the thick armrests of the chair so hard I was sure they would break.

"You were second to last in your academic results and, even with your better scores from combat training and passing environmental with little physiological stresses shown, it still puts you into the bottom four."

The president looked up from the tablet and studied me from under his hooded brow. His ginger eyebrows knitted together as thick fingers stroked his jowls.

"You understand my predicament here?" he asked me. "Two must go today, and already Angelo has been dismissed because he can't read or write properly. It's very apparent that you have the same issue. Not that you're dyslexic, which would be an automatic dismissal, but that you're illiterate for the most part. There are others who didn't score as well as you in combat, but excelled in academia. Tell me," he said leaning toward me. "If you were in my spot, what would you do?"

Part of me wanted to shout, screw the others and let *me* go. Another part of me wanted to admit defeat and allow the better-qualified people to save us. I toiled with the dilemma and something inside made itself known. A little voice, not shouting, not meek, but confident and strong, took hold of my nerves with a steady hand.

"I can't make that decision for you," I replied, meeting his probing gaze. "You have to do what you think is fair, what you think will provide us with the best chance for survival. But I'm strong and healthy. I'm determined and have come from the pits of hell to be here. No one else in the team knows what it's like to fear for your safety every minute of every day. I do. If anyone can make it in a hostile alien environment, I know I can. In my opinion, choosing someone over me would be a mistake."

The president studied me for a long time. I sat still in my chair. My gaze never left his. Even though my heart pounded in my chest, my breathing remained even. The corners of my armrests dug painfully into the palms of my hands as I waited for his judgement.

"Hmm," he said, rubbing the ginger bristles on his chin. "You see, that's part of my issue with you, Zoe. The fact that you're from such a harsh tier, I worry you might not be able to conform to a world where you don't have to fight all the time. Your fellow cadets have all spoken well about you, but some of them seem scared, intimidated even. Not everything is a war, you know?"

I gripped the chair even tighter.

"Why should I be held responsible for *their* misconceptions about people from Tier Five?" I answered, trying to hide the defiance in my voice and failing.

"Well, you haven't given them much cause to think otherwise," the president said, leaning back in his chair and resting his interlocked hands on his sizable belly. "So far, you've mostly kept to yourself, argued with the general in front of the others, and even killed a fellow cadet." I winced and remembered Amile's broken body as she was carried out of the gym.

"That was an accident," I said quietly, trying not to look away from the president.

Eye contact showed honesty, but I wasn't innocent despite my attempt to convince us both. I had let my anger take over that day, and it *was* my fault that she died. I had let my anger take over when I pummelled Nathan, too, but the president hadn't mentioned that yet and it made me curious. If Nathan's aim was to get rid of the competition, why wouldn't he have reported me? *Maybe he wanted something else. Maybe he wanted his own string to pull.* I shook off the idea. *No one could be that calculating.*

"Anyhow, I don't see how keeping to myself is a bad thing," I said.

"My dear Zoe," he said, smiling broadly. "You'll be hurtling through space with the rest of this crew, exploring a new world with them, and maybe even spending the rest of your lives with *only* them. How are they supposed to trust you with their safety if they don't know who you are? Life is a show, darling. A long succession of smiles and performances so the general public never finds out the horrible truth of it all. Some people might call that being fake, but I like to think of it as being protective. After all, what kind of world would it be if there was no hope?"

The president waited for my answer, but one didn't come. I hadn't thought about it before. I disliked the president's showmanship, but I was beginning to see the purpose behind it. In a small way, I understood the theatrics and was even a little grateful for them, too. He was right. If I was going to spend the rest of my life with only my fellow cadets, I ought to be more approachable. To be honest, I hadn't realised that I wasn't, before now.

"I'll tell you what would happen if the people had only stark honesty," he continued. "There would be chaos, Zoe. Chaos, thievery, and crime. The human race would be lost to fear and desperation. I know this because those in Tier Five live without hope, do they not?"

I nodded slowly in the realisation of what a world with only Tier Fives would be like. It was everything I was fighting against. I wanted equality, not opportunists who would deplete or horde our resources for themselves.

"Our social experiment proved that even those in Tier Three and four had too little to create a stable socio-economical civilisation. We humans are naturally greedy and need more; more food, more medicine, more everything. And we can't get that here."

"Wait, what do you mean by *our social experiment*?" My back became erect and my eyes narrowed. "Do you mean to say that Tier Fives didn't need to suffer as much? Could they have had more food and medicine? Is that the true reason behind the tier system, to figure out at what level our humanity would return to us?"

I hadn't meant to, but toward the end, my voice reached pitches I had never heard before. The armrests of my chair creaked as outrage stirred.

"No, no, of course not, Zoe," the president said, shifting nervously in his chair. "Well, what I mean to say is that it didn't start out that way. Truthfully, Tier Five was a place to put the criminals, as I said before. But after the criminals died out and the next generation emerged, well . . . it became an observational study. And the experiment yielded results that were troubling. So troubling, in fact, that it warranted further study." I gritted my teeth and breathed tersely through my nostrils. "Please, don't think badly of me. That's the way things were when I came into power and, in truth, it did help us."

"Well, I'm glad the suffering and starvation of so many people was so *useful*."

"Zoe, you must understand. There were a number of other planets to choose from. Some far closer to us than Kepler 452b. But from our limited knowledge of the other planets, we gauged that their resources wouldn't have been adequate to sustain our people. The tier system helped us pinpoint the nearest planet with enough resources so we wouldn't escape this hell only to face this problem again."

I felt sick to my stomach. Images of my mother suffering in her bed, my father passing away in the most horrendous pain, flashed in my mind. I figured their experiment was also the reason citizens couldn't move from tier to tier. Allowing their test subjects to think there was a chance of escape, to hope for something other than what was available, would be counterproductive. What would be the point in putting a mouse in a maze if there were no walls?

I couldn't make a fuss. The president was looking for cadets who would shut up and follow orders, regardless of their feelings. I took a deep breath and held it while I smiled sweetly at him.

"I understand," I said, letting the breath out slowly so as to not sound furious. "But in the interests of ensuring the survival of the human race, and given everything you've just said to me, how is it that your son will move onto the next phase? He doesn't speak with us and he doesn't train with us. I'm not sure he even took his combat exams. Surely he is, socially, in a worse state than me?"

The president leaned forward, crossing his arms on the desk in front of him, and smiled a brittle and dangerous smile.

"Are you blackmailing me?" he asked.

"No, no, that's not what I meant at all," I said, my eyes wide and my mouth suddenly dry. Blackmailing the person deciding my fate wasn't a smart move. "I just wondered if that's why you were having a difficult time deciding. I can understand if it is between me and your son."

My heart pounded so hard in my chest I was sure the president could hear it.

"I have to say, I'm a little disappointed in you, Zoe," he said, leaning back in his chair again. "There's a certain naiveté about you, an innocence about how the world really works, and I was worried you might be oblivious to the truth. I wouldn't care if you *had* tried to blackmail me. It wouldn't have worked, but I wouldn't have cared. If you had, though, it would demonstrate your understanding of politics. He who has the most leverage stays in control, after all. And isn't it better to have someone good in charge."

But does the end justify the means? I thought, not daring to say it aloud. *And who determines the goodness of our leaders, themselves?*

"My son does have issues with touching people or being near people," he continued. "I'm sure you already know this because he doesn't even try to hide it. But Liam is no exception to the training either; he does his separately to everyone else. As far as his phobias are concerned, that will get better once he's on the new planet."

"How can you be sure?"

The president smiled that dangerous smile again, his eyes almost disappearing beneath his brow.

"I just am, Zoe," he said. "In fact, maybe you can help me with that. If you could befriend Liam and help him connect with the other cadets, I'm sure both he and I would be very grateful. You'll have to keep your distance, of course, but even just including him in conversations might help. Will you do that for me?"

I didn't see any harm in helping a fellow cadet. I nodded.

"Well, that's just wonderful," the president with a chortle. He raised his hands in the air in triumph. "You see how this works, Zoe? You scratch my back, and I scratch yours. Welcome to the next phase of your training."

Had I gotten into the next phase by agreeing to befriend Liam? Had I just jumped into the murky waters of corruption? He had made such a trivial request of me, I wasn't actually sure. I remembered then, Nathan's warning of the puppet strings he said the president liked to have wrapped around his fat fingers. I hadn't felt the tug, but perhaps he had pulled one of mine . . . the compassionate one that my parents had put on me.

Regardless, I smiled, relief washing over me from head to toe.

"I have one final question before I let you go," the president said, scanning his tablet again. "I'm asking each cadet whom they would like to see as the leader of the mission. I was surprised that Sam picked you, but not so surprised that Angelo did. He seemed fond of you, and it's a shame he couldn't continue. But now I'm asking you. Which of your fellow cadets can you follow and trust? Which would you like to see lead this team on your mission?"

So that's what Sam had meant when he said I could thank him properly later. He would be sorely disappointed when I didn't become the leader and he couldn't hold it over me. The only other person who might vote for me was Otto, and three votes wouldn't be enough. Unlikely as I was to become the leader, I didn't have to think twice about my answer.

"Tristan," I said.

The president smiled, made a note in his tablet, and gestured toward the door. I got up, my legs a little shaky, but my heart flooded with the relief and happiness. The feeling spread across my face in the form of a large grin. I opened the door and Otto was the first to look at me. I couldn't help but give him the thumbs up. He smiled and silently punched the air while my unburdened chest swelled and inhaled the free, albeit plastic tainted air.

"Miss Ruthland?" the president called after me.

I turned and faced him, still standing in the doorway and smiling like an idiot.

"I thought you might like to know, your mother passed away three days ago." My heart stopped beating for what seemed like an entire minute and an ache began to crush my chest. The walls of the president's room closed in around me, trying to suffocate me. I felt my face drop and that was the last thing I physically felt. "I didn't want to tell you sooner because I thought it might distract you from your testing. But take solace in the fact that she died peacefully, and your brother is responding well to his treatment for leukaemia."

The president's eyes never left mine. The corner of his lips curled into a half-smile, and his finger hovered over his tablet. He was testing me, seeing if I could hold it all together. The door was open and everyone had heard my terrible news. As my heart broke into thousands of pieces, I returned his smile.

"May I see her?" I asked almost in a whisper. "To say goodbye."

"I'm sorry, my dear. Your mother has already been recycled," he answered. "And your brother is in isolation until his immune system regenerates. I think it's better if you leave him that way."

I took a moment to stifle the sob that threatened to unmask my calmness.

"Thank you for letting me know," I said, my voice quivering audibly. "May you find health this day."

"And you," he said, lifting his finger from where it hovered and placing the tablet back down again, almost with a look of disappointment. "Larissa Chang!"

Larissa stood from her chair and brushed past me, squeezing my arm just before she closed the door behind her. I didn't know what to do. The sadness rose inside me like a death chamber filling with icy water. I looked at Tristan. He only glanced at me for a moment before closing his eyes and leaning his head back against the white wall behind him. *Nothing? Not even a single word?* I wasn't expecting much, but even Larissa had managed a quick squeeze of my arm.

Feeling the tears burning at the edges of my eyes, I walked quickly toward the door.

"I'm so sorry," Otto said as I left.

I didn't answer him. I didn't look back.

I ran.

Beneath the waxing and waning buzz of the drones, and between the intimidating figures of the Tierless, I ran, trying to hold in the anguish until I found someplace safe to let it out. Through my blurry vision, and after bumping into a few soldiers along the way, I found my way to the barracks. I was hoping Angelo might still be there so I might have a friendly shoulder to cry on, but the Tierless were nothing if they weren't efficient. His bed was already cleared out, empty as if he had never existed. His absence wrenched at the deep sadness inside me and I collapsed, belly first, onto my bed and buried my head into my pillow.

I must have cried there for hours before Otto came in and asked if I wanted to talk. I told him to go to hell. After a pause, he left with a quiet sniffle. People milled in and out of the room, picking up belongings from their beds before disappearing quickly again, but none of them spoke to me. I guessed Otto had spread the word. Each time I heard someone come in, I suffocated any noise of me crying into my pillow. I didn't want their sympathy. I just wanted to be left alone so the hole in my heart could let my life-force escape and I could die.

Later into the day, the unmistakable sound of heavy boots echoed in the room as someone entered and sat on the edge of my bed, shifting my mattress. A strong, wide hand rested gently on the small of my back, rubbing it in slow circular movements to comfort me. His touch tingled my skin beneath my tunic and I knew who it was.

I'd been so selfish, expecting Tristan to react to my terrible news. Of course he wouldn't. He needed to keep himself together so he could face the president, and comforting a distraught friend was emotionally draining. He was only ensuring that he didn't drown alongside me. His kindness now, released a deluge of tears and deep sobs that prevented me from breathing properly.

"I wasn't th . . . there," I blubbered into my pillow. "My poor mother died alone and, and I wasn't there to s . . . say goodbye. She never wanted to die alone, she told me so. She must have been so scared."

Tristan's hand reached up and stroked my hair with such gentleness and care that my sobs turned into howls. I couldn't breathe. I couldn't understand why my right to be with my mother had been taken from me, like everything else in this world. It was the one thing I thought was secured, even when I tried so hard to run away from it. The memories in Tier Five when I just wanted her to shut up, tore at my heart until all that was left was a rawness and pain.

Tristan hooked my hair behind my ear, the gentle brush of his fingers against my lobe sending an electric tingle down my neck. It surprised me because I hadn't felt anything like that from him before. He wiped a tear from my cheek with his thumb and I heard him breathe heavily, as though he felt the sting of my pain and was desperate to take it away. It made me cry more.

"Shh, everything will be okay," Nathan said.

A sharp shock of horror washed over me as I realised it was Nathan, not Tristan, who had been brushing my hair and rubbing my back. I spun around in my bed, sickened that he had tricked me. Tersely

177

wiping the tears from my eyes, I focused on his blurry silhouette and viciously tried to kick him off my bed again and again. My foot found the centre of his chest a few times and he grunted with the impact, but didn't move. That was all I managed before he clamped my foot between his chest and his arm.

"Leave me alone," I shouted, freeing myself from him. "What do you want from me? Can't you just leave me in peace for one day? My mother just died . . ."

But my mother hadn't just died. She'd been dead for three days. I slowly brought my knees up to my chest and buried my face in my hands. I didn't want Nathan to see me cry. I didn't want him to see that vulnerable side of me. I wanted him to leave, but he never moved.

"Is it really so hard to believe that I just wanted to make sure you're okay?" he said, his voice quieter than normal.

I peered at him through my fingers.

"I thought you didn't like Shadows," I said with as much venom as I could muster. "Wasn't I supposed to have dropped out by now or have had an accident?"

Nathan pulled at a loose thread on my blanket, his eyes avoiding mine.

"Yeah, sorry about that," he said. "Guess I might have had some misdirected anger."

"What do you mean? How did *I* make you angry?"

I never understood his hatred toward me, and thinking about it was a welcome distraction from the pain tearing at me from inside my chest. Nathan took a deep breath in, his powerful chest rising and lowering in resignation. His eyes stayed fixed on the stray thread, and his Adam's apple bobbed as he swallowed deeply.

"My parents didn't die of radiation poisoning. They were killed in tier four."

"Wait, I thought Tierless soldiers didn't have parents?" I said, taking my hands away from my face.

"Of course we have parents, Zoe. Where do you think we come from?" Nathan said, sheepishly glancing at me and smiling.

"No, that's not what I meant," I said, wiping my eyes and sitting up more to face him. "I thought most of you were born here, in the Tierless compound. But you said your parents were from tier four?"

"Take a look around you," Nathan said, gesturing around the room. "Have you seen any nurseries here? Or for that matter, have you seen any women?"

I'd never thought about it before, but I hadn't. Tierless soldiers were always male and, although I had seen young Tierless boys wandering about the corridors, I had never seen any younger than four or five-years-old.

"We're all born on other tiers, but we're meant to be taken at a young enough age so we don't remember our parents or siblings. And only boys, so there aren't any distractions . . . or complications. It's an exchange, you see? Our parents are given certain privileges, or items they normally wouldn't have, if they give us up."

"That's awful," I said, clasping my hand over my rebreather. "So you and Tristan were both sold?"

"We *all* were. But it wasn't really that bad," he said, looking up from the thread. "I got to live someplace where I would be fed three times a day, and my parents would get medication for my little sister."

"You have a sister?"

Nathan nodded, his brow furrowed and his jaw clenched.

"My sister isn't well," he said quietly. "She needs lots of medicine just to stay alive. She's getting that medicine now that I'm here, but before winning the lottery, I could only get her a small amount . . . too little really. Teresa has diabetes!"

Nathan appeared different to me then; more human, vulnerable even. If he was capable of caring for his sister, then maybe he wasn't the jerk I thought him to be. Maybe he *did* have a softer side to him and he *did* want to make sure I was okay.

"I'm sorry to hear that," I said honestly. "You still visit Teresa? I thought Tierless weren't meant to have any allegiances to other tiers or the people in them?"

"We're not, but I wasn't taken until I was six. I still had . . . have, strong ties with my family. I kept in touch when I could, but my parents died and now it's just me and my sister."

"Why are you telling me this?" I asked. "You know that if I told the president about you visiting her, you'd be kicked out of the group and probably thrown into Tier Five?"

"I know," he replied, bowing his head, the corner of his lip curling into a handsome smile. "But I didn't report you for starting a fight the other day, and now I'm trusting you to not tell on me."

"But why?"

Nathan sighed and stood from my bed, throwing his hands into the air.

"I donno. Honestly, there's something about you that makes me want to . . . goddammit. I can't explain it properly, but it's like . . . it's like . . . I know I can trust you. Which is really weird seeing as how you're a Tier Five, you know?"

"No, I don't know. You've been cruel to me for so long, and now you can suddenly trust me? Why were you so mean?"

It was the question he had avoided answering the first time I asked, and it made him flinch, squirm even. Nathan turned his back to me and didn't answer for a long time. He crossed his arms over his chest and his shoulders slumped. His voice became low when he finally spoke.

"It's not something I like to talk about. I can't always . . . get the words out." Nathan took a few more breaths before continuing. "My parents were murdered by Tier Five citizens trying to escape." His words were hesitant and his arms squeezed around his chest more tightly. "I had gone back to see them that day. I guess I must have been nine at the time, and my sister was only little." Nathan paused, his head shook, and his breathing became uneven. "I . . . I couldn't protect them. I'm supposed to be this big Tierless soldier, but I was just . . . too scared." Nathan's voice broke into a whisper.

"When they came, I, I dragged my sister under the bed with me . . . and I watched. All I could do was watch." Nathan inhaled deeply, holding his breath for a moment. "They raped her," he said, his voice laden with sorrow and pain. "They raped her, then slit her throat right in front of me. And I did nothing. She screamed, God how she screamed, and then she went quiet."

I understood why he had hated me at first sight. I was a reminder of that terrible day; a day, I'm sure, he had vowed to despise all Tier Five monsters for eternity. I would have done the same. It also explained why he hated Tristan so much, too.

"Every night I see her eyes in my sleep, looking at me and Teresa under the bed, begging for me to help her," Nathan said, stifling a sob at the end.

I rose from my bed and took the few steps between us until I stood behind him. My hand rested on his powerful arm. He flinched and cocked his head over his shoulder to look at me. I caught sight of a tear falling from the edge of his eye before he wiped it away quickly with the back of his hand.

"You couldn't have done anything, Nathan," I said, feeling my own tears well for both our losses. "You were only nine, and this is an awful place to be a child."

"But I'm Tierless. I'm supposed to die to protect the people. That's why I'm here," he said, turning to me, the corner of his lips turned down and his eyes glistening with unshed tears. "I'm a coward, and I failed to do my duty more than once. That's what the tattoos are for. Each one is a reminder of someone I didn't protect."

His tattoos were hidden beneath his red tunic. Only the tip of a wing protruded above his collar on the right side of his neck. Where once I had disliked them, thinking them badges of honour for him, now I knew them to be so much more. I was ashamed that I had been just as prejudiced against him as everyone else had been toward me. He had a funny way of showing his true feelings, but at least he showed them, unlike Tristan.

"Tierless does *not* mean fearless," I said, before pointing to his neck and asking, "May I see them?"

Nathan hesitated and locked eyes with me for a long time, perhaps wondering if he should reveal so much of his vulnerability to me. His mouth opened slightly as if to say something, but nothing came out. Slowly he reached up to the toggle under his chin and unzipped his tunic. The powerful muscles of his bare torso moved gracefully as he peeled the tunic off his shoulders. His chest bore three symbols of his sorrow, but the rest of his muscular torso was unmarked; the tattoos predominantly covering his arms.

Without thinking, I ran the tips of my fingers gently over his chest. In the centre was a heart drawn in an elegant pattern of swirling black lines. Presumably, that one was for his mother. A dolphin engulfed in flames became dappled with goose bumps as I glided my hand over it. The last one, a fiery dragon's head on the other side, did the same as I trailed my fingers along Nathan's chest. I saw him hold his breath, and he swallowed like his mouth had gone dry.

"Who is this one for?" I asked.

It took Nathan a while to answer.

"A boy," he whispered, then cleared his throat. "A tier four boy who loved dragons. He died in a riot I couldn't stop."

His words dripped with regret and culpability. My heart ached to hear it. He and I had more in common than I ever imagined. We both took the weight of the mission on our shoulders, and we both felt our failings deeply.

"How could you stop it?" I said, sliding my hand up past the graceful swallow on his neck to rest on the side of his face. He half-closed his eyes and leaned into my hand just a touch; not enough to make anything of it, but enough that I noticed.

"I was the commander on duty that day," he said quietly. "It was my job to control it."

"The world will be what it wants to be and you alone can't change that," I said. "You can't stop everything. You're here to protect us, not die for us. And as far as I can tell, you *did* do your duty when your mother was attacked. You saved your sister."

Nathan let out a small laugh, almost as if it was from relief, and bowed his head. He didn't deserve to be weighed down with the expectations set upon him by an unfair world. Neither did I. I wanted to bite my tongue about the corruption of the WCC while people died and suffered under their feet, but it was becoming increasingly difficult. Now, after everything that had happened today, the unfairness of not being told my mother was dead and the control the president seemed to hold over us all, some part of me needed to rebel.

"Nathan?" I said, sliding my hand off his cheek again.

"Yeah?" he said, his eyes half closed and his speech muffled like he was drunk.

I looked around the room for a drone before continuing. Thankfully there was none.

"I'm tired of seeing people suffer, aren't you? I'm tired of jumping through hoops for the president and following orders like a soldier. I want to do something. I want to help the people in the worst place of Bunker Twelve. I want to help Tier Five."

"How do you plan on doing that?" he asked, raising an eyebrow.

"I don't know yet, not exactly. But when I do—" Uncertainty screamed at me to shut my mouth, but I couldn't be quiet. Not long ago, Nathan had been my enemy, and now I was trusting him with another secret that could see me kicked out. I bit my lip, took a step away and looked him dead in the eyes. "When I do, will you help me? It might involve breaking a few rules."

Nathan's gaze raked over me, as if he was seeing me properly for the first time.

"Tier Five?" he said incredulously. "After everything I just told you, you want me to help the scumbags who killed my mother?"

I dropped my head and fiddled with the hem of my tunic. *Was I asking too much from him?* I felt bad, but I needed the help.

"We're not all like that," I said quietly. "At least half of them are like me, just wanting food, medicine, and to die painlessly. But it's a lot to ask of you, and I understand if you want to say no."

Nathan breathed tersely through his nose. I could feel his anger exude from him like a heat that threatened to burn me if I got too close. Surprisingly, he didn't leave the barracks shouting foul names at me like I expected. Instead, his fists unclenched and his voice became softer.

"I'd be lying if I said I had never broken a rule or two," he said. "But you know what this could mean if we get caught, right? What it would mean for your brother and my sister?"

"I do," I said, slightly disappointed that he was edging toward a *not on your life* answer. "But I can't take it anymore. You and I both know that there's more than enough food and medicine for everyone, at least for two years. No one deserves to die like my father. I can't stand by and do nothing anymore . . . but I understand you have to protect your sister."

Nathan took a long, deep breath, and scowled at me.

"Well, seeing as how you're such a terrible thief and an even worse liar, I suppose I *should* help you," he said with a crooked grin.

"You mean, you're in?" I asked, the shock clearly written all over my face.

"Sure, why the hell not?"

He smiled at me, and for the first time since we had met, I found myself not hating him. All that remained to be seen was if he could be trusted.

Chapter 12

The plan was afoot, or as afoot as I could make it. The truth was, I was just the idea-man . . . or woman. I couldn't deny being an awful thief. That much was evident from my attempts to steal when we passed through the labs, but with Nathan and Otto's help, I was hoping this time I might be more successful.

Although Otto declined to actually come with us, which was probably best given his nervous disposition, he was willing to design a way for us to open the sealed doors of Bunker Twelve. Swishing imaginary designs and calculations in the air above his head, and muttering incoherently to himself, Otto finally settled on the idea of creating a master key. Working in secret in the Afterhours club, he estimated it would take a week to complete the task, which gave Nathan and me plenty of time to plan.

Finding a quiet spot to huddle with him and whisper felt strange. I was still getting used to the idea that Nathan wasn't as bad as I first thought. Although the general had said as much, I hadn't quite believed him, until now.

Nathan's approach to things was rough and always defensive, but deep down his intentions appeared to be good. Even now, as we sat in our corner of The Tin whispering quietly, he would often call me names. I was *almost* sure he didn't mean them.

"How will we get past the guards in the main stairwell?" I asked. "Maybe we could slip them something to make them sleep?"

"Don't be such an idiot. Do you really think someone hasn't already tried it?" he replied, raising one eyebrow. "The Tierless are trained to expect juvenile tricks like that."

"Well, what would you suggest then?" I said, sighing loudly and scowling at him.

Nathan's lips curled unexpectedly into a smile.

"What, are my plans so bad they're funny?" I asked hotly.

He let out a laugh and reached forward, brushing a stray hair away from my eyes. His fingers grazed my skin as he tucked it behind my ear. His touch sent a tingle through me and made me flinch. Nathan froze, like he'd just became aware of how close he was to me before snatching back his hand.

"No," he said, shifting in his chair. "Angry suits you, that's all."

I didn't quite know what to say. Even if I did, his touch had clammed my mouth shut. Never in a million years would I have suspected that Nathan had a gentle side, and it disarmed me every time I saw it. I noticed that he only ever seemed to show it around me, however. Whenever anyone else was nearby, his guarded rude demeanour returned.

"I have some people in the Tierless who owe me," he said. "There's a few more who can be bribed with medicine. Let me see if I can get them all on duty at the same time. That way we can pass through the tiers while the drones are down."

"You can do that?" I said. "I mean, will they take the bribe and not tell on us?"

"Zoe," Nathan said, giving me a bemused look. "You remember where you are, don't you? People in this hellhole will do anything for medicine. It's a currency, and only slightly less valuable than food. Trading in stolen meds happens all the time. If they blab they'll be blacklisted from any future dealings. In this place, no one can afford to be blacklisted because you never know what you might need."

Nathan seemed to have extensive knowledge of the illegal trades, something I never knew existed outside of Tier Five until he told me. I wondered if it was his worldliness that had made him such an expert or something else.

"Is that how you got your sister's meds?" I asked quietly.

Nathan was silent for a time. He let his eyes drop to the table before he spoke again.

"It is," he said, his voice dropping low. "Do you think I'm bad now, a criminal no better than the convicts you lived with in Tier Five? You know what?" he said, looking at me with defiance. "I don't care. I did what I had to do. Sorry I'm not Mr. Perfect, like Tristan over there."

"I never thought you were perfect," I said, resting my hand on his shoulder and smiling. "In fact, I thought you were a huge ass until recently, so you've come a long way since then."

Nathan laughed loudly and his broad smile crinkled the corner of his eyes. He was at his most handsome when he smiled.

Even though I had come to like Nathan, there was still something more about Tristan that drew me to him. I wasn't sure if it was just a kinship for a fellow Tier Five or a comfort that came with finding a close friend. Either way, his name brought an idea into my mind.

"Should we ask Tristan if he'll help? With him being a Tierless, too, he might have some connections," I asked.

Nathan sat up straight and took his folded arms off the metal table, letting my hand slip from his shoulder. His smile faded and his lips pursed together.

"No, definitely not," Nathan said soberly. "You tell him and he'll use it against us. He'll tell the general and we'll both get kicked out."

"No he won't," I said, dismissing Nathan's concern with a small laugh.

"Yes, he will," Nathan snapped, standing to walk away. "Listen, if you want my help, I'll help you. But leave me out of it if you're going to include that . . . that . . ."

Nathan didn't finish his sentence. With clenched fists and jaw, he turned and left me in The Tin. The other cadets took sheepish glances in my direction, including Tristan who was sitting by himself again as he ate. I knew they weren't staring because they'd overheard us, Nathan and I had been careful about that. More likely it was because of the sudden change in our relationship. Seeing us together, they couldn't help but gawp, although Tristan glared more than anything.

"Are you okay?" Larissa asked, plopping herself on the chair next to me.

"Yeah, I'm fine," I said, ignoring the others. "So, what gives?"

Larissa's smile told me she already knew the answer as she nudged me playfully with her elbow. I didn't know where to start, so I didn't.

"I don't know what you mean," I replied.

"Please!" she said, batting a hand in my direction. "A few days ago you two were at each other's throats. I'd never seen anyone hate another person as much as you two hated each other. And now, you guys are what, best buddies?"

"I wouldn't go that far," I said with a snort. "For the sake of the mission we put our differences aside, that's all."

"That's not the way it looked to me," Jax said, throwing his leg over a chair opposite mine and sitting down. "You two looked cosy as hell."

"Get lost, Jax," I said, trying to hide my hot cheeks behind my hair as Otto and Thelma joined us, too. I was surrounded by prying eyes and pricked ears. It seemed the whole room also wanted to know what was going on. "We're just sorting out our differences, that's all. And if you didn't notice, he kinda left in a huff."

"Bah, that's just a lovers tiff," Thelma said. "I saw the way he looked at you and brushed your hair. How can you not see that?"

My mouth opened and I expected to hear some kind of rebuttal, but nothing happened. The fact was, I hadn't noticed the way he looked at me, or anything else. Perhaps Nathan had gained a certain amount of kinship toward me, or something, but nothing more. Certainly not love.

Unlike my conversation with Nathan, this one wasn't so quiet. All of the cadets were listening, even those I didn't know so well. So, too, was Tristan, and he didn't seem impressed. He stood with his tray in-hand and, without saying a word, glared at me as he walked past. On his way out the door, he shoved the tray roughly through the recycling slot and it landed with a loud clatter on the other side.

"Geez, what's got his knickers in a twist?" Otto said.

"No! Do you think? Not him as well. I mean, maybe he could?"

"Larissa, would you stop talking to yourself and please make some sense so the rest of us can understand what you're waffling on about?" Jax said, rolling his eyes.

"Em," she began, looking between me and the empty doorway. I instinctively didn't like where this was going, but before I could open my mouth, she did. "I think Tristan likes Zoe, too. I think he's mad, or jealous, of Nathan."

"Don't be daft," I said with a laugh. "Neither of them like me. You're just reading too much into everything."

"Whether she is or isn't is kinda redundant right now," Thelma said, pointing at the other cadets who were filing out of The Tin. "We'd better move and get to the professor's lab before we're late."

Loitering in one of the labs with men dressed in pristine white coats and red rebreathers, I couldn't help but take awkward looks at Tristan and Nathan. Both seemed at odds with me, and neither returned my gaze. I tried to figure out what I'd done wrong, but concluded that I'd just never understand boys. Sighing deeply I turned my attention to the professor instead.

I was hoping we might get to finish our tour of the Kepler One, but apparently security was even tighter than ever and we would have to wait until launch day for that. The closer we got to it, the higher the risk of a stowaway.

The professor had another *treat* lined up for us instead. Laid out on a metal tray were eighteen syringes all primed with a blue liquid. The professor stood behind them, furiously tapping on an electronic tablet in his hand. He scratched his head a few times and slid his glasses back up his nose before he addressed us.

"Right, so, okay," he began. "Today we're going to give you a vitamin booster. This is a long-acting inoculation. It will be activated after emerging from stasis and will help you survive without food for a about a week. As of yet, we're unfamiliar with the vegetation on Kepler 452b and don't know if there'll be anything edible before terraforming."

"That's if there *is* any food," Sam said under his breath.

I threw him a pointed look. Things were hard enough without him chiming in on the disquiet. We all knew we might die before we got there. We all knew we might explode on re-entry, too. We all knew that the planet might be nothing more than a barren rock . . . but what was the alternative?

"Now, this is a strong medication," the professor continued. "So expect some discomfort, like a cold feeling in your vein, maybe some itching throughout your body, but that should be about it." The professor paused for questions. There were none. "Right, em, I suppose we should just get started then."

No one told us we needed shots, but I couldn't complain. Given the poor state of my nutrition to date, I could probably use a booster. The others didn't argue either and I wondered if it was because vitamin shots were common in their tiers.

The professor took the first syringe and approached Nathan. Using the back of his hand, he tilted Nathan's head to the side, then unsheathed the needle. Without hesitation, he slid it into a prominent vein in Nathan's neck and pushed the blue fluid into his body. Nathan's hands clenched.

"Wasn't that bad, was it?" the professor asked, withdrawing the needle and placed a cotton ball on the small dot of blood left behind.

Nathan took the cotton ball and gave him a scathing look. He turned a paler shade than normal and clenched his stomach as though he was about to throw up. It didn't reassure any of us.

Next was Tristan. As I expected, Tristan gritted his teeth, but made no qualms about the ordeal. Jax sucked air in sharply between his teeth, and Larissa let out a squeak as the needle punctured her skin. Most everyone put up a brave front. All except Otto, who was hysterical even before the shot happened and whimpered through the entire thing, but he didn't faint like we all thought he would. I was proud of him for that.

"Right, you're next," the professor said to me.

I tilted my head to the side as he approached. I could feel my hands getting sweaty and a tremble start in my fingers. I clenched the bottom of my tunic to hide my fear. A sharp prick shot electricity up my neck as the professor pierced my skin. The liquid was cold enough that I could feel it travelling through my vein. It ran up into my head, and down all the way to my heart. My skin itched instantly, and the feeling of cold spread throughout my body, making my muscles cramp.

"All done," the professor said, pressing a cotton ball into my neck.

"It hurts," I said, squeezing my eyelids tightly together.

"Well, I just injected you. It's going to hurt a little," he replied glibly.

Pain erupted through my body, into every muscle and every cell, and my brain pulsated as though it was going to explode. My blood felt like it was literally boiling inside my body, and fear gripped my stomach tightly.

"No, it hurts!" I cried out.

I collapsed onto my knees, held my neck where the professor had injected me, and screamed with the pain. The feeling of small, sharp metal tendrils ran the length of me, scoring my innards and puncturing my organs. I had never felt pain like this before, and I screamed again as it intensified.

"What's wrong with her?" I heard Tristan demand from the professor.

"I . . . I don't know," he stumbled.

"Well you'd better find out, and fast," Nathan shouted at him.

Someone wrapped an arm around me and I cried out. The pressure on my skin sent a deluge of sharp needles plunging into my body. Even kneeling was almost too painful to bear. I held my head in my hands as it pounded relentlessly, and I crumbled into the foetal position on the ground. The tears streaming from my eyes burned into my cheeks as the agony overwhelmed me and dark spots danced around the edges of my vision.

"Help her!" Nathan shouted at the professor, panic audible in his voice.

The sound of a handheld scanner beeping was like being stabbed in my ears with a needle. Without warning I felt my muscles tighten and my breathing quicken uncontrollably. My jaw clenched of its own accord. My back arched and every muscle in my body screamed in agony as though someone had placed me into a vice and was slowly squeezing the life from me.

I couldn't breathe!

"She's seizing," was the last thing I heard the professor say before darkness surrounded me.

Muffled noises of Otto crying and Nathan demanding that the professor do something became a distant echo. They soon drifted away, too. In the darkness there was no pain, just peace, emptiness, and quiet. There was no sensation of up or down, no colour or temperature, just the nothingness that suspended me and caressed my skin in its viscous pleasantness. I wasn't sure if my body floated right-way-up or swirled in every direction, but I was aware of some movement even if I couldn't pinpoint it.

I'd known this darkness before, in dreams on Tier Five. I escaped into them often, but they had never been so visceral. Drawn to an amity I'd never known, I didn't want to leave the darkness or question it. I didn't want to return to that terrible agony called life. Had I died? A small sadness fluttered throughout my being. Jason would be upset. *Poor Jason,* I thought. *I hope he . . . I hope . . .*

My thoughts melted out of my brain through my ears and joined the darkness. I floated for what seemed like many years in the ambience, content to lose myself. But, like all good things that happened to me, my peace didn't last.

A low thud reverberated all around me, like the deep warm tone of a timpani drum. The sound shifted and moved the darkness in a rippling wave which reverberated through my being. I snapped to attention, straining my ears to hear what had made the noise. Squinting into the nothing, I tried to see something other than the black, but I was alone as far as I could tell, and the sweet lulling silence returned.

After some time, the beat of the drum sounded again, but this time it was joined by a second beat. I listened, waited. This noise was not meant to be here. If I had a heart it would have been thumping wildly in my chest, but surreally my chest remained as still as the darkness.

I felt nothing but the ripples left in the wake of the strange noise. The darkness wasn't so welcoming anymore. There was something here with me, something I couldn't see and it was watching me. I couldn't see it and I had no reason to believe that anything was there, but somehow I knew it was.

Again the low timbre, deep and foreboding, shook my dark world, churning its black ocean with large, wild waves. The beats were coming faster now, closer together until it began to sound like a sluggish heartbeat. *Relax,* I thought. *It's just your own heart you're hearing.* A ball of electricity in my stomach raised the hairs on the back of my neck and didn't agree.

The drumming was interrupted by another sound. I knew I should have been terrified from the beginning of it, but at first, all I heard was a small squeak mixed in between the heartbeats like someone far away had opened a rusty door. Almost unnoticeably to begin with, the sound repeated itself over and over.

"Resuscitate her," the nasally voice of the professor echoed in my head.

Slowly the squeaks turned into long, grating shrieks, like nails down a chalkboard. That was when fear took hold of me properly. I turned in every direction, trying to see where the noise was coming from, to no avail. The shrieks became deafening and were joined by a series of clicks and throaty thuds. The beats quickened, and I now knew it wasn't my heart for sure; every beat had three thumps instead of two.

I covered my ears as the sound of the metallic beast shrieked out its disdain for me. It became unbearable, so loud and piercing that I was sure my ears must have bled. I screamed, but no noise came from me. I kicked out at the darkness trying to swim away, but the nothing came from my efforts and I stayed glued in the soupiness.

"Clear!" I heard someone say.

Without warning, something crashed down on my heart and lungs. Almost as soon as it landed on me, it leapt off again and I was left clutching my chest. The shrieks died away for a moment, but they came back again . . . louder than ever and seemingly more desperate, too.

"Clear!" I heard someone shout again, this time his voice more distinct.

The creature that punched me in the chest did it again. For a split second, the darkness receded, and I saw the blurred silhouette of the professor and one of his lab assistants hovering over me. Behind them, Tristan's normally stoic features were creased with worry. But the darkness wasn't done with me yet. It pulled me back down into its murky world and held me fast. Greedy, lonely, shapeless hands grappled with my essence and refused to let me go.

That was when it happened . . . the darkness blinked. Converging from the far reaches of my vision, a pair of dark-green, fleshy eyelids came together and encapsulated me. There were no lashes to speak of, but the lids were dotted with small glowing puffs of what looked like pollen clinging to the skin. Bulging veins pulsated in rhythm to the bizarre heartbeat as the lids stayed closed around me.

It only lasted a second before they retracted gain. Only when I recognised the darkness as the black eyeball of some imagined creature did I see myself reflected in its glassy surface. My blonde hair fanned out and swayed as though I was underwater, while my body was suspended limply in the black. Whatever the professor had given me, it was seriously trippy.

"Clear!" I heard again.

"Come on, Zoe," Nathan's desperate voice whispered.

Again something punched me in the centre of my chest, and my body was hit with a blow that threatened to make me scream, if I could scream. The bright lights of the professor's lab evaporated the strange eye and pulled me back into my world. My chest burned and my body ached for air. I arched my back and took in a deep breath, thankful that the searing pain in my muscles seemed to have subsided, although not completely.

"Oh, thank God," Larissa whimpered.

As the world spun around me, I heard Otto sobbing among the panicked whispers, and the professor's frantically bleeping scanner. I managed to open my eyes just enough to see Nathan kneeling by my head, his face in his hands, and his chest heaving with the effort of breathing quickly before I passed out again.

Pain etched through every limb, and my chest felt as though some lard-ass had used it as a trampoline. A gentle, rhythmic beeping brought my consciousness into a glaringly white world that smelled like new plastic. My head spun in deep, unrelenting waves until my churning stomach was the only thing which registered. I opened my eyes and raised a shaky hand to my throbbing temple. Trying to breathe deeply, my ribcage objected in deep squeezing pain. Nothing seemed real to me. It was all muffled and distant, like I was waking up from a nightmare only to find myself in another, less frightening, dream.

"Good morning, Ms. Ruthland," a woman's kindly voice whispered.

I focused on the blur milling about to my left. The lady's grey hair was pulled into a loose bun behind her head, and her pristine white uniform almost blinded me in the bright lights of the Medbay. Her translucent red facemask mirrored the stark red lipstick she wore on her lips.

"What happened?" I said, my voice raspy.

When I spoke I realised I was no longer wearing my rebreather. My eyes went wide as I sucked in a breath and expected to feel the suffocating atmosphere of Bunker Twelve envelope me. It didn't. I tested the air again and again, unable to trust my senses. It was full, refreshing even, something I wasn't expecting.

"Don't worry, my dear," the nurse said, tapping the plastic dome around me that I'd been too groggy to see before. "All patients with severe illnesses are provided with oxygen tents. It's more comfortable that way."

Tier one patients, you mean? I thought sardonically.

"Wait . . . severe?"

"Yes, dear," she replied, entering something into a touchscreen above my head. "Your heart stopped and you had to be resuscitated. The professor thinks you had an allergic reaction to the vitamin booster."

My heart stopped? As ironic as it was living in a world that was killing me, I had never paused to *really* think about my own mortality. The thought of dying was terrifying. All at once, I began to question the meaning of life and the existence of the hereafter, wondering if the blackness was all that was left. I came to know and understand the fragility of my body in one blinding flash of panic.

"I'll send food in shortly," she said. "I'm sure it won't be long until that Tierless friend of yours comes in to visit again."

She smiled sweetly at me, like this was meant to offer some comfort. I wondered how she knew he was Tierless, given the fact that we all wore the same uniform now. I suspected she might have treated the Tierless once or twice over the course of her career. That, and Tristan and Nathan were still the most imposing of the group. A dead giveaway.

"Tierless friend?" I asked, my attention drawn back to the here and now.

"Yes, you know? The dark foreboding one, with the eyes," she said, fastening a scowl on her expression that could have mimicked either Tristan or Nathan. "He's been here the whole time, watching over you. I think he popped out to get something to eat, but I'm sure he'll be back soon."

To be honest, I wasn't entirely certain who she was talking about. Both Nathan and Tristan were foreboding to those who didn't know them better, but Tristan's eyes were brown . . . dark. Her descriptive skills left a lot to be desired, and I doubted if there was any point in asking her to try again.

I raised myself onto my elbows, the tent only high enough to allow me that much, and glanced around Medbay. The nurse attended to the three other patients in my room; two men and a woman, each cradled in their own plastic tombs. They looked gaunt. Their skin donning an unhealthy waxen huge. They were dying. I had enough experience with death to recognise it, but unlike my mother or my father, they weren't in absolute agony . . . and this pissed me off royally.

I was more resolved than ever to do something for the poor souls in Tier Five. It wasn't fair that they had to suffer while the rest of the citizens were free to

202

suck up the failing resources of Earth. Even tier fours had some degree of dignity afforded to them at death.

When I was younger, when my father was dying, I prayed every night that someone from another tier would have the compassion to help him. My childish prayers were left unanswered, but if I could answer for some other little girl it would be worth the risk. I wanted to help the other tiers, too, but that would draw too much attention, and there was only so much Nathan and I could carry. Better to help the worst of us and complete our mission to save the rest.

Through the open door at the end of our four-bed ward, I could see the blanket-covered feet of four more patients in the room opposite mine. Each was encased in the same oxygen bivouac as my own. For the most part the Medbay was quiet, save for the low tones of other nurses chatting to themselves. This wasn't death, not the death I knew anyhow. It wasn't dark. It wasn't ugly or filled with coldness and desperation.

It was then I realised the opportunity handed to me.

"Nurse?" I called across the room.

"Hmm?" she replied, keeping her focus on the lady across from me.

"Is my brother here? His name is Jason and he's thirteen-years-old. He's being treated for leukaemia."

"I'm sorry, dear. All patient files are confidential," she said. "But most likely he is in the oncology wing." Seeing my disappointment, she added, "It's a good thing that you won't find him here. This wing is only for respite care." She leaned toward me, the back of her hand hooking around her rebreather, and whispered, "You know, for those on their last legs?"

I guessed she was trying to spare the feelings of the other patients by not saying it out loud, but I wasn't sure the other patients would have cared or noticed. The copious amounts of drips running various liquids into their veins saw them comatosed.

The doldrums of the ward were broken by the groaning of a metal door being opened and the sound of heavy boots stomping along the granite floor. The nurse winked at me, like she knew who it was, before leaving my room to meet him in the corridor.

"Oh, hello," she said. "Yes, she's in there, but I was expecting someone else."

Tristan's broad frame turned into my room.

"You're up?" he said, a broad smile under his mask. "How you feeling?"

"Like crap," I replied, rubbing my throat. "How long have I been here?"

"'Bout a couple of days, but you can't stay much longer," he said, straddling the chair beside my bed. "We're learning how to fly the ship now, and everyone's finding their position. If you miss too much training, you ain't gonna be able to catch up."

"What do you mean, their position?"

"Well, that friend of yours, Otto, seems to have a real knack for computers and stuff. So, they've made him an engineer. Larissa is tactical, Liam is medical, and Jax is the pilot. But ain't nothing set in stone, yet. They keep changing everyone around to see where they're best suited."

Some of the positions surprised me, but Liam being on medical almost seemed natural. As a germaphobe, I wouldn't have expected to see him anywhere but the cleanest place on the ship. I worried about how he might cope if one of us actually got sick, though. Would he be able to touch us if we needed stitches? What happened if one of us got a cold or a severe infection? Would he bail on us?

"Where have they put you?" I asked, knowing full well he'd be ranking somewhere high.

"Command," he replied, smiling broadly again. "There's only two spots, one for a captain and one for a first lieutenant. You, me, and Nathan have been put in the running, but if you don't get your ass outta bed soon, they'll send you back to Tier Five."

If I had been put into the running it meant more people voted for me to lead than I first realised. It also meant that Sam might be calling in some kind of favour later. The idea made my stomach churn even more. Regardless of what Sam might ask of me, and obviously be refused, one thing was clear. I couldn't lounge around in bed anymore. I was losing out on precious training which wouldn't be repeated.

"Right, hand me my clothes and mask," I said, reaching for the zipper of the tent.

I pulled on the toggle and it collapsed around me. The suffocating air invaded, leaving me gasping as I sat upright. Tristan jumped up from the chair, reached into to the locker beside my bed, and quickly found my mask. He pressed it onto my face, his fingers resting on my cheek, and held it there for a moment. Again, there was no tingle like when Nathan had brushed my ear. Part of me liked Tristan more than Nathan, but now I realised it wasn't in the same way.

"Woah, take it easy," he said, his brow crinkling with concern. "You gotta get out of bed, not run a marathon."

I nodded, fearful that speaking might reveal the truth about my lack of feelings for him. I didn't want to hurt him or push him away. Tristan was a loyal friend, and I wanted to keep it that way.

He let his hand slide from my mask and took my elbow to help me walk. I rose tentatively onto legs that felt as though they hadn't been used in years. Everything ached and wobbled. My chest refused to allow me to breathe without pain and my head spun. The cold air of Bunker Twelve wafted up my hospital gown and made me shiver.

"What do you think you're doing?" the nurse shrieked as she bustled into the room.

"I'm leaving," I replied, grasping the edge of my locker.

"Are you mad? You've just been brought back to life. You have to take it easy and recover. Your heart isn't strong enough yet."

"And if I was just a Tier Five, what then?" I snapped at her. "Would you be so concerned for my well-being? Would I even have been allowed into a place like this?"

The nurse looked affronted, but not surprised by my outburst.

"We do what we can for those we can," she said, pursing her lips. "Leave if you must, but the professor said to expect side-effects from your ordeal. It would be better if you were here to be observed, but I can see I can't stop you." She turned and left the room in a series of undignified stomps. On her way out the door she threw back one last scathing remark. "Don't say I didn't warn you."

She didn't really care. Her complacency toward Tier Five citizens and her unwillingness to do anything about the injustice, fuelled my anger even more.

"I'm so sick of this crap, aren't you?" I said as Tristan steadied me.

"Which crap, exactly, are you talking about?" he asked with a small laugh.

"*This*," I snapped, gesturing to the patients around me. "I'm sick of people trying to justify the way this place is run. I want to do something about it. I can't swallow it anymore. Will you . . . will you help me?"

Nathan's warning about not trusting Tristan made itself known in my mind. That and the fact that he said he wouldn't come if I involved Tristan. But what Nathan didn't know, until the last minute, wouldn't hurt him. Tristan was a fellow Tier Five. If anyone could understand why I was doing this, it would be him. Nathan would just have to get over it because we needed the help. The more hands we had, the more food and medicine we could carry.

"What are you gonna do?" he asked, a sceptical look crossing his face.

"Nathan and I have a plan to take some food and medicine down to Tier Five. He has some Tierless friends who will let us pass through the levels undetected. Will you help us?"

I expected there to be some resistance from Tristan. I knew he wasn't one for breaking rules, but he became beyond furious, which confused me. Tristan scowled dangerously at me, and his eyes exuded a deep anger that I had never seen on anyone before. He visibly shook with rage, his knuckles turning white as his fists clenched. He became a thing of fury and heat, threatening to become violent at any stage. For the first time since I met him, I was frightened.

"Was it Nathan who put you up to this? Did he suggest it?" Tristan demanded, squeezing my arm too hard.

"No, Nathan had nothing to do with it," I answered, my voice higher than normal as I tried to pull away. "Why are you being like this? I thought you would want to help."

Tristan let go of my arm roughly and backed away. His jaw muscles tightened repeatedly as he stood staring at me, holding in the terrible things I could see he wanted to say.

"You think because I was born there that I got some kinda loyalty to them?" he said, the bitterness clear in his tone. "What have they ever done for me? Nothing. No one has ever done anything for me. My parents threw me away and I had to fight, tooth and nail, for everything I got now. But you want me to jeopardise it all, for *them?*"

"Tristan, everything we're doing is for them," I said, feeling tears sting at the edges of my eyes. I hated that he was mad at me, but I hated it even more that I might cry in front of him. "That's what this whole mission is for, isn't it?"

"The general didn't train me to be a leader just so I could throw it all away because I went soft," Tristan said in a voice too cool for his demeanour. "He didn't make me stand on one foot for hours so I could use those feet to walk away. He didn't drill the rules and laws of combat into me so I could give up my chance to command the greatest feat in human history. He trained *me* for that position, and I ain't gonna to let those dirty, thieving, scumbags take it away from me. I ain't gonna let *anyone* take it away from me."

"Tristan, they're not dirty, thieving—"

"Shut up. I don't wanna hear it," he said, slamming his fist into the side of my bed before backing toward the door. "I thought you were smarter than that. This whole thing smacks of Nathan and his sympathy votes from the *bleeding-heart brigade*. That's how he became commander, you know? Acting like Robin Hood. *I* should have had that command. *I* was the better leader. But that's what you get when you let soft-hearted idiots have a say in how things are run.

"He made mistakes because of it, too. And he's gonna make more mistakes, wait and see. I don't want you following him, Zoe, because you're gonna get caught up in his mishaps. Someone's gonna find out and report your little plan to the general. *Then* what will happen to you?" Tristan leaned closer and pointed his finger at my face. "You're a fool if you think otherwise." After a moment he straightened and took a long, deep breath before speaking again. "Just promise me you won't go back to Tier Five or have anything more to do Nathan."

I could feel the heat of my tears slowly teeter off the edges of my eyes. I knew Tristan, in his own way, was only looking out for me, making sure that I made it onto the Kepler One, but his demeanour was threatening. It was clear that there was more to Nathan and Tristan's animosity than I first realised, and it wasn't helped by Tristan's irrational need to succeed.

I couldn't tell if this need was solely for himself, or if it was a deep-seated desire to prove worthy in the milky eyes of the only father figure he'd ever known, despite how poorly the general treated him. Regardless, my strange connection to Tristan despised the way he looked at me now and I wanted it all to go away. I nodded, a tear running along the rim of my rebreather.

"Good," he said, heading toward the door again. "It's time to grow up, Zoe. This ain't an ideal world and ain't no one gonna to take a fall for you. The sooner you realise that and do what's smart for yourself, the easier this will all be. Get dressed."

Tristan barked the last bit and then left. Clutching my bedside locker for balance, tears continued to dampen my cheeks. I wiped them away slowly with shaking fingers, and found my clothes like an automaton following its program. Was he right? Was humanity really so lost that there was no hope for us anymore and I shouldn't bother caring? But Nathan was willing to help me and jeopardise his freedom and his sister's health, too. Nathan clearly believed that there was some hope left, a reason to risk it all. Was he foolhardy to think such a stupid plan was worth it, and by extension, was I?

I felt the pull of their stances as though they were icebergs floating in opposite directions. Stuck over the widening crack, I had to choose which one to get on, but I didn't know which would melt under my feet and let me drown.

Dressed, I sat on my hospital bed for a moment, collapsing the tent underneath me. I needed to rest my aching body and calm myself before I left the room. I didn't want anyone else to see me cry. As I looked at the other patients in the ward and remembered my father's eyes wide with pain and sunken into his head with starvation, my decision was made for me. I didn't care what Tristan thought. I couldn't allow myself to be complacent in the disparity of Bunker Twelve. If *I* didn't try, who would?

I stood and tugged at the end of my red tunic, straightening it. With the back of my hand, I wiped away the last tears that threatened to fall, then sucked in a deep, aching breath. My legs shook and my head spun as I took the first few steps out of the ward past the silent, transparent coffins of the nearly dead.

The corridor was empty. No one called out to stop me from leaving, not even my nurse who busied herself by searching through a large white cupboard full of linen in another room. She just looked at me and pointed to the other end of the corridor with a disgruntled air.

I followed her directions, my legs threatening to buckle under the weight of my body at every step. I suspected that my heart wasn't happy with being asked to work instead of rest, but I had little choice. I couldn't afford to be left behind in training, not after the president had told me I was at the bottom of the group.

I don't know what made me look into one of the other wards as I neared the exit, but I did. To my right was a room with no discernible difference to any of the other rooms I passed, save for one exception. Lying in his own oxygen tent in the bed next to the door was General Stonewall.

He looked terrible, like a demonic creature had sucked the life from him, leaving some of his bones prominent under his weakened muscles. Dark rims circled under his eyes, and the gunmetal grey hair that normally stood to attention was messy and dishevelled. "*All patients with severe illnesses are provided with oxygen tents*," the nurse had said. General Stonewall wasn't just blind, he was dying. Whatever had clouded his eyes was killing him, that much was obvious now.

I stopped and stared for a long time. Tristan hadn't mentioned that the general was in here. If he knew, his visit today wasn't long enough to have stopped in here, too. I didn't know the general well enough to feel sad for him, but part of me was. He was a tough, proud man who hated the use of his seeing-eye captain. By the looks of him, he had hidden the severity of his disease well enough that no one realised just how close to death he was.

I wondered if I should pop in and say hello or offer to bring him something. That thought was immediately squashed as I remembered him pulling his arm away from me when I tried to steer him toward the gym door. If his own adopted son didn't visit, perhaps that was the way the general wanted it. As quietly as I could, I continued walking and pushed open the heavy steel door of Medbay.

The darkness beyond the door swathed me in its gloom and wrapped its colder cloak around me. I shivered and it took a moment for my vision to adjust to the darkness. I hadn't realised, as I'd never been here before, but Medbay was located inside the Tierless compound. It made sense, though, as most of the injured would come from the Tierless . . . most of the injured who would be treated anyhow.

The corridor was unfamiliar and one end of it was identical to the other. I had no idea which direction to head. A few Tierless soldiers gave me scathing looks as they crossed in front of me. Deciding that moving in the wrong direction was preferable to standing around looking like an idiot, I turned right and started down the poorly lit passageway.

"Goddamn red-coats," a Tierless said to me under his breath, bumping into my shoulder.

I stumbled sideways a couple of steps. My mouth dropped open, and I couldn't help but stare at his back as he kept walking. Animosity was something I was used to as a Tier Five, but his slant was toward the uniform I wore, not me. Didn't he know that we were risking our lives for him?

"Don't mind them," Nathan's voice came from behind me, making me jump. "They're just miffed they don't get to escape Earth, too. That's all."

"Nathan!" I said, trying not to sound surprised to see him. "What are you doing here?"

"I came to see *you*, dumb-ass," he replied, elbowing me hard enough to make my weak legs stumble again. "Whoa, take it easy." Nathan grabbed me around my waist with one hand and hauled me upright again. "Are you sure you should be walking about? I mean, it was only an hour ago that you were still unconscious."

Nathan's voice dripped with concern and his eyebrows knitted together.

"How did you know I was still unconscious?" I asked, realising that it must have been him sitting beside me all along, not Tristan. I was unable to hide my smile. "How do you know I wasn't in and out of consciousness?"

Nathan's mouth opened as if he was going to say something, but the bustle of the corridor remained unbroken by his voice. As he slid his hand from around my waist, his fingers brushed along the small of my back making my skin tingle with an electricity I had hoped to feel from Tristan. He glanced at his hand as it froze, then back to me, before pulling it away sharply.

"Sorry," he mumbled, taking coy glances at me, his cheeks reddening like a child caught stealing from the cookie jar. "Em, I, em . . ."

"You're starting to sound a lot like the professor," I laughed, enjoying seeing him squirm. "Come on, walk me to training and catch me up on everything."

Nathan smiled, his awkwardness evident in the small laugh of relief he let out.

I was only able to walk slowly through the Tierless compound, giving Nathan plenty of time to tell me everything that happened since my ordeal. There wasn't much that Tristan hadn't told me already, but, unlike Tristan, Nathan did his best to teach me what he had learned. He glossed over the responsibilities of each station and described the consoles as best he could. Some if it made sense, while other parts were complete gobbledygook. By the time we came to corridors I recognised, I had a vague understanding of what he was describing.

"By the way," he said, stopping me outside a set of doors which had been locked before, the whirr of the machines inside still piquing my interest. "I've organised the Tierless shifts. We should be good to go in two days . . . that's if you're still up for it? If you need more time to recover, I understand. I just don't know if I'll be able to co-ordinate it all again before we . . . you know . . . blast-off."

I smiled and, without thinking, reached up to wrap my arms around his neck, pressing my head against his. I felt him stiffen under my embrace for a moment before his warm arms encapsulated me around my waist and pulled me toward him. His powerful torso pressed gently against mine and I could feel him breathing. He was strong, careful not to crush me, and I felt a comfort, a peace I had never known before. I felt . . . safe.

"What's this for?" he asked. The stubble on his jaw tickled my cheek as he spoke and send that delicious tingle down my neck again.

"To say thank you," I answered, unwrapping my arms and sliding them onto his broad shoulders. He didn't release his grip on my waist. He kept me pressed close to him, like he didn't want to let me go. "I know what you're sacrificing if it all goes wrong, and I think you're brave for doing this. Not many would."

Nathan hesitantly unlocked his hands from around me and rested them gently on my hips. His hazel eyes stared at me for a long time, like he was deciding something about me again. He smiled a handsomely crooked grin, then let me go. My hands slipped from his shoulders as he took a step back. Everything felt colder without him.

"Yeah! I don't know if it's bravery or stupidity, but you make me want to be . . . well . . . not a complete ass. You're a bad influence on me, Zoe Ruthland," he said, pushing the door to the whirring room open. "Just remember to use your power over me only for good, okay?"

"I promise nothing," I said with a wide grin before stepping into the room ahead of him.

Chapter 13

What I eventually came to know as the simulation room was predominantly beige, oval, and more brightly lit than the corridor outside. Taupe plastic pedestals swelled from dark grey floors and coalesced into walls dotted with a plethora of touch screens. The largest screen, directly in front of me, displayed an expanse of stars and nebulae, and interrupted the continuum of beige.

Two command chairs, each with an arm rest of flashing buttons, sat empty in the centre of the room. An eye-catching console with more keys and lights than I had ever seen, was perched stoically in front of these chairs. Occupied by Jax, I assumed this was the helm. His normally spikey, green-tipped hair was flattened by a headband supporting a translucent, glowing screen across his eyes.

"Zoe!" a few people called as I entered the room.

Otto, positioned next to the door, was the first to reach me. He wrapped his pudgy arms around me tightly and squeezed.

"I'm so g-glad you're okay," he said with a small voice. "I thought you were dead."

"I'm okay," I groaned. "But not so hard, please."

Otto's grip, while not the strongest in the world, made me feel as though every bone was about to shatter.

"Sorry," he said, releasing me immediately.

Larissa, Thelma, Jax, and a few others clapped me on the back and remarked at how "well" I looked. I didn't feel well, but seeing as how the last time they saw me I was knocking on death's door, I supposed I probably *did* look a damn sight better.

The sound of someone clearing his throat sent them scurrying back to their positions. Captain Michael Stansfield waited in the centre of the room, his hands clasped firmly behind his back. Tristan stood just behind him, his face thunderous and deadly again. Tristan's whole physique oozed a disdain I could only assume came from the fact I had walked in with Nathan right after promising him I would have nothing more to do with him . . . or our plan. I hated that he was still angry with me.

"Welcome back, Zoe," Captain Stansfield said. "I'm glad to see you're doing better. As the others already know, I'll be taking over for General Stonewall for a time. He has some, eh, business to take care of." I knew what that business was, but from everyone else's blank expressions, I guessed I was the only one. "Please, join us as we run through battle simulations.

"This is an exact replica of the bridge on the Kepler One," he continued. "It will allow you to become accustomed to the workings and feel of the ship before take-off. Larissa is at the tactical station, over there," he said, gesturing to where Larissa sat. "Otto is on engineering behind you. Emily is Navigation to his right."

As I followed the direction his hand waved, I noticed that Liam was, once again, nowhere to be seen. How did the president expect me to befriend him if he was never here? I could only assume that he was in Medbay, learning the ins and outs of being a medic . . . or at least, for all our sakes, that was where I hoped he was.

"Over here, where Jax is sitting, is the helm. This is also where the O.O.W. will sit during downtime."

"The what?" I interrupted him.

"The officer of the watch," he relied. "The O.O.W. is responsible for the safety of the ship and waking the captain to any anomalies while the crew rests. That position will be taken by the ship's android."

I imagined the severed head of the android perched on the chair, smiling haplessly at the screen. Although I knew it wouldn't just be a head, it was all I could imagine.

"Why not just send the android to do our job?" I questioned.

The captain looked at me for a long time before offering a small smile.

"Artificial intelligence is just that, artificial. While the android is programmed with certain parameters it knows humans can tolerate, it has no appreciation for the need of comfort, safety, and many more things. To truly know if the human race can settle on this alien world, we need a human's perspective."

"Screw that," Sam yelled from a console to my left. "I don't want a stinking robot to decide my fate for me. Those things would kill us just because some numbers don't add up."

"Well then," the captain said calmly while tapping on the armrest of one of the command chairs, "feel free to leave the programme at any stage, Mr. Wilkens."

The sour look on Sam's face nearly made me laugh. Despite the general's dislike of his curly-haired seeing-eye captain, *I* liked him. He was direct and no-nonsense. Sam had a point, however, as much as I hated to admit it.

Androids were clinical and calculating, not capable of feeling emotions or understanding the value of life over exceeding defined parameters. The captain had as much as admitted it himself. Remembering how the bots in the maze just lay down and died when shot them, I worried it mightn't fight hard enough to save us all. It might decide to allow half of us to die so the other half could live, but which half and why? Which of us were more useful to the mission? I knew I wouldn't make the shortlist.

"Miss Ruthland, seeing as how you haven't had a turn yet, how about you take command today," he said, gesturing to the larger of the two chairs. It wasn't a suggestion so much as a direction. "I realise you've had no time to prepare, but captaining a crew is more about character and instinct than anything else."

I swallowed the dryness in my throat. Everyone was watching me, so I slowly made my way to the chair. It was good to sit, but I'd rather have had some time to get my bearings before being left to decide the fate of humanity, real or not. At least this was a simulation and people wouldn't *actually* die before they realised what a terrible captain I would make.

"Tristan, why don't you take the first lieutenant's chair, and Nathan can take tactical with Larissa."

Nathan crossed the room to stand next to Larissa and gave me a reassuring nod along the way. Tristan sat in the chair next to mine and neither spoke nor looked at me.

"Right," the captain began. "Displayed on the screen is what we believe the planet will look like. I've positioned the ship at the point we believe it is safest to emerge. To get any closer would run the risk of damaging the ship on the asteroid belt here," he said, pointing to a mass of grey specks that circled the planets within.

"Your objective is to fly around the asteroid belt and land safely on Kepler 452b. Easy, right?" No one answered. "You have over one thousand tactical drones capable of holding down heavy fire for thirty or so minutes. After that point, their ammunition will be spent and they will shut down. I'm sure I also don't have to tell you that it's imperative you don't fly through the asteroid belt itself. Any damage to the ship might breach our hull and see our mission fail. You're our last hope for survival, so you can't afford to do that. Do I make myself clear?"

"Aye, Sir," they roared.

I tried to swallow the dryness again, with little success.

"Captain Ruthland," Captain Stansfield said, turning to me. "Take us home."

My stomach lurched and my heart beat faster than it wanted to go, aching in my chest. *Home?* I thought. *Was this really going to be home?*

"Okay," I began, thankful I was sitting down. "Em, okay, so I suppose, Jax, let's go?"

220

"Use fifty-percent propulsion to take us toward the asteroid field," Tristan ordered.

Jax shot him a dubious look before turning to me.

"Are those your orders, Captain?" he asked me.

Tristan threw a scathing look in Jax's direction, but it was Jax and Captain Stansfield staring at me expectedly that made me nervous.

"Yes," I said in a meek voice.

Jax's fingers danced over the console in front of him, and the sound of engines hummed to life in the small room. The floor vibrated as the universe outside the screen began to move behind us. We glided toward our destination with the same graceful movements as a feather floating toward the ground. The ship travelled faster than I was expecting. Although the professor had explained the advancements of nuclear speed, I hadn't understood the significance of it, until now. Large planets, tumultuous and wild to the eye, sailed silently past our periphery as we neared the asteroid belt.

"Take us over it," I said, my voice still no louder than before.

"Aye, Sir," Jax replied.

The room tilted backward, and the spinning horizon of icy rocks dipped below the screen. Although I knew it was only a simulation, it felt real. I glanced at Tristan again, hoping for some reassurance, some hint that I was doing okay. He ignored me, his jaw muscles still clenched tightly.

"Unidentified vessels, bearing 330 mark 15," Nathan said suddenly.

"Red Alert," Tristan ordered.

Nothing happened.

"I said, Red Alert," Tristan shouted at Nathan.

"Captain?" Nathan asked.

I didn't answer for a long time. I could feel everyone's eyes on me, waiting to see if I would fail just like I did with the math.

I glanced at Captain Stansfield wanting to ask if there really was a possibility of meeting aliens this technologically advanced. The prospect had never occurred to me, and it scared the heck out of me.

I had assumed the planet would be derelict, just waiting for us like a Garden of Eden. Human arrogance! But what if there were aliens and what if we never made it to the planet's surface because of them? Would humanity die, and Jason along with them? My questions spun wildly and in diverging tangents.

I looked at Nathan, my mouth open and my eyes wide. He raised his eyebrows and mouthed, *are you okay*? Something woke up inside me then. I don't know if it was an inbuilt need to survive or the need to impress Nathan. Whatever it was, it took hold of my innards and held them still.

"Red Alert," I ordered loudly, gripping onto the soft fabric of my captain's chair. The lights of the bridge swathed us all in red as adrenaline took hold. I ignored the profanities Tristan continued to grumble toward Nathan. "Bring us around to face them."

I could feel the tension from my crew as Jax responded to my command. Slowly, as though stuck in quicksand, the ship turned and the room levelled out. As we sailed above the asteroid belt, hundreds of alien ships descended quickly from above. These ships were smaller, faster, and appeared to be made from a mesh of organic exoskeleton. Between the small holes in the spikey, white vessels, a green skin glowed in the darkness of space, and something suddenly flashed in my mind. I had seen this kind of skin before, in my anaphylaxis-induced nightmare.

"Send the drones out and take a defensive position," Tristan ordered.

"No, wait," I said, standing from my chair to get a better look at the alien ship. "They haven't shown their hand yet. How do we know they're hostile?"

"Because we've done this before, and every time they've attacked us," Larissa said, her finger poised above a red flashing button.

"Has anyone *tried* to talk to them first?" I said, squinting to pick out the finer detail of the ship. "I mean, what are they doing here? How did they see us coming?"

"You're wasting time," Tristan replied angrily. "Shoot them before they shoot us. It's just a stupid program anyway. You ain't gonna actually kill anything."

I turned to Tristan and stared at him for a long time. He couldn't help himself, I knew it then. He had to prove himself, but to who? The general was dying, held up in the Medbay somewhere, and there was no one here to prove his worth to, save the captain. The way the captain kept staring at me, he didn't look remotely interested in what Tristan had to say. The only one left was whoever was watching us through the eyeball hovering over our heads.

The unwavering hand holding my spine erect refused to be dominated by him. This wasn't Tristan's turn to decide things, it was mine. I *finally* got to choose. Despite caring for him, I was tired of everything being out of my control.

"Tristan, you'll let me command or you *will* leave the bridge. Is that understood?"

I couldn't believe those words came out of my mouth, but they did. My stomach churned and my heart beat faster as I watched him stare at me with disbelief. I could see the disbelief soon change to pure rage as his eyes burned into me, but he said nothing. He clenched his fists over his armrests and pushed himself back into his chair as far as he could go.

"Captain, a second mass is emerging from the rear, bearing 180 mark 180," Nathan said, a graveness in his voice. "It looks like they're surrounding us."

"Do we have anything we can use to communicate with them?" I asked.

Otto ran from one side of the room to the other. With his eyes wide and his fingers trembling, he hammered buttons clumsily on the wall.

"Lines of communication o-open on all channels," he said.

"This is . . . Captain Zoe Ruthland," I began, feeling the weight of the title. "We're a rescue vessel, and mean you no harm. Please respond."

The speakers in the bridge crackled as we all held our breath and waited. I didn't know what I was expecting to hear, perhaps the same screeching noise I had heard in my dream. Silence was the only response, and part of me was glad. I could safely chalk up the similarities between the ships and my nightmarish eye to coincidence.

"Zoe," Larissa almost whispered. "They've surrounded us on all sides now. We're trapped between them and the asteroid belt."

It's just a computer simulation, I thought. But my recent dalliance with mind-bending drugs made it difficult for me to believe that.

"Please respond," I said again, unable to hide the higher pitch of my voice.

I made the mistake of looking back at my crew then. I didn't know which was worse, Otto's terror or Tristan's smugness as he sat in his chair grinning, his arms crossed over his chest.

Without warning, a bright light flashed across the screen and the whole room shook violently. My legs, unable to keep me upright, buckled, and I found myself gripping onto Captain Stansfield's arm.

"Guess they responded," Tristan derided.

A heat of anger flared inside me and, without apologising to the captain, I righted myself again. I gestured for Otto to end communication and took long strides back to my chair. I managed to plop down into it just as another explosion rocked the bridge.

"Deploy the drones around us, fan them out like a dome and keep us low to the asteroid belt," I ordered. "Otto, how's the ship?"

Otto, panicked and taking a couple of seconds to run back to his post, almost shouted the answer. "The damage is m-minimal, for n-n-now. But a few more hits like that and w-we'll breach our hull."

"Emily, find a gap in their formation," I yelled to the navigation officer.

"Yeah, you're doomed," she said, examining her nails nonchalantly. "They got us covered."

Emily's apathy irked me beyond reason. I stood and faced my crew, goading them to meet my furious gaze. Emily continued to pick at her nails, Otto avoided my eyes, and while the rest stared at each other in confusion Tristan smirked as if to say, *I told you so*.

"This may just be a simulation," I stormed, "but you're stupid if you think that's all it is. This isn't just another lesson to pass or another step we have to climb to get onto the Kepler One. This is a testament as to how we'll function together as a team when we're *really* out there." Another explosion rocked the bridge, and I only barely managed to stay upright.

"It doesn't matter who the captain is, it doesn't even matter that the aliens aren't real. If we can't work together, if we can't follow something as simple as the chain of command, then you're right, Emily, we *are* doomed . . . we're all doomed to die, and that includes the family you left behind."

Silence followed my words, but I noted that Emily's eyes finally found mine.

"How many times have you done this before?" I asked her.

She looked sheepishly at Sam before answering. "Maybe five or six times?"

"And how many of those times did you survive?" Emily didn't answer.

"None," Nathan replied softly.

"And did you *all* truly work as a team?" My question was met with silence. "If it means we survive this simulation, I'll step down and allow whomever you choose to be the captain. I'll follow their orders without question. But if you still want me, the Tier Five scum, to give it my best shot, then I expect nothing but the best from you all, too. Understand?"

"Yes, Sir," most of them replied in unison.

"Oh, why the hell not!" Emily said with a snort.

I was careful not to let the smile inside show. Emily's retort was the closest I'd ever gotten to a friendly word from her.

I sat back down in my chair and faced the carnage unfolding on the screen. The drones fired doggedly at the enemy above us. When one was shot down and tumbled away from the rest, the others quickly packed themselves in tighter to fill the gap, but they were almost spent and our cover was disintegrating. If I was going to do something, I needed to do it fast.

"Find me an exit, Emily."

I heard her furiously tap the console behind me.

"There's one, but you're going to hate it," she said. "The only way out is to go through the asteroid field below us."

"What are the chances a ship this big will make it through, Otto?"

"Wait, you can't go through there," Tristan protested.

Quicker than I've ever seen him do before, Otto turned his eyes to the ceiling and completed his calculations in seconds. "About sixty-seven percent likelihood of finding g-gaps wide enough for us to travel through. Out of those, about a forty percent chance of finding them all the way through."

"Larissa, do the drones have a self-destruct?" I asked.

Larissa held her breath for a long time as she flew through schematics on a wall console. Picture after picture glided off the screen with a swipe of her hand.

"No," she said finally.

"Wait," Otto interrupted her, making his way over to the console she was using. "You're r-right, there's no self-destruct. But I can r-remotely r-reconfigure their weapons to overload. That will ignite their core and *act* like a self-destruct."

"Otto, you're a genius," I said, offering him a broad grin.

"Did you ever have any doubts?" he replied, confidently polishing his nails on his red tunic.

I was proud of him then; not just for solving the problem, but for finding his place and his voice. It was like watching a baby brother become a man before my eyes. I wanted to hug him, but time was not my friend and I knew it.

"Right, here's the plan," I said, ignoring Tristan. "Otto, start redesigning the probes. Larissa, bring the drones in tighter to us, use them to block us from the enemy's vision. We're going to tunnel our way through the asteroid belt. Nathan, use the ship's weapons to blast any asteroids we can't go around. Emily and Jax, find us a way through and bring us out the other side."

"Wait, but you can't. That's cheating," Tristan said, gesturing for the captain to interfere with my plan. The captain remained silent as he watched things unfold.

"Otto, what are the chances we'll survive if we *don't* go through the asteroid field?" I asked, keeping my eyes locked on Tristan.

"Less than three percent."

"The captain also said we weren't allowed to fail. So, I'm disobeying one order to obey another. I think you'll agree that a forty percent chance is better than three, right?" I said to Tristan before lowering my voice and placing my hand on his arm. "Don't fight me on this, please. I know I'm only a Tier Five and I haven't got the experience you do, but whether I'm right or wrong, I need your support. This is the only way I know how to do things, to run away. Anyway, when I fail they'll know you're the better captain, okay?"

After a moment, Tristan rested his hand over mine and squeezed it gently.

"Okay, Zoe," he said with a small smile. "Sorry. I ain't good at all this trusting business, that's all. I just don't wanna see you do something stupid."

I knew he was talking about more than just my command ability then. I smiled. The honesty in his voice and sincerity in his brown eyes made my heart melt, and I couldn't be angry with him anymore.

"I know," I whispered, letting his arm go and turning back to the screen. "Well, what are you all waiting for? Hell has already frozen over," I yelled.

"Aye, Sir," they roared.

I didn't quite know what was happening, but for the first time since the lottery, I didn't feel any hatred or fear toward me. They were listening to me, trusting me. A lump formed in my throat, and my confidence, something I never knew I was capable of feeling, grew.

"Descend, bearing 0 mark 270," Emily shouted.

As though we were really inside a spacecraft, the room groaned as we descended into the mass of tumbling ice-rocks. Some of the asteroids scraped the side of the imaginary ship as we went, and a metal-twisting screech of protest rang out inside the bridge like a banshee's wail.

"Bring the drones in tighter. I don't want them seeing what we're doing," I ordered Larissa.

"Aye, Sir," she replied.

As the drones disappeared above the screen, I saw them clamp together like a silver shield of small round balls. *Well done, Larissa*, I thought.

Emily continued to direct Jax in a frantic succession of coordinates. Our ship pitched and straightened a few times as we weaved our way between asteroids, some of which were five times the size of the Kepler One.

"I can't see a way," Emily said after a time, her fingers feverously tapping the console. "There's too many, and they're moving too fast."

Without warning, a bright light flashed across our screen again, and I held my breath as I waited for the impending *boom* to rock the bridge. Nothing happened.

"That any better?" Nathan asked.

Emily didn't respond to him. Instead, she continued to bark directions at Jax. Jax almost preceded her commands, as though he knew what she was going to say before she said it.

"When I say," I said in the steadiest tone I could managed, "I want you to send the drones toward the nearest ships and keep them as close as you can, Larissa. Otto, you turn them into bombs and take out as many enemy ships before the drones run out of ammo. Then it's up to you, Larissa, to fire on the rest of them and keep us safe. Have we got all that?"

I had never seen them all so edgy or quiet before. Each stared intently at the screen, and each of their jaws clenched as they gritted their teeth. An equal amount of determination and trepidation was evident in all their expressions, including Tristan's.

"We've never come this far before," he whispered into my ear. "Well done."

My chest swelled with a deep satisfaction and pride at his praise. I knew now that I wasn't too unlike Tristan; I craved his approval the same way he craved the general's. It was a bizarre kinship. Part of me was sad, however, that this person, whom I seem to resonate with so deeply, would never be anything more than a friend.

"Right," I said, keeping my eyes focused on the screen. "Let's tear them a new one!"

"Aye, Sir," they all responded.

Like a well-oiled machine, the crew of Kepler One carried out my plan. The drones suddenly dispersed and found the nearest alien ship to cling to. We were mostly unsheathed, save for the asteroids above us.

The aliens seemed confused and remained motionless when it was revealed that their treasure was no longer there. With heavy finger taps, Otto got to work, and moments later the drones exploded in a succession of bright red flashes. They took out half the enemy fleet, and illuminated the asteroid belt with the bright light of their fiery deaths. The crew erupted into cheers.

"Quiet," Tristan ordered. "We're not done yet."

He was right. The explosions only caused a momentary skirmish among the alien fleet before they found us again and came straight for us. A hail of torpedoes and pulse beams streaked toward our position. Tumbling ice rocks were blasted into pieces or sent careening into bigger ones, upsetting the flow of the asteroid belt and making it more difficult to navigate.

Jax dipped and dove around giant balls of ice, as if he knew where they were even before Emily. Deep throaty drumbeats sounded out the release of our own weapons; silent fireworks in the screen's periphery the only evidence of a hit. Together we fought and together we prayed that we would come out of this alive, lost in the illusion that gripped us so fiercely.

The red glow of the bridge, punctuated by brighter flashes of light from enemy fire, became eerie and poignant. The groans of the Kepler One as the exterior scraped against the moving asteroids made us clench our teeth and hold our breaths as we waited for the hull to breach. For what seemed like forever, we engaged in a dogfight with a smaller, quicker enemy ships. Sweat poured from every possible place on me and the nanites in my uniform struggled to keep my armpits dry as we widened the gap between us.

The asteroid field suddenly closed in around us, and Jax brought us to a halt. Our luck had run out. The only exit was being filled with enemy ships, and they were almost within weapons range.

"There's no way out!" Emily shrieked.

"Nathan, use our weapons to drill through the biggest asteroid in front of us," I said, pointing to the largest rock of ice and stone. "Otto, see if you can help him pinpoint a weak spot."

Together, Nathan and Otto began their assault on the enormous asteroid, blasting a hole through it as ordered, but time ran out and the enemy spilled into our prison, surrounding us on all sides.

"Larissa, hold them off as best you can," I said, pulling myself so close to the edge of my seat that I was practically off it. "Jax, take us into the hole when it's big enough. The asteroid will shield us while bottle-necking the enemy, too. That should make your job easier, Larissa."

Like the mistimed arrhythmia of a dying heart, the ship sounded out Larissa and Nathan's weapons fire. All I could do was watch as Jax took us slowly into the centre of the spinning asteroid. Meter by meter we crawled through, all the time waiting for the inevitable end. There was a definite feeling of claustrophobia as the sparkling grey walls closed around the screen, blocking everything else from sight. The feeling was made worse when the alien ships entered behind and the bridge rocked under their fire. Time and time again, Larissa shot at them to cull their numbers, but there were too many. The sweet taste of possible victory turned bitter in my mouth. I held my breath and waited.

"We're through!" Nathan yelled suddenly.

"Get us out of here," I roared, standing from my seat. "Turn everything we have on the asteroid. Everything! Empty our weapons into the hole. Now!"

Only a few alien ships made it out of the asteroid before the full might of the Kepler One was unleashed. Hundreds of beautiful balls of light sailed through the inky sky and entered the dark cavern we had made, disappearing from sight. I held my breath as I waited for signs of failure, or success.

The surface of the asteroid cracked and broke, like a glass shattered by a high-pitched sound. Its surface, a hatching of brilliant blue light that glowed against the dark background. The asteroid crumpled, then sagged beneath the invisible hand crushing it before exploding violently. Shards of ice, stone, and alien ships shot out in every direction from the glowing core our arsenal had created. Alarms on the bridge wailed when debris hit our hull, and the ship was rocked sideways with the force of the blast.

We waited.

"Scan for enemies," I said, clasping my hands together as I examined the space around us for any sign of ships. An expanse of clear black sky, punctuated with stars and one large, predominantly green planet, met my vision.

"We're clear," Larissa said, relief audible in her voice.

"Kepler 452b is dead ahead," Emily said.

"Damage?" I said with my breath still held.

"We'll live," Otto replied.

After a moment of stunned silence, the bridge erupted into a clamour of cheers and applause. I stood numbly in my spot, not really trusting that we *had* survived. Under the disapproving glare of Tristan, Nathan waltzed over to me and picked me up. He crushed me against his chest and I lost my breath.

"You did it," he said quietly, putting me down again. "You actually did it."

"I did?" I replied, my mind still in the throes of battle.

The red lights on the bridge turned back to their normal glaring white and the alarms were silenced. The screen went blank, and the captain stood stoically in the centre of the room.

"What happened?" I asked, whirring around to face the captain.

"You're done," he replied with a wide grin. "All of you can head back to The Tin and have some chow. I have some data to go over."

The door to the bridge opened again and the dark corridor outside destroyed the illusion I had created.

Reality sucked. Knowing we hadn't actually reached the planet and that we were still being contaminated by the radiation on Earth was depressing.

The others began to file out of the room, each clapping me too hard on my back along the way. Only Nathan hung back. I could see he was waiting to speak to me privately, and I didn't have to guess about what.

"Well done," Tristan said from beside me. I turned and was caught by the expression on his face. It was an odd mixture of happiness and dejection. "You did well today."

"Thanks," I replied. "But it wasn't just me."

Tristan nodded solemnly. I didn't get the impression that he believed me. He tried to smile, failed miserably, then followed the others out of the room. I felt bad. I knew he wanted the command of the mission as badly as I wanted to escape Earth. My success was a spanner in the works for him, but I couldn't let that make me lose my place on the Kepler One. I had to try my best in every training exercise, even if that meant only getting as far as the last day of training.

"What's up with misery guts?" Nathan asked as we left together. "Looks like someone just shot his puppy."

"I don't know," I lied.

We walked silently beside each other for a time. Nathan's eyes darted up and down the corridor before he spoke again, making sure we wouldn't be overheard.

"So, will I finalise the plan then?" he asked.

In all the drama I had forgotten our plot to help the Tier Fives. I'd also purposefully neglected to tell

Nathan that Tristan knew all about it. I was sure that both Tristan and Nathan would forgive my little fibs once they saw the good that came out of it.

I nodded.

"Okay. Well, in that case, I'd suggest we head to bed early on the night," he said. "The sooner everyone gets to sleep, the easier it will be. Just tell them you're still tired from everything that happened and maybe they'll hit the sack early, too."

It wouldn't be a difficult lie to tell. My body ached all over, and I expected it would do for a while. I could have easily gone straight to bed without supper, but I hadn't eaten since I woke up, and regaining my strength for our secret mission was important. This was the only chance I would get to help the children of Tier Five and that was tomorrow night.

A flashback of my own time spent cowering in the worst places of that hellhole came flooding back to me.

"Okay," I said, feeling adrenaline energise me once more. "Okay, let's do this."

Al's culinary skills missed the mark again. The slop I was given to eat tasted like cardboard boiled with vomit chunks. My stomach was thankful for the sustenance, regardless. Despite going to bed early and the rest of the cadets now sleeping, too, my mind wouldn't let me join them. I wasn't sure if it was the excitement over my success in the simulator the day before, or the adrenaline pumping through my veins as I waited for three a.m. to arrive. Maybe it was the fear that Nathan and I would sleep past the hour and miss our opportunity.

I lifted my head and looked at his bed across the room from mine, my eyes heavy and sandy. Nathan appeared to be dead to the world. With his blanket tucked under his arms, I could see his powerful chest rising and lowering rhythmically. If I hadn't known to look, I would have missed the shape of his boots under his dishevelled blanket. He suggested leaving our clothes on so we wouldn't have to dress in the dark and risk waking the others. Our red tunics lay at the foot of our beds, ready to be grabbed, and the sight of them made my heart beat faster.

What if it all went wrong?

Breaking curfew was punished harshly in Bunker Twelve, everywhere save Tier Five. If we were caught tonight, we'd end up getting kicked out of cadet training at the very least. If we were caught stealing resources on top of that, we might end up dead, or worse, back in Tier Five.

The distant sound of drones patrolling the corridors outside the barracks didn't ease my anxiety. I turned toward Tristan, perhaps for comfort or maybe out of curiosity. Lying in the bed next to me, his breaths fogged his rebreather in an even succession of cloudiness. He seemed so relaxed and calm. He wouldn't be when he found out what Nathan and I had done. In my head, I played out the conversation we would have when he discovered that I had lied to him.

"I'm sorry, Tristan, but it was something I had to do."

"Really? Did you really have *to do it? Why did you lie to me, Zoe? I thought you understood that I was only protecting you. I thought you liked me more than that."*

"I couldn't live another day without at least trying to help the poor wretches in Tier Five."

"I ain't ever gonna trust you again, Zoe."

No matter which way I played it out, the conversation never ended well, and it made my stomach churn. I didn't want to lose him, I didn't want him to hate me again, but I *had* to do this. If Nathan found out that I had lied to him, too, would he hate me as well? I'd come so far, befriending more cadets than I ever thought I could, and now I was jeopardising it all. Was Tristan right? Was it really worth it? I closed my eyes against the sight of him sleeping peacefully, unaware of my betrayal. *What am I doing?* I thought.

An unwelcomed memory came back to me as my eyes remained closed. I was cold, small, and folded tightly into myself as I hunkered in the darkest corridor of Tier Five. Seedy characters whose interests lay only in the shadows, eyed me with a want in their expression. My outreached hand trembled and remained empty save for the large dollops of contaminated water which dripped from the ceiling.

I remembered the fear that rooted me to the spot. I remembered the fetid, cankered skin of toothless men as they leaned closer to examine me, only to then cast me aside for being too thin . . . or a boy. I also remembered the words I repeated for weeks on end, pleas that went unanswered, the same ones I echoed for my mother three years later.

"Please help me. My father needs medicine. Please!"

A hand gently rested on my shoulder, and my eyes flew open in a moment of panic. No, I wasn't back in Tier Five begging for medicine. I was in my bed, and Nathan was trying to wake me. I must have nodded off for a few moments, lost in the childhood memories that rapaciously fed my fear.

I couldn't see Nathan properly in the dark. Steeling myself against the lingering images in my mind, I pulled back my bed covers, careful not to make too much noise. Throwing off my t-shirt and donning my red tunic, I tip-toed silently behind Nathan's broad silhouette as we left the barracks in the dead of night.

The corridor was almost pitch-black, darker than it had been with Otto. I wondered if that was Nathan's doing, too. The only light saving us from walking into the walls were the illuminated keypads of the locked doors either side of us.

"You okay?" he whispered once we were far enough away from the others that they wouldn't hear. "You looked like you saw a ghost back there."

"I'm fine," I replied, wondering how he'd seen me in the dark.

"You know, you *can* pull out if you're not up to this," he said. "It's not too late, and you've been through a lot."

"I'm fine, really," I said, pushing past him. "This is the only chance we're going to get. I'm good."

I couldn't see his scowl of disbelief, but I felt it billowing behind me like a dark presence that mistrusted my every word. I ignored him and continued walking. Before we reached the end of the corridor, he held my elbow and stopped me.

"We need to go here first," he whispered.

I heard him rustling through his pockets. He took something dark and rectangular out, about the size of his palm, and pressed it against the keypad next to me. Were it not for the green glow of the number pad, I wouldn't have seen it at all. With a beep and a clunk, the door opened and he quickly pulled me inside, closing the door behind us.

"That was too loud," he said.

Without warning, the harsh lights of the room flickered on in a series of blinking flashes. Nathan's hand stayed resting on the light switch for a moment while we both squinted against the brightness. In his other hand he held a thin, black card with no discernible marks or blemishes.

"Where did you get that?" I asked pointing to the card.

"Your friend, Otto," he replied, slipping it into his pocket again. "He thought it would take him longer, but since our vitamin shot . . . since you nearly died . . . he focused all his attention on it. Guess it gave him something else to think about other than the fact that we . . . *he* nearly lost you," Nathan said, taking sheepish glances at me.

He cleared his throat and grabbed a couple of rucksacks from a corner of the room. I recognised where we were. The Afterhours training room, or rather the Tierless storage room.

"He said he made it using the nanites from our tunics," Nathan continued. "Something about reprogramming them to open electronic locks when they're placed on them. He's pretty smart, you know?"

"I *do* know," I replied, taking one of the bags from Nathan's outreached hand and slinging it onto my shoulder. "So does that mean we have access to the labs and the hydroponic garden, too?"

"We have access to everywhere," he said, and with a cheeky grin added, "So, where would m'lady like to go for our first date?"

My cheeks flushed with heat as Nathan bowed to me, like *I* was someone special. He was truly handsome, and in that moment, any erstwhile thought I'd had of him being an ass faded away. He was exciting, he was unpredictable, and, yes, a little dangerous, too. He was nothing like Tristan, who was steadfast, methodical, and calculating to the last.

"Take me to the treasure, Robin Hood," I replied, smiling as the excitement of rebellion tingled every nerve in my body.

"Who?" he asked, raising one eyebrow.

"You know, Robin Hood? Steals from the rich and gives to the poor?" I answered.

My reply was met with silence. I thrust my hands onto my hips and glared at him with the disbelief that he had never heard the story before. By the blank expression on his face, however, I could tell he truly hadn't. *I can't be the only one who's heard that story, can I?* Perhaps my bedtime tales were just another way for my parents to teach me about morality and sacrifice, but then I remembered Tristan mentioned the same story in Medbay. Maybe it was just a Tier Five thing.

I sighed and reached for the door handle.

"Never mind, come on."

"Wait," Nathan said, his arm reaching around me and to hold the door closed so I couldn't get out. I froze, still gripping onto the handle as he slid himself between me and the exit. His hazel eyes focused intently on me as his chest accidentally brushed against mine. There was a moment of awkward surprise in his expression, like he hadn't meant to get so close, but despite any discomfort, he didn't pull away. Our faces were only inches apart, and if it weren't for the rebreathers I was sure I'd be able to feel his breath on my lips.

"Got to switch off the lights first," he said after a while, his voice low and deep.

My hand tightened over the cold metal handle, immobilised by his closeness. I could feel his powerful chest rising and lowering against mine, and I knew he could feel me, too, but still he didn't move. He *wanted* this closeness, and it disturbed a rabble of butterflies in my stomach, and set my innards alight.

From the corner of my vision, I saw his hand flick the light switch off and we were plunged into darkness. An electricity ignited inside my belly, and my hands began to tremble. I'd never been this close to a man who didn't want to kill me before, not alone and in the dark. I could feel his breathing become heavy and slow. He didn't want to move away. I didn't want to move away either. I wanted to press myself against him further, to bring us closer. I didn't dare and not just because we had a job to do, but also because I was too scared.

Regardless of my fear, I couldn't help sneaking in a moment to exploit the position he put himself in, mostly out of mischievousness. I leaned in closer, purposefully brushing my cheek against his.

"Thank you," I said. His head turned toward mine in response and our masks touched. I didn't pull away. "For everything you've done."

I removed my mask just long enough to press my lips gently on his cheek. He stopped breathing. His chest became motionless and rigid as my lips grazed his bristled jaw. But before he had a chance to react, before we lost our reason, I pulled away, giving him the room to move from the door. Although I couldn't see him, I knew he was still standing there, frozen by my touch. I wanted to kiss him again, properly this time, on his lips, but time wouldn't wait for us, and he knew it, too.

"Em." His voice shook and lacked the usual confidence. "I . . . em . . . sure. Anytime."

I heard him stumble to my right. With my broad smile hidden by the dark, I swung the door open. I was elated and curious about how a single kiss on the cheek could disarm him so readily. The daunting Commander Nathan McColl, reduced to an ungainly mumbling simpleton by a slip of a girl. It was the first adorable thing I'd seen of him, and I wanted to do it again.

"Where to first?" I asked, heading down the corridor like nothing had happened. "Labs or hydroponics?"

"Labs first," he replied, not quite recovered from our coquetry and jogging to catch up with me. "The hydroponics is at the other end of Tier One."

"Okay," I said, adrenaline and excitement making me skittish.

Chapter 14

We walked in silence, passing the eerily quiet gym and through a set of large doors. Bright lights stung my eyes again as we entered the adjoining hallway between the Tierless compound and Tier One. Two guards dressed in black with large guns crossing their chests, stood stoically either side of another set of doors. Nathan walked toward them without hesitation. I was a little slower to react, but followed closely on his heels.

The young guard on the left saw us and raised his gun. The one on the right whispered something to him before turning and walking away. Hesitantly, he lowered his gun as Nathan approached.

"May you find health this day," Nathan said, holding out his hand.

The guard reached out and shook Nathan's hand, his eyes narrowed and his finger still resting on his gun's trigger. I saw something slip between the two, a small bottle of liquid with the word *insulin* clearly written on the label.

"May you find health this day," the guard replied, pocketing the small vial before turning away like his companion, leaving the door unprotected.

"Come on, we've got to hurry," Nathan said, taking my hand and leading me through the doors into Tier One. He laced his fingers through mine and squeezed my hand slightly as we slipped through the door.

"Where did you get that insulin?" I asked, already suspecting the answer.

"It's my sister's," he replied, not looking back at me while we navigated the luxurious corridors. "I stole it to bribe Tom."

"But Teresa needs that . . . Nathan,"

Nathan let my hand drop to push open another set of heavy doors. I was expecting to be met by a sea of drones hovering overhead. Thankfully there were none and the corridors of Tier One remained silent, save for our footsteps.

"Don't worry about it," he said. "Because I'm a cadet they'll make sure she has enough. Once we get into the labs, I can swipe another bottle and replace it before they know it went missing."

"And if you don't?" I asked, following him as he took off down another corridor. "They'll accuse your sister of selling her meds . . . they'll accuse you of selling it for her."

"Well, I guess we'd better make sure that this all goes smoothly then," he said.

I wasn't convinced the price he'd pay was worth it anymore, not now that I had come to care about him.

We emerged into the Central Pavilion, and at that stage it was too late to turn back. Another weight landed on my shoulders and it made it more difficult for me to breathe. Nathan, on the other hand, seemed light-footed and so sure of himself, sure this plan would work. For all our sakes, I hoped he was right.

The door to the tram lay unguarded as usual. Nathan and I both glanced at it and then at each other before crossing the central stage. I was sure the same question went through both our minds; how easy would it be to break in there? Tempting as it was to try, we both knew the answer . . . not very.

Now quiet, the ghosts of unsuccessful lottery hopefuls appeared before me, ones that might have made better cadets. The angry face of the Tier One boy named John weaved in the periphery of my vision as I crossed the central stage. He knew I was nothing but a thief, and here I was proving him right. John's spectre sneered knowingly at me before being dispelled by the voices of the guards outside the labs.

"About time, Nathan," the sable-haired guard said as he engulfed Nathan in a tussling hug. "I was beginning to think ya'd chickened out."

"Hey, the only yellow belly around here is the one belonging to your mother," Nathan replied with a wicked grin. "Took off running when she gave birth to your ugly mug."

"Oie!" the guard replied, slapping Nathan roughly on his arm. "Enough lip outta you, ya eejit. Ya've got ten minutes to grab what ya need and get to hydroponics. We'll clear out the guards for yer ugly ass, but ya won't have much time before the next lot come in. So get a move on."

The guard turned to the other soldier and waved him away.

"Thank you," Nathan said.

"Don't say I never did nothing for ya," he replied, slapping Nathan on the back before turning toward me. "And don't let that fella get ya into trouble, young miss," he said, wagging a finger toward Nathan. "He does some stupid stuff sometimes."

"Hey!" Nathan's injured tone fooled no one.

"I'll keep both eyes on him," I replied with a grin.

"Whatever happened to innocent until proven guilty?" Nathan called after his friend as he disappeared the same way the other guard had.

"Nothing innocent about you," he replied.

Nathan laughed and pushed the doors to the labs open. I followed, feeling as though I didn't truly know Nathan even though we had become closer. Among the Tierless, he seemed well-liked, popular even. It surprised me as I had pictured him as this angry, no-nonsense, dictator when we first met. But he hated me then, hated every Tier Five, and with good reason.

Inside the lab we scavenged through the cupboards, grabbing fistfuls of tablets and throwing whatever we could into our rucksacks. I wondered if trusting me was one of the "stupid" things his friend warned me about. I ignored the niggling thought and ransacked the coolers for injectable drugs. Coming across a few more bottles of insulin, I shoved one into my trouser pocket while the rest went into the rucksack. I wanted to make sure to keep one separate for Nathan, so his other *stupid* act didn't get him into trouble, too.

I tried to only pick medication I knew was pain relief—antibiotics were of little use to the dying—and came upon some shelves I recognised. This was where Nathan had caught me stealing the day of the lottery. I stood still, remembering how scared I was that day, how alone and desperate. The hate in his hazel eyes burned in my memory, too.

A hand gently rested on my shoulder, dragging me from my thoughts.

"I'm sorry for being a dick," he whispered, realising why I was staring at this particular spot. I turned to face him, and his hand slipped off my shoulder. His eyebrows were knitted together and his eyes wouldn't meet mine. "I judged you and let my emotions take over."

"It's okay," I said. "We've both come a long way since then. I mean, look at you now. Who would have thought that *you*, of all people, would be willing to help the Tier Fives?"

More so than Tristan, I thought.

"Crazy, right?" he replied with a small laugh. "But I guess if half of them are like you, they aren't so bad after all."

A canister of pills crashed to the floor and made us both jump. Nathan moved quickly to put himself between the noise and me. We waited to see soldiers rush at us, but there was no one there.

"Must have just fallen, or something. Come on. We need to keep moving," he said, heading toward the door.

I took one last glance at the mess we'd left behind. Drawers were half open, and countless pills were strewn all over the pristine floors.

"They're going to know we were here," I protested as we pushed through the doors. "We should go back and tidy up."

"They count every single pill, Zoe. They're going to know we were here no matter how neat we leave it," he replied.

"What about the guards? Won't they get into trouble?"

We ran down a corridor I'd never been in before and came to a domed glass ingress, barricaded by a succession of glass doors. Each had a keypad and each was thicker than the next. Nathan placed Otto's card onto the keypad and, one by one, they opened for us. Upon closing again, we were sprayed with a fine, cold mist I assumed was meant to cleanse whoever was entering.

"Who's to say which guards were on and which were off when it happened?" Nathan said as we passed through yet another door. "If they all say they weren't on that night, what's the general going to do, court-martial them all? No, the only way this works is if they *all* deny it. And they will."

I felt only slightly more relieved that our secret would be safe.

As the last glass door closed behind us, I was amazed at how large the hydroponic compound was. All the walls, doors, and fixtures were made of glass. Glowing blue and yellow wires—pumping thick liquids—crawled between the walls; the only obstacle in an otherwise gorgeous view. We could see right through the compound and into the luscious agrarian tiers which housed our most important resource.

Leafy fingers stretched through hazy air toward lights that dangled above them, teasing them with only enough light to allow them to grow. I noted that Tier One was more brightly lit, and I wondered if the lack of light here was by design or default.

Looking closer, I also noticed that the leaves of some of the plants were wilted and yellowing around the edges. Some plants were stunted compared to others, while one appeared misshapen beyond recognition. The farm animals, on the opposite side to the entrance, had large growths protruding from their backs, and chickens with no wings pecked at invisible corn beneath them. Worst of all, massive tanks of irradiated water housed fish with two tails or no eyes, or just a body with a mouth. The rumours were true. The food in the hydroponics compound was mutated and tainted.

"This way," Nathan said, directing me toward one of the stores.

Tainted or not, the sight of shelves and shelves of food, some already prepared, made my mouth water despite not being hungry. Loaves of bread were stacked one on top of the other, vegetables toppled out of blue boxes, and cured meat hung from metal hooks on the ceiling. Tier Five would never normally see this kind of food.

Nathan pressed the card to the keypad and it opened without a sound. An overwhelming sense of exhilaration consumed me as I thought of the joy we would bring to those children with nothing in Tier Five. I couldn't help smiling as Nathan and I stuffed our bags. Whatever amount of food we took, it just didn't seem like enough, but time was running out and our backpacks were near bursting point.

"Okay," I said, trying to cram another carrot into my bag. "Let's go."

Without needing another word, Nathan threw his bag onto his back and we headed out. We had to stop at each corner because the drones were restarting their rounds. I was thankful that Nathan seemed to know how to avoid them. It was slow going, but we had to make sure.

Finally reaching the doors I had come through over two weeks ago, we slipped into the concrete stairwell. It was strange to see them again, to be climbing them once more. The cracks were small here; hairline fractures only hinting at the deadly water behind it. The further we climbed, however, the wider the gaps became.

Slowly the steps became narrower and, tier by tier, the guards let us pass with a solemn nod. Nathan returned the gesture silently and we continued to climb. As we passed tier four, large fissures distorted the middle of the steps. The cracks in the walls became wide enough to fit a hand through and the drip, drip, drip, of water was the only other audible noise, save for our boots.

The gates to Tier Five loomed ahead. They were rusted, old, and warped in places. A cold draft wrapped itself around me as we neared, welcoming me back to Tier Five. The two guards, each with their rifle inserted into the Tier Five compound through holes in the gates, didn't move to greet us. Watchful eyes, ever prepared for the unpredictable nature of the Tier Fives, stayed locked on the happenings beyond the door.

Nathan stopped and fished out two bottles of pills from his rucksack. He opened one of the many pockets of the soldier's vests and slipped a bottle into each. The soldiers didn't move, didn't even blink, and for a split second I thought they would turn their guns on us and shoot.

Undisturbed by their stony demeanour, Nathan shrugged the rucksack onto his back again and leaned his full weight onto one of the doors. It groaned open, loudly. Rusty powder dislodged from the joints, floated through the air, and peppered one of the soldier's backs with a red snow. He moved with the door, keeping his focus squarely on the inhabitants behind it.

"You ready?" Nathan asked, waiting for me to lead the way.

"As I'll ever be."

Tier Five was darker than I remembered. Accustomed to the brighter lights of the higher levels, my eyes took a moment to adjust. There wasn't much to see. The corridors around the exit were deserted. Too often the temptation of escape drew the desperate close, and it was all too easy to make a bolt for the door when it was in the line of sight. Most Tier Fives stayed away to keep that temptation at a good distance. There was also the pot-shots to avoid that Tierless soldiers would sometimes take at a passing citizen. Why not? Who would demand justice for a Shadow? Murder was common here, and the temptation to dip one's toe into sin was prevalent on both sides of the doors.

Tier Five was colder, too, something I hadn't noticed as I'd never known warmth before the lottery. The brisk, damp air moistened the skin on my face and tingled the tips of my fingers. Were it not for my tunic keeping me warm, I would have found it difficult to cope with the frigidness. I wondered how I ever survived it in the first place.

"Which way?" Nathan asked.

"Follow me," I replied, turning down the corridor to my right.

The concrete walls looked the same as I remembered them, grey and bleeding brown groundwater. The cracks were wider, though, and I'd never noticed the rusted pipes that ran overhead before, probably because eye were better kept scanning for attackers than admiring the lofted ceiling.

Aside from the slap of our shoes on wet floors, the only sounds cultivating the air around us were of whispers, punctuated with distant screams. There was no chatter of normal conversations in Tier Five, the singing of a child's laughter rarely graced these halls. The smothering timber of fear and desperation muted all but the whispers and the screams.

Nathan said nothing as we walked. His eyes darted left and right as we passed the opened doors of some Tier Five residences. People in grey recoiled as we encroached into their world, our red uniforms a warning that all was not right. Suspicious eyes hid behind dirty hands, and in the dark recesses that Tier Five allowed, Shadows found their hiding places.

I didn't stop. I was taking Nathan to the worst part of my home, the seediest and deadliest corridors in all of Tier Five. A place known as The Reaper's Snare. Only the desperate, the stupid, or the insane ventured there. For a fleeting moment, I wondered which *I* was.

The Reaper's Snare was home to the worst criminals in Tier Five, a catchment of evil and depravity. Controlled by the only people who could get what was needed in a world where there was nothing to be had, this was the place to go for medicine and food . . . but there was always a price to pay. Not many could afford that price, and like I had, they took their chances begging for mercy from the merciless.

As we rounded another corner, the numbers of grey people in the penumbra, grew. Dirty sheets hung from the rusting pipes overhead and dripped contaminated water onto my head. The whispers grew louder and I recognised the word they spoke. "Chantar."

Chantar was a Tier Five word, made up in the absence of English. It was the most commonly used word and had many meanings; outsider, danger, hurt, pain, and all the negative things associated with a potential threat. The word swirled in the air around Nathan and me, following us like a belligerent nimbus that wouldn't dissipate. I came to realise the people I'd grown up with didn't see me as one of their own anymore. All they saw was the red uniform, a portent for further persecution.

Raiders ransacked a room to our left, fighting among themselves for the meagre chattels of an old man. His skeletal body lay cold and grey in the middle of his room as they argued, oblivious to his death and to the tears of his wife sobbing gently beside him. Nathan's pace slowed and his eyes widened as the macabre scene unfolded. I laced my fingers through his and pulled him forward before he could say anything.

"We can't help her," I whispered.

I could feel him staring at me, even though I didn't look back. I knew he was thinking that I was callous and heartless, but I had passed by many scenes like that before and no good ever came out of interfering. No good had come when they arrived at my father's room the night he died and I had objected. Were it not for my mother dragging me away like I dragged Nathan away now, I suspected they would have killed me instead of just beating me to near death.

Turning one last corner, the Reaper's Snare opened up before us and I unlocked my fingers from Nathan's, reluctantly. Gaunt and scrawny children huddled in the shadows behind the bony legs of promiscuous ladies who offered "fun" in exchange for anything a passer-by was willing to part with. At the other end of the half-mile-long corridor, bloated men with sloping foreheads and leering smiles swilled the only alcohol in Tier Five. They wiped their mouths on soiled sleeveless tunics and perused the ladies. Turning them around to examine them like property, they slapped the ladies on the rear for good measure. Some even cupped the terrified faces of the children hunkered by the ladies' feet, a menacing lust in their eyes.

"Wh . . . where do we start?"

Nathan's voice was uneven and quiet. His cool, untouchable exterior broke under the horrifying reality of life in Tier Five. Now he understood, now he knew why I had to do this. I shrugged my rucksack off my back and pulled out a loaf of bread.

"Start with the children," I said, breaking the bread in half and approaching the nearest child.

From my periphery I could see Nathan standing in the same spot, watching me. Paralysed by the sight of the pitiful beings who cowered from us, it took him a moment to follow my instructions, but he did. He hurtled his rucksack to the ground and tore it open, fishing out our ill-gotten-gains and handed them to the smallest children. I smiled as he took the wall opposite mine and we began to work our way through the ravenous, gaping maw that was the Reaper's Snare.

At first, the children were wary, but the sight of food soon abolished any caution they had. Snatching the bread from my hand, they tore into it at a ferocious rate. Before long, whispers alerted the other children, and they began to swarm. I had made my way farther up the corridor than Nathan, so they came to me first.

"Medicine, please, please," some of them pleaded.

I rooted in the bottom of my bag and thrust fistful after fistful into their grabbing, grateful, hands. Arms wrapped themselves around my waist, squeezing me for a moment before withdrawing and disappearing altogether. Wails of "be tanking you" shouted at me from a distance as they scurried off before their prize was taken from them. Joy rang through the most desperate part of Tier Five, probably for the first time ever, and I couldn't help but smile. The wave of the desperate reached Nathan and surrounded him, too.

"Medicine?" a woman's voice said from beside me.

I wheeled around to find the source of the voice and was surprised, not by who was standing there, but by the expression on her face. One of the ladies-of-pleasure's hand was outreached toward me. It trembled, and her eyes glistened with the hint of tears. Her face, too rawboned to hide the lines of age and worry, held an expression that told me her life story . . . and it was tragic.

Her hair, dishevelled and sparse, was tied in a loose bun on top of her head, revealing her impossibly thin neck. The grey tunic, opened at the front to allure men, exposed an atrophied figure supporting a too-large black bra. It was a wonder she was able to hold herself up at all.

I stared at her for a moment, unsure. I wanted to keep the food and medicine for the children, but who was I to judge which citizens were worthy of help and which weren't? To deny her what I was offering the children would make me no better than President Tucker. Her face exuded desperation and my heart couldn't bear to say no. I handed a bottle of pills to her and she took it with a withered, disbelieving smile.

"Be tanking you," she said with a trembling voice. "Be tanking you all my days."

The courtesan hugged the bottle of pills close to her emaciated chest and ran from the corridor the same way the children had. Within moments, more ladies coalesced with the throngs of children pressing against me. Nathan and I were surrounded, wedged in a sea thickening with the discarded debris of Bunker Twelve. He looked at me, a solemn nod acknowledging his understanding of why I had to come, before I lost sight of him behind the wave of outreached hands and desperate eyes.

I smiled and turned my attention back to the growing number of people. Word had spread to the end of the corridor, and now there were a few seedy characters beginning to edge the crowd. A panic untethered the joy I was feeling and I came crashing back to the harsh reality around me. I knew they would come . . . those who took from everyone. The children and the ladies knew it, too. It was the reason they fled and didn't ask for more. Better to leave, than to risk losing it all to *him*.

"Nathan, we have to go," I shouted.

I wasn't sure he heard me. I wasn't even sure we could fight our way through the mob in time either. Still handing out food and medicine, I craned my neck over the crowd but I wasn't tall enough to see him.

"I be wanting some," a gruff voice said.

I felt the heat of the crushing crowd disappear from around me and the whispers of chantar return. I turned slowly, not ready to face who I knew was waiting for me. A man, one of the bloated, alcohol-swilling men with more hair on his shoulders than his head, leered a toothless grin at me. His sleeveless grey tunic was stained with many things; his last meal, the drink he still held in his hand, and the fresh blood of whomever he had last met.

I knew this man. His name was Ubel. If ever anyone had the misfortune to be engaged by this man, it was a certainty that something bad was going to happen. I could feel a tremble start in my fingers, so I balled my fists trying to hide my weakness. The crowd farther behind me hadn't yet become aware of his presence, and the jovial sounds of children and ladies still thanking Nathan for sharing his wealth seemed out of place now.

I swallowed deeply, my throat dry and my tongue incapable of moving the way I told it to. Taking a deep breath to steady myself, I reached into my bag and pulled out a bottle of pills, keeping my eyes locked on Ubel at all times. Trying my damndest to not let the shaking of my hand sound out my fear by the rattling of pills, I held them out to him.

Ubel's grey eyes trailed lazily down my arm and rested on my offering. He grinned, then slapped the pills from my hand. The bottle exploded and tablets scattered onto the concrete floor. They were quickly gathered by the smallest of the children, who then weaved their way through the crowd and away from the monster they all feared.

"Give me," he said, pointing to my rucksack.

Ubel wanted all of it.

"It be mine," I said with more defiance that I thought I had.

Ubel wiped the side of his chin with his filthy, hairy arm and took a step closer. I couldn't be afraid; I had to show him strength. I had to talk like a Tier Five and behave like a worthy adversary if I was to survive this. Ubel preyed on the weak, but like any bully, was more cautious of those who could do him harm. On my own I could do him little harm, but he didn't know that.

"Give me," he demanded, throwing his alcohol to the ground.

The bottle smashed into pieces, and the sound of it made me jump. He saw.

"It be mine," I roared at him, trying to make up for my jitters. "I tinking you leave now, or I'll be having me blaster on you."

Ubel paused for only a moment. The threat of a blaster was the one thing I knew would scare any Tier Five. With the arrival of two of his equally inebriated and formidable cohorts, however, my warning lost its weight.

Ubel gestured for the man on his left to take the bag from me. He lunged and I jumped out of his way, raising my knee to meet his head. A crack of bone and a spurt of blood from his mouth signified his broken jaw. He howled in pain, cupping his chin in one hand while still trying to grab me with the other. Again I dodged it.

Ubel's second man managed to grab a fistful of my hair, dragging me back toward his master. Pain tugged at my head as I twisted around and threw a punch at his groin. He released me, staggering to his knees and whining like a beaten puppy. I straightened my hair and threw the bag onto my back. I tried to melt into the crowd behind me, my fists clenched and my stance crouched, ready for Ubel's next attack.

I was quietly surprised I'd lasted this long against him and knew I had the general's training to thank for that. For a moment, nothing happened. The sounds of the worshipers around Nathan seemed too far for me to reach.

"NATHAN!" I yelled, the panic in my voice giving me away.

Without warning, three pairs of hands grabbed me from behind. I looked over my shoulder to see who it was, and my eyes went wide in disbelief. The ladies-of-pleasure, those I had helped, were back, and they were siding with Ubel. Even the first lady who had been so grateful before now held me fast, her expression hard and uncaring. I didn't understand. I helped her, and now she was betraying me?

"What are you doing?" I gasped.

"Sorry," the blonde-haired lady said, not looking at my eyes. "Ubel is boss."

Following the unspoken edict of her master, she gripped me more tightly and thrusted me toward Ubel and his two cronies. I crashed straight into Ubel's chest and fell to my knees. His toothless grin grew wider, letting his saliva flow over his cracked lips and pool in his mask.

"Ubel is king. Everybody knows. And now you, too," he said.

He was right and we both knew it. His rule over Tier Five was known to everyone who lived there, and no one would dare cross him to help me. Safe in his totalitarian rule, he stepped closer, almost bowling me over, and sneered with maliciousness. He grabbed my arms and dragged me up until I was off my knees, pressing me against his filthy chest.

I could see it in his cold eyes as they came closer, the rapacious want that didn't just stop at my rucksack. My heart galloped and my breathing tremoloed with fear. I had imagined my death at the hands of this man many times before, and now, it seemed, my time had come.

The bloodied face of a man with a disfigured jaw came into view beside Ubel. His eyes glared at me as though he was imagining which of the many ways he would kill me first. Another pair of rough hands grappled with the rucksack on my back. I refused to give in easily, and he pulled at it until the straps snapped and tore at my shoulders. I gasped in pain, and this seemed to excite Ubel.

The crowd around me watched and did nothing as Ubel crushed my arms under his iron grip and dragged me all the way to my feet. Through his rebreather, Ubel breathed heavily and licked his thin lips. His two comrades seemed to know what he was thinking and edged closer to me, replacing his grip on my arms. They were stronger than he, and my arms burned as they twisted them and held them out wide.

"Everytin is mine," he said, reaching around behind me and putting his hand on my rear.

"No!" I whispered, too scared to speak aloud.

He was going to rape me, I knew it beyond any doubt. He was going to rape me in front of everyone, to show them his power and authority. *No, no, no, no, no*, my mind screamed. I struggled against my captors, but it was no use. I kicked out at Ubel, at his cronies, at empty space . . . at anything. Tears blinded my vision as I twisted and turned in their grip, lashing out viciously. But I couldn't get free. More hands grabbed at my legs to keep them still, and fear erupted inside.

"NATHAN!" I screamed, hearing the terror in my own voice.

Ubel stepped behind me, wrapping the crook of his arm around my neck, and squeezed it hard enough to only allow a small sliver of air into my lungs. My voice went silent, and my tears flowed freely as he gently caressed my hair with his free hand. His cronies lifted my legs off the floor and the crowd looked on, ladies, and children, and all. I struggled, twisted, and soon my body ached for air.

"No, stop," I gasped inaudibly.

I stretched out my hand to the lady who had betrayed me, silently pleading for her help. She turned her head away and slunk back into the crowd as more men surrounded me. There were too many to count, some less formidable than Ubel, but with an equally depraved leer. They blocked my view of the crowd beyond them. They blocked any chance of escape.

A hand reached up and cupped my breast through my tunic. I wheezed in as much air as I could and screamed. I used every last morsel of energy to fight them off, but I was trapped. Ubel loosened his grip on my throat, allowing me a second to breathe, as he fumbled with the toggle of my tunic before unzipping it in a fast ripping motion. Cold air cascaded over my torso, bathing me in the icy reality of what was going to happen. Someone tugged at my bra, pulling it off, and I screamed again as hands grasped at my chest.

"Zoe!"

I heard Nathan's voice before I saw him. Sheer panic and horror coalesced with my name as he spoke. A commotion erupted behind the wall of men who blocked my view and the hands suddenly ceased their exploration. Something sharp and cold replaced Ubel's arm against my throat; a knife. I froze, breathing heavily, crying, waiting for death to come, but Ubel's knife didn't move.

Through my teary vision, I saw the heads of the leering men disappear one by one as Nathan made his way toward me. Grunts and screams of pain precursored the hurling of Tier Five men across the room. Between the thinning wall of perverts, I caught a glimpse of Nathan viciously uppercutting a man under his jaw, sending the man's teeth and head flying backward. Nathan was outnumbered. I didn't believe he could fight off that many, but he just kept coming. He clenched his teeth and exuded an unyielding rage, his powerful fists pounding anyone who came near.

Ubel's minions fought back, throwing vicious punches at Nathan. He absorbed each blow as if it only served to fuel him more. He was determined to reach me. The closer he came, the more I witnessed the deadliness and fury exuding from his hulking form—an air that sent many men scurrying away. The men who held my arms and legs, however, held me tighter as he came within feet of me.

My tunic opened, I wanted to hide from Nathan's gaze. His eyes didn't rest on me long, however. They flashed a savage warning to Ubel, who pressed his stubbly cheek against mine to hold me steady. The feeling of Ubel against me made my skin crawl and I whimpered at his touch.

"Let her go," Nathan ordered, his voice deeper and more menacing than I had ever heard.

"She be mine," Ubel hissed at Nathan, sliding a hand down my chest to prove it. I struggled and cried out against his touch as he cupped my breast.

"STOP!" Nathan yelled, reaching a hand toward me before freezing as Ubel pressed the knife further into my neck. His hand trembled and his eyes went wide and I realised something. His mother was raped in front of him by Tier Fives, too, and he was reliving the worst part of his life. "Please!"

The change in Nathan's demeanour seemed to shock Ubel and his army into silence. For whatever reason, they became still and waited for Nathan to speak again. Maybe they enjoyed his fear, my fear, and wanted to relish it a little longer.

Through my blurred vision I saw Nathan reach behind and take his rucksack off his back. It shook slightly as he held it out to Ubel. He swallowed slowly as his eyes flicked between me and my captor.

"Take this," he said. "*She* can't get you any power, but this can."

Ubel nodded to the cronies holding my arms and legs. They let me go and I dropped to the floor, still captive under Ubel's knife. My unsteady legs wouldn't let me stand, so I stayed crumpled on the ground with Ubel hunkered behind me.

I immediately grabbed my tunic and pulled it closed with one hand, while the other held Ubel's arm steady for fear he would slit my throat by accident. The men snatched the bag from Nathan and rummaged through its contents. A grunt signified their satisfaction. Ubel grabbed me around my waist and hauled me upright again.

"I be tanking you," he said, sneering at Nathan. "Now, everytin *is* mine."

Ubel began to drag me backward, deeper into the Reaper's Snare. I struggled as best I could, but with the sharp blade at my neck there was only so much I could do. If it came to it, however, I was fully prepared to slit my own throat rather than let him take me.

The sound of gunfire exploded in the corridor, making everyone cower. This included Ubel, and he dragged me down with him. Nathan was the only one left standing. In his hand, he held the smouldering barrel of the gun pointed to the ceiling. He never told me he was bringing a gun, probably because he knew I would object to him shooting Tier Fives, but now I was glad he did. Slowly he lowered his weapon and pointed it at Ubel, taking purposeful strides to narrow the gap between us.

"You let her go," he said, his voice warning and dangerous again, "or I'll shoot you with my . . . what do you call it? Ah yes, my blaster."

Against my back, I could feel Ubel's chest rise and lower more quickly at the sight of Nathan's gun. It was the one thing never traded in Tier Five. It was the one thing Ubel could never get hold of. To the criminal element living in this squalid cesspit, it signified absolute power and authority.

"Give me, for her," Ubel demanded.

"No. You'll just take it like you took my bag," he replied, taking another step closer. "Either give her to me or I'll shoot."

I could feel the rage exude from Ubel as his knife pressed a little harder into my neck. Something warm ran from the blade and trickled slowly down my half-covered chest; blood? Nathan's eyes followed the blood, and I could see him trying to hide his anger.

"Fine," Ubel shouted, lifting the knife and thrusting me toward Nathan.

I landed at his feet, gasping, crying, and immediately tried my best to close my tunic again. My hands fumbled on the toggle as Nathan bent down and cupped my face, turning it toward him. I pulled away, not wanting to be touched by anyone. Nathan said nothing. Instead, he stood to face Ubel.

Giving up on fastening my top, I tried to get onto my feet, too, but found that I couldn't. My legs buckled and I truly felt how pathetic and weak I was. How was I supposed to save the human race when I couldn't even save myself?

I eventually looked up at Nathan. His eyebrows furrowed together, but the rest of his face was stoic. Even though his gun was still pointed at Ubel, his eyes never left me.

"Be ready!" he whispered.

Ready for what? I shook my head, alarmed that I had no idea what he was planning.

"You want this gun? Well, maybe I'll just give it to this guy over here," Nathan said, pointing to the man whose jaw I had broken. "If he has the gun, you'll lose your power, won't you? And I know you don't want that. Or maybe I'll just throw it into the crowd and whoever gets it can kill you. Then one of *them* can take your place. They might even make a better leader than you." Ubel threw scathing looks between Nathan and the crowd around him. Nathan paused for a few moments, letting the idea sink in to everyone's minds. "You know what? I think that's what I'll do."

Without warning, Nathan hurled the gun into the thickest part of the crowd. There was a moment of incredulous silence before the madness ensued. People dove over each other and fists slammed into faces, the most ferocious of them all being Ubel's. Nathan's strong arms slid under my legs and around my back, hauling me up to his chest. Before I realised what was happening, he took off running down the corridor using the hysteria as a distraction. A few people gave chase, but soon gave up, succumbing to the lure of power the gun provided.

Slowly the sounds of yelling and screaming faded behind us, and that was when it hit me. I hooked one arm over Nathan's shoulders and pressed my head into his chest while keeping my tunic closed with my other hand. I sobbed, big unattractive shudders of anguish and heartache. I felt dirty, spoiled. It was my fault. I knew what these miscreants were like, and shouldn't have been there in the first place. They betrayed me. They had no courage, no morality. Tristan was right; we owed these monsters nothing. Now I truly understood why Tier Fives were so hated, and I began to hate them, too.

Nathan pressed his chin against my forehead as we headed toward the exit. His powerful chest rose and fell rapidly with the effort of carrying me, but he never slowed, not once. It was only as we came to the corner just before the exit that Nathan finally stopped. He lowered me, and my unsteady feet found the ground. I hiccupped desperate breaths and slid my arm off his shoulder to hold my tunic closed with both hands. I couldn't look at him. I couldn't stand to see the pity I knew was in his eyes.

"Zoe," Nathan said, trying to cup my face again. I pulled away. "Zoe, I'm so sorry this happened, but . . . you have to pull it together now."

His statement, while not made harshly, was more heartless than I was expecting and sobered me from my nightmare. I looked up at him and blinked away the tears. He must have seen the shock and disbelief in my expression, because his face crumbled under my stare. He fixed his eyes on the ground instead.

"They can't know, not the guards, not even Tristan," he continued, only looking at me occasionally. "The only way this will work, the only way nothing gets reported, is if it went smoothly. If you act any differently, if you hint that something happened . . . There'll be an investigation into the theft, Zoe, and they'll be looking at how we all behave to find the culprits. It'll be your brother and my sister who pay the price."

I couldn't believe what he was saying. I had just been attacked, nearly raped, and in the next heartbeat *that* was what he was thinking about? He didn't care about me, not really. I was just another of his stupid mistakes he kept making. When it came down to it, he only cared about himself and his sister. Nathan was no more loyal or caring than the lady-of-pleasure who had betrayed me. He was right, of course. I couldn't act any differently; I couldn't risk going back to Tier Five.

Nathan ran his hands through his hair tersely and stared at one of the stained walls.

"How could I have been so stupid? If I didn't make it back, who would have looked after Teresa?"

And there it was. His admission that I had led his plans astray—plans that never involved me in the first place. Tristan was right about it all. He understood people better than I ever could. He knew Nathan was impulsive to a fault, that his gallantry was usually ill-thought-out and reckless. Tristan also knew that when it came down to it, Nathan's self-interests would come first.

They were very much alike in that regard. The only difference between Tristan and everyone else was he didn't hide it behind some stupid mask of friendship. He didn't lull me into a false sense of security for the sake of gaining allies or asking for a favour in return. He didn't make me care about him either. He told me flat out that he was looking after himself only. He was honest. I began to wonder what Nathan would ask of me in return for his help today.

"You're right," I said weakly. "It *was* a mistake."

A single gunshot resounded from the corridors behind us. Someone had claimed the gun and if it was Ubel, he would be coming after us. I fumbled with the toggle of my tunic, but my hands still shook too much. Seeing my difficulty, Nathan reached forward to help. I slapped his hand away as hard as I could and started toward the exit.

"I can do it myself," I snapped, finally finding my grip and zipping it quickly. "We'd better go before Ubel finds us."

Remembering the insulin I had kept in my pocket and stopped to fish it out. Without looking at him, I took the few steps between us and slapped the bottle squarely into his chest, pulling my hand away just as his reached up to grab it. The insulin fell into his open palm.

"There. Now it's like nothing ever happened."

"Zoe, I . . ."

I had already turned and walked away, leaving Nathan and his sentence behind me. I vowed then that *this* would be the last time I'd cry, the last time I'd care, and the last time I would try to help anyone. Tristan was the only one who was truly looking out for me. He was right about everything, and I should have listened to him in the first place.

Chapter 15

The next morning, the Tierless compound was abuzz with the news of the heist. Many theories circulated as to whom the culprits were. All of them were wrong. Only Nathan, Otto, me, and by the looks of his thunderous expression this morning, Tristan, knew the truth. I didn't care what he thought of me anymore. I was numb to it all.

Shepherded by the professor into one of the previously locked rooms, he ordered us all to strip. I was reluctant to undress after my ordeal, but I had no choice. Of all the things he could have asked me to do today, this was the worst.

We stood semi-naked in our standard black underwear, and the bruises on my arms and the cut on my neck were insanely obvious, as were those on Nathan. People threw a few inquiring glances at my injuries. Otto even asked if I was okay. I dismissed him coldly, telling him that I was doing some extra training with Nathan and we took it too far. I knew he didn't believe me, but when I followed it with a warning glare he slunk quietly away, a scolded expression held fast on his chubby face. My harsh rebuke didn't go unnoticed, and the rest of the cadets also gave me a wide berth.

Two things inevitably struck me as we waited for the professor to stop his fiddling. The first was how much colder it was without my warm tunic. I shivered, my feet aching as I shuffled against the cold cement floor. The second, deciding what on Earth the strange human-sized chambers in front of us were for.

Six pill-shaped, glass sarcophagi with circuits and copper wire crisscrossing over their surface, were morbidly (or perhaps preemptively) laid out like coffins in front of us. Filled with a churning, purple and viscous liquid, each hummed quietly; the rhythm reminiscent of a sluggish heartbeat. Professor Salinski milled between them and periodically tapped on a small control panel located on the top of each, making the goo churn more vigorously.

"Okay, well, hmm," he said, standing and scratching his head. "These are the, em, the stasis chambers. This is what you'll all be travelling in for the majority of your journey. As you know, the ship will be bombarded with radiation and gravitational pressures that would tear all organic material apart," he said calmly, as though he had just told us the weather outside was balmy. He picked up a red plastic box and fiddled with the latch. "Surviving it would only possible if the inertial dampener was powerful enough to protect both the ship, and the life inside. It would require a power source we just don't have on Earth. As it is, em, we've calculated that only the inorganic substances, like the ship itself, will survive.

"This bio-responsive stasis gel will provide you with not only the buffer needed to keep your bodies in one piece, but all the necessary nutrients to sustain you, too. With no way to store the organic food, this will be the sum total of your sustenance. It also means that you must arrive within days of Kepler 452b's orbit, too, as there will be no food stores on board.

"Because the gel must be absorbed through the skin, it's necessary for you to be, em, you know, undressed." The professor's cheeks tinged pink as he gestured toward us. His words made me wrap my arms tighter around my bare midriff and shiver against the memory of last night. "It will also provide you with a sedative so that you'll remain asleep during your journey. *These* pods, however, are only being used for the purposes of training, so they don't have a sedative."

The professor opened the small plastic box and began fixing a white circular sticker from inside to the centre of each of our chests.

"Because you'll spend a long time inactive and in a low gravity environment, too, you'll also be sporting self-adhesive electrodes that will stimulate your muscles while you sleep. They will protect you against too much muscle loss and make your transition from stasis sleep to waking, much easier. Eh, but we won't need those today, either."

"Wait, how are w-we supposed to breathe?" Otto interrupted.

And did you really just say we're going to be electrocuted throughout our journey? I thought with a healthy dose of trepidation.

"Ah, yes, a good question, young man. Along with everything else, eh, the gel will provide you with oxygen, too. And that brings us to the reason we're here today," he said. "What we're about to do goes against every natural instinct your body has. You'll have to fight against the need to survive and train your bodies to relax. This isn't an easy thing to do and so it's necessary to ensure you can all do it before you leave."

The professor tapped a control panel at the back of the room, and the stickers flashed to life in an array of blinking lights. The wall behind the stasis chambers lit up, and eighteen blue silhouettes of our bodies appeared. Each had a heartbeat, blood pressure, breathing rate, temperature, and something called cortisol. Under each body was the name of a corresponding cadet. Otto's elevated stats had turned his avatar red.

"Hm, I think you need to calm down a little, son," the professor said to Otto, flicking his over-the-glasses gaze between Otto and his avatar. "To pass this part of your training," he said, addressing us again, "you'll need to be able to breathe the substance in the pod. From the studies we've done, it's been proven that absorbing the oxygen through the skin alone results in hypoxia, and eventually death. Breathing the gel will feel much like drowning, but you mustn't give in to the sensation. You mustn't give up."

I wondered if his studies had been theoretical or practical.

"Why not just put a breathing tube in there?" Larissa asked, her voice slightly higher than normal.

"Because the pod must be sealed completely to ensure your safety. Even a hairline crack will compromise the integrity of the chamber. So, we can't very well have a tube coming out of it, now can we?" Nothing he said reassured me that the journey through space wouldn't inevitably end in disaster. "Time is short. With less than a week left, you'll each have two attempts to pass this part of your, em, training. You must do your best to not panic, because it will do you no good." *You don't say.* I rolled my eyes. "It should also be noted that, in this phase you're also on equal footing for the first time. Not even the Tierless have been trained in stasis sleep before."

I had a feeling that the cadets who would find it most difficult would be the Tier One and Twos. They weren't used to having to struggle to breathe. To my amazement, however, it was Jax's stats which indicated higher levels of stress. They weren't high enough to turn his avatar red, like Otto's, but the numbers were clearly elevated.

I picked him out from the rows of shivering cadets beside me. His face was paler than I had ever seen, and beads of sweat dotting his brow glistened the harsh lights of the room. I watched him walk toward one of the pods, fear etched on his features, his green-tipped hair shaking from more than just the cold. I remembered he had the same reaction when we were scanned on our first day.

"Zoe Ruthland," the professor called out.
"What?"

I was aware he was talking, but I hadn't actually been listening.

"Join the others please."

I swallowed hard, feeling a tremble start in my knees. Standing beside the other coffins with Jax was Otto, Thelma, Ariel, and Liam. In only his underwear, it was alarming how thin Liam looked. If I hadn't known about his phobias and nervous disposition, I would have sworn it was an illness that had made him so gaunt.

"Now, em, take a moment to acclimatise to the cooler temperatures of the stasis pods," the professor said, gesturing for us all to step inside. "It has to be cold because your metabolism needs to be slowed to prevent cell damage."

The lids of the coffins slid open and I took my place between Jax' and Liam's pod. Liam's thin arms folded around his reedy frame as he eyed the purple liquid under a furrowed, hooded brow. He looked so pathetic, so emaciated, like one of the miserable children in Tier Five.

"Good luck," I said, smiling at him.

His thin lips stretched under his mask in what I could only guess was a smile, and his eyes quickly skimmed over me. No sooner had he acknowledged my speaking to him, than he ignored me once again.

It was a smart thing to do, make friends with the president's son. I was beginning to see how this kind of leverage would help and why Tristan said, *"You gotta make smart choices here, Zoe. And figuring out who's most beneficial to befriend is more important than you realise."* He was right, and I had been so stupid . . . about everything.

I turned my attention to my bath of churning gloop and wondered if I was going to be able to do what was asked of me. *I have no choice,* I reminded myself. *If I don't, I go back to Tier Five, to Ubel.* Some part of me acknowledged that my reasons for success had changed. I no longer wanted to succeed for Jason's sake or Angelo's. A deep shivering sickness washed over me at the thought of Ubel, but it motivated me enough to lift my right leg and submerge it into the sucking, sticky substance.

It was ice-cold and immediately my foot cramped. I ignored the pain and lifted in my other leg. The ache stabbed me from the soles of my feet and ran up both shins. It felt as though my bones had turned to ice and were freezing me from the inside out. I waited for the others. We lowered ourselves into the coffins together; a united act in consolidation of our mutual discomfort. Otto breathed more quickly than the rest of us; I didn't have to look at his avatar to know that. His huffs and puffs rang out in the silent room as the others looked on.

While most of the cadets flicked their eyes between us and the monitors behind, Sam's unrelenting gawping at my chest brought up a mix of repulsion and fear. A shiver ran up my spine as he licked his lips and sneered at me. He was trying to unnerve me, make me freak out and fail. He reminded me of Ubel, and that was enough to bring a tear to my eye. I bit my bottom lip, trying to quell the quiver that had started there.

While I knew most of the onlookers would put it down to the cold and nerves, Nathan was the only one who knew why Sam's leer affected me so much. I could feel Nathan's eyes on me, but when I glanced at him his stare wasn't angry despite my outburst this morning. Pity, sorrow, regret, and a whole host of other emotions I didn't want to see, crossed his face. I didn't want anyone's pity or their charity. I could do this on my own, without anyone's help and without owing anything to anyone.

He had tried to talk to me a few times at breakfast, but each time I pushed him away with some flimsy excuse designed to not be believed. If he wanted to protect himself and pretend like nothing happened, then I was going to pretend *nothing* happened. As far as I was concerned, we never went to Tier Five, I wasn't nearly raped, and I never had any feelings for him. In fact, I was going to disown Tier Five altogether and make it onto the Kepler One. I was never going back.

"Now, em, remove your masks and when you lie back, the stasis chamber will close," the professor touted as he strolled between us. "It won't open again until you're either comfortably breathing, or your oxygen levels reach eighty percent. Allowing them to get that low is, em, more than uncomfortable, but it's necessary to force your bodies to accept the new environment."

Otto's avatar flashed red and blue repeatedly, sounding an alarm.

"Son, please, calm yourself. We haven't even started, yet," the professor said.

"Sorry," Otto replied in barely more than a whisper.

"When you're ready," the professor said, giving us a nod.

I waited, taking deep breaths in and out. So did everyone else. In the quick glances I took, I found that everyone was watching me, waiting for me to go first. *Goddammit.* I looked to Tristan for some reassurance, careful to avoid Nathan and Sam's eyes. I couldn't endure the ignominy of looking at either of them again. Tristan, however, kept his focus on the avatars behind us, oblivious to my needs. As was the way with our friendship to date, I expected no less.

Gripping my mask, I filled my lungs as much as I could before pulling it off. With my chest bursting with the last breath I might take, I held my hand over the edge of the stasis pod and dropped my rebreather onto the floor, there was no turning back now. My heart quickened, and the cold that surrounded me crept up my spine. Before I had a chance to think about it too much, I squeezed my eyelids shut and pushed myself back into the thick gloop.

I felt a shift in the gel as the rhythmic thudding of the stasis chamber quickened. I pushed my hands upwards, pressing them against the clear glass and feeling along the edges for the opening that was there a moment ago. It was gone now, and I was trapped.

My heart galloped as the freezing goo invaded my body, weighing my hair down and filling my nostrils and ears. As though I was returned to the womb again, hostile and cold this time, I curled into the foetal position out of reflex. I had to breathe it in. I had to get it over and done with. If I stayed in here much longer, I would panic.

Letting the air out of my lungs, my chest felt as though it was being slowly crushed by a vice. I waited. For how long? I don't know. The need for oxygen brought a burning ache to the muscles in my legs arms, and that was the only way I could gauge the time. My mind screamed at me to breathe, my lungs threatened to collapse, and my heart pounded inside its crumbling citadel. I opened my mouth and allowed the churning goo to fill it. It tasted like meal bars and plastic. With nothing else left to do, I inhaled.

My lungs spasmed, my body arched, jerked, and twisted, as I fought against the goo. I coughed, inhaled, and coughed again more violently. I was drowning; I was dying; I was suffocating. Ubel flashed in my mind. His sweaty, meaty arm crushing my throat came back to me, and I panicked. My lungs wrenched and filled once more. My heart beat so hard I thought it would burst, but still I fought against it. I slammed my fists against the glass as hard as I could, though the thick liquid didn't allow me the satisfaction of a solid thump.

I'm going to die!

I clenched my teeth and fought harder, bracing my hands against the lid to try and push it open. My body was useless against the goo. My skills in combat lay worthless against its might. How something so simple and mundane could have defeated me was demoralising. I was powerless, just as I'd been with Ubel, and I was going to die because of the professor's ineptitude. Perhaps his testing *had* been solely theoretical and I was the first victim of his practical study.

I accepted my fate with a modicum of relief that my fight with the world, which wanted me dead, would end. I became still and let my arms and legs float in resignation within the goo.

A calmness washed over me as the screams for air, and help, died. It was reminiscent of the lulling darkness the first time I nearly died, only instead of feeling nothing, I felt everything this time. It was then I realised my body wasn't aching for oxygen anymore. My lungs began to push the liquid in and out. I could breathe, and it was the most bizarre sensation I had ever experienced.

Slowly, and with the odd spasm or two, I became accustomed to the strangeness. It took a lot more effort to breathe liquid than air, but my body relaxed and my heart slowed. I hadn't realised, but I had kept my eyes closed the entire time. The truth was, I didn't know if I *should* open them. I suspected the cold gunge might give me a headache, if not worse. Curiosity got the better of me, however.

I was right. Within seconds, my frontal lobe ached as brain-freeze took over, but thankfully that was all. I waited until it passed, which didn't take as long as I thought. Suspended, not floating, in the life-preserving phlegm was surreal. It was as if I was in an alternate reality, looking through a purple haze at a world I once knew; a world that could no longer hurt me.

Outside, Tristan and Nathan-shaped blurs stood watch over my coffin. A scrawny red-headed impression floated in the pod next to mine, seemingly as calm as myself. Liam *had* passed his test, and he did it without his father's help, too. My assumptions of him might have been wrong, like most everything so far.

My head moved slowly through the gelatinous substance as I turned to look at the other pod next to mine. In Jax's pod I could only see half a body, as though he was still sitting up, or perhaps he had already finished. Beyond him, I could just make out Otto's larger frame, thrashing around in the goo. After a time, he, too, became still.

Just as I started to enjoy the quietness, a wave of movement shifted the goo around me. I reached up to touch the lid and my fingers broke the surface, grasping at nothing but air. I tried to sit up, but the liquid was too thick and I couldn't move. A strong hand took mine and pulled me out.

My head, shoulders, and chest emerged into the room again where the air felt colder than ever. I attempted to breathe, but my lungs gurgled and tried to drown me again in a mixture of half-liquid, half-air. I coughed and hacked, pulling myself over the edge of the pod to try and expel the goo.

Two strong arms lifted me from the coffin and rested me on the cold cement floor. I rolled onto my hands and knees, convulsing as I expelled the gunge from my lungs. The air I tried to replace it with was thick, unrefreshing, and made my lungs ache once more. Black dots started to form around the edges of my watery vision as my consciousness started to slip away.

Something covered my mouth and nose. It wasn't until the crushing feeling in my chest began to subside that I realised it was my rebreather. I grabbed the strong hand of whoever was helping me and pressed the mask more tightly into my face. Long, slow breaths saw my senses return.

Shivering from head to toe, the biting coldness marched through my skin and invaded my muscles, coming precariously close to my already frozen bones. Someone threw a blanket over me and I was grateful for the coverage as well as the warmth. I clung to my helper's hand, even though my breathing had eased, and couldn't let go because of his warmth. Lifting my head off the floor, I leaned into his torso to collect the rest of his heat.

His free arm slipped under my blanket and wrapped around my waist, pulling me closer to him. It sent a different kind of shiver through me and only then I felt the bareness of our two bodies pressing against each other as he held me close. Part of me succumbed to the safety of his embrace, while the other part shuddered against his touch. After wiping the goo from my eyes, I made out the dragon tattoo my head leaned against, and I knew the identity of my helper.

I tensed under his embrace. Nathan had witnessed the most humiliating and terrifying moment of my life, and had been all business about it afterward. I didn't want him near me, but the safety of his hug was beguiling. As much as my head ordered me to, I couldn't pull away from him, not until I heard Otto hacking up a lung from the far end of the room. Still shivering, I let go of his hand and lifted my head from his chest.

"I'm fine," I said, keeping my eyes fixed on the blanket I clung to now.

I heard him sigh gently. Nathan's arm stayed securely around my waist longer than it should have. Slowly he let me go, his fingers trailing lazily along my bare back as though he didn't want to.

"Is everyone okay?" I asked. "Did everyone do it?"

"Nearly," he said, helping me stand again.

I looked around at the pods. Four others were empty, the evidence of use on the floor beside them. Jax, however, was still sitting in his. The ground around him was dry, as was his green spikey hair. His avatar flashed red as he breathed too rapidly. The professor tried coaxing him out of the goo, but each time Jax slapped away his hand and glared at him.

"You can try another day," the professor said.

"No, no, I have to do it. If I don't, I'll never get to the other side. I have to get to the other side. I have to get to the dark mountains," Jax repeated over and over, tears brimming on the edges of his brown eyes.

He made no sense, and no one hid their concern. Not even Otto's gentle persuading could snap Jax out of whatever fear-induced trance kept him glued to the pod. It was only when I noticed Jax's lips turning blue that I realised his fear might have frozen him in place, but high levels of carbon dioxide had caused his confusion.

Out of instinct more than reason, I pushed past Nathan, my arms wrapping the blanket around my body more tightly. Picking up Jax's mask from the floor, I slipped behind him and pushed it onto his face. He fought back instantly and shoved me so hard in my stomach that I went careening into the screens behind me. The wind knocked from my lungs, and my blanket discarded, I gasped for air again. Before I could sit upright, both Tristan and Nathan were by my side.

"Are you okay?" they asked in unison, each giving the other a scathing look.

"I'm fine, you dolts. Hold him down for me."

Tristan immediately went to Jax and hooked him under his arm, wrapping his hand behind his shoulder to immobilise one side of him. Nathan helped me to my feet first, then joined Tristan.

"Let me go. Let me go," Jax roared, fighting wildly against them both.

I picked up Jax's mask again and stood behind him, far enough away this time that he couldn't hit me. His spikey hair flailed around as he tried to escape the iron grip of the two Tierless. I reached around his head, and after a moment or two of trying to place the mask over his face, I finally succeeded, but not without a vigorous protest from Jax.

"Hold him steady," I yelled.

To my surprise, Tristan and Nathan followed my orders without question. They widened their stance and squeezed Jax between them like a vice. Jax screamed, but was forced to breathe heavily into the mask. After a while, his lips lost their blue tinge, and his eyes began to focus on the people around him.

Everyone was staring. The professor was left scratching his head while the other cadets either held their hands over their rebreathers or across their hearts with relief.

"What . . . what happened?" Jax croaked.

"It seems fear got the better of you," the professor said. "Never mind, maybe next time?"

Jax looked at the two holding him, then back at me. I'd let go of his mask now that he had regained most of his senses wasn't in danger of knocking it off again. Along with his senses came a sadness in his eyes that I recognised from Tier Five; defeat.

"Let me up," he said in a quiet, but deep voice.

Tristan and Nathan looked to me.

"Let him up," I said quietly.

Jax shrugged them off and clambered awkwardly out of his pod.

"There won't *be* a next time," he told the professor. "I can't do it."

"Jax, don't be silly," Larissa said, taking a few steps closer to him. "All you need to do is clear your head and everything will be fine. It's just the shock."

"It's not the shock," he said harshly, balling his fists. "I can't do it. I can't. I'm claustrophobic. I know what failing means, but I just can't do it, okay? Just leave me alone, all of you."

Jax tried to hide the tears welling in his eyes as he pushed past the professor and the other cadets. I didn't see him leave the room through their bodies, but the loud bang of a door as it slammed shut told me he had.

A thick silence of disbelief filled the room. Giving up wasn't an option for me; it was do or die trying. I suspected it was same for most people. I liked Jax, and I didn't want to see him fail, but to walk out like that, to give up, was selfish, unthinkable, and cowardly as far as I was concerned. I'd expelled enough energy trying to help people like him. I was done.

"I'll go after him," Thelma said, concern clearly written across her face.

"Wait, no, you still have to do your test," the professor urged. "You only get two chances."

Thelma furrowed her brow, her eyes flitting between the pods and the door that Jax had just exited.

"We can't just let him leave," she said, looking around at us all.

Silence followed her plea. It seemed I wasn't the only one irked that he had thrown in the towel so easily. General Stonewall's words came flooding back to me. *"Your body will do as your mind tells it. And if it tells you to let go, y'all will end up like Chuck, with two broken legs and a one way ticket back to hell."* He was right! Jax hadn't even tried, he had just quit.

"I'll go," Otto said, wrapping a blanket around himself before heading out the door.

"Right. Okay, so I suppose we should carry on then," the professor stumbled, scratching his head again. "Em, let's have Tristan, Nathan, Thelma, Emily, Larissa, and Sam next."

The rough fabric of my blanket rubbed against my shoulders as someone draped it over me again.

"Thought you would have gone after him," Nathan said, tucking the blanket under my chin.

"If he wants to quit, who am I to stop him?" I replied, snatching the blanket from him and stomping off to join the other spectators in the room. I couldn't have Nathan so close . . . I just couldn't cope. Everything was still to raw, and the mortar on my walls was still drying.

"Wait," Nathan whispered, holding my arm through the blanket to stop me. "You can't mean that."

He was trying to keep the conversation just between us, but in a room full of enquiring and frightened people, he was failing miserably.

"Why wouldn't I?" I demanded. "Why should I care if he fails?"

"Zoe," Nathan whispered even lower, closing the distance until he was leaning into my ear. "You're just upset over what happened in Tier Five."

I shoved him as hard as I could in the centre of his chest. Winded and unsteadied, Nathan stumbled backward a few paces. I glared at him with as much rage as I could muster, but it wasn't nearly as much as I'd liked.

This was his reason for helping me, was it? He wasn't going to ask me for anything in return, he was just going to hold it over my head? Control me and my actions. Was I to become the latest recruit in his army of yes men in return for his silence? Was that how he got so many Tierless to help him?

"You, shut up," I yelled. "Just shut up."

Nathan's expression held a picture of confusion and hurt. I might have believed it was genuine had I not been educated in the manipulative reality of Bunker Twelve—ironically by him. I spun on my heels and swung the door open, letting it slam satisfactorily against the wall before leaving.

"Leave her be, Nathan," Tristan said.

"Commander McCall, if you leave the room we can't wait for you," professor Salinski's nasal voice warned as it followed me down the hall.

"Zoe, wait," Nathan called after me.

"Go back or you'll miss your turn," I shouted.

"I don't care," he said, his voice coming closer.

I ignored him and quickened my pace, but the sound of his feet slapping on the concrete floor kept tempo with mine. I didn't want to talk to him. Whatever about not helping people, it was far more naïve of me to think I could stop us becoming either enemies or lovers. The way I was feeling now, it would most likely be enemies. I was so angry that if I stopped, I wasn't sure I'd be able to control myself . . . but I was running out of corridor.

Slightly ajar, I could see through the barracks door at the end of the hall. Jax gently sobbed into Otto's shoulder as they sat on a bed. I didn't want to join them; I didn't want to have to utter the platitudes I knew they'd be expecting. I just didn't care enough.

"Zoe, will you *stop* and just talk to me," Nathan said, his exasperation clear.

"What if I don't want to talk to you?" I demanded, stopping dead and whirling around to him.

"Don't I get a say in who I talk to, or doesn't that matter to you?"

"What the hell, Zoe?" he said, halting a foot away from me and boring his hazel eyes into my furious gaze like he could see through me. "What the hell did I do? What happened to you was awful, true, but I wasn't the one who . . ."

Nathan caught himself before he finished the sentence. Even without the last few words I knew what he meant to say. He wasn't the one who tried to rape me. This close to him, and only a thin blanket covering my shivering body, the desperation and fear induced by Ubel's touch revisited me once more. I felt the sting of tears burn at the edges of my eyes and a shake start in my hands, then I recalled the way Nathan had dismissed my ordeal afterward and it all turned into a fiery ball of fury that threatened to burn my insides.

"I'm sorry," he said more quietly than I had ever heard him speak before.

"Don't," I snapped, wiping the tear away tersely. "Don't pretend you're sorry, because I know you're not."

In the darkness of the corridor I watched as Nathan's brow slowly drew together. His mouth opened just a touch, but no sound came out. In a movement so small that I almost missed it, he shook his head from side to side in disbelief. His fists slowly clenched, and the muscles along his arms and chest went taunt.

"How can you say that, after everything I risked for you?" he whispered.

"What did you risk? Really?" I laughed, almost hysterically before sobering. "You're Commander

Nathan McCall. If we got caught, your little Tierless friends would deny you were ever there. They'd have to, otherwise the general would know they were complicit, as opposed to just inept—which is more forgivable. I was the only one *really* risking anything. It would be your word against mine if I said otherwise, and who the hell would believe a Tier Five scum like me anyway?"

Nathan's nostrils flared and his jaw clenched repeatedly until he opened his mouth to object, but I didn't give him the chance. I kept talking.

"Your sister was in no real danger, was she? You have enough power and influence in this hellhole to weasel your way out of anything. But that led me to ask the most important question. Why the hell *would* you help me? What could you possibly gain from it? And then it came to me, just then when we were in the stasis training room. You wanted leverage, a puppet string of your own to hold. I wonder, am I your only marionette, or are there others?"

"Zoe, that's not why I helped you," Nathan said, taking a step closer.

Infuriated beyond reason, I opened my hand and slapped him across his face as hard as I could. His head turned away with the force of my blow. My palm stung satisfactorily.

He didn't retaliate, he didn't rub his jaw, and he didn't look at me. Nathan kept his face turned away, but I could see his rage building.

"Don't pretend like you actually care, Nathan, because I know you don't," I yelled. "If you really cared about me, you would have shown me some semblance of compassion after . . . after . . ." I wasn't able to finish the sentence. "Most normal people would ask if I was okay before thinking of themselves. You never did. You only cared about not getting caught. You don't care about me. No one does."

I couldn't hold in the small hiccup of a sob at the end. It was quiet and barely audible against the echoes of my raised voice, but it was there and Nathan heard it. His eyes found mine and he stood frozen in his place, like he'd been unmasked and didn't know what to do about it.

"Goddammit," he shouted, turning away from me and punching the wall behind him.

I wasn't expecting this reaction, and it made me jump. He cradled his hand against his chest, but didn't turn to face me again. His chest heaved incessantly as he breathed through his teeth. He was so angry I was sure he'd hit me next or throttle me.

"I wanted to kill him, Zoe," he said more quietly than I was expecting. "I wanted to tear him limb from limb, or shove my fist all the way down his throat and pull out his black heart. I wanted to burn his hands over the hottest fires of hell for touching you the way he did. I wanted to rip his bloody eyeballs from his head so he could never look at you like that again."

Nathan whirled around to me, locking his eyes on mine and exuding an anger laced in desperation. His nostrils flared, his jaw muscles clenched repeatedly, and his scowl darkened. Every visible muscle in his torso strained with the effort of containing himself, and I truly knew how powerful he was then. He could snap my neck effortlessly if he wanted to, and that scared me.

He didn't speak again until his breathing calmed.

"You don't know how much I wanted to do those things, but I couldn't." He closed the distance between us until there was only a few inches left. "There was more of them than there was of me. Even if I had tried to shoot my way out, they would have overwhelmed us at some point. I had to bait them away with the gun so I could get you out of there."

Nathan raised his bruised hand toward me, only pausing momentarily when I flinched, and pushed some of the gooey hair from my face. His touch sent tickles cascading through my skin and my knees became unsteady. When I didn't pull away he took another step closer, and my hands emerged from the blanket to rest on his bare chest. I wanted to push him away, but his fingers trailing down my neck sparked a fire inside that I so desperately needed . . . and not just for the heat.

Beneath his powerful torso, his heart thumped rapidly against my trembling hands.

"I didn't know what to say after it happened," he whispered. "And I'm sorry for that. It's something I'll regret for the rest of my life, but I didn't know what to do. I worried that if I said what I was really thinking . . . you'd know."

"Know what?" I asked, unable to hide the tremble in my voice.

Nathan paused for a moment, his hand resting on the side of my neck. His eyes searched mine as he swallowed slowly. His other hand reached inside my blanket, slid around my waist, and rested on the small of my back. He pulled me close until our two bodies pressed against each other. Leaning his head toward mine, our masks touched. If it weren't for them, our lips would have brushed together.

"You'd know how much I *really* care," he whispered, before taking a deep breath and removing his mask with the hand that had been on my neck.

I had just enough time to take my own breath before Nathan removed my mask, too, and held them both to the side. He leaned into me and pressed his lips against mine. They were warm, inviting, and electrified the rabble of butterflies in the pit of my stomach. He parted my lips with his, and we kissed deeply.

I couldn't help it. Despite my brain telling me that I needed to breathe, I leaned into him and kissed him back. One of my hands followed the line of his neck to cup his face, while the other slid down his muscular abdomen. He groaned at my touch as I moved my hand around behind him and pulled him against me.

The blanket slipped from my shoulders and fell to the floor. His body, strong and taunt, pushed me against the wall behind me and he pinned me against it with his body. I slid my hand down and he groaned against my touch again, setting my innards alight with a renewed fire. I craved him, and not even the desperate need to breathe could pull me away at that moment.

Nathan's hand found my collar bone, then my chest, and undauntedly brushed over my breasts. The terrible memory of Ubel doing the very same thing flashed in my mind. It was too soon for this. I pushed away immediately and tried to put some space between us, but Nathan held me tightly in his arms, confident, unhurried, and unwavering.

"Nathan, I can't," I whispered, gasping for air.

Trapped in his arms, he replaced my mask first, then his. He leaned his forehead against mine and smiled softly as we both panted, refilling our bodies with oxygen.

"I understand," he said finally. "After everything you've been through, I understand, Zoe. We can take it slowly, if you like?"

As much as I loved the sound of my name on his lips, this couldn't continue. I steeled myself against the addictiveness of his encompassing embrace and the lulling sound of his deep voice. I braced myself against the delicious heat of his body and walled up the feelings I never knew I had for him.

"No, you *don't* understand," I said firmly, pushing away and freeing myself from him. "I just don't feel that way about you. You need to go back to the professor and finish your stasis training. And I need to just look after myself."

"Zoe, it's okay," Nathan said, moving to hold me again. I stepped around him, picking up my blanket and backing down the corridor we had come from. His face dropped as did his arms.

"I'm sorry if you got the wrong idea," I said, barely able to keep my voice even. "I didn't mean to, but this can't happen. I won't let it happen."

"You can't deny that you feel something for me. I felt it when you kissed me. And I can't deny it either . . . not anymore." Nathan stared at me, and I could see what he was about to say. "Zoe, I—"

"No, you don't," I interjected before he could make the words real. "You think this is some kind of fairy tale and everyone is going to live happily ever after? All the fairy godmothers died of radiation poisoning, along with our real mothers." My voice caught in my throat with that one, and it took a second to speak again. "When people die here, they're dead. There's no magic dust that will bring them back to life, no prophecy that will ensure the future of the human race, and no fricken Prince Charming to rescue the damsel in distress. The only one who's going to rescue us, *is us*. And your feelings will only get in the way of that. So, just leave me alone."

I turned and hurried down the corridor away from Nathan. He didn't call after me or try to stop me. I heard nothing but the sound of my bare feet smacking the cement. I couldn't let him in. I couldn't have another weakness to exploit. It was bad enough that I had Jason and Angelo depending on me, weighing me down.

Cutting Nathan off was the right thing to do, I knew it was, but my chest ached with regret and my body refused to let go of the physical memory of him, regardless. In five days the final list of cadets for the Kepler One would be announced, and I was going to be on that list come hell or high water. I couldn't face staying on Earth. I couldn't face going back to Tier Five, to Ubel. There was no way Nathan *wouldn't* get on the list, but my chances were slim.

My heart sank into my chest at the thought of Nathan leaving Earth without me. Tears erupted, and I covered my head with the blanket as I wandered aimlessly through the Tierless compound. Soldiers, young and old, stared at me as I stifled my sobs. I couldn't deny my feelings for Nathan. If President Tucker was sending him into space to die or drift for all eternity, I wanted to be on the ship with him. To do that, I couldn't be distracted by him. I couldn't let my feelings get in the way.

Chapter 16

It was Otto who approached me that evening as we readied for bed. Only he, Thelma, and Jax still slept on the floor, waiting to either be kicked out of training or take the bed of a cadet who met that fate instead. It was alarming to see only three where once there had been so many. With less than a week left until launch, I was surprised they hadn't gotten *my* bed. When I first arrived, I was convinced that I'd fail or someone would have murdered me in my sleep. Yet, here I was, and I was going to stay.

"I think Jax n-needs some help with his s-stasis training," Otto whispered as he sidled up beside me on my bed, resting his chin on one raised knee the way worried children did. "He's agreed to stay and try again."

"Has he?" I replied coldly.

Otto furrowed his sandy-blond eyebrows and stared at me in confusion.

"So . . ." he said, trying to lead me to what he thought I was going to suggest.

"So, what?" I replied, kicking my boots off and shoving them under my bed. "If he can overcome his

297

fear, that's great. If he can't, he should just step out of the way for someone who can."

Otto, slack-jawed and taken aback, stared at me as though I were someone else.

"I-I . . ." Otto stammered.

"You, you, what?" I mocked. "You think I should come with you to Afterhours and help him? Why the bloody hell would I do that?" I noted the widening of Otto's eyes. "If you want my help, here it is. Get someone strong to hold him down. He'll either learn to breathe or drown."

My eyes never left Otto's as he slowly leaned away from me, the fear and disdain he had when we first met, returning. His studied me for a long time and I waited. I didn't know what for, but he didn't leave my bedside for longer than I wanted him there.

"You u-u-used me," he said quietly. "You n-n-needed to learn to read. That's all you wanted from us, wasn't it? You don't w-w-want to be my friend at all."

"That's r-r-r-r-right."

I was as cruel as I could get at that very moment, a moment I will never forget or forgive myself for either. I felt horrible and filthy as soon as my mouth shut. My innards repulsed against my whole being, but I couldn't take it back. I hadn't used him, at least I didn't think I had. I cared a great deal about Otto. His innocence and youth reminded me of Jason, and I didn't want to be his friend because of it. I didn't want to be *anyone's* friend.

Otto jumped to his feet and huffed heavily as he scowled at me. He said nothing else. He turned and headed toward Thelma's bed where Jax and a few others had gathered. He whispered loud enough that it was insanely obvious what he was saying. I had become the outsider again and, judging by the other's outraged expressions, I was no longer welcomed among them.

"Ignore them," Tristan said from the bed beside mine. "You're better off."

"Am I?" I whispered, the beginnings of doubt creeping in.

"Listen," he said, pulling the covers from his chest and sitting up to speak to me. "If they got a mind to cling onto each other, hoping they'll survive, they're as dumb as a bag of rocks. You need your arms and legs free to climb outta a lava pit, and your mind, too. What use will they be to anybody if they jump right back into Satan's bath to save the other one? Instead of just one dying, they'll *all* be dead."

I knew he wasn't just talking about Otto and his group; he was talking about the heist and my attempt to help the people of Tier Five. The meaningful look in his dark eyes told me so. It was clear he knew I had broken into the labs and hydroponics bay, but I didn't feel any judgement from him. I smiled weakly and nodded. He returned my smile and lay back in his bed, turning over to sleep and end the conversation.

I ignored the whispers and scathing glances as I undressed, but as I lay down and threw the sheets over me, I couldn't help noticing that Nathan's bed was still empty. I hadn't seen him since I left him in the corridor, and part of me wondered where he might be. A sickening lurch grabbed my stomach and turned my body cold as a terrible thought clawed at my mind. *Had he dropped out of cadet training?* I shook the thought from my mind. He wouldn't do that, he had his sister to think about.

Right on cue, Nathan strolled through the barracks door, his long strides seeing him reach his bed quickly. His jaw clenched and his movements were terse as he shrugged off his tunic. As he did, I caught a glimpse of a new tattoo etched onto his right shoulder blade, and it explained why he was gone so long. It was small and looked raw, but I could make it out clearly; a rucksack, surrounded in barbed wire. Poking out from the opening of the bag was a flower, as delicate and as pretty as I had ever seen. My heart sank. *Is this me?* I thought. *Am I another person he couldn't save?*

The sight of Otto approaching Nathan interrupted my thoughts. The two had never been friendly that I knew of, so it was a curious sight. Otto spoke quietly to him, more quietly than he had spoken to the others. I strained my ears to hear, to no avail. I understood then. He wanted me to hear what he was saying to the group, so I would know that I was no longer welcomed among them, but the conversation he had with Nathan wasn't meant for my ears.

I saw Nathan nod and reach into his pocket. He took out the black card Otto had given him to open the locks of Bunker Twelve. Otto moved his body to block my view, throwing a cautious glance back at me. I pretended to be asleep and saw him push the card back into Nathan's pocket. Gentle murmurs of more imperceptible words floated between the two, and eventually Nathan nodded and Otto smiled. That was the end of their conversation.

Otto returned to the floor and Nathan finished dressing for bed. Even though I knew I shouldn't, I couldn't help but watch Nathan. His head seemed just that little more bowed, his shoulders a little more slumped, and his movements curter than normal as he climbed into bed

Plunged into darkness, I felt more alone than ever, but I was exhausted and sleep came quickly to take me away. After nearly drowning in goo and my time in Tier Five, I was in no condition to argue with it. Regardless of how much my body yearned for the tranquillity of peace, however, my night was anything but.

Nightmares plagued my dreams. They turned the memories of a life I wanted to escape into something else altogether. In my mother's room, smoke churned in thick, dirty clouds, only parting to show me her gaunt face. Almost as an echo, I could hear her coughing again. I couldn't see her, but through the tumbling nimbus she pleaded with me to save her.

Over and over again, her words pulled at my consciousness, bringing me closer to her as I, too, choked on the smog. I didn't want to get close; I didn't want to see her sunken green eyes tear up with disappointment; I didn't want to see that desperation again.

I fought against her pull, trying to edge closer to the door, but I was stuck in the quicksand of her making. Her will, her power, or whatever it was that stopped me from running away was stronger than I was, and it brought me closer to her. My mother began to scream at me, demanding that I save her life. I couldn't, and tears erupted from my eyes. I reached behind me, scrambling for the door beyond the billowing, choking clouds invading my mask.

"No," I yelled. "Leave me alone."

A second presence made itself known then. Ubel sneered outside the door as I fought my mother's grip. His skin mottled and darkened, as though someone had thrown him into a fire and it had charred him. His teeth grew into sharp points, and where there had been only a few, now he had a full set of deadly gnashers. Bones and muscles bubbled beneath his dark skin until his former portly physique was no longer recognisable. Leaning lazily against the frame of my mother's door was a creature with the same want in its emerald-green eyes as Ubel . . . but this was *not* Ubel.

My mother's cries drew my attention back to her. They had turned into the screeches, clicks, and throaty thuds of the creature I imagined when I nearly died.

Slowly at first, like the billowing black smoke around me, her eyes turned dark. She reached out a green hand toward me, grasping at my tunic and catching the edges with elongated fingers. Her mouth opened so wide that her jaw cracked and broke. It drooped downward, like a melting candle, coming to rest on her chest. Her rebreather sagged and expanded with every breath she took, dissolving into a membrane punctuated with a multitude of holes. She screamed that ear-piercing scream, and I covered my ears.

"Stop it," I roared at her. "Stop it."

I lurched forward in my bed, my eyes wild and darting all over the room looking for the creature that had pretended to be my mother. I wanted to call out to her, to make sure she was okay, but then I remembered she wasn't.

Sweat and tears dampened my skin, but it wasn't enough to cool me. I panted hard, balling my blanket in my fists as if it were a life vest. My heart thumped violently as I searched through darkness for something familiar, something to ground me again. The room, swathed in shadow, took a long time to come into focus and return me to reality. If I had made enough noise to wake the other cadets, they didn't show it. I wasn't expecting them to care.

Only one pair of eyes met mine as I struggled to control my breathing, however; Nathan's. He lifted his head off his pillow just enough to look at me and stare, but said nothing. For what felt like a long time, we locked eyes on one another in silence. His face was rigid and remained so until he lay his head back down again. Before today he might have come over to check that I was okay, but not anymore. I had seen to that.

Trying to still the shaking that took over my body, I lay down and wrapped the blanket around me tightly. I knew I wouldn't sleep again, not after such vivid and terrifying images. Were these the side effects the professor had predicted from my reaction to the vitamin shot? Even if it wasn't, given everything I'd been through it was no wonder I was having trouble sleeping.

Hours must have passed before I heard anyone stir, but stir they did. It began quietly at first. The rustle of bed clothes. The accentuated whir of the hovering engines under the cots as someone got out. The gentle whispers of a boy with a stammer. I stayed still, pretending to be unconscious, and through my barely opened eyelids, watched as Otto, Jax, Thelma, and Nathan stole past my bed. They were going back to the stasis chambers, to help Jax.

Part of me wanted to go with them, but the hardened wall I had built around me refused to allow me up. *It'll be worth it in the end,* I convinced myself. *If they get caught, they'll be kicked out. I won't, because I'll be safe in my bed.* They left and I comforted myself with that thought. Beside me, the gentle breaths of Tristan and the quiet snores of the other cadets, my only company.

I closed my eyes, but was careful not to sleep again. I didn't want those terrible images of my mother and Ubel to return. Nightmares were nothing new to me, but I had never experienced ones as real and vivid as these. Despite my best efforts to not think about them, however, that's all I could do as I waited for the others to return.

I waited through the coldest part of the night, until people began to groan and turn over in their cots. When the morning alarm screeched through the concrete corridors of the Tierless compound, the others still hadn't returned. By the time I had dressed, I was starting to get worried. I couldn't help thinking that something had gone terribly wrong with their training, that maybe one of them was injured. Even if that was the case, who could I tell? Who could I trust to not turn them in? No one!

I followed Tristan as we made our way toward The Tin. Lurking along the corridor in pairs of at least two, were some murmuring junior Tierless. Amidst the scuffle of shoes on concrete and the din of normal conversations, I heard a few of them whisper.

"Really?"

" . . . how'd they get in?"

A lump formed in the base of my throat, and I caught my breath as I strained to hear.

". . . 'cos General Stonewall is beyond pissed," one boy whispered to his friend as they passed me. "They'll get kicked out for sure."

"Maybe we'll get to take their place on the Kepler One," the other said.

I stopped in my tracks, the lump in my throat now squarely sitting in my chest.

"Who are you talking about?" I demanded of the second boy. "Tell me!"

His eyes narrowed and he trailed them up and down, scrutinizing me.

"I don't have to tell you anything, Shadow," he said, disgust evident in his tone.

Even now, after I had disavowed my caste, it seemed to make no difference to those around me. How did they know? Was I doomed to be recognised as a Shadow my whole life? The thought enraged me.

My fist swung at the second Tierless faster than his squinting eyes could perceive and my knuckles collided with his jaw. He howled in pain. Grasping his chin in his hands, he collapsed to the floor, sobbing in high-pitched wails.

"Guess this Shadow is a bit more solid than you're used to," I said, clenching my fists. "Tell me who you're talking about or you'll find out first-hand how solid I can be."

"Woah," Tristan said, grabbing my arm to hold me back. "Take it easy, Zoe. They're just kids."

I shot a scathing look at Tristan before turning my glare back at the two soldiers. The first had his arms wrapped around the second's shoulders, but both were fighting back tears. Both were no older than eleven. *How could I not have seen that?* I thought, a swell of self-loathing surging from my stomach. My fists unclenched and I took a step away from the two children.

"I'm sorry," I said quietly.

Tristan let his hand drop, and the two boys stood straight again, albeit at a lean away from me.

"Some of your people were caught breaking into the training rooms last night," the first one said quickly. "I guess that means they'll be sent to Tier Five."

The lump that had accumulated in my chest exploded into a cascade of cold dread, spilling all the way to my toes. I stood transfixed. The two boys took my distraction as the perfect time to scurry away from me. *No, this can't happen.* I could feel the heat drain from my face and my stomach want to lurch.

"Maybe it's for the best," Tristan soothed.

"WHAT?" I shouted. "HOW COULD THIS BE FOR THE BEST?"

I turned on Tristan, my fists clenched again. *How could he say that? Doesn't he know how I feel about Nathan?* But of course he *did* know. I could see it in his eyes, and that was the real reason he said it. Nathan was his competitor, his rival, and my affections were just another trophy to win.

"You got a real shot at making it, Zoe," he tried convincing me. "Nathan, Otto, and the others, have been a distraction to you. You ain't been concentrating on your training in the last while. You could be so much more without them. I . . . I guess what I'm trying to say is . . . I don't want you to stay here. I want you with me, on the Kepler One. I . . . I really like you, Zoe."

There was a hint of genuineness in his eyes, but it was as fleeting as his stare and I didn't trust it. How could I when he had shown me nothing but indifference before? The rapid thud of someone's boots closing in on us didn't allow me to question him further. I looked behind Tristan in the direction of the determined trot and was surprised to see a crop of curly brown hair headed our way.

"Zoe, Tristan," the captain said, his voice low but authoritative. "The general wants to see you both. Now!"

My throat went dry and my hands began to tremble. After one last glance at Tristan, I nodded to the captain. *If they've caught Nathan, he's probably told the general everything about our heist,* I thought. *The general's going to kick me out, but why would he want Tristan, too?*

As I followed the captain and Tristan, my mind swirled with panic-driven reasons, none of which were comforting. In all of my time here, I'd never heard of anyone being summoned by the general before. The last I saw of him, he was in a terrible state in Medbay; lying inside his oxygen tent in the ward reserved for the dying. Had he recovered enough to return to his duties?

The captain led us through a set of Tierless corridors I'd never seen before and stopped outside the only door painted in a bright orange colour. It was the first splash of anything other than black I'd seen in a long time. Stencilled on it in big bold letters was the name General Cormac Stonewall. I wondered if the orange was the general's personal homage to the tier he was born in, Tier Three.

The captain pressed a button to the right of the door and it swished open seamlessly. Through the opening, the first thing that drew my eye was a battered wooden desk. Organised into neat little piles and lined up perfectly with the corners was a small collection of pens, papers, and other items no longer used in Bunker Twelve. Swivelling gently in a dark grey chair behind the desk loomed the general. His square chin rested on tented fingers as he waited for us to enter. An aura of billowing darkness surrounded him, invisible but present, and its electricity tingled my skin. He was furious.

"Come in," he said, his voice low, powerful, but with a quietness to it that revealed his physical weakness.

Tristan gestured for me to go first. I did and was surprised by the sight that unveiled itself just beyond the door. I wasn't expecting to see them there, yet, here they were. Held like prisoners under the unwavering point of two Tierless's rifles, Otto, Thelma, Nathan, and a soggy looking Jax knelt in a line with their hands behind their heads. Aside from Nathan, they all looked terrified and their wide eyes followed me as I entered the room.

"It seems that we got some criminals in our midst," the general said.

The general's usual steely demeanour was no more. A tired, defeated mask hung on his face, along with the pain he was obviously trying to hold back, and it painted a greyness over his skin. He looked so ill that I couldn't mistake the look of death about him. Even his barrel-chest seemed little more than that of a frail old man now.

His illness didn't mean I feared him any less, however. He still had the power to kick us all from the program and back to Tier Five. The thought made my knees shake as I stood to attention in front of his desk.

"We got word that some of y'all were ignoring curfew and breaking into rooms that are off limits," the general said, sighing heavily. I glanced quickly at Tristan, but if he had been the one to squeal on us his expression never showed it. "I didn't wanna believe it. I didn't wanna believe that anyone would be so *stupid* as to throw away their only chance to escape this hellhole. But after the heist, after someone blatantly stole food and medicine from the mouths of the good, hardworking folk around here, how could I not?"

I swallowed deeply, trying to get rid of the dryness, and waited for him to accuse me of being one of those criminals. I was a Tier Five, after all. What other kind of evidence did he need? But his milky eyes didn't rest on me. Instead, they stared with as much disappointment as I had ever seen in anyone, at Nathan. Nathan avoided looking at him by fixing his gaze on a spot on the ground.

"What are we gonna do with them?" the general asked, turning to Tristan and me again. "As the only two in command who ain't broken the rules, I'm leaving this in your hands."

My mouth dropped open and my legs stopped shaking, more out of shock than anything else. Nathan hadn't told on me, nor had Otto. I couldn't understand why. They had both come to hate me again. Surely if they wanted to stay as part of the Kepler One crew, sharing the blame would ensure there were too many cadets to punish. It was the smart thing to do. I would have done it. No, I'd have done it now, not before.

"They should all be kicked out," Tristan said, a smug grin curling the corners of his lips. "There's only one place for criminals in Bunker Twelve, and that's Tier Five."

"No," I interjected, amid Otto's whimpering.

"No?" the general questioned, raising one eyebrow and focusing whatever sight he had left on me. "Why not? That's what woulda happen to any other Tierless soldier. The laws are here to keep us safe, and Nathan, above all, knows that," he said, throwing a scathing look in Nathan's direction. "Why shouldn't they get the same punishment as any other soldier?"

"Because not all of them are soldiers," I blurted out, scrounging for some plausible excuse to save them. "Granted, Nathan is, but the rest of them were just trying their best to find a way through the training. Besides, there's not enough time to train any more cadets. Even if there was, you'd never be able to replace Otto's skill with computers or Jax's navigational expertise."

I purposefully left out Nathan's abilities, mostly due to the fact that I was still mad with him, but also because I didn't want anyone to have the slightest hint that there was anything between us. Not that there *was* anything there, I had seen to that.

"Hmm." The general pressed his steepled fingers against his mask for a moment before answering again. "If I were to make you captain, Zoe, what punishment would you dole out?"

"This is just hypothetical, ain't it?" Tristan asked, a laugh of disbelief in his words.

"I would take Nathan off command," I replied quietly, ignoring the alarmed glances Tristan shot between me and the general. "If he's in the habit of making mistakes based on emotions, then he shouldn't lead."

From under a darkened brow, Nathan shot a hard look at me then. I lifted my chin and kept my gaze on the general.

"What about the rest? Should they get off scot-free?" asked the general.

"No. They should all be flogged," Tristan answered harshly. "And why ain't you asking me?"

"Because I've made my decision. Zoe Ruthland is now the captain of the Kepler One, and you're her first lieutenant," he said, a calm and serious expression holding fast against Tristan's building fury.

The captain approached me at the general's signal, tapping a small console he held in his hand and waving it over my right shoulder. My tunic buzzed and for the first time, I *felt* the nanites as they worked. Slowly, a strip of gold materialised over my shoulder and ran the length of my tunic on one side in the same way the general's did. I shook my head in disbelief and opened my mouth to protest, but Tristan beat me to it.

"What? WHAT?" Tristan raged. "Her? Ain't I done everything you asked of me? Ain't I followed all your rules? I ain't a thief or a liar, but you want *her* instead?"

"Tristan, I . . ."

I was about to say that I didn't like what he was saying, but the wild-eyed glare that screamed *don't test me or I'll tell him* shut down my outrage. I was positive then, that he had been the one to inform the general about the heist. Although I was *almost* sure he didn't mention my name. He most certainly would have mentioned Nathan's, though. That's why they got caught, someone was waiting this time. It was only by looking out for myself that I wasn't there, too.

"You can't do this. The president—"

"The president, what?" the general interrupted. "For my part in training y'all, I was granted the sole right to appoint the captain of this mission. Nothing else; not the first lieutenant, not the tactical officer, nothing. The president decides the rest. And if that's the only say I got in this mess, I intend to pick the right one. I was hoping it was gonna be Nathan. But, as we can see from where he's landed himself, he ain't the one for the job. Neither are you, Tristan."

"You never liked me," Tristan yelled at the general, thumping both fists on the table. "Even though I took your orders without question and was the most loyal solider you got, you always liked Nathan more." A terrible and cold expression masked Tristan's face in what I could only describe as pure maliciousness. "I hate you, old man. I hate you more than you can know, and I'm glad you're dying. I hope you die slowly, painfully, and alone."

"Tristan!" I gasped in horror.

He had said the words with such loathing and sincerity that it couldn't have *not* hurt the general's feelings. The general bowed his head and took a few breaths before continuing.

"You think they should be flogged?" he asked me, ignoring Tristan.

"I . . ." The words in my heart battled furiously with the words in my head. I needed Tristan to stay on my side. He was my first lieutenant now. Tristan glared at me, his arms crossed tersely over his chest. I had to give him something. I had to give him some say in the matter.

"Yes," I replied. "One lash each."

Otto whimpered and the others threw dagger-eyes at me. Those I could take, those I expected to see, but Nathan I couldn't look at. To see those kinds of stares coming from him might break me altogether, so I focused on the general instead.

"No," Tristan said, slamming a hand on the general's desk again. "That ain't enough. Not for Nathan, anyhow. He's Tierless, and a commander, so he should know better. Five lashes for him."

The general waited for my decision. My mouth became arid and my heart sagged in my chest. Tristan had me between a rock and a hard place, and he knew it. Unable to say it out loud, I nodded slowly.

"Five lashes for the commander," the general said in a low voice. "Guards, you can take them to the gym and wait for the captain to oversee the punishment." No, I didn't want to oversee it. It was bad enough having to give the punishment, but to have to enforce it, too? Tears burned behind my eyes. "Tristan, go with them and leave me to talk to Captain Ruthland for a moment."

Reluctantly, and with an indignant snort, Tristan helped the Tierless soldiers haul the others to their feet. He shoved Nathan roughly out the door before following.

I fingered the gold stripe on my tunic absently. It was thin and if you didn't know to look for it, you might have missed it. In the general hub of the Tierless compound, I could go unnoticed, but it was still there.

The door slammed, jolting me out of my daze. Alone with the general, I wanted to plead with him to change the orders, but I knew he couldn't. I was their leader now, as much as I didn't want to be, and he would not undermine my authority.

"It ain't easy," he said quietly. "Heavy is the weight of that command stripe, but your burden is bigger than most, Zoe. Being a leader sometimes means doing what's right, instead of protecting those you care about. Then again, sometimes it means protecting them, too. You, and you alone, have to figure out what's right and I don't envy your position. Only a fool would. I'm sorry I had to put this on you."

"I don't understand. Why did you pick me?" I said weakly. "*Anyone* would be better than me."

"Now, that ain't true," the general said, resting his clasped hands on his chest. "Nathan might have been better, but he leads too much with his heart. He's passionate and temperamental, not good traits for a leader. The rest of the cadets look naturally to you. The captain told me so after you beat the simulator.

"You're a Tier Five, and you've come from the worst of the worst. Many more woulda given up or buckled under the hateful treatment you got. But you didn't, so I know you're a fighter. The others respect you for that, and a leader needs respect."

I winced. The cadets might have looked to me for leadership before, but not after the way I cut them off. The distance I created, however, might not be such a bad thing. It was hard to be fair when I cared about some more than others.

"You didn't want Tristan then. Why not?" I asked. "I mean, he follows your orders without question. He never breaks the rules. He's the perfect soldier."

"Exactly," the general replied with a defeated tone.

As though he had been holding himself up before, the general sagged into his chair and exhaled loudly. His whole demeanour changed. All power, all authority lost to the agony clearly etched on his face. I recognised that agony. It was the same that I saw on my father's face before he died.

"Tristan is the best soldier a leader could ever wish for," he said. "He does exactly as he's told by a figure of authority. I suppose that's kinda my fault. You see, when he came to us, he was older than the other kids. He was lost, abandoned by a family he remembered, and that led him to start lashing out at everyone. I took him under my wing, paired him with Nathan for company, but I guess I aint great at being a father.

"In case you hadn't noticed, I aint exactly the warm and cuddly type," he said, a small smile stretching his lips. "I put everything I had into him, but I only ended up turning him into a robot. Unlike you, he ain't capable of deciding when to break the rules. He ain't capable of deciding differently for himself. Heck, if that boy had an idea of his own it would die of loneliness."

The general was trying to make light of the situation, but I could see the guilt in his expression.

"I thought I was doing good," he continued, his head bowed. "I thought I was creating the perfect leader for a mission like this. But two years ago, I came to understand my mistake."

"What happened?" I asked after the general paused for too long.

"Tristan and Nathan were on patrol," he began quietly. "They were checking the hydroponic bay. When they got there, they found a young Tier One girl inside. Tristan told me he thought she was stealing food, and that's why he shot her. He said it was a mistake, that he just reacted outta instinct."

"But it *was* an accident, right?" I asked.

The general paused again before looking me in the eye as best he could.

"Nathan knew her. He knew that the girl sometimes wandered from her parent's quarters to sniff the flowers. But Tristan didn't know that about her. He don't know much about anyone around here, not unless they're of some kinda benefit to him.

"Nathan said he yelled at Tristan not to shoot. He said that Tristan heard him, but shot the girl anyway. Ain't no one supposed to be in hydroponics at night, you see? It's breaking the rules, and rule-breakers get shot. Tristan followed his training, without thinking or caring. I can't trust him, and neither should you."

I was beyond shocked by his warning. Now I knew what had happened to make Nathan hate Tristan so much.

"If you don't trust him, why make him first lieutenant? Why let him go at all?"

"Because, at some point, every leader needs a loyal soldier who will just follow orders," he replied. "I hope you never have to use him, but if you do, he will do whatever the highest authority there orders him to do . . . and that's you, Zoe. I'm sorry for landing such a burden on your shoulders, but you're the only one I believe can bear it and do it right."

"But I'm no leader," I protested. "They hate me."

"That might have been true in the beginning," the general said, leaning forward in his chair and resting his elbows on the table. "But they've come to see you the way I do. Whatever you think they hold against you, they'll get over it pretty quick. Even if they're pissed at you for breaking the rules and going back into that infernal hellhole you came from. I'm sure they're well miffed that they got into trouble and you didn't."

I rocked back on my heels. *He knew. He knew Nathan and I went back to Tier Five.*

"I . . . I don't know what you mean," I stammered.

"Oh, don't piss on my leg and tell me it's raining," the general said, leaning back into his chair with a lethargic flop. "I know what you idiots did. I might be blind, but I ain't stupid."

My mouth opened to protest, but then closed again. If the general wanted to kick me out, he would have done it earlier. He would have sent Nathan and me back to Tier Five. If he did that, however, then he'd have to appoint Tristan as captain of the Kepler One, and that was the last thing he wanted. How did he find out? Deep inside my gut, a coldness gripped my stomach.

"Who told you?" I asked quietly.

The general smiled at me, as much as he could in his weakened state. It was then that I noticed his chest heaving harder than before, the effort of sitting up drained the colour from his face. He wasn't going to last long, maybe a week or two. I knew it because I had become an expert in predicting death by cancer.

"*That* is the right question to ask," he said, huffing. "*That* is the reason I'm making you captain. You can feel it, can't you? That cold, sticky sensation of betrayal."

I didn't answer. My jaw clenched and my fingernails dug into the palms of my hands.

"Who do you think told me?" he asked.

"Tristan," I replied, the word sending a cold ripple over my skin.

The general nodded slowly. I wanted to cry. I wanted to slam my fists against the table and demand that he change the answer I knew couldn't be changed. The truth became apparent. Tristan's ambition superseded any loyalty he had for me, for his fellow cadets, or for humanity. Nathan wasn't the only one who tried to warn me about him, which lead me to believe that betrayal wasn't something knew for Tristan. His true nature shown to me beyond any shadow of a doubt, dug deeply into my heart. He had betrayed *me,* despite his encouragement and his intentions before.

"What will you do now that you know?" the general asked, narrowing his eyes.

"What can I do?" I said, more calmly than I was expecting. "As you said, the mission needs him. All I can do is be more wary in future."

"And now you see the predicament he put me in," the general said, letting his head flop back into his chair. "He's a dangerous person to trust. I've broken my own rules to keep him from becoming both the commander of our army, and the captain of the Kepler One.

"I ain't got no children of my own. So when I die, the only legacy I leave behind is the success or failure

318

of this mission. I won't live to see the rescue ships return, but you know that already, don't you?" I nodded solemnly. "With you in charge, Zoe, I believe they'll return. I believe that you'll succeed. And maybe if we live, people might remember my part in all of this. Promise me that you'll do everything in your power to save those left behind," he said, gesturing with a nod to beyond his door. "They all need you, Zoe. It's a lonely job, but they need you to do what they can't."

I didn't know what it meant to be a leader. I'd never been led by anyone in Tier Five, so I had no idea what made a good one. Should I be distant and adhere to the laws rigidly, like Tristan suggested? Should I be friendly and let them get close to me, like I had before? No. A leader wouldn't be either. I couldn't allow my judgement to be swayed by hatred, loyalty, or love. I couldn't pardon Nathan and the others. They had to accept their punishment . . . but I couldn't leave them to take it on their own either.

Without answering him, I turned on my heels and left the general's office. Part of me hated him now, too. I hated that he chose me to bear this burden. It was so heavy, and I didn't want it.

"We need you, Zoe," he called after me.

I entered the gym, careful to hide my stripe under my hair. My steps were weighted as though my shoes were made of lead. A small crowd of Tierless soldiers had gathered in the centre of the room, occluding my view of what was beyond them. I pushed past the gathering of black—which was randomly punctuated by cadets in red.

On the other side of the mass, Otto, Nathan, Thelma, and Jax were lined up against the far wall. News of the punishment had travelled fast, and more Tierless soldiers followed me into the gym.

A goliath of a man, more wide than tall, waited beside the four cadets. Wrapped around his chest like an honorary sash was a worn, braided leather whip. His face, too small for his trunk-like neck, carried a gormless smile as he gently stroked his whip. His eyes, slanted and innocent, found mine as I approached.

Tristan stood statuesque in front of the prisoners, his expression judging them and finding them lacking. Despite not wanting to be anywhere near him right now, I chose to stand close to him, albeit at an arm's length away. *He's my first lieutenant,* I told myself over and over. *I need him to not hate me, too.*

One by one, my friends were shoved forward and ordered to remove their tunics by the goliath. Otto was the last to comply, his face rubicund from the embarrassment at having to bare his ample frame to the world, but no one mocked him. There were no sniggers echoing in the large hall, no derisive whispers fluttering about the air. In fact, the gym was more silent than I had ever heard it before. Save for the scuffle of boots as more Tierless soldiers made their way in, all that reached my ears was Otto's whimpers.

The goliath commanded them to kneel, their hands clasped together on top of their heads. No doubt, his way of keeping their arms out of the way so he could get a clean strike at their backs. He unfurled the whip from around his chest and let it slide fondly through his fingers until it dropped lazily onto the ground. With a wide sweep of his arm, its snake-like form danced in the air above his head, then snapped loudly. We all jumped, including Tristan.

At the sound Tristan's face wore an almost imperceptible smile beneath his stoic mask. He was enjoying this. He hated Nathan so much that he would take pleasure in other people's pain just so long as Nathan suffered, too.

"Don't worry," an unfamiliar voice said from the other side of me. "They know this needs to happen."

I turned and was momentarily stymied to see Liam's slight frame standing there. His hooded brow was furrowed more than usual and, judging by his pallor, he wasn't a fan of this kind of punishment. He must have heard the gossiping in the hallways and come to see what was going on. Behind him, nearly every Tierless soldier, too. The collective exuded a dark nimbus which cumulated in the air above me. They hated someone for this, and I felt their disdain as palpable as if it was a living creature, pacing, waiting to find its target.

"I hope so," I whispered back.

"You're their captain," he said, his voice deeper than I expected. "You had no choice."

I caught my breath, realising something too late. "How—"

"How did I know you were made captain before the general announced it?" he said. "You forget who my father is. Nothing happens in this place without him knowing about it or without him having a hand in it somehow." Liam stared meaningfully at me then. "Nothing! Not in the Tierless compound, not even in Tier Five."

I almost laughed. No one had that kind of power. No one could control so many people, especially not in Tier Five. If he could, then he would know about my heist, about Ubel's attack on me. *Maybe the president orchestrated the attack? Was that what Liam meant by not even in Tier Five?* I shook my head in disbelief. If he could do that, I would *not* be standing here. I'd be kneeling next to Nathan, or have died by Ubel's hands. But maybe Nathan was the kink in his plan to have me removed from the running. Maybe he wasn't expecting anyone to save me?

"I don't know how you did it," Liam continued. "But I've never seen him so mad. He didn't want you to make it through cadet training, you know? But you did, and somehow the general got the final say on who was to lead the mission. I don't know what he's holding over my father's head, but it must be pretty damn juicy."

The lengths and interconnections of the marionette strings the president pulled started to become more obvious to me. But there were other people pulling strings now, too, and my head hurt trying to figure it out. I was in shocked disbelief that anyone, let alone the president, could be so conniving or have that much power.

"I have to go to Medbay . . . for when these guys are done," he said, half-turning away from me. "Just watch your back, Zoe Ruthland. I'm afraid the general might have painted a rather large, gold target on it."

I fingered the command stripe wondering if there was a way to take it off, before covering it further with my hair.

"Why are you helping me?" I asked before he left.

He stopped just long enough to say one thing without looking back.

"Because I'm not my father."

With that, he continued toward the gym doors. I didn't know what to make of Liam. This was the first time he'd ever spoken to me, to anyone. Why now? *Because you're the captain, that's why.* He was helping me because he was "not his father." He didn't have any power or influence of his own, and soon he would be catapulted into space without his father's protection. *That* was why he was aligning himself to me. Part of me wanted to call him out on his painfully obvious tactic, but another part of me realised that I needed allies as much as he did.

Tristan cleared his throat, and I turned my attention back to the four. Behind them, the goliath waited impatiently, his whip licking the floor in little swirls and flicks. He gestured to the four with his head and raised his eyebrows a touch. I knew what he wanted; he needed the captain's go ahead to begin the punishment.

My stomach churned and I nodded slowly. Aside from Otto, who squeezed his eyes closed, I was on the receiving end of a room full of harsh stares that imagined many ways to hurt me. None of those stares came from my fellow cadets, however. They couldn't bear to look at me.

With my nod, the Tierless soldiers now knew that I was the captain, the one responsible for hurting their fellow Tierless brother. Though they would never dare to step out of line and actually do anything to me, they could still imagine it, and I felt their hatred crawl all over my skin, making it burn.

The goliath stepped behind Otto and his whip swirled high in the air before coming down with an ear-splitting crack. Otto cried out in pain and dropped onto all fours. A red welt stretched from his shoulder to his hip and contrasted brightly against his pale skin, but at least it wasn't bleeding.

I hated this. I wanted it over and done with as quickly as possible. I nodded and the whip was circled in the air once again. Jax, still soaked in goo, grunted but remained still as it came down across his back. He squeezed his eyes closed tightly and clenched his jaw muscles. I felt my bottom lip begin to tremble, so I pursed them together to hide it.

Thelma, who was bare from the waist up save her bra, breathed rapidly as the goliath ambled behind her. I nodded. The sound splintered the air and she arched her back, grimacing with pain, but made no sound. A few Tierless soldiers whispered words of admiration, and Thelma smiled weakly. Along with Otto and Jax, she stood and gathered her tunic, choosing to hold it in against her chest rather than put it on. The three of them waited for Nathan.

The leviathan flicked his whip a few times and licked his lips as he squared himself behind Nathan. The others he didn't seem to care about so much, finishing their punishment as quickly as possible, but his enthusiasm seemed to become more intense as he eyed Nathan's bare back. He and his beloved whip were going to have some proper fun.

I nodded.

With a quick smirk and a gleam of delight in his eyes, he circled the whip overhead and brought it down hard on Nathan's back.

"One," I breathed softly to myself.

Nathan didn't flinch. His already taut muscles remained locked in place like a rock. The goliath's disappointed expression turned more resolute as he secured his stance and raised the whip once more, this time giving it more height.

"Two."

Nathan grimaced, but remained stoic. I had never prayed before, but I prayed that this would end quickly. I knew it wouldn't, though. I knew this would be the longest moment of my life, probably of Nathan's life, too.

"Three." Tears brimmed at the edges of my eyes.

Nathan grunted and arched his back, the pain now clearly obvious as he breathed heavily and struggled to regain his composure. The goliath waited for him, waited for him to be in the perfect position and draw it out more.

The next lash sounded the loudest of all and made my innards run cold.

Nathan bared his teeth, doubled forward, and muffled a cry of pain. My hand flew over my rebreather, and I took a sharp breath in. The last one had drawn blood, and small rivers of it began to run over his back as he panted hard. He tried to right himself again and failed on his first attempt.

Four, I mouthed, unable to say the actual word.

Nathan raised himself up slowly and took his position again. He breathed rapidly through clenched teeth, a tremble visible in his clasped hands as he raised them slowly above his head. The man behind him began to swing the whip around and around his head to gain momentum. The whip hummed in the air longer than necessary before coming down hard on Nathan's back.

The electric sound ripped through the air and Nathan cried out. He fell to his hands, gasping, exposing the red welts and the two long gashes along his back. His arms shook and he collapsed to his elbows. He groaned and struggled to regain his breath. *Too much, too much,* I cried inside.

"Five," I said aloud, dropping my hand. "That's it, no more."

The goliath bowed his head, but seemed almost disappointed that he couldn't get an extra one in there. Otto, Thelma, and Jax went to Nathan's side to help him up. He shrugged them off tersely taking a few more minutes before he spoke.

"I'm fine," he said through clenched teeth.

It took a long time, but he managed to stand after faltering a couple of times. None of the Tierless rushed to his side to help him, like I wanted to. None of them moved until he stood on his feet again. It was a matter of pride for him, I came to realise, and I didn't want to hurt that, too.

I could see the glisten of tears at the edges of his eyes as he hobbled after Otto, Jax, and Thelma, toward the Medbay. The sea of Tierless soldiers behind me parted way for them. Just as Nathan walked past me, I reached out to touch his arm.

"Nathan, I'm sorry," I whispered.

Nathan pulled his arm away roughly and didn't acknowledge me. I watched him leave, feeling my own tears begin to form. I wanted to give him time to get to Medbay before I rushed past. I didn't want him to see. Regardless of my resolve not to cry, my vision blurred and tears dampened my cheeks.

"Zoe, you did the right thing," Tristan said. "You did what a captain should."

"I DON'T WANT IT," I yelled, wheeling around to him. "I don't want any of it, do you hear? I just wanted to get off this planet. I wanted to run away from responsibility like I've always done, not get *more* of it. And now what? I'm responsible for the whole world? Well, the whole world can look after itself. I don't want to be captain."

I took off at a run, not seeing where I was going, and bumped into a few Tierless soldiers along the way. They took the opportunity to give me a hard shove, retribution for hurting their brother, no doubt. I ignored them and ran to the barracks. It was quiet, and I was glad there was no one there to bother me as I flopped onto my bed and sobbed harder than ever.

"I can't do it," I said, weeping into my pillow. "I just can't do it."

"Yes you can."

Too blinded by tears to see properly, I had missed Larissa sitting on her bed in the corner of the room. I was in no mood for her pleasantries. She was always so nice and always so bloody caring. My mother was dead, and I didn't need Larissa taking her place. I cried into my pillow harder. What I wouldn't give to be back in Tier Five now, back to just looking after myself.

"Go away," I yelled at her.

"I. Will. Not," she replied, equally as determined to stay as I was to have her leave. "If you want me out, get up off your butt and make me."

Some part of me wanted to laugh, but the laughs in my head turned into hysterical cries. I was done, defeated. It was all too much. A weight shifted my mattress as Larissa sat beside me.

"Sit up," she ordered.

There was no niceness about her tone, no overly caring mannerisms.

"What?" I raged, sitting up and facing her. "What do you want from me?"

I saw her take a deep breath before she started speaking.

"You're not alone in this, you know?" she said, using her sleeve to wipe my face. "Believe it or not, there are other people here, too, and we *all* feel the pressure to save the world. If we mess up, then we mess up. And Nathan messed up by getting caught. That's not on you. He knows it and I know it, too. Heck, everybody knows it. It's the number one rule of sneaking around . . . don't get caught. When his pride is done being sore at the world, he'll get over himself and will realise that this wasn't your fault."

She was right in one way. Nathan and the others knew what getting caught would mean. That, I wasn't responsible for, but I knew more now. The general was using me to do his dirty work. I was a pawn and I had allowed myself to be used, allowed people to pull my strings.

The general was right; Tristan shouldn't lead, and I was the only one bold, or stupid enough, to speak my mind throughout the process. But now I was beginning to wonder if that hadn't been taken away, too. Had someone moulded my thoughts and opinions without me realising it? Was I jumping through their hoops like a trained dog, reaching the lofty heights of captaincy only because they allowed it? I just didn't know anymore, and it was that idea which broke me. My mind was the only thing I had left in this world, but it didn't matter anymore.

"They'll never follow my orders now," I said quietly, my head bowed.

"Of course they will," Larissa said, her tone lighter than before. "They know you, they chose you, and eventually they'll forgive you."

"I hope so," I said, wiping my cheeks with my sleeve.

Larissa sidled up beside me and wrapped an arm around my shoulders.

"Nathan really does care about you, you know? I don't think he could hate you forever anyway, no matter what you did to him," she said, a knowing tone in her voice.

I hoped and prayed she was right.

Chapter 17

I stayed huddled in my bed between training sessions. I avoided the others. I didn't speak to them either, not unless it was an order. There were only two days left until take-off, and I couldn't afford to make matters worse.

Jax managed to pass his stasis training and I was genuinely happy for him. Another cadet had failed, which meant there were two places still in jeopardy. Simulation training was the hardest. Nathan, who refused to speak to me, was removed from command and demoted to, ironically, the communications officer. I wasn't sure there was a need for a communications officer. In the grand scheme of things, I didn't actually believe that aliens existed, despite the simulator training, but communication was apparently a big complicated thing to understand.

I came to learn that the Kepler One was equipped with a sophisticated communications array. I was surprised when Captain Stansfield told me that it wasn't for the little green men I imagined. The array consisted of individual satellites that would launch periodically through our journey, to bolster our signal across vast distances. As long as we stayed within a certain range, we would be able to communicate with the president back on Earth and receive messages from home, albeit at a snail's pace as messages would take many months to reach us.

Part of me was delighted that I would be able to keep an eye on Jason, while another part was distraught that the president would still be able to keep an eye on us. *From so far away, could he still pull strings? Could he still manipulate us all into doing what* he *wanted? Of course he could,* I realised. *He had all the leverage back on Earth.*

I turned over in my cot just as Otto came into the room and walked by me as though I didn't exist. As much as I wanted to say something to him, I couldn't bring myself to even look into his eyes. He was just a child, no older than Jason, and I had allowed him to be beaten. I should have protected him better. I should have put a stop to this Afterhours club. I had failed him.

Otto did something peculiar then that forced me to speak to him. He hobbled over to his little corner of the room, gathered his things, and threw them onto a cot that belonged to another cadet.

"What are you doing?" I asked, so quietly that I barely heard it myself.

Otto hovered over the cot, pawing at his belongings absentmindedly. A long, awkward silence became almost solid between us.

"They've eliminated two others," he said, keeping his back to me. "If you'd been in The Tin w-with the rest of us, you'd know that w-we're the final fifteen."

I sat bolt-upright, my mind racing.

"Who? Who was eliminated?" I asked, my heart racing, praying that it wasn't Nathan.

"Matthew and Natasha, two Tier One kids," he said, abandoning his belongings and turning to face me. His eyes were dry, hard, and scrutinizing. "But don't w-worry, you didn't know them. Guess you don't know anyone here, n-not really."

My mouth dropped. Had I been standing I would have rocked back onto my bed. His words cut through the joy I should have felt at making it onto the Kepler One. Even though I didn't known Natasha or Matthew, like he said, he clearly did and was upset at their leaving.

"Otto, I . . ." I stopped.

My mind went blank. What could I say? He was right.

He waited for me to answer, and when it became apparent that there was no retort coming, he huffed and turned away again. Without much care, he gathered his belongings and shoved them into the footlocker of his cot, wincing because of his back.

"Otto, please let me help you," I said, standing and making my way toward him.

"No, I think you've helped enough," he snapped. I flinched against his words.

Otto pulled back the sheets of his bed and grappled with the mattress, trying to turn it over so he could sleep on the cleaner side. Halfway through his task the hovering bed jolted to one side. He arched his back because of the pain and lost his grip. The mattress flopped dangerously toward him. I ran the last few feet and caught hold of it before it sent him careening to the floor.

"I can do it," he said tersely, finding his grip again and taking hold of the mattress.

"I know you can," I replied softly.

I let go and backed away. He threw a questioning glance over his shoulder at me before tackling the mattress and triumphing. Only a little out of breath and stretching his shoulders gingerly, he regarded me through sideways looks and with a little less disdain than before.

"Listen," he said with a sigh, pulling the sheets back over his bed again. "The president is having a celebration tomorrow n-night, to announce us to the rest of Bunker Twelve. It'll be on the monitors on every tier. He's providing everyone with fancy clothes and stuff. I dunno, m-maybe he thinks it'll boost m-moral or something. Anyway, I just wanted to let you know, that's all."

Otto brushed past me, heading toward the door.

"Thank you," I called after him. "For letting me know."

His pace slowed and he cocked his head over his shoulder, but he didn't stop. He didn't answer me either, just gave me a weak smile. Larissa was right; Otto was sore, but he didn't hate me, not really. With only one day left before our flight there wasn't enough time to repair our friendship, but that's not what I wanted anyhow. I just was hoping we could at least be on speaking terms after the celebrations.

Hope was all I had left as I waited for night to come.

My stomach churned wildly as I stood behind the billowing floor to ceiling curtains in the middle of the Central Pavilion. The president's bloated voice and theatrical speech about how we were "the best of the best" seemed comical. The buzz of the unseen crowd believed him, however, and whispers of adulation and wonderment reached my ears. I questioned if I was ever that gullible before.

The president had a way of spinning words until they coalesced to form a gently swaying pendulum that transfixed whoever listened. Perhaps that was how he won his post, by charming his way to the top. Regardless of his hypnosis over the crowd, however, I had never felt so uncomfortable in my life and I knew I wasn't hiding it well . . . or at all really.

The president's "people" surprised me after our last training session with the captain. They dragged me off to a part of Tier One I had never been to. I was on the receiving end of questioning and disgusted glances from passers-by with white tunics and haughty expressions. Metallic automatons mimicked their masters' expressions, as best their rusty faces could, before my kidnappers shepherded me through a pair of large golden doors.

I can't say exactly what happened behind those doors, because most of it happened so fast that I didn't see. Tunics were pulled off. I was thrown into a swivelling chair, and my hair was lifted and curled repeatedly. Powdered stuff exploded in my face in a bloom of scented chalky smog that blinded me. Things were painted, preened, tucked and plucked until I felt stripped naked, but apparently I was a "vision" and looked "fabulous, darling."

I didn't have time to find out if it was true, they whisked me off again before I had a chance to look into a mirror. I felt ridiculous mostly because I was wearing a dress, I had never worn one before. I didn't quite know what to do in it. It squeezed my stomach too much, and the plunging neckline didn't help my awkwardness either. My body had grown muscular with the training and I found it hard to believe that it made me look feminine.

I was only slightly relieved to find that I wasn't the only victim. While the boys were dressed in a military type uniform, black trousers and red tunic with gold trusses, the girls were dressed in similar sleek, red gowns as my own . . . only mine had a gold thread woven throughout the fabric, making it shimmer more than theirs. The perks of captaincy, no doubt. I felt like a prized lady-of-pleasure about to be auctioned up to the highest bidder, and I expected the trained eyes of Tier One citizens would find me to be the fraud I was.

I shifted the dress this way and that, trying to find where it was supposed to rest. My cheeks grew hot, and I huffed in frustration as I failed to find the right place. My spikey disposition wasn't helped by Tristan scrutinizing me, judging me as the crew's representative. By his sour expression, I was guessing he found me too inimical for the position.

"Smile," he said, exaggerating his own smile. "The president wants the world to be confident in us and you look like you're about to throw up."

"I *am* about to throw up," I said, giving up on my dress and resorting to just holding my stomach instead.

"Ladies and gentlemen," the president boomed from beyond the curtain. "While I know you all love to hear about my plans for the colony on our new Earth and about how much *my* training has shaped and moulded the bodies and minds of our cadets," I rolled my eyes. "I think it's now time to meet our saviours. Please, put your hands together and welcome . . . the crew of the Kepler One."

The president clapped his hands twice and the white curtain around us rose toward the ceiling. As music trumpeted our appearance, the curtain's silky folds waved as though a summer breeze had moved it, hiding us, revealing us, toying with viewers on the other side. I held my breath and tried not to pass out as a sea of mostly white tunics met my wide-eyed gaze.

To my surprise they applauded. Broad grins and cheers of adoration sounded throughout the crowd. Ladies pointed at me, at my dress, and whispered behind their hands with smiles on their faces. Had they forgotten that I was a Tier Five? Perhaps they had come to accept me, or perhaps I looked nothing like my former self and they didn't recognise me as the dirty Shadow they had scorned before.

As ordered, I smiled and waved, mimicking the president's own head-tilting, teeth-clenching demeanour. I must have looked ridiculous, but the rest of my crew followed suit so at least I wasn't the only one.

"Thank you, thank you," the president said into the silver microphone he gripped fiercely. "Now if you please, Captain Ruthland, a few words to the people of Earth before your journey tomorrow."

My hand froze mid-wave and my smile sagged as though I were made of slowly melting wax. No one told me I had to make a speech. I felt the heat drain from my body and dark stars dance around the periphery of my vision. Alarmed, I focused on the steel-blue eyes of the president and shook my head, silently pleading with him to forego this part.

"Come, don't be shy," he said, reaching a pudgy hand toward me. "As the captain, I'm sure you have something to say on behalf of your crew!"

From the looks of his reddening face and teeth that were clenched just a little too hard, it wasn't so much a request as a demand. I moved my foot forward. To my surprise I didn't collapse with fear, so I followed it with another step. I could feel the eyes of my crew on me; the eyes of the president and crowd, too. My head spun just enough to make my steps awkward, but not enough to let me pass out. How I wished I could have passed out.

"Captain Ruthland," the president said with a snigger as I reached the mic. "You don't need to keep your hand up."

I hadn't noticed, but I had forgotten to put my hand down. *What an idiot,* I thought as I hid it behind the folds of my dress. The crowd laughed, so did some of my crew behind me, namely Sam. My face burned hotter than ever.

"Sorry," I mumbled into the mic.

"Now tell us, Captain Ruthland." He said my title with a hint of derisiveness. "It being your last night on Earth, is there anything you'd like to say to those you leave behind?"

Like an automaton unable to run away without being told, I leaned closer to the mic. My head scrambled for something intelligent or poignant to say. All I could think about, however, was the sound of my heavy breathing over the mic as the room went silent.

"Em . . . Thanks," I said finally.

If crickets still lived, they would have been the only thing heard. The faces that had once been solidified in hope and awe, drooped in a wave of disbelief. Inside, I kicked myself repeatedly, calling myself every name under the irradiated sun. The burning in my cheeks flushed down my neck.

"Thanks?" the president questioned, grabbing my upper arm and squeezing it tight, maybe so I didn't run away. "I think what you mean to say is that you will, unquestionably, succeed in your mission and before too long, we'll *all* be joining you on Kepler 452b. Right?"

Again I leaned and, like a gormless idiot, breathed into the mic for too long.

"Right," I replied, feeling bile creep up from my stomach.

The president stared at me with such ferocity that I could feel his disdain, even if I couldn't see his eyes beneath his furrowed brow.

"A woman of few words," he said, spinning around to the crowd and knocking me away with his arm. His face, as taciturn as his personality, smiled brightly at the worried crowd. "After all, who needs eloquence to conquer an uninhabited planet? Better that she's a great shot than a great spokesperson. Am I right?"

The crowd, soothed by his reassurance, applauded loudly. I melted back toward my crew, trying to control my stomach as best I could, and bumped into Sam along the way. He caught me by the upper arm and held me there for a moment.

"Nice speech, Shakespeare," he said, pushing me to the side and letting me go again.

I ignored him. Instead, I focused all my attention on staying conscious. I didn't know how long I stood there, breathing deeply and clenching my fists repeatedly to raise my blood pressure, but after a particularly boisterous applause the rest of the crew began to fan out among the crowd.

Amidst the white columns of the Central Pavilion, several tables of food and drink had been laid out for the enjoyment of those who were invited. The president, with obnoxious deep-belly laughs, milled around the sea of people, moving from group to group just as their accolades would became stale.

"Psst," Larissa hissed at me from the steps of the stage. "What are you doing just standing there like an idiot?"

It took a couple more seconds to realise that everyone else had left the stage and I, like the idiot Larissa had so observantly pointed out, had remained rooted to the spot.

"Damn."

I headed toward Larissa as quickly as my heels and dress would allow. If I was red before this, I was positively scarlet as questioning stares followed me off the stage. I even heard someone wonder if I was "all there."

"You moron." Larissa laughed, not meaning to be cruel. "Go get something to drink before you faint. You're almost the same colour as your dress."

I smiled weakly, grateful that at least one of my crew was kind enough to snap me out of my fear-induced trance. Larissa shoved me toward the tables at the back of the room and I followed her advice. I ate the tiny sandwiches, the miniscule pies, and drank the thimbles of wine. I got a few queer looks, too, only realising too late that this was "posh food" and not meant to be eaten like a meal. I wasn't sure it was meant to be eaten at all as countless Tier One dignitaries seemed content to just hold their thimble of wine and not sip from it.

Salvaging any remaining sliver of decorum with a firm grasp, I swallowed my mouthful and patted my chin delicately with a napkin. After straightening my dress, I followed their example by holding the wine I wouldn't drink with two hands close to my chest, just as they did. I felt stupid. More than that, I felt isolated. The rest of the crew had branched off into various groups. They chatted and laughed together, like old friends. I was even envious of the companionship Sam and his cronies seemed to have, but, as captain, it was better that I remained distant . . . wasn't it?

I heard Nathan's voice to my left. He and the rest of my former friends were deep in a jovial discussion, oblivious to my presence three feet away. Nathan held himself stiffly, not because of his company, but undoubtedly because of the pain in his back. I saw him wince on occasion. Despite that, he still smiled when the others joked, crinkling the skin around his hazel eyes.

God, he was handsome. An irresolute side of me tried to will my feet to walk toward him, pat him gently on the shoulder, and then when he turned, kiss him with as much passion and fierceness as I could muster. But the part of me that had suffered the ignominy of recent events laughed hysterically, almost madly.

"Zoe?"

The voice was female, meek, and behind me. Whomever it was, I could have kissed her for pulling me from the mad debate that was tearing my resolve apart. I turned and was met by a mousy-haired Tier One girl. I knew her from somewhere, but where? The only Tier One's I had ever met were the cadets, and she . . .

"Sarah?" I said, my mouth opening a fraction.

"You remember me, I'm so glad."

Sarah beamed, her eyes glistening with a hint of tears. She was crying the last time I saw her, too. After our first body scan, she was told to return to her tier because she couldn't have children. I couldn't imagine what her life must have been like after that. To not only lose her place on the only escape from hell, but to be told that she couldn't have children either. I wondered if she had cried every day since. I would have.

"How are you?" I said, resting a hand on her arm gently.

"Pregnant," she replied with a small gasp of a laugh.

My mind went blank and my jaw dropped, as did my hand.

"What? What do you mean? I thought . . . I thought you couldn't . . . you know?"

Sarah spread her arms wide and shook her head. A tear fell from the corner of her eye and she didn't bother to wipe it away.

"I don't know," she said, her voice trembling. "When I was told I couldn't have children, I kind of gave up and went off the deep end. I'm ashamed to say it now, but I had sex, *a lot*, and with whoever I wanted. I mean, why not, right? I couldn't have children and I'd probably die alone on this rock anyhow. Why not have some fun while I'm at it?"

My mind couldn't comprehend what Sarah was telling me. I looked around for someone to help me process it all, but my eyes were immediately drawn to President Tucker. Taking grandiose bows and wafting off the half-hearted attentions of his audience, the president announced over the din of the crowd that he would be leaving the party to finish some important work.

"Did you tell the president?" I questioned, turning my attention back to Sarah. "They must have made a mistake."

"I told no one," she said quietly, taking a step closer. "You don't understand, Zoe. I'm a Tier One, and we don't get pregnant by accident. I've ruined my chance to marry well. To tell you the truth, I'm not even sure who the father is. If anyone finds out, if they only knew, I'd be moved to Tier Two, and I can't do that to my baby. I have to stay as long as I can in Tier One, to get proper nutrients for it, you know?" Sarah stifled a sob and blinked away tears. "It's too late now anyway. They won't let me travel while I'm pregnant."

I had no idea that the privileged Tier Ones had such restrictions put on them, but it made sense. What would be the point in pairing the most renowned minds of our world with the village idiots? Diluting their perfect gene-pool like that would be seen as lunacy. Pairings must be carefully orchestrated, both for genetic and political reasons, and with Sarah's diagnosis she was probably cut from the running. My heart went out to her.

"How far along are you?" I asked with concern.

"Only a week or two, but I'm not here for your sympathy," she replied, straightening herself again and wiping a tear from her cheek. "I'm here because I need you to succeed. My baby and I need you to succeed. We don't stand a chance in Bunker Twelve. As soon as I start showing they'll move me to Tier Two, maybe even Tier Three. The only chance we have is if we can start again on the new world."

"I'll do my best, but I—"

Sarah interrupted me with a raised hand. Her eyes had dried and a determined look hardened her features. She never struck me as a strong person, but something about her now changed all that. I suspected it had to change, for the sake of her unborn child.

"I'm not here to listen to promises you might not be able to keep," she said, her tone hard and even. "You need to know something. If someone else was the captain I'm not sure I'd be saying anything at all, but I've come to admire you. I've heard lots of stories about you from the men, you see? That's the only positive thing about my dalliances; they tell me things afterward.

"You see, I wasn't just having sex for the fun of it, although it was the *main* part of my rebellion. I had planned to deal in information and find a place for myself that way. But none of that matters now."

Sarah took me by the arm and pulled me away from prying ears.

"You're not being told the truth," she whispered. "None of you are. I don't know what the truth is exactly, but the president is hiding something big, and it has to do with your mission."

I opened my mouth to say something, to protest and demand she reveal the name of her informant so I could interrogate him, but nothing came out. My throat went dry with fear. From what I knew of him, it wasn't farfetched to imagine that the president was hiding things. He was a politician after all, but what was he hiding about the mission and what did it mean for us? *Are we all going to die in space like I first thought?*

A fierce anger started to bubble inside me. I was angry at Sarah for putting these doubts into my head the night before we launched. I was angry at the president for whatever he had done. I was just plain angry, and I wanted answers.

"What's he hiding?" I demanded of Sarah a little too loudly.

"Shh," she hissed, pulling me farther away from the people around us. "I don't know, I told you. But there's someone working for him on your crew. Someone who believes in his agenda, whatever that is. I heard whispers of a spy."

"Liam!" I said, my anger clenching my fists. "It has to be Liam."

"It's not Liam," she said, shaking her head and sighing impatiently.

"Of course it's Liam. He's his son. How could I have been so stupid?" I said, running my hand through my hair and dishevelling a few curls.

"Oh my God, you really *are* stupid," Sarah replied, grabbing me by the shoulders so my vision focused on her instead of the president's ample frame leaving the Central Pavilion in a whirl of waves and bows. "It's not Liam, because Liam is dying."

That caught my attention.

"What? Liam's not dying. He just has a few problems, you know, in the head."

Sarah released me and crossed her arms over her chest. She pursed her lips together and raised an eyebrow.

"Liam *is* dying," she said flatly. "He's undergoing a treatment for leukaemia which destroys his immunity. *That's* why he doesn't like touching people. *That's* why he's been missing from training so much. And that's also the reason why he was made a medic, so he can have easy access to meds when he needed them, no questions asked."

Everything she was saying made some kind of bizarre sense. It all fit, but I still couldn't wrap my head around the idea that the president would risk the entirety of the human race by swapping a perfectly healthy girl, for his sick son. If what Sarah was saying was true, then that's exactly what he must have done. He must have fabricated both her scan results and Liam's, too. He must know that Liam might not survive the rigors of space travel in his condition, though. Surely?

"If Liam isn't the spy, who is? And what is this agenda the president has?" I asked, feeling my rage continue to build.

"I don't know," she replied. "All I heard was talk of some kind of underground cult or something. You can't trust him, Zoe. You can't trust anyone in your crew, do you hear? I need you to succeed." Sarah placed a hand on her belly and leaned closer to emphasise her point. "*We* need you to succeed and come back for us."

"You and everyone else," I said, spinning on my heels and heading for the door the president had disappeared behind.

"Zoe, wait," she called after me.

I already knew what she was going to say. She was going to beg for my silence, but *this,* I couldn't be silent about, not anymore. I ignored her and kept walking. Nathan and the others threw me a few inquisitive looks as I stormed past them. I didn't stop for them either. I was tired of people's manipulation and nothing was going to stand between me and the truth. Not even Tristan's outreached hand as I approached the small white door. He said something about not being allowed in there, but I ignored him, too.

I dodged his grip and pushed open the door, making it slam loudly against the wall. Tristan called after me as I stormed down a narrow passageway toward a sole white door at the end. He wouldn't follow; I knew that because he would never risk breaking the rules. I stopped outside the door, panting heavily.

The murmurs of the president's voice mixed with the nasally tones of the professor were muffled, and I couldn't make out what they were saying. I tried the handle, but the door was locked. With as much force as I could muster, I rapped loudly on the panelling. The voices behind it became quiet and I heard the sound of another door opening and closing. It was closely followed by the distinct clink of a lock turning.

"Yes?" the president said after a few moments.

I stormed inside and was surprised to see him standing there alone. The room appeared to be another office of some kind, although I knew it wasn't his. In countless cubby holes, yellowing papers and dusty books took residence. Accompanying them in the centre of the room was a careworn desk that looked as though it had been made before the war. A green leather top, crinkled and peeling, was burdened by more books. This all rested on four cracked wooden legs, each of which looked ready to give out. It was a thing of old eloquence, and it was far too drab for the president's eccentric tastes.

"Where's the professor?" I asked, boldly circling the room like a predator that had finally cornered its prey.

"I think, on the eve of your departure, you can imagine that he has a great many things to do," the president answered, seating himself on the corner of the desk which groaned alarmingly. "But I believe you have far more pressing things on your mind than the whereabouts of a dithering scientist. What's the meaning of this trespass, Captain Ruthland?"

I laughed a little hysterically as a madness took over me. Perhaps it was the pressure that had finally made me crack, but crack I did. I could feel the wildness of my eyes on the president, and I could see the fear in him as he did his best to keep his back to the wall while I circled.

"What's this about?" I repeated. "Shall I tell you what this is about? I mean, do you *really* want to know or are you going to just pay lip service to it like you do everything else?"

"Captain Ruthland, you're not yourself," he cooed, trying to smile through jowls that wobbled with angst. "I wouldn't want to have to reconsider your appointment as captain."

His threat was hollow, not because he didn't mean it, but rather because I didn't care. I laughed unrestrainedly and the president's hooded brow lifted. His tiny blue eyes shifted from side to side as the weapon he thought would disarm me with, clattered to the ground.

"There you go again," I shouted at him, my hysteria giving way to fury in an instant. "Taking credit for other people's work. Hmm? Well, I don't want to be captain, so go ahead and take it."

I stopped pacing and crossed my arms tersely over my chest. The president spluttered and stammered, but nothing of any consequence came out of his mouth.

"You can't, can you?" I said, seething from every pore. "Because you weren't the one to appoint me, the general was. You're a blowhard, a big bag of hot air. That's all you are, aren't you? You're a figurehead with no more power in this world than the professor. You're a phoney."

The president shot to his feet, fuming.

"How *dare* you, you impudent little child." The president shook with rage. "You've no idea what I'm capable of. I'm a very powerful man, Ms. Ruthland, and you would do well to steer clear of me and this conversation."

It was Ms. Ruthland now. No longer did I deserve the title of captain, even if he hadn't given it to me.

"I believe you," I said so flatly that the hairs raised on the back of my own neck. "Because I know what you did."

"Do you?" he said, eyeing me with a cool squinting stare. "And what, exactly, have I done?"

"You altered the results of Sarah's scan so that Liam could take her place," I said. "You told her she couldn't have children. But that was a lie, wasn't it? You also altered the results of your son's scans, didn't you? You made him appear healthy even

348

though he's not. You've lied, manipulated, and have probably done far worse to get him onto the ship, haven't you?

"But the general saw right through you." I cringed slightly with the unintended pun. "He knew what you were like. Hell, he probably knows the real reason you got promoted to Tier One. He messed up your plans to get rid of me, didn't he? Tell me, not that I care much but out of curiosity more than anything, why don't you want me here? Wasn't a Tier Five good enough for the mighty president?"

The president leaned back on the table, and it groaned with a louder protest this time. His lips curled into a half-smile, and he crossed his pudgy arms over his chest as best he could.

"Zoe, I didn't want you for the very same reason that the general *did* want you," he said softly. "You're unpredictable."

I huffed.

"We're all unpredictable. That's what makes us human," I said.

"Yes. But you're unpredictable in a different way, and that puts our mission in jeopardy," he continued. "If I were to tell you the truth about this world and how we came to live beneath the ground, you wouldn't sleep well ever again. People, unpredictable people left in charge of weapons that should never have been created, were responsible for our demise. Yes, the world was in crisis after the meteorites fell, but there was hope. Unable to see the bigger picture, these unpredictable leaders unleashed death as easily as they breathed. And when they were done, all that was once beautiful and right with the world, died with them.

"We're the only ones left, Zoe. And I couldn't trust that you would do what was required. I couldn't trust that you would follow the lead of someone who's wiser, and older than you," he said, pointing to himself. "It's true, I wanted Tristan to become captain. He, at least, can follow an order without questioning it every two minutes. But I never tried to have you thrown out of training. Regardless of my thoughts on your leadership skills, you're a valued member of this team. We need you, Zoe."

"Stop blowing smoke up my ass," I said. "It'll get you nowhere."

"My apologies if it sounded like that, but it's the truth whether you choose to believe it or not," he continued. "Our world was plunged into a nuclear winter because of greed and paranoia. And now our children will never breathe freely again. We will never feel the warmth of sunshine on their skin. That's no kind of life to live.

"I've worked hard to make sure no one ever has that kind of power again. The general disagreed with my tactics. Perhaps I held the reins too tightly, but my intentions are good . . . I promise you." I wasn't sure I believed him. "I didn't alter the scans for that Tier One girl. If there were mistakes then it must have been a glitch in the machine or something. It happens from time to time because of the radiation. But you're right, I am guilty of something."

The president stood and took a few steps toward me, his eyes fixed on the concrete floor. As a matter of instinct I clenched my fists, ready for whatever he threw at me.

"I did alter my son's results," he said quietly, meeting my gaze. "My poor Liam *is* sick. And so what if I manipulated people to get my son on board? He's my *son.* He's all I have left in this wretched world and before he dies, I wanted him to be free, to feel the warmth of sunlight on his skin and to breathe untainted air. Wouldn't you have done the same for your mother?"

I couldn't believe he had admitted it. My fists clenched so hard that my fingernails dug into my palms.

"I would have done a lot of things, but not at the cost of everyone else. You think you're any better than those who dropped the bombs?" I said. "You manipulate people to get what you want. You're the epitome of everything you say you're against. I bet the general knew more than what you're telling me, too. That's why you let him choose the captain, why you had no choice but to leave me in charge. It was either that, or you'd be shipped off to Tier Five for whatever crime you committed, wasn't it? How am I supposed to trust a leader like that?"

"No one said you had to trust me," he said, his voice becoming low and menacing. "God knows your parents never did."

My heart stopped for what seemed like three whole seconds. Something that felt like panic, or fear, rose inside my chest, the electricity of it restarting my heart again.

"What do *you* know about my parents?"

Some part of me prickled with fear, like he knew secrets that they had hidden from *me*, their daughter. The prickling sensation soon turned hot. *My parents had nothing to hide.* But they must have known him a little, well enough to not trust him.

"Oh, I know a great deal about your parents," he replied, a bulging smile slowly crossing his face. "In fact, I know all about your family. You say you'd never do the things I did, you'd never risk the lives of other, more deserved people? But you're a liar, Zoe Ruthland. You did the very same thing for your brother, Jason."

My mouth went dry. I could see where he was going with this.

"I don't know what you mean," I lied.

"Your brother is being treated for the very same cancer as my son, right? He has all the luxuries of a Tier One even though he's not one of them. He's taking up valuable space in Medbay meant for someone who could potentially save us," the president said, edging closer to me and leaning into my ear. "Only he's not your brother, is he?"

I backed away and the wild rage that had fuelled me died in a cascade of cold realisation. *He knows.* I panicked. *He knows and now Jason will be thrown back to Tier Five.*

"Don't worry, my dear," the president cooed. "Unlike you, I understand the complexity that family and friendships can bring. We're not perfect, none of us. But now you have a choice to make, and his fate will rest on your decision. I wonder," the president said with a small laugh. "Will you be as stringently adherent to the same rules you'd like *me* to follow, or will you keep my secrets for the benefit of your brother, and the mission?"

The president's smile irked me beyond anything I'd ever known. How I wished that I'd kept my cool and my mouth shut. But I was impetuous, unpredictable, like he said, and no match for this

Machiavellian Prince. I had taken on the most powerful man in Bunker Twelve, and I had lost. Turned out that the morality and integrity my parents cultivated in me, was as incorruptible as the president's.

Chapter 18

It was the nightmares that woke me first. Strange creatures trying to adorn the faces of dead people I knew, tore at any peace I might have. I wasn't surprised. It happened most nights now. After that, it was my worries for Jason which stopped me from falling back into the nightmares.

The president had me between a rock and a hard place, and he knew it. Whatever naïve idea I had about making moral choices, it had become clear that the only choice I could live with was to protect the ones I loved by doing what the president wanted. It also reaffirmed that I was right to push the others away.

I couldn't afford to give the president any more leverage over me. Especially not now that we had a new understanding of each other. There was no more pretence between us, no more niceties that would excuse the lies. Lies were just lies now, and he could ask me to do anything, threatening my brother if I didn't comply. I suspected it was the main reason he wanted to keep in contact with us on our journey, too.

Nathan warned me about this, about the fact that we all had something that he could use against us. I wondered how many of my sleeping comrades were also under the same duress. I wondered which of them was the supposed spy and if they were voluntarily snooping.

None of that mattered now. We were all going to be strapped inside the same tin can and blasted off into space in the next few hours. Once we broke orbit, *if* we broke orbit at all, we would either sleep for the next year or die. *That* prospect alone needed no allies to keep me awake.

Even though it had been six weeks, it felt like only a few days since training began. I wasn't ready, *we* weren't ready. There was so much we didn't know, so much we couldn't control, yet. I was afraid of what was coming, afraid of failing, but time marched on and refused to answer my call to cease its journey.

Without warning, someone burst through the barracks door.

"Rise and shine," the captain's voice boomed. "Time to liberate you from this world."

I jumped out of bed, an explosion of electricity igniting in my stomach as I realised what the captain's reveille meant . . . it was time to go. But we weren't supposed to be getting up this early and a few people questioned him. He replied with a bark to *just get ourselves ready*. No one needed telling twice, and it wasn't long before the others threw off their blankets.

Dressed, and nervous beyond belief, we were quickly led from the Tierless compound behind the determined pace of Captain Michael Stansfield. It was eerily quiet in the corridors, and at least six Tierless soldiers stood guard by each of the entrances to the other corridors. That was odd in itself because normally the other corridors had minimal security, but today was different and we all knew it.

The plan, according to the president's proclamation last night, was to have one last send-off before a mid-day departure. By the coldness in the air, however, and the emptiness of the Tierless compound, I imagined it was still very early morning. Too early to be getting ready for take-off.

"Where are we going?" I asked the captain.

"To the launch pad," he replied, quickening his pace. "There's been a change in plans. Rumours of an uprising from Tier Five have reached us. We've secured the passages, but we need to secure you in the spacecraft before the alarm is sounded. There's a long line of people who want to stowaway on the Kepler One and they'd use the confusion to their benefit."

The isolated cadence of our boots marching in the quiet halls, separated us from reality even more. I worried about the riot in Tier Five and if it was Ubel and his cohorts deciding that the Kepler One was his, too. More pressing worries rose in my mind, however.

Are we going, really going? Now? Like this? I wasn't sure what I expected, maybe a line of familiar faces, smiling, waving us off. Maybe a chance to visit my brother and say goodbye, but there was no one and nothing. It felt like I was still dreaming, and by the looks on the faces behind me, my crew thought so, too.

We were getting off this fetid rock and blasting into space. Not for one moment did I ever dare to believe it would actually happen. My life of disappointment wouldn't allow me to think about it before now, but the uncomfortable butterflies in my stomach confirmed that it was real.

The captain turned down another corridor and I knew where we were going. Everything was happening so fast. I wasn't ready for it, *we* weren't ready for it. Didn't they know that we were only kids?

"Things have changed above ground, too," the captain continued. "And the president feels it would be better if we launched sooner, rather than later," he said, pushing open the doors to the empty Central Pavilion.

"What things?" Nathan demanded as the captain waved us past the main stage.

I was shocked to discover that the door to the launch pad was open, as was the inner door. Beyond the recess, now guarded heavily by Tierless soldiers, a tram offloaded workers in green overalls and white hats. The workers stared open-mouthed at the Central Pavilion, evidently in awe at seeing something other than the launch pad. Perhaps they never knew Bunker Twelve existed? The captain waited for the last worker to exit before ushering us inside.

"Weather conditions," he replied, wrapping his wrist through the hoop on the ceiling just as the tram took off at speed. "The professor is closely monitoring a storm overhead, and has left me to escort you on board. He isn't sure if it will increase the density of ash in the atmosphere or not. If it does, it might affect the engines make it more difficult to take-off."

"The ash?" I asked, sure I wasn't the only one confused.

"After the meteorites hit Earth and the nuclear bombs b-burned everything, the black carbon it produced b-blocked out the sun," Otto explained. "Without the sun, the Earth's temperature dropped and p-plunged us into permanent winter. Sometimes the amount of carbon is thicker in one area than another, e-especially if there's a storm. There's a chance that the carbon might clog the engines, and if that happens we could end up plummeting back to Earth."

"What the hell?" Sam said in a high pitch.

It appeared that I wasn't the only one not paying attention during *that* lesson.

"Don't be alarmed Mr. Wilkens," the captain soothed. "The professor assures me that it's all perfectly normal."

"Normal for what?" he mumbled.

The tram fell into an uneasy silence after that. Like me they were undoubtedly wondering if this was the last day we'd see Bunker Twelve, see each other. As much as I wanted to hold Otto's hand or hug Larissa tightly, I felt like I had to keep a respectful distance between my crew and myself. But, damn, it was hard not to steal a glance at Nathan.

I did, once or twice, under the guise of looking around the tram one last time as it hurtled through the darkness. In the moment when the electricity sparked below us and illuminated the carriage, Nathan's hazel eyes met mine. I flinched before turning away because of the powerful emotion behind his stare. It wasn't hateful, or even accusing, but rather it was something raw and burning. In that glance, that one scowling onslaught of rawness and honesty, I realised

I had broken him, perhaps beyond repair. *I* had done that to him . . . me.

Nathan's nature was more emotional than mine. He seemed to feel responsibility more deeply, perhaps even felt love more deeply, too. Seeing his suffering tore at my heart, and I could feel my resolve falter, so I focused my gaze in front of me instead.

We emerged into the launch bay and I expected there to be a skirmish of people rushing about to ready things for the last minute departure. The cylindrical room was silent, save for the occasional hissing of water from the pipes circling it. Puffs of smoke rose upwards into the far reaches of the room whose ceiling was occluded by a darkness my eyes couldn't penetrate.

The workers had been evacuated, the drones, too, and all that was left was the Kepler One and us. It hummed rhythmically, its rings sliding more quickly over one another than before. I was expecting one to collide into another at any moment, but it didn't. Precise, dangerous, and beautiful, it waited on reverberating thrusters, its gangway already deployed.

I hadn't noticed the silence so much. It was only when Captain Stansfield cleared his throat that I realised we had all been staring, slack-jawed and wide-eyed, at the Kepler One. I closed my mouth and followed the direction the captain's eyebrows gestured.

In long, swaying steps, aptly done on heels almost as long as my forearm, waltzed the ship's android. As unbelievable as it was, this beautiful, graceful, creature, with the same androgynous features as the computer avatar, made its way across the deserted platform toward us. No longer was he just a head on a

359

block, he was complete and oddly mesmerising as he sauntered toward us.

Figure-hugging trousers gave no indication as to his sex, and if it wasn't for the low-cut top, I would have never know he was male. At least, I was almost sure he was male. Regardless, he was a sight none of us were ready for.

Men dressed as women, or the other way around, was outlawed in Bunker Twelve. Man needed to impregnate woman, and that was the law we all lived and died by. Objections were met with a one way ticket to Tier Five, where such lifestyles were exploited in the worst way. But this creature was no human. Its alabaster skin was far too perfect for that, so the rules apparently didn't apply to it.

"Hello," he said, his voice boyish and airy instead of tinny this time. "May you all find health this day."

None of us quite knew what to say. Part of me wanted to respond, but, like my crew, I remained dumb.

"My apologies," the android said with a small laugh. "I suppose you are used to only seeing parts of me. I am the Ship's Automated Mobile Unit, or SAMU. Although, many have taken to calling me Sam."

"Hey, look at that, Sam." Emily snorted. "You have a sister! And it looks as if she got the good looks in the family while you got beaten with the ugly stick."

"Shut up," Sam snapped, elbowing Emily in the ribs.

A few others sniggered under their breaths, much to Sam's apparent annoyance.

"Although I was modelled in the image of my creator, who was male, I am predominantly designed to evict the usual sense of male or female," the android said, tilting his head elegantly to the side and blinking once. "But I can see where two Sams would be confusing. You may call me Samu instead."

There were many things I wanted to ask Samu about his appearance which piqued my interest, but there were more pressing matters to concern myself with.

"When is the launch window then?" I asked the captain.

"Now," he replied, gesturing for us to make our way to the ship. Samu took the lead and we followed his long elegant strides across the launch bay, his perfectly swaying hips making me feel mannish and inadequate. "You can launch as soon as you're able. The president is remaining in the Tierless compound to quash the uprising and ensure things go back to normal. He won't be here to see you off, but he sends his best wishes."

Samu sauntered over the grated gangway without hesitation. I admired the automaton's ability to not get a spikey heel stuck in the grate, but then again, he was a robot and probably calculated the perfect spot to place his foot every time.

"And the general?" Tristan asked, his voice slightly harder than normal.

"I'm afraid the general won't be able to make it either."

Captain Stansfield didn't offer any explanation for the general's absence, but I knew why. If Tristan was aware of his surrogate father's declining health, he never let on. He snorted a laugh and clenched his jaw, as though he was annoyed at the inconvenience of the general's illness.

"He'll send you a message once you're all safely on your journey, I'm sure," the captain replied, trying to reassure us. It was a futile exercise at this point. Things had gone off plan so much that I accepted the unexpected easily. It wasn't a good start to an already precarious journey, but at least it was a start.

As I entered, I couldn't help but run my hand over the mercury-like hull again. It felt solid as it had before, but with a bit more energy beneath it this time. Were it alive, I expected the buzzing feeling beneath my hand to suddenly bite me.

The captain cleared his throat. I let my hand fall, and regarded him for a moment as the rest of the crew filled in. His expression was pinched as he stood just outside the Kepler One. This was the closest he was ever going to get to freedom, and I admired his strength for not trying to stow away himself.

He would have to return to the horrible, savage world we were leaving. He would be burdened with the death of the general and the vacuum of influence it would leave. Greedy, power-hungry people would try to take his rightful place as the general's successor. For the first time since I met him, I felt the true weight of his responsibilities. It would be his job to hold down the tumultuous fort until our ships came back. I envied his position less than my own.

"May you find health this day and all the days until we return," I said quietly.

The captain nodded, his bottom lip pressing firmly against the top. He struggled to turn away from the Kepler One, one foot not following the other, but eventually he moved. Descending the gangway slowly, he hesitated once more before both feet found the dirty concrete of the launch bay. The gangway retracted, severing any chance he had of escape.

"When the bay doors open, the launch bay will be flooded with radiation," he yelled after me as the silvery curtains began to close, melting into one another like a wound healing of its own accord. "As a result, the radiation in Bunker twelve will increase twofold. So . . . hurry . . . please."

I nodded and the captain disappeared behind a beige wall that bubbled and eventually solidified. I touched the wall where the door had been and was awed to find that my hand couldn't pass through it anymore. A firm and unshakeable resolve to complete my mission steeled itself in my heart then. I would do what everyone needed me to do, follow the rules they wanted me to follow until the mission was over, and then I would be free.

"Okay," I said, turning to Samu and my crew. "Let's get this bucket of bolts moving."

Instead of leading the way, Samu smiled innocently and tapped his nose three times, saying nothing. I stole a glance at Otto, Larissa, and Tristan behind me, but they looked as confused as I did.

The automaton's smile broadened, like a child with a juicy secret he just had to share. He leaned in closer and reached up to my face, taking hold of my mask. My hands wrapped around his wrist as he suddenly pulled my rebreather away.

Tristan and Nathan jumped up beside me and grabbed his arm, too, but to no avail. He was stronger than them both, which should have alarmed me at the time, but I was preoccupied by the fact that I no longer had my rebreather on and was about to die.

They struggled with Samu, urgency evident in their attempts to dislodge my mask from his hand. All the while Samu watched me with a wide grin, unperturbed by their efforts.

Nathan swore at Samu. I waited to feel that hot, sweaty, insufficient air invade and smother me. I waited to crumble under the crushing weight of my chest . . . but nothing happened. I glanced at Samu, a mixture of incredulity and outrage evident on my face as I breathed freely.

Touching both Nathan and Tristan's shoulders gently, they released the droid once they realised I was not in any danger. The android laughed a child-like, innocent laugh, seemingly unaware of the glares Nathan threw at him.

"This ship's atmosphere is far higher in oxygen than the environment outside," he said, clasping his hands behind his back and swaying his shoulders like an excited schoolgirl. "You don't need your masks. Not anymore. Isn't that wonderful?"

Part of me felt incensed because of this creature's audacity, while another part of me saw the innocence in its actions. It didn't know fear, it could never know fear, and it meant no harm. It was only a child, born for the sake of our mission and unused to human interaction.

"Samu," I said firmly. "You can't do that. You have to ask permission before you do anything to us. You scared me."

Samu's mouth opened slightly, then his smile faltered.

"I apologise," he said quietly. "I did not know. I thought it would make you happy."

"That's okay," I replied, taking my mask from his hand and holding it with a tight grip. "You know now. And I'm sure the rest of the crew will be glad to get rid of their masks, too."

I nodded to Tristan first, not daring to look at Nathan again. The excuse that Tristan was my first lieutenant was a convenient one for that. Tristan took a deep breath and removed his mask, holding it only an inch from his face as he let the air out of his lungs. Slowly at first, he breathed.

"It's good," he said to the others.

They, in turn, followed his lead and removed their rebreathers, but daren't drop the masks onto the ground. After a lifetime of wearing them, I wasn't surprised. It was strange to see their faces clearly and some part of me didn't recognise them. Like me, I'm sure they felt naked without their rebreathers.

Like a fool, I glanced at Nathan. It was only for a split second, but it was long enough to ensnare me. I couldn't look away. He was handsome to begin with, but now, unencumbered by a sheath of plastic over his mouth and nose, he was nothing short of arresting. The joy of breathing freely for the first time in my pathetic life was lost, and I was happy to lose them.

I must have stared too long, because it was only when Larissa poked me in the back that I realised Samu had been talking for quite some time. Samu twirled, with precision rather than flare, and sauntered down a corridor muttering something about strapping in for take-off. His words sounded so final, like nothing else was going to happen beyond that. We would launch and then what? Live, die?

My stomach churned, I was terrified but I never let on. *Everything is going to be fine,* I told myself.

We're not going to die on take-off. We're not going to die while in stasis. We're not going to die trying to land, and we're not going to die on a strange planet we know nothing about. There was a lot of dying in those thoughts, and the butterflies in my stomach didn't believe me.

"Engineers should make their way to their station while I escort the others," Samu said, gesturing down a corridor to our left. "Once we are in orbit and are prepared for wormhole travel, I will show you to way to the stasis chamber, Sam, Ariel, Thelma, and Tony."

Sam threw his robotic counterpart a scathing look, but was soon distracted as he followed Ariel to engineering. Her curly brown hair, now down past her lower back, swished back and forth, drawing Sam's eyes to her rear end. I shuddered, not wishing to be in her shoes.

Thelma rolled her eyes and skipped ahead of them, closely followed by Tony, an athletic, softly spoken guy with sallow skin and wary look in his eyes. He was someone I didn't know too well. As captain, I felt bad for not knowing him better and vowed to change that once we landed on the new planet.

Samu led us to the elevator, but before we clambered in, a niggling thought disturbed me.

"Samu, how volatile is this terraforming device?" I asked as the elevator doors closed. "We've learned virtually nothing about it other than how to turn it on."

"I a-asked the professor about that," Otto said. "He wouldn't tell me anything about it either."

"In its current state it is completely inert, Zoe Ruthland," Samu replied. "None of you have anything to worry about. It is completely secured."

"I'd like to check it myself, Samu," I said unapologetically.

It was one thing flying with armed drones and mechanical leviathans in our cargo bay, but I drew the line at mysterious bombs.

"Of course," he replied, smiling sweetly.

The elevator came to a stop and the doors swished open revealing another beige corridor. I recognised it immediately, mostly because of the number fifteen branded on the wall opposite the elevator.

"Auxiliary personnel should exit here and make their way to the cargo hold," Samu said, gesturing out the door with his hand while remaining in the elevator. "Please remember to strap yourselves in securely before take-off."

By the sour look on Simon's face as he moved to leave, he didn't like being lumbered in with the title "auxiliary crew." Everyone knew it meant that there was no specific job for him. Auxiliary were the labourers, the donkeys to carry the loads, or rather the extra genetics needed to widen the gene pool should we be stranded.

I knew two of the others joining Simon only by name. Majella, a year or two younger than I with short blonde hair and dazzling blue eyes, and James, a quiet unassuming boy about Otto's age. Two more I would have to get to know once we landed. I nodded reassuringly at them, but only Majella and James returned my gesture.

Without warning, the elevator took off at rapid speeds. It only seemed like a second before it came to a halt again and it opened its doors.

"Medbay," Samu said. "Please strap into your chair Mr. Tucker."

I heard Liam take a deep breath before exiting the elevator. Before the doors could close behind him, however, I stuck my hand out and stopped them.

"Okay, Liam?" I asked.

I could tell he was nervous about being left alone. If our launch was a disaster, he would be the only one to die alone. Now that I knew he was sick, I felt it was my duty to make sure that didn't happen, like it had happened to my mother. He smiled meekly and nodded, clasping his hands together in front of his chest tightly. I returned his nod and left him to find his way to Medbay.

Samu gave me a curious look as I took my hand off the elevator door. The concept of fearing loneliness must have been foreign for Samu, if he could recognise it at all. A robot can't crave company, can it? I ignored his looks and stood in the centre of the elevator, ready for the next level, a level we had never explored before.

The now familiar feeling of my innards hitting my boots as we rose, struck again. At one point the elevator jerked to the right and I lost my balance, accidentally leaning against Nathan. He caught my arm, his grip strong but gentle as he steadied me, and my eyes found his.

Even though he still carried that pain, his hand was slow to let me go, his fingers trailing along my arm long after I was righted. I smiled weakly, soliciting no response from him. The awkwardness between us was palpable and grew in the silence of the small elevator. It mercifully came to a halt, and I practically ran after Samu as he exited.

This corridor was different. Instead of the usual beige walls, it was swathed in a deep blue. Samu led us passed various rooms, one of which was lined with pulse rifles. I hoped and prayed we would never need to use those, but I was glad they were there regardless.

Samu stopped outside a metal door with a small circular panel at its centre. There were no buttons on this panel, no locks, no retinal scanners, no DNA samplers. It consisted of a pool of the same liquid metal as the ship's hull, held upright by some unseen force. Samu placed his hand on the panel and the liquid metal engulfed it for a moment, before letting go again.

"I am the only one capable of opening this door," he said as cogs began to turn and clonk. "I am the only one with the permission to remove the device from this ship. But I can only do that with the captain's orders."

I wasn't wholly reassured by that. The door groaned open and inside a small room was a sight I wasn't expecting. Held in a bizarre structure of pipes interlaced with multiple force fields was a ball of tumultuous black substance that twisted, jumped, and thrashed wildly. It was stormy, dangerous, and looked as though it wanted to break from its restraints and kill us all.

I took a step toward the room only to be stopped by Samu.

"You cannot go in," he said, tilting his head to the side. "There is a great deal of electromagnetic energy in there, not to mention that it is also devoid of air. You will cease to function inside this room, Zoe Ruthland."

I glanced at Samu before turning my attention back to the violent energy inside the vault. I'd never seen anything like it in my life and I worried it *would* escape and kill us all while we slept. By the expression on most of the faces around me, I guessed I wasn't the only one. I nodded and allowed Samu to escort us to command.

We soon emerged into a corridor adorned in red fixtures this time. Beyond an unassuming set of double doors was an exact replica of the simulator, or rather the template it was modelled after. It was so familiar and so exact that I half expected to turn around and see the darkened corridors of the Tierless compound behind me. The only difference was an extra chair beside Jax's navigation console.

"I would suggest that we get underway before the storm above ground gets worse," Samu tooted, sauntering his way toward the screen.

He eased himself elegantly into the extra chair and waited, seemingly unaware of the gravity of what he was asking. It wasn't as if we were moving a table from one side of the room to the other. Any miscalculations and we would hurtle toward our deaths, but thinking about it too long did no one any good either.

"Jax, take the helm," I commanded, making my way to the captain's chair and perching myself on the edge of it, unable to relax. "I'm going to need you to become psychic here and counteract the headwinds before they happen."

Jax didn't answer as he and the crew took their seats like they had done a hundred times before in the simulator. The same fear that hollowed out my chest and made my rapid heartbeat reverberate against my ribcage was mirrored in their expressions. All save Tristan, who leaned back into his chair, pulled the straps over his shoulders and clicked the lock in place, like this was just another simulation.

"You gotta strap in this time," he reminded me.

In my mind I slapped my hand against my forehead and cursed for making such a rookie mistake. It wasn't a good start to my leadership, but it wasn't a disastrous one either, at least not yet. Taking a sweeping glance around the room before securing myself, I was glad to see that at least the others had the sense to copy Tristan.

"Okay," I said, feeling the knot in my stomach twist my innards painfully. "Otto, let's get out of here."

Chapter 19

The rumble of the ship's thrusters was more visceral than I imagined. I took a few deep breaths and focused on the bridge viewer to distract me. It wasn't a window so much as it was a projection of the environment outside. The image was still sharp enough, however, that I couldn't tell the difference—not that there was much to look at. The concrete tube encircling the ship still disappeared into an impenetrable darkness, and that was the extent of our vista.

"Open communications with the crew," I said to Nathan.

Nathan pressed a couple of buttons and a loud whistle signified his compliance. He still refused to speak to me, however.

"Good morning, crew. As I demonstrated last night, I'm not one for speeches," I began, managing to get a few chuckles from the bridge crew. "We all know why we're here. We each have loved ones in Bunker Twelve who need us to succeed. Some are healthy for now, while time is running out for others. We can't afford to make anyone wait longer than they have to.

"We've worked hard, overcoming obstacles we never thought possible, and Earth can be proud of the ambassadors she sends to a new world. *I'm* proud of you. But this is just the first step in a journey that will be difficult, maybe even deadly. I'm humbled that you call me captain. I don't deserve the honour, but I'll work hard to become worthy of it."

I shifted in my seat, hoping some glorious words would flow from me and inspire my crew to not be afraid. There were no such words in existence.

"To that end, all hands prepare for launch," I ordered. "And may you *all* find health this day."

It was rare that I ever meant those words, but with the future of the human race resting on our success, it was imperative that we did not die. A mantra, a prayer, a hope for survival was all we had left.

I nodded to Nathan and he cut off communications, offering me a small, unexpected smile. My heart did a flip, and I couldn't stop myself from returning his gesture. Tristan shot irked glances between us both, but said nothing.

"When we're ready, Otto, bring the thrusters to full power," I ordered, focusing on the viewer in front of me.

A series of beeps from Otto's station preceded the rumbling and trembling of the ship itself. Our chairs shook violently as the silver behemoth gathered power.

"Open the bay doors," I shouted over the noise.

I didn't hear the beeping of console buttons anymore. It was lost to the ferocious timbre of the ship's launch engines. Through the bridge viewer, the ceiling of the launch bay slowly spiralled open in the same way the entrance to the tram had. Where there had been a secreted darkness before, now a dull twilight revealed the opening to the world outside. I half expected to feel the extra radiation burn us all, but of course, there was nothing as the silent and deadly poison flooded the launch bay.

Bits of metal and damaged ceilinging, which had hung undisturbed for many years, fell onto our vessel. Their descent to the ground below us rang out in a series of clangs and alarming clatters along the shell of the ship. Flying my fingers over the small console on my chair, the readings indicated that no damage had been done. I tried to breathe a sigh of relief, but couldn't relax enough to do so.

Flurries of white snow floated and swirled into the launch bay, like a sluggish tornado illuminated by the fires of our thrusters below. The flakes danced and floated like they had a consciousness which didn't want to find the ground where they were bound to die.

I had never seen snow before. It was beautiful, elegant, and delicate. I wanted to reach out and touch it, but its beauty was a lie, and I knew it only harboured death.

"Bring us up, Jax," I shouted over the roar.

The silvery mammoth shuddered and rumbled as its powerful engines flared to a new intense level of life. The Kepler One fought gravity in slow increments to start. Gradually the walls of the battered bunker sank either side of the ship's screen as we climbed higher and higher, emerging from the icy tomb many once called home.

The air was heavy with turbulent flakes blown up by the engines. Through it, a blanket of snow and ice covered everything that was once visible, save the half-buried skeletons of ancient buildings. They reached their many twisted metal fingers toward the sky, solidified in frozen agony. Enormous icicles hung from their digits, some of which cracked and tumbled to the ground as we climbed higher. *How many died in those buildings?* All around us, the world that had once been so vibrant, so full of colour and movement, was white from horizon to horizon, and eerily still.

Our speed gathered as the icy Earth began to recede from the edges of the viewer, pressing us into our seats. Thick black clouds choked out the minuscule disc of orange that gave the only a modicum of light, and we headed straight for it.

"Emily, what are the winds like?" I shouted.

It took her a moment to answer, and I only barely heard her over the engines.

"I don't understand," she said. "The winds are steady at ten miles per hour."

I glanced back at her over my chair, hoping to find some hint of a joke. Her brows were furrowed over her dark eyes.

"Where's the storm?" I demanded.

"That's what I'm trying to tell you," she snapped. "There's no storm. Sensors indicate that we're in an area of steady high pressure. If it wasn't for the nuclear winter, it would be a beautiful bloody day."

I stared at Tristan beside me. He looked as confused as I did.

"Samu, the president said there was a storm coming. That's why we had to launch early," I shouted at him. "So where's the storm?"

Samu shrugged, then smiled his sweet smile again.

"Maybe he was mistaken. Radiation interferes with Earth's instruments all the time. Sometimes the information received is corrupted and humans resort to taking an *educated* guess," he answered, doing air-quotes and everything. "Perhaps this guess was incorrect."

Samu slipped his hands between his slim legs and focused his attention on the screen again, like he was a spectator instead of part of the mission. This was the second time the president had made an error due to instrument malfunction, and I never trusted coincidences.

I wanted to slap Samu then and demand an answer. He was once the bunker computer, or still was, I couldn't be certain. But surely he should be privy to all the unheard conversations, secret messages, the underhanded tactics of everyone in Bunker Twelve? Perhaps he wasn't permitted to talk about the president's reasons for an early launch, or his plans. It would be stupid to send up a database full of incriminating evidence with a bunch of wilful teens who held his rescue in their hands. The president was anything but stupid.

The ship tilted to the side and the black clouds in the viewer thinned. They surrounded us on all sides now, a blanket of dark twilight blinding our view. We accelerated faster, and I felt my innards being pushed into my back as Jax made the final push to break free of the Earth's gravity. I gripped the armrests of my chair and was surprised to find Tristan's warm hand covering mine a moment later.

I looked at him and he smiled reassuringly, like he knew everything was going to be okay. I closed my eyes and gripped his fingers as they laced mine.

Despite his cruelness, I couldn't help but be reassured by his touch. There was something about Tristan, something solid that made me feel at ease . . . when he wasn't angry with me.

Without warning, the ship's thrusters dulled and the pressure pushing my body into my chair, eased. My innards floated inside my torso, and for a moment I thought we had died. The sudden clunk of the ship's thrusters disengaging brought us all out of our disbelief.

"We're out," Jax said, sounding as surprised as I felt.

I opened my eyes and an inky-black horizon dotted with dazzling stars and a blazing sun, met my vision. I had to squint against it until the viewer compensated for the extra light. Never in my life had I seen anything so beautiful, and I went numb as a cheer erupted from the bridge. We were free. I had escaped. No more cancer, no more Bunker Twelve or Tier Five. I had escaped, and no one could send me back there now.

A tear floated away from the corner of my eye, drifting gracefully through the bridge. Tristan squeezed my hand and a broad smile crossed his face. I held back the deep sobs that threatened to bubble over and leaned my head onto his shoulder. His free hand cupped my face and pressed me against him. I couldn't believe that fate, which hated me so much before, had seen fit to let me live this time.

It was then that I saw Nathan staring at Tristan and me. He didn't seem angry, but he wasn't rejoicing along with the rest of us either. I pushed Tristan away and tried to right myself. My hair floated across my eyes, and my arms and legs wouldn't quite turn as I told them.

"Otto, get the artificial gravity going," I said.

The sound of unseen engines coiled around the ship and my feet were sucked to the floor. It wasn't the same as Earth's gravity, not nearly as strong, but enough to keep me rooted to the ground and put my hair back into its rightful position.

"Crew check," I said, not looking at Nathan, instead just waiting for the whistle. "Engineering, all personnel still okay?"

"Unfortunately," Ariel said with a snort over the intercom.

I almost laughed. Her disdain for Sam was clear in her voice.

"Auxiliary crew, how about you?"

"Majella puked, but yeah, we're still here," Simon said.

I cringed. The idea of vomit floating around in space uncontrolled was more than I was willing to think about right now.

"Medbay, everything okay?"

There was a pause too long to stop me from worrying.

"Medbay?"

"Yes, yes," Liam answered meekly, sounding flustered. "I'm good."

I breathed a sigh of relief. The last person on this ship I wanted hurt was Liam. If I let the president's son get killed, who knows what he would do to Jason in return.

"All right," I said, gathering myself again. "Everyone stay strapped in for the moment. When we reach our first wormhole entry point Samu will escort you to the stasis room. Engineering, take whatever time you need to make sure everything is in order before we jump."

I swallowed deeply, wondering if that would be the last command given on the bridge of the Kepler One. Once we were in stasis, all decisions would be left to Samu. Watching the apathetic expression on his face while all others cheered or cried, I wasn't reassured that I could trust him.

Jax guided the ship farther from the Earth. As we journeyed beyond the moon, which was dotted with discarded, ancient satellites, I couldn't help but feel sad as I watched the ball of tumultuous grey clouds we called Earth disappear. Somewhere down there were desperate people, praying for a rescue. We were their last hope.

The Kepler One sailed deep into the inkiness of space, guided by Emily's directions as she located the nearest gathering of negative energy. Strangely, the closer we came to it the more I noticed Jax breathing more quickly. Behind the glowing visor covering his face, I spotted beads of sweat on his brow. I put it down to his nerves about going into stasis again.

"Here!" Emily said, triumphantly. "Dead ahead, we should be able to open a wormhole."

"All stop," I ordered, wiping my hands on my trousers. The ship's engines whirred as we slowed and everyone waited for my next order. I swallowed deeply. "Otto, open the wormhole."

Otto squeaked, almost inaudibly, as his fingers flew over the console. A deep thud reverberated throughout the ship and on the screen, a beam of searing white light shot into the nothing. After a small skirmish of electricity branching over an unseen object ahead, there was a sudden flash of brilliant light. The shields around the ship sparkled like a sheet of diamonds as it absorbed whatever exotic material that was spewed out.

The searing beam of followed one of our probes as it passed through a rotating, violent vortex. Like a torch, the beam illuminated a set of different stars in its centre of the vortex, and beyond that, hovered a small planet that shouldn't have been there.

"It w-worked," Otto said, his eyes wide and his mouth open. "The wormhole is stable."

"Of course it is," Samu replied, getting up from his chair. "But it won't stay open forever. Might I suggest you make your way toward the stasis chamber now?"

"Yes," I said, my voice breathy as I released the straps on my chair and stood to follow Samu. "Yes, stasis chamber."

I wasn't sure when my fear had turned me stupid, but it had.

The stasis room wasn't too unlike the one in the Tierless compound. Clean beige walls replaced the dirty concrete, and the body avatars were newer with a few more readings that meant little to me. Fifteen pill shaped pods, instead of six, rested in three rows of five, each churning the purple goo we would spend the next year in. Save for that, the only difference in the room were the fifteen metal lockers that adorned the wall opposite the screens. They had our names stamped into them, solidifying our place aboard the Kepler One.

When we disrobed and placed our uniforms inside the lockers, something unexpected got everyone talking. A helmet, half of which was glass, hung from a thin hook in each locker. Attached to the helmets were shiny black suits. They reminded me of an empty snake skin dangling limply from its perch. There was no bulk to the suits, and the hexagonal patterned material slipped easily through my fingers.

"These are your EMU suits, or Extravehicular Mobility Unit suits," Samu explained when asked by the others. "Should the need arise to exit the ship and repair it, these suits will provide you with protection and life-support. Each also has an arm monitor capable of identifying items that might be dangerous or poisonous to you humans. This is also what you will wear when we first arrive on the planet, to protect you until we can determine the planet's safety, you understand?"

"Protect us?" Larissa said, her voice much higher than normal. "I can't see these things protecting us from a stiff breeze, never mind an alien planet."

"I assure you that even though they look thin, these suits have a tensile strength that would rival the best bullet-pceiling armour known to man," Samu said, tilting his head to the side and smiling again. "They are also air-tight and firepceiling."

Larissa scrunched her nose and scrutinized the suit again. "Really?"

"Let's hope we never have to find out," Tristan interrupted, throwing his boots into his locker and slamming the door shut.

The sound jolted me from the daze I'd been in since we opened the wormhole. I shook my head and finished undressing expecting the air and the ground to feel cold on my bare skin, but it didn't. Another stark reminder that we were no longer in Bunker Twelve.

Bunker Twelve. Some part of me was sad that I'd never see it again, but it was only a fleeting emotion. Given the choice, I'd rather be on the Kepler One. But everything seemed so rushed this morning. I wasn't in control, and the feeling unsettled me. Soon I would be relinquishing all control to Samu, and *that* notion terrified me beyond belief.

While waiting for the others to undress, Samu approached and placed the same small sticky sensor onto my chest as Professor Salinski had. My avatar flashed to life in a succession of numbers I didn't understand, save maybe the heart rate. So far, it told me I was relatively calm, as was Nathan, Tristan, Thelma, and Otto, the latter surprising me most.

Samu followed it with a series of red stickers which he attached to each of the major muscle groups on my legs, arms, torso, and, embarrassingly, my buttocks. I'd forgotten the professor said that our muscles would be repeatedly shocked so we wouldn't lose too much mass. I hadn't realised there would be so many and wondered if I'd end up feeling like a fly caught in a zapper. *One portion of fried Zoe, coming right up.*

Samu finished and moved onto the next person. "Zoe?"

The sound of Nathan's voice behind me made me jump. I wasn't expecting to hear him say my name again. Stilling the nerves that wanted me to tell him everything, I slowly turned and looked him straight in the eyes, but he wouldn't meet my gaze. His head hung, and he preoccupied himself with one of the red dots on his arm. God, he was handsome.

"I get it," he said quietly, taking a sheepish glance at me under his brow. "Can't say that I understand your choice, but I get it."

"My choice?" I asked, shaking my head in confusion.

"You and Tristan," he answered. "I get why you and I can't . . . why you pulled away. I just wanted to let you know that I'm not angry, and I won't try to kiss you again . . . not unless you want me to." Nathan paused, half turning away from me. I nearly told him that I *did* want him to kiss me; that I truly *did* have feelings for him. I *would* have said it, had he not spoken again. "I just want you to be happy, and I'll do whatever it takes to make sure you are . . . even if it means it's with him instead of me."

I watched him leave and head to the stasis pods with the others. His back was still red and sore from the lashing he received at my orders.

I had no romantic feelings for Tristan, of that much I was certain now, but if believing it kept Nathan at arm's length, maybe it was better for the both of us to let him think that. I couldn't trust myself to keep a good distance between us otherwise, and I couldn't face having to hurt him again. The president held my strings tightly, and I had many hoops to jump through before I could be free.

I stood, burying my emotions deep inside as I watched my crew be submerged into their pods. They went willingly, but the goo seemed thicker this time, and Samu had to help lower each person by pressing on their chests and pushing them under. At least he asked everyone if it that was okay this time. He'd learned from our rebreather encounter and that fact made leaving him in charge while we slept, less terrifying.

Aside from some thrashing from Jax, all members of my crew made the transition into their pods easily. All except Tristan who waited with me as I walked among the crew, checking that everyone was still alive. Everyone was. They were already asleep from the sedatives, and I stole that moment to rest my hand on Nathan's pod. He was so peaceful and handsome as he slept. My heart dropped into my stomach as I wondered if I would ever see him again.

"You wanna go next?" Tristan asked.

I shook my head.

"I'm the captain," I answered quietly. "I'll go last."

Tristan bobbed his head in agreement and made his way to his pod. The truth was, I wanted to spend the last few minutes with Nathan, alone. I don't know why. It's not as if he could hear me. Maybe it was because I was too scared to enter my own pod.

Tristan paused for a minute, Samu's hand resting on his chest as he sat in his pod.

"Whatever happens," he said, glancing at me. "I'm proud of you, Zoe. You did good. Ain't no one can take that away from you now."

Tristan smiled before allowing Samu to help him the rest of the way into the gel. His cocoon closed, and I watched as his chest spasm a few times before becoming calm. His eyes closed and his body stilled. I was alone, save the android we were entrusting our lives to.

"Are you ready, Captain Ruthland?" he asked, his rose lips parting to reveal his perfect teeth. "The ship will meet the event horizon in one minute and twenty-three seconds. You are running out of time."

I didn't respond. I took one last look around at the people who had started off hating me, fearing me. Those same people who had become my friends, and I prayed that I would see them again someday. Walking to my pod I was glad mine was between Nathan and Tristan. Being close to them, although they could do nothing if the worst happened, made me feel safer.

The thick meniscus of the goo was difficult to break as I stepped in. That same freezing ache climbed into my bones and crawled up my body as I lowered myself into it.

"May I help you?" Samu asked, his smile never flinching.

"Yes," I said, breathing deeply. "Just make sure you look after us," I added as his hand rested on my chest. His skin was colder and more rubbery than I was expecting for such a life-like automaton. "Make sure as many of us live as possible."

"Of course," he said, blinking twice and pushing my torso into the stasis pod. "May you find health this day."

My head submerged, and the encapsulating coldness made a panic rise inside me. Out of reflex I struggled to sit up again, thrashing wildly, but the goo and Samu kept me in place. I couldn't move, I couldn't scream. My lungs filled and I choked. Samu smiled while he watched me floundering for breath. When I was completely submerged and still, he removed his hand.

I felt the usual shift as the lid closed above me. A disassociated calmness made my limbs heavy. I watch through the purple liquid as Samu receded from my pod. *Would he make the right choices, human choices? Or would we be the subjects of probability?* I would find out when we emerge a year later, if we emerged at all. A year? That was too long a time.

The unnatural heaviness made my eyelids droop. Cemented in the goo, there was no way out now. Only one thing stayed with me as the cold strangled my senses and the black began to take my consciousness.

Is this when I die?

Also by TP Keane

The Paladins of Naretia
Book one in the Naretia series (fantasy)

Dear Bob, The Misadventures of Petunia Pottersfield
Book one in the Petunia Pottersfield children's series

*For more information on publications
or contacts, please visit
www.tpkeane.com*

Printed in the USA
CPSIA information can be obtained
at www.ICGtesting.com
LVHW011552200224
772364LV00010B/461